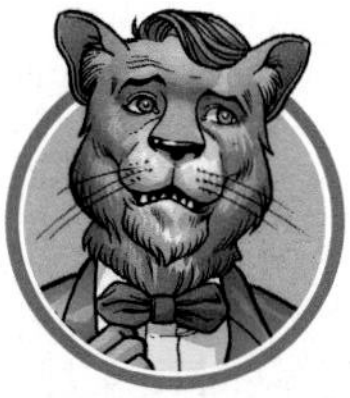

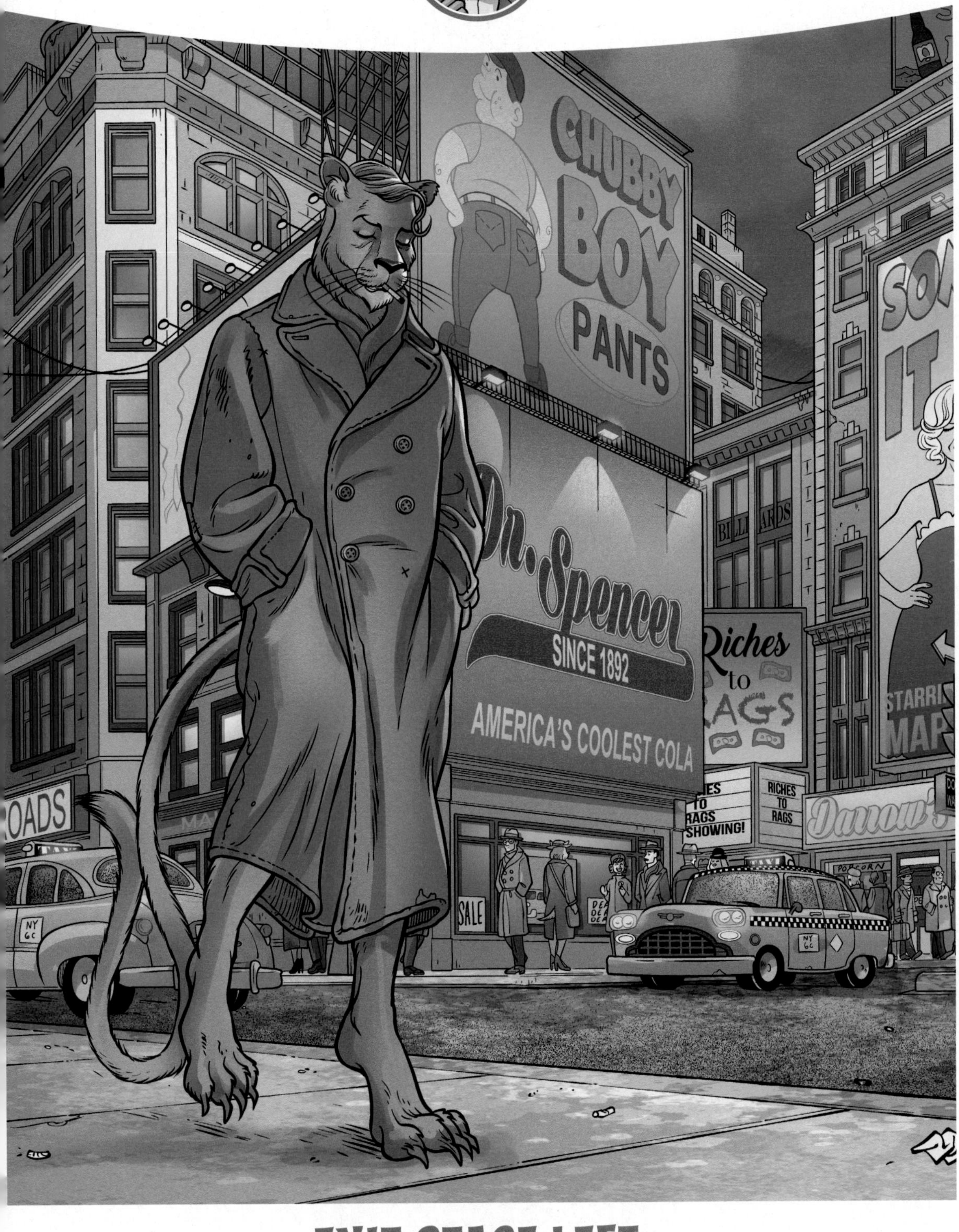
CHUBBY
BOY
PANTS
Dr. Spencer
SINCE 1892
AMERICA'S COOLEST COLA
Riches
to
BILLIARDS
RICHES
TO
RAGS
RAGS
SHOWING!
SALE
Darrow's

EXIT STAGE LEFT:
THE SNAGGLEPUSS CHRONICLES

EXIT STAGE LEFT:
THE SNAGGLEPUSS CHRONICLES

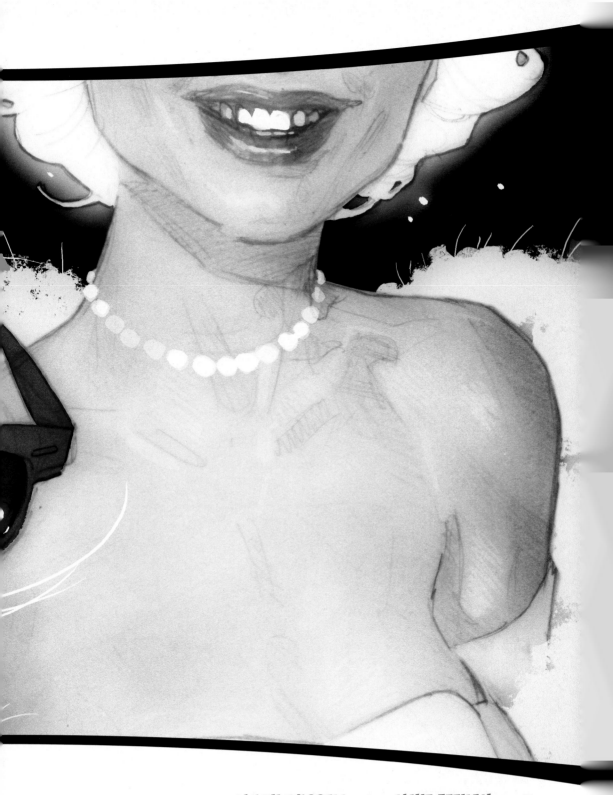

MARK RUSSELL writer **MIKE FEEHAN** penciller

MARK MORALES SEAN PARSONS JOSÉ MARZÁN JR. inkers

PAUL MOUNTS colorist **DAVE SHARPE** letterer

BEN CALDWELL series and collection cover artist

PROLOGUE by **MARK RUSSELL** writer **HOWARD PORTER** artist
STEVE BUCCELLATO colorist **DAVE SHARPE** letterer

PRESS

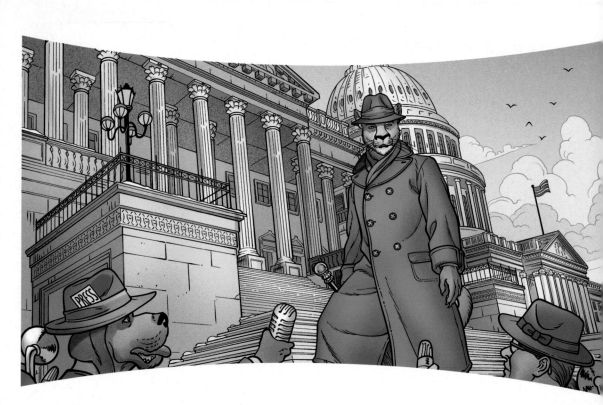

MARIE JAVINS Editor - Original Series
BRITTANY HOLZHERR Associate Editor - Original Series DIEGO LOPEZ Assistant Editor - Original Series
JEB WOODARD Group Editor - Collected Editions ERIKA ROTHBERG Editor - Collected Edition
STEVE COOK Design Director - Books CURTIS KING JR. Publication Design

BOB HARRAS Senior VP - Editor-in-Chief, DC Comics
PAT McCALLUM Executive Editor, DC Comics

DAN DiDIO Publisher JIM LEE Publisher & Chief Creative Officer
AMIT DESAI Executive VP - Business & Marketing Strategy, Direct to Consumer & Global Franchise Management
BOBBIE CHASE VP & Executive Editor, Young Reader & Talent Development MARK CHIARELLO Senior VP - Art, Design & Collected Editions
JOHN CUNNINGHAM Senior VP - Sales & Trade Marketing BRIAR DARDEN VP - Business Affairs
ANNE DePIES Senior VP - Business Strategy, Finance & Administration DON FALLETTI VP - Manufacturing Operations
LAWRENCE GANEM VP - Editorial Administration & Talent Relations ALISON GILL Senior VP - Manufacturing & Operations
JASON GREENBERG VP - Business Strategy & Finance HANK KANALZ Senior VP - Editorial Strategy & Administration
JAY KOGAN Senior VP - Legal Affairs NICK J. NAPOLITANO VP - Manufacturing Administration
LISETTE OSTERLOH VP - Digital Marketing & Events EDDIE SCANNELL VP - Consumer Marketing
COURTNEY SIMMONS Senior VP - Publicity & Communications JIM (SKI) SOKOLOWSKI VP - Comic Book Specialty Sales & Trade Marketing
NANCY SPEARS VP - Mass, Book, Digital Sales & Trade Marketing MICHELE R. WELLS VP - Content Strategy

EXIT STAGE LEFT: THE SNAGGLEPUSS CHRONICLES

DC Comics, 2900 West Alameda Ave., Burbank, CA 91505. Printed by LSC Communications, Kendallville, IN, USA. 2/25/19. Second Printing. ISBN: 978-1-4012-7521-1

Library of Congress Cataloging-in-Publication Data is available.

DCC041211

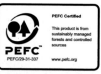

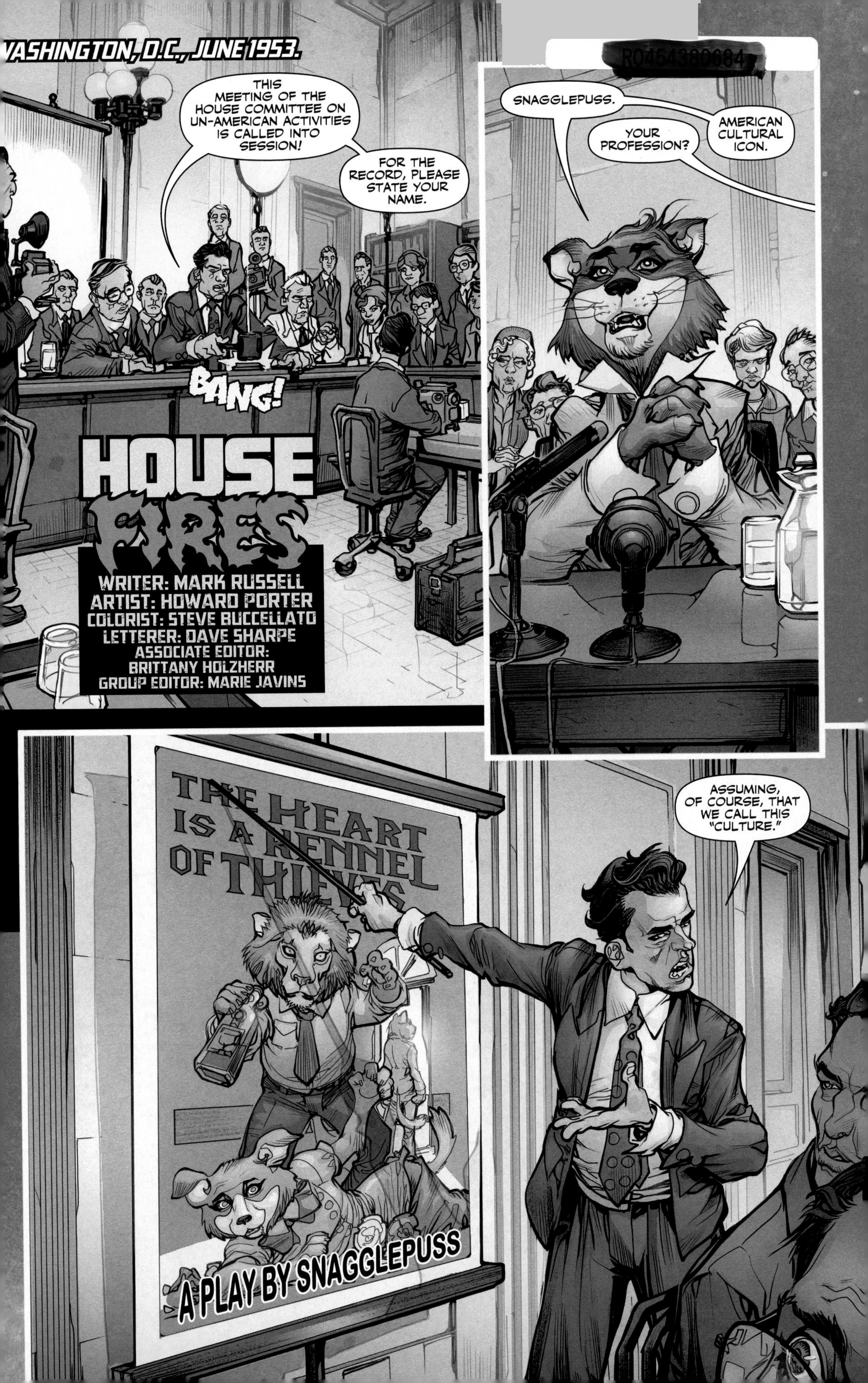
WASHINGTON, D.C., JUNE 1953.
THIS MEETING OF THE HOUSE COMMITTEE ON UN-AMERICAN ACTIVITIES IS CALLED INTO SESSION!
FOR THE RECORD, PLEASE STATE YOUR NAME.
BANG!
HOUSE FIRES
WRITER: MARK RUSSELL
ARTIST: HOWARD PORTER
COLORIST: STEVE BUCCELLATO
LETTERER: DAVE SHARPE
ASSOCIATE EDITOR: BRITTANY HOLZHERR
GROUP EDITOR: MARIE JAVINS
SNAGGLEPUSS.
YOUR PROFESSION?
AMERICAN CULTURAL ICON.
THE HEART IS A KENNEL OF THIEVES
A PLAY BY SNAGGLEPUSS
ASSUMING, OF COURSE, THAT WE CALL THIS "CULTURE."

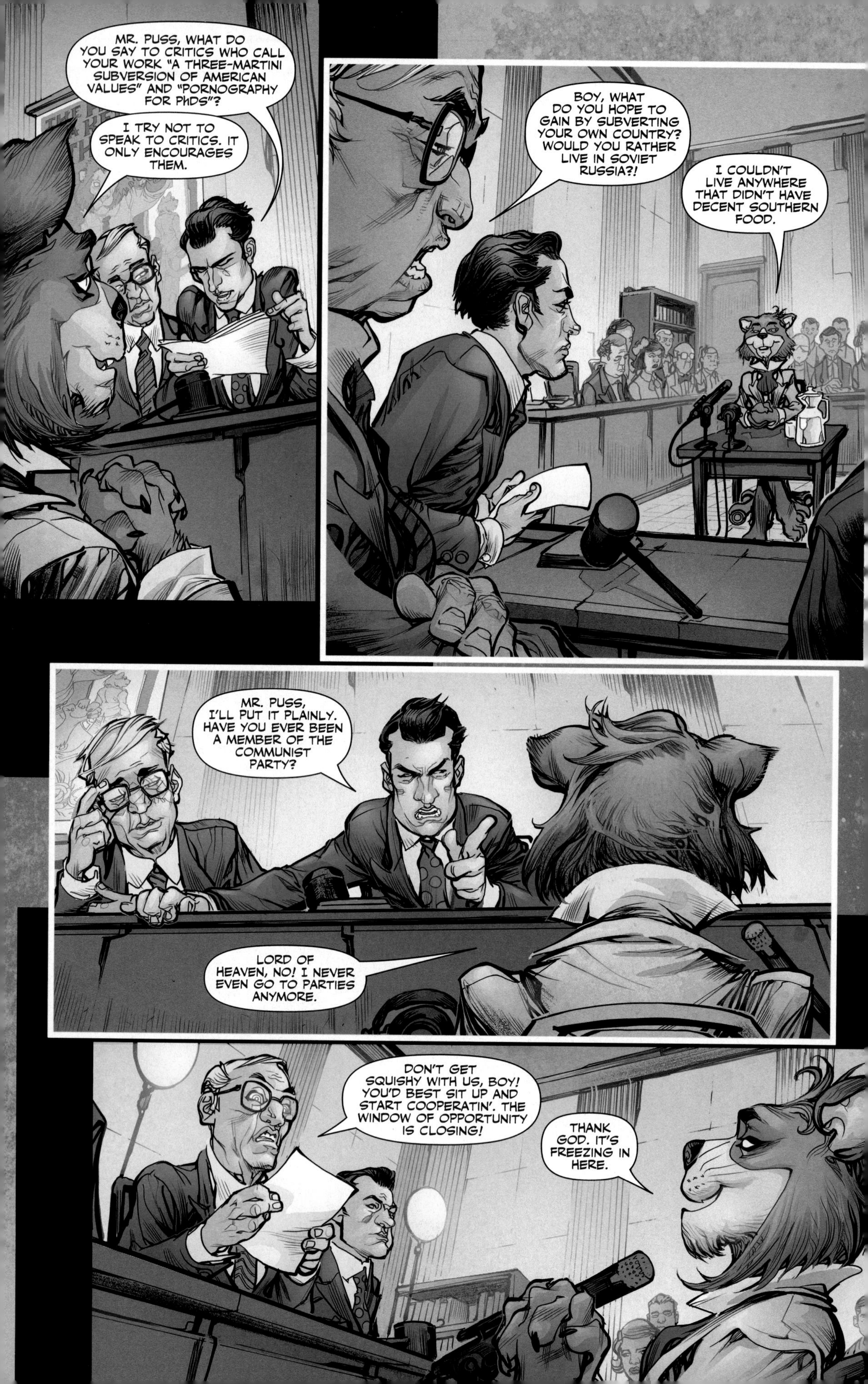
MR. PUSS, WHAT DO YOU SAY TO CRITICS WHO CALL YOUR WORK "A THREE-MARTINI SUBVERSION OF AMERICAN VALUES" AND "PORNOGRAPHY FOR PhDS"?
I TRY NOT TO SPEAK TO CRITICS. IT ONLY ENCOURAGES THEM.
BOY, WHAT DO YOU HOPE TO GAIN BY SUBVERTING YOUR OWN COUNTRY? WOULD YOU RATHER LIVE IN SOVIET RUSSIA?!
I COULDN'T LIVE ANYWHERE THAT DIDN'T HAVE DECENT SOUTHERN FOOD.
MR. PUSS, I'LL PUT IT PLAINLY. HAVE YOU EVER BEEN A MEMBER OF THE COMMUNIST PARTY?
LORD OF HEAVEN, NO! I NEVER EVEN GO TO PARTIES ANYMORE.
DON'T GET SQUISHY WITH US, BOY! YOU'D BEST SIT UP AND START COOPERATIN'. THE WINDOW OF OPPORTUNITY IS CLOSING!
THANK GOD. IT'S FREEZING IN HERE.

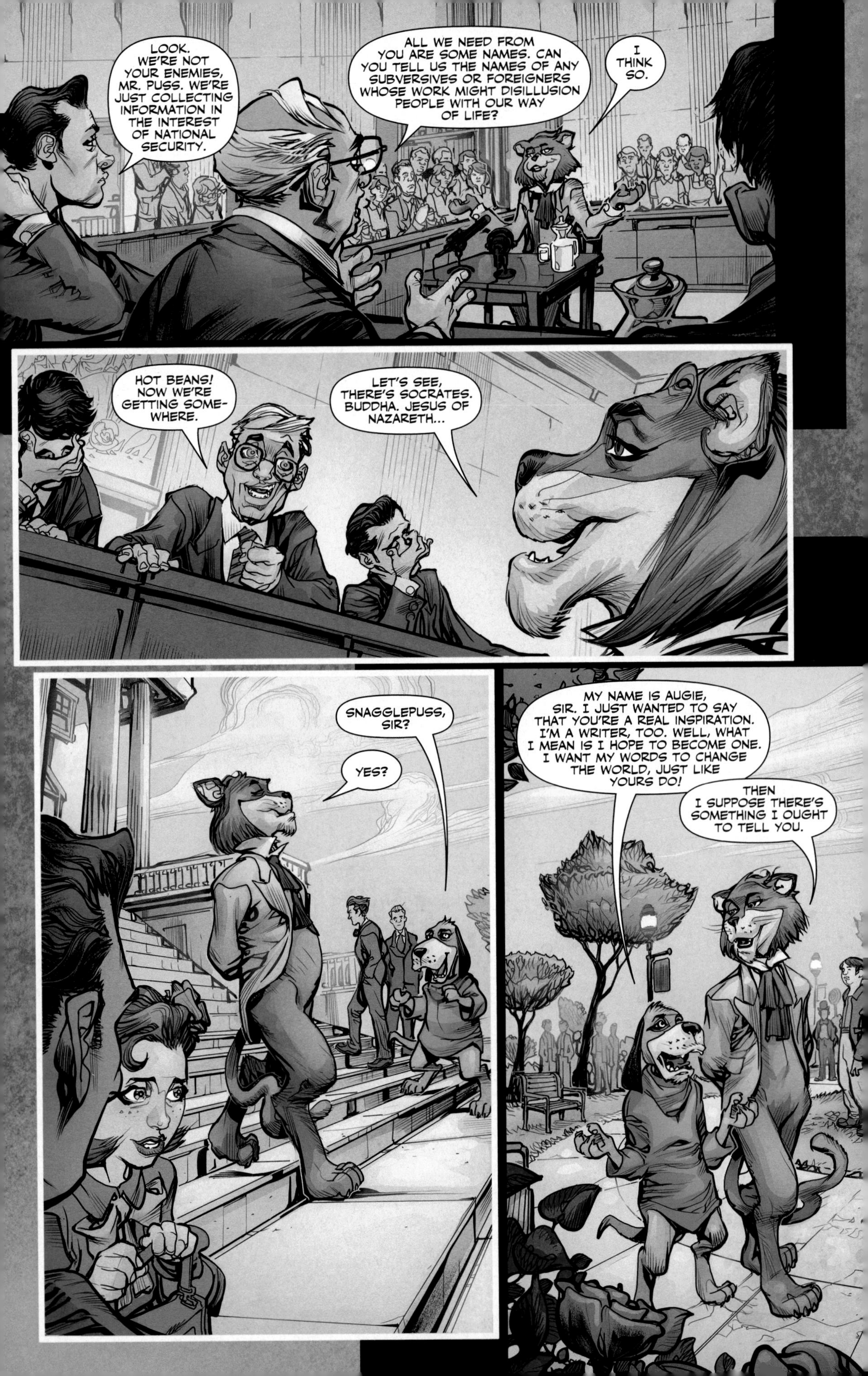
LOOK. WE'RE NOT YOUR ENEMIES, MR. PUSS. WE'RE JUST COLLECTING INFORMATION IN THE INTEREST OF NATIONAL SECURITY.
ALL WE NEED FROM YOU ARE SOME NAMES. CAN YOU TELL US THE NAMES OF ANY SUBVERSIVES OR FOREIGNERS WHOSE WORK MIGHT DISILLUSION PEOPLE WITH OUR WAY OF LIFE?
I THINK SO.
HOT BEANS! NOW WE'RE GETTING SOME-WHERE.
LET'S SEE, THERE'S SOCRATES. BUDDHA. JESUS OF NAZARETH...
SNAGGLEPUSS, SIR?
YES?
MY NAME IS AUGIE, SIR. I JUST WANTED TO SAY THAT YOU'RE A REAL INSPIRATION. I'M A WRITER, TOO. WELL, WHAT I MEAN IS I HOPE TO BECOME ONE. I WANT MY WORDS TO CHANGE THE WORLD, JUST LIKE YOURS DO!
THEN I SUPPOSE THERE'S SOMETHING I OUGHT TO TELL YOU.

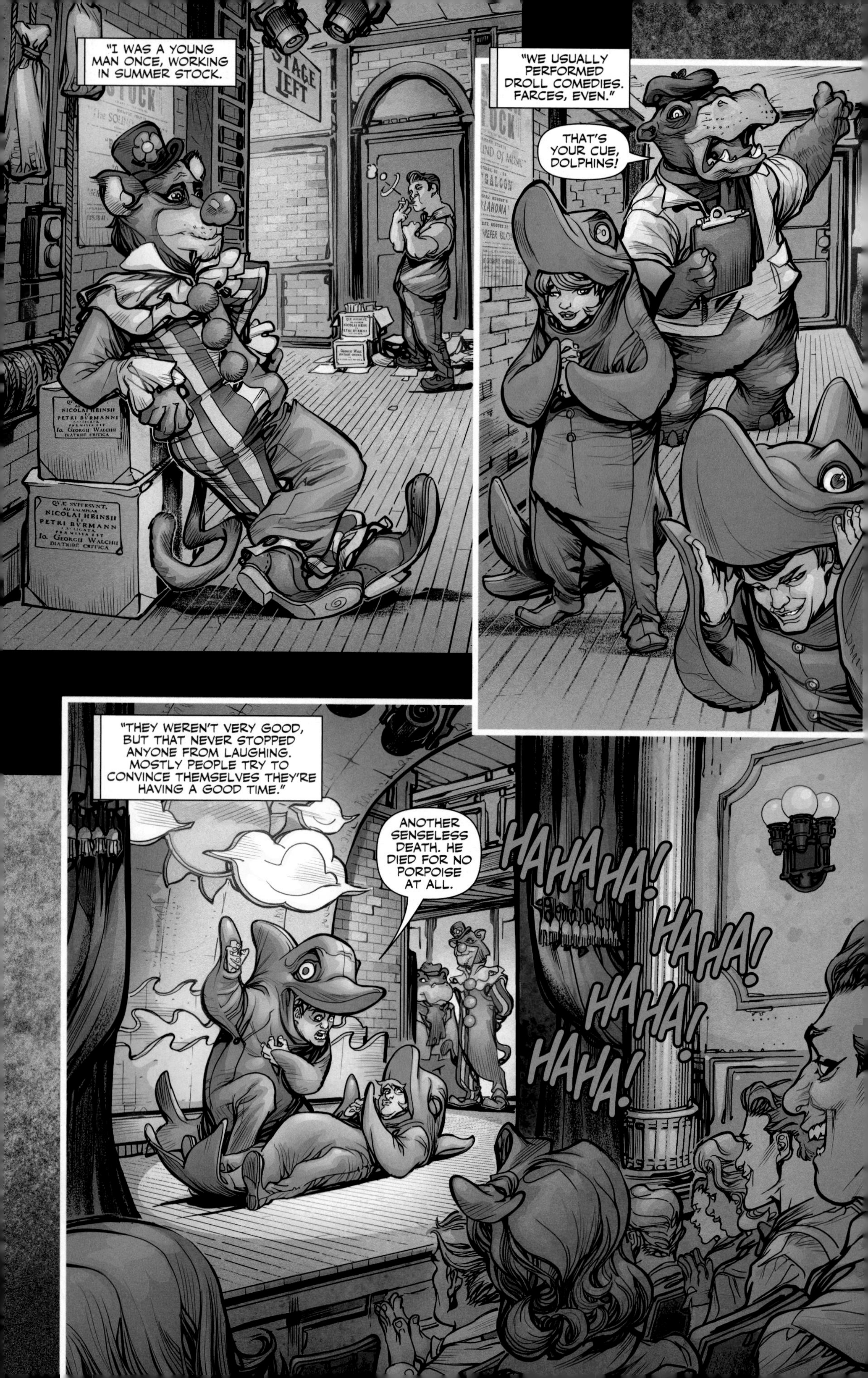
"I WAS A YOUNG MAN ONCE, WORKING IN SUMMER STOCK.
STAGE LEFT
"WE USUALLY PERFORMED DROLL COMEDIES. FARCES, EVEN."
THAT'S YOUR CUE, DOLPHINS!
"THEY WEREN'T VERY GOOD, BUT THAT NEVER STOPPED ANYONE FROM LAUGHING. MOSTLY PEOPLE TRY TO CONVINCE THEMSELVES THEY'RE HAVING A GOOD TIME."
ANOTHER SENSELESS DEATH. HE DIED FOR NO PORPOISE AT ALL.
HAHAHA!
HAHA!
HAHA!
HAHA!

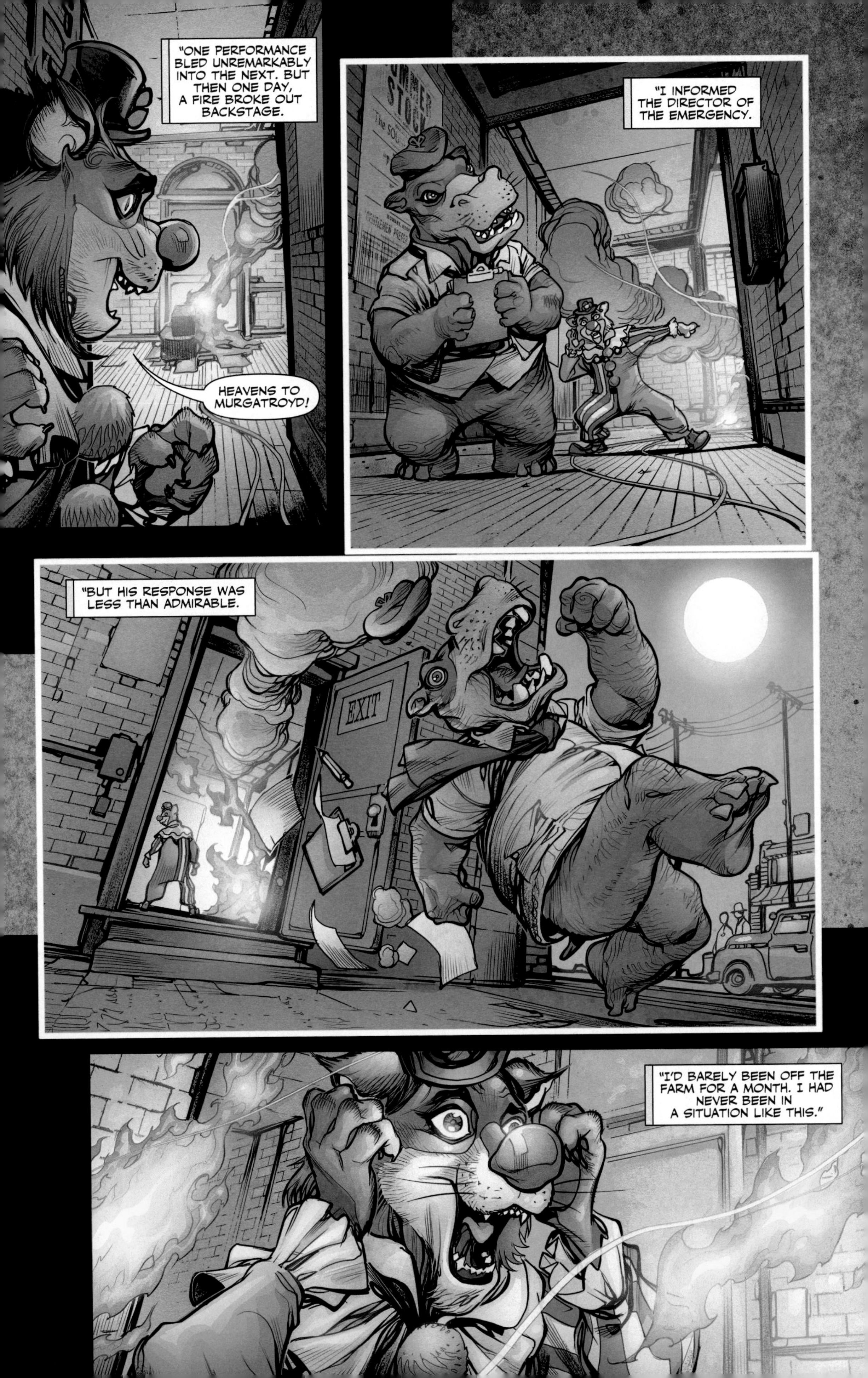
"ONE PERFORMANCE BLED UNREMARKABLY INTO THE NEXT. BUT THEN ONE DAY, A FIRE BROKE OUT BACKSTAGE.
HEAVENS TO MURGATROYD!
"I INFORMED THE DIRECTOR OF THE EMERGENCY.
"BUT HIS RESPONSE WAS LESS THAN ADMIRABLE.
EXIT
"I'D BARELY BEEN OFF THE FARM FOR A MONTH. I HAD NEVER BEEN IN A SITUATION LIKE THIS."

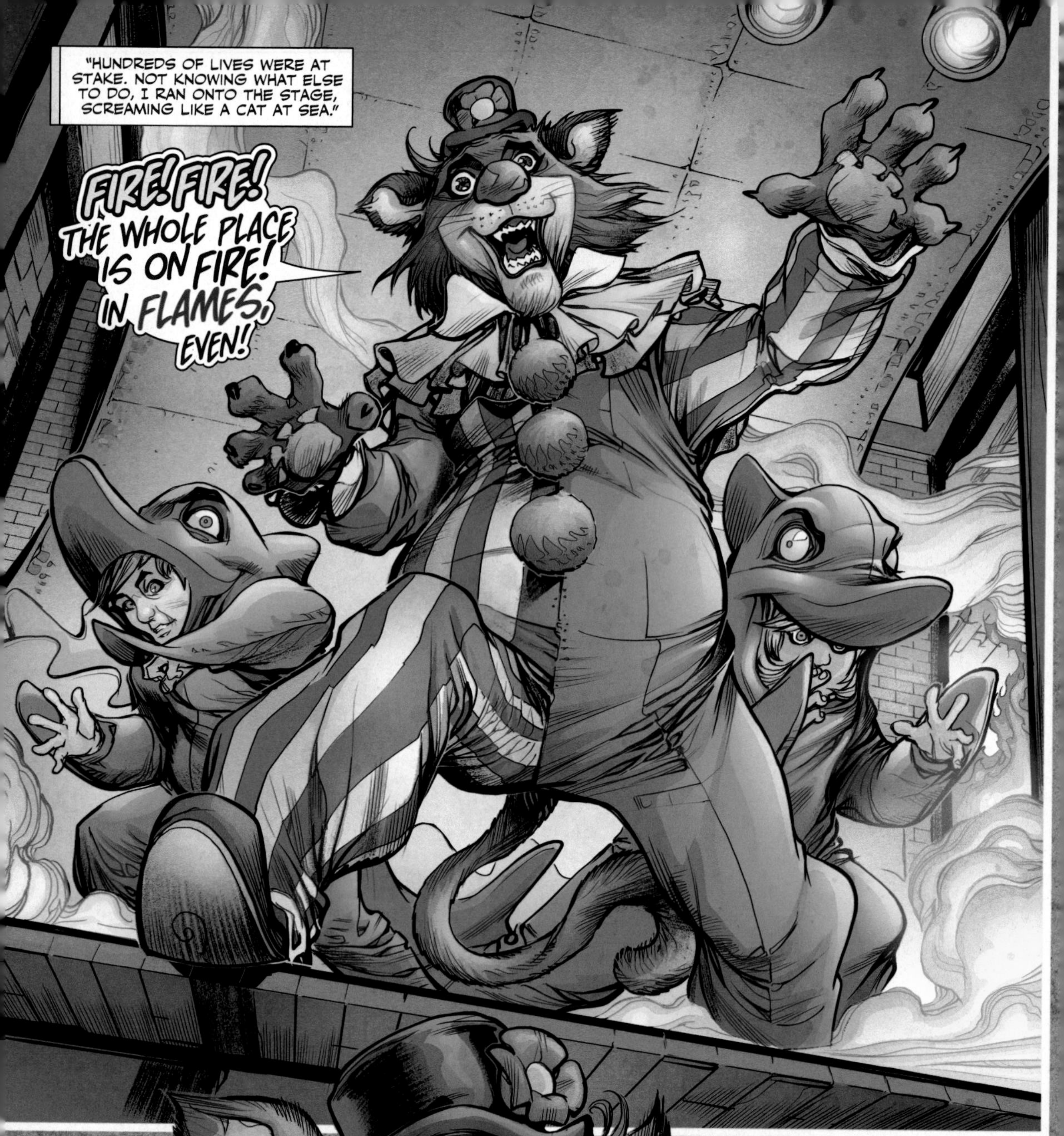
"HUNDREDS OF LIVES WERE AT STAKE. NOT KNOWING WHAT ELSE TO DO, I RAN ONTO THE STAGE, SCREAMING LIKE A CAT AT SEA."
FIRE! FIRE! THE WHOLE PLACE IS ON FIRE! IN FLAMES, EVEN!

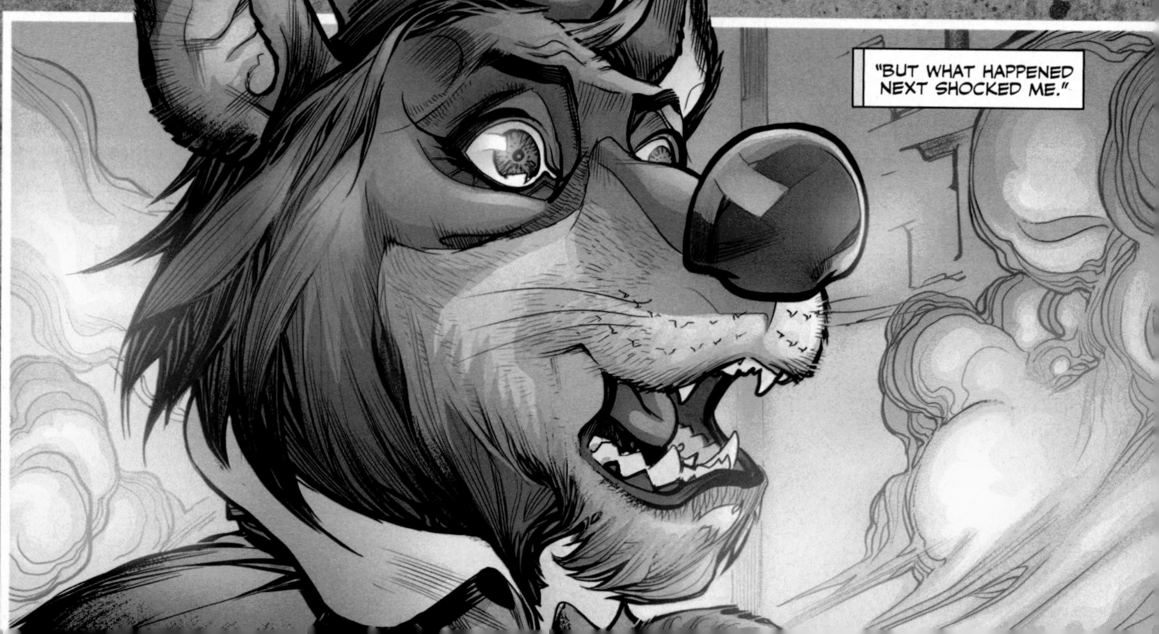
"BUT WHAT HAPPENED NEXT SHOCKED ME."

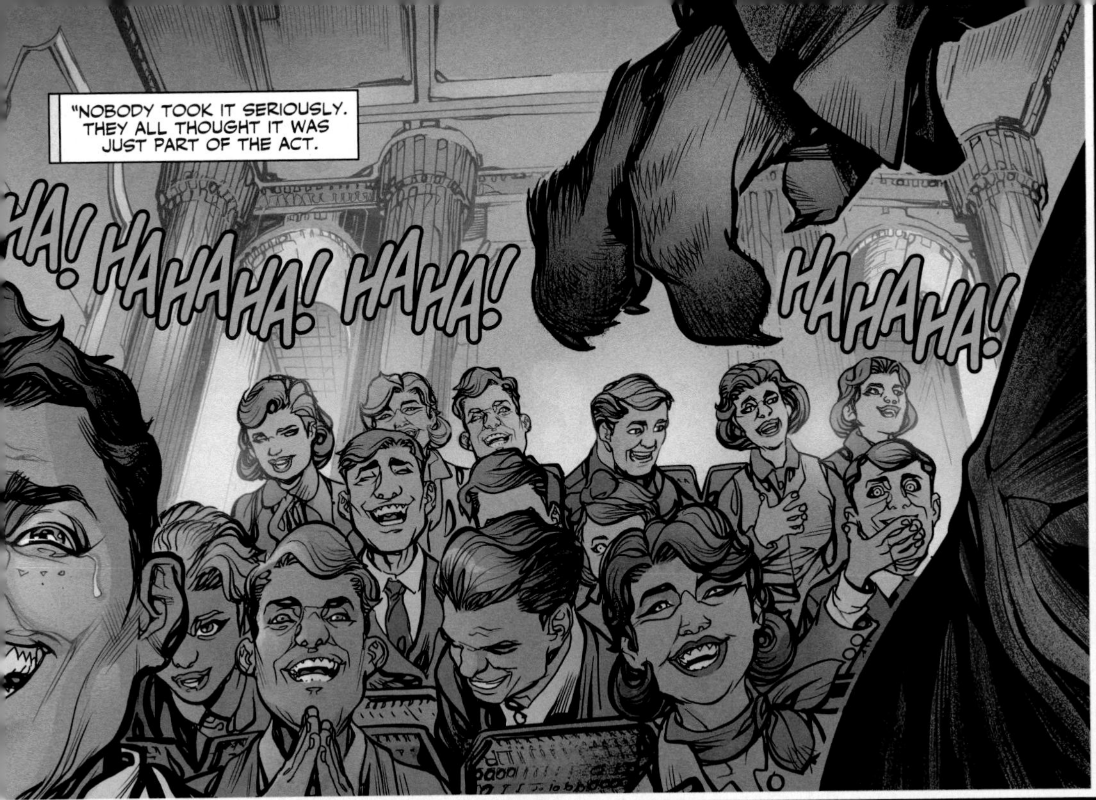

"NOBODY TOOK IT SERIOUSLY. THEY ALL THOUGHT IT WAS JUST PART OF THE ACT.
HA! HAHAHA! HAHA!
HAHAHA!

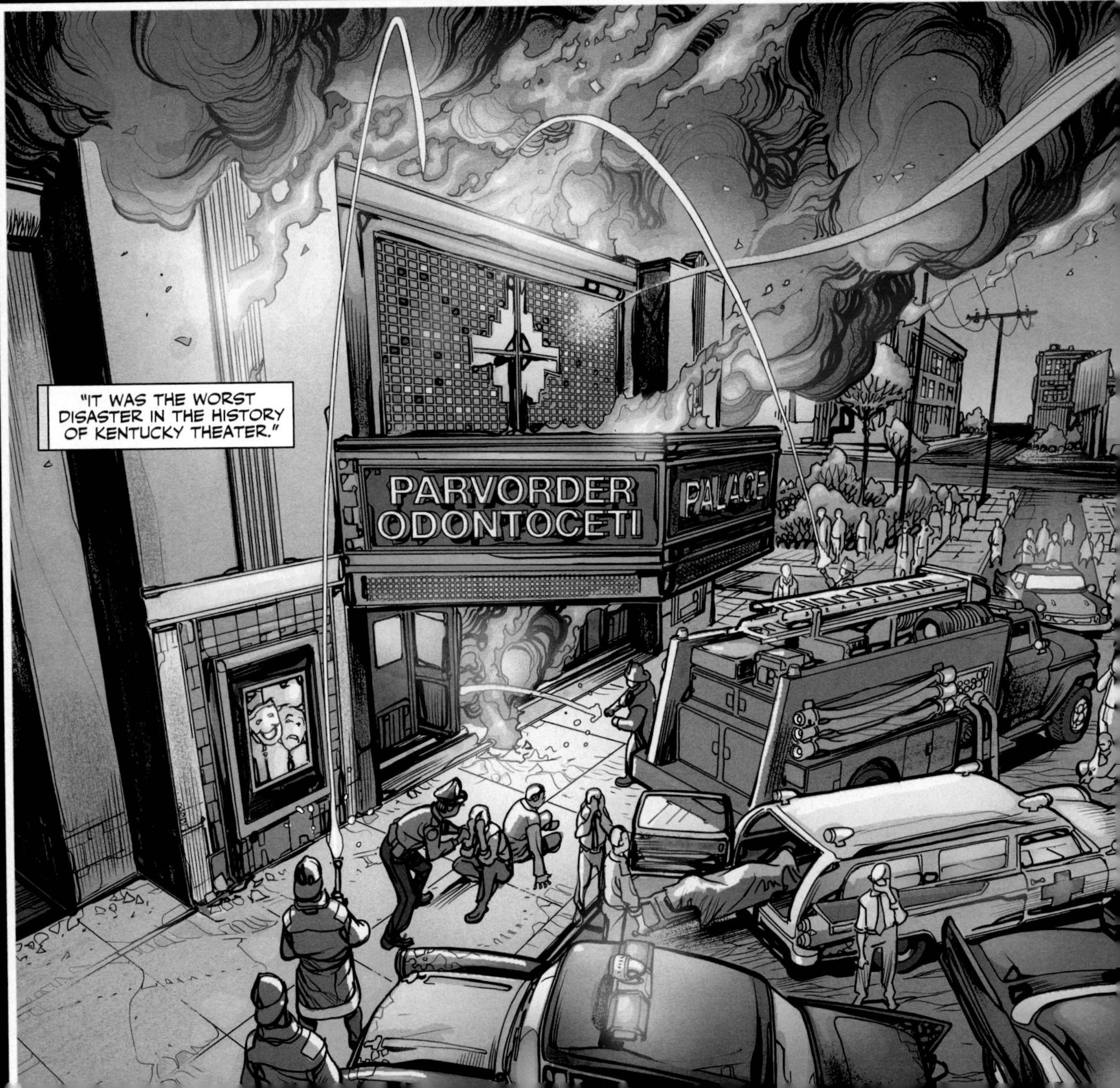

"IT WAS THE WORST DISASTER IN THE HISTORY OF KENTUCKY THEATER."
PARVORDER ODONTOCETI
PALACE

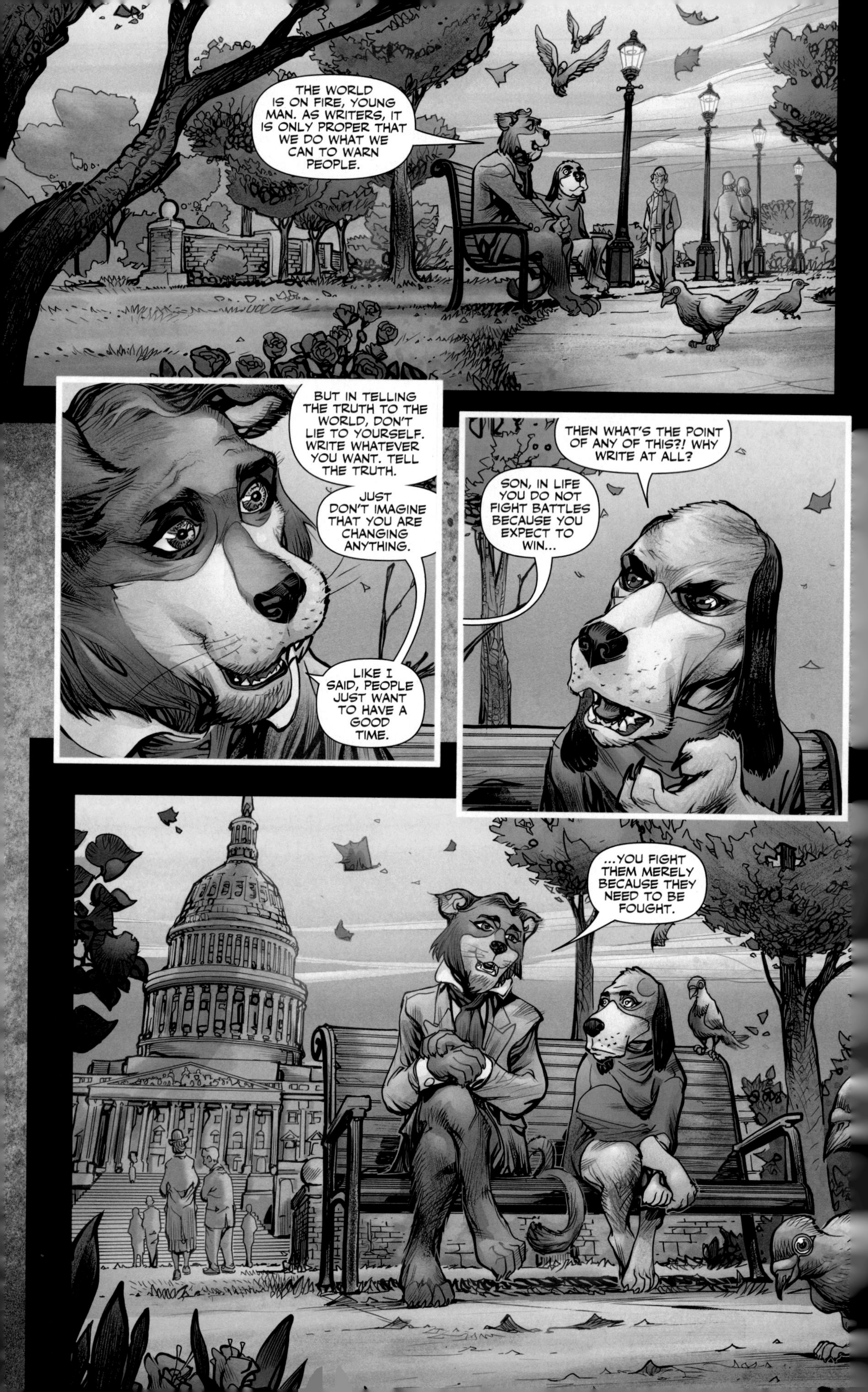
THE WORLD IS ON FIRE, YOUNG MAN. AS WRITERS, IT IS ONLY PROPER THAT WE DO WHAT WE CAN TO WARN PEOPLE.
BUT IN TELLING THE TRUTH TO THE WORLD, DON'T LIE TO YOURSELF. WRITE WHATEVER YOU WANT. TELL THE TRUTH.
JUST DON'T IMAGINE THAT YOU ARE CHANGING ANYTHING.
LIKE I SAID, PEOPLE JUST WANT TO HAVE A GOOD TIME.
THEN WHAT'S THE POINT OF ANY OF THIS?! WHY WRITE AT ALL?
SON, IN LIFE YOU DO NOT FIGHT BATTLES BECAUSE YOU EXPECT TO WIN...
...YOU FIGHT THEM MERELY BECAUSE THEY NEED TO BE FOUGHT.

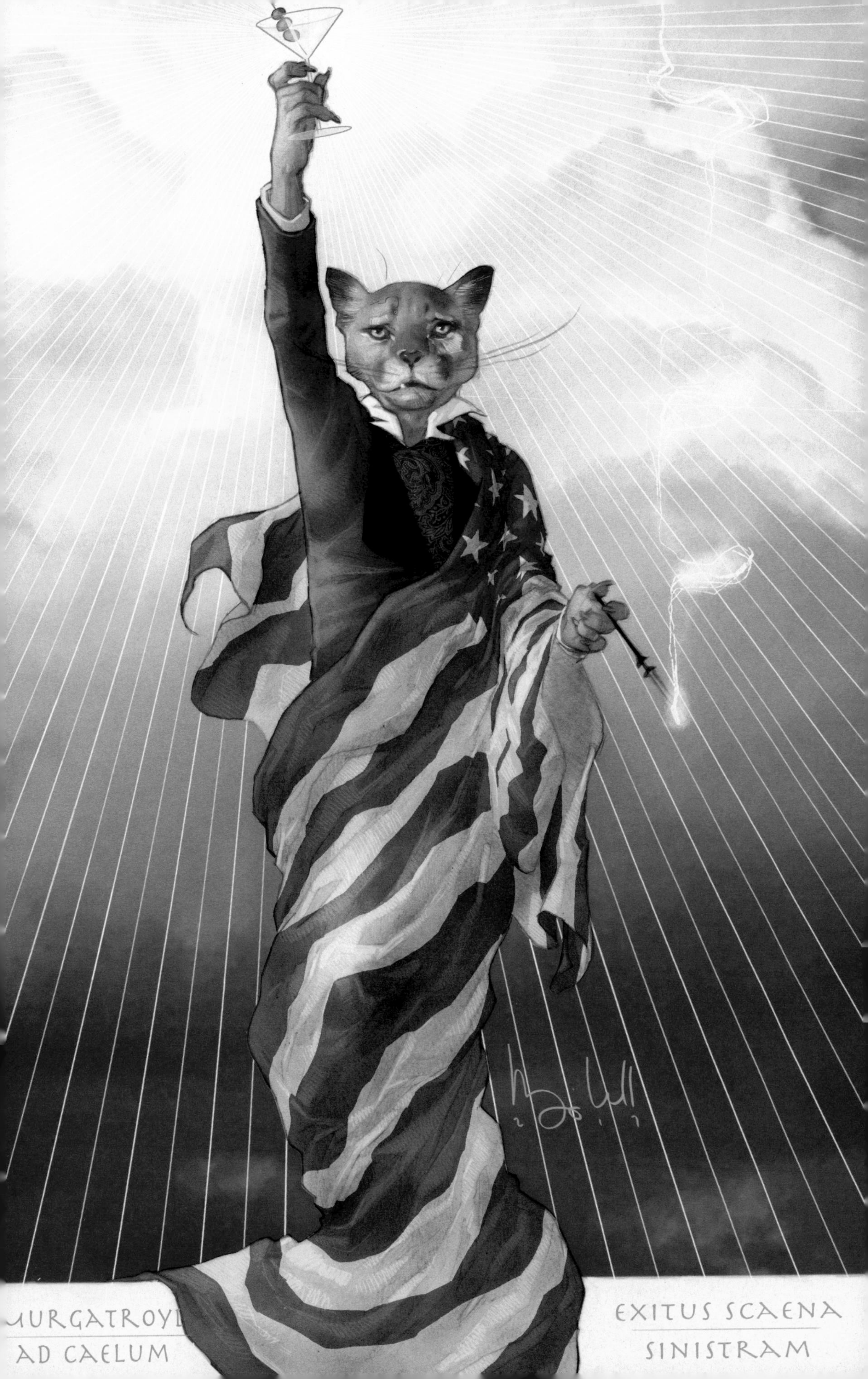
MURGATROYD
AD CAELUM
EXITUS SCAENA
SINISTRAM

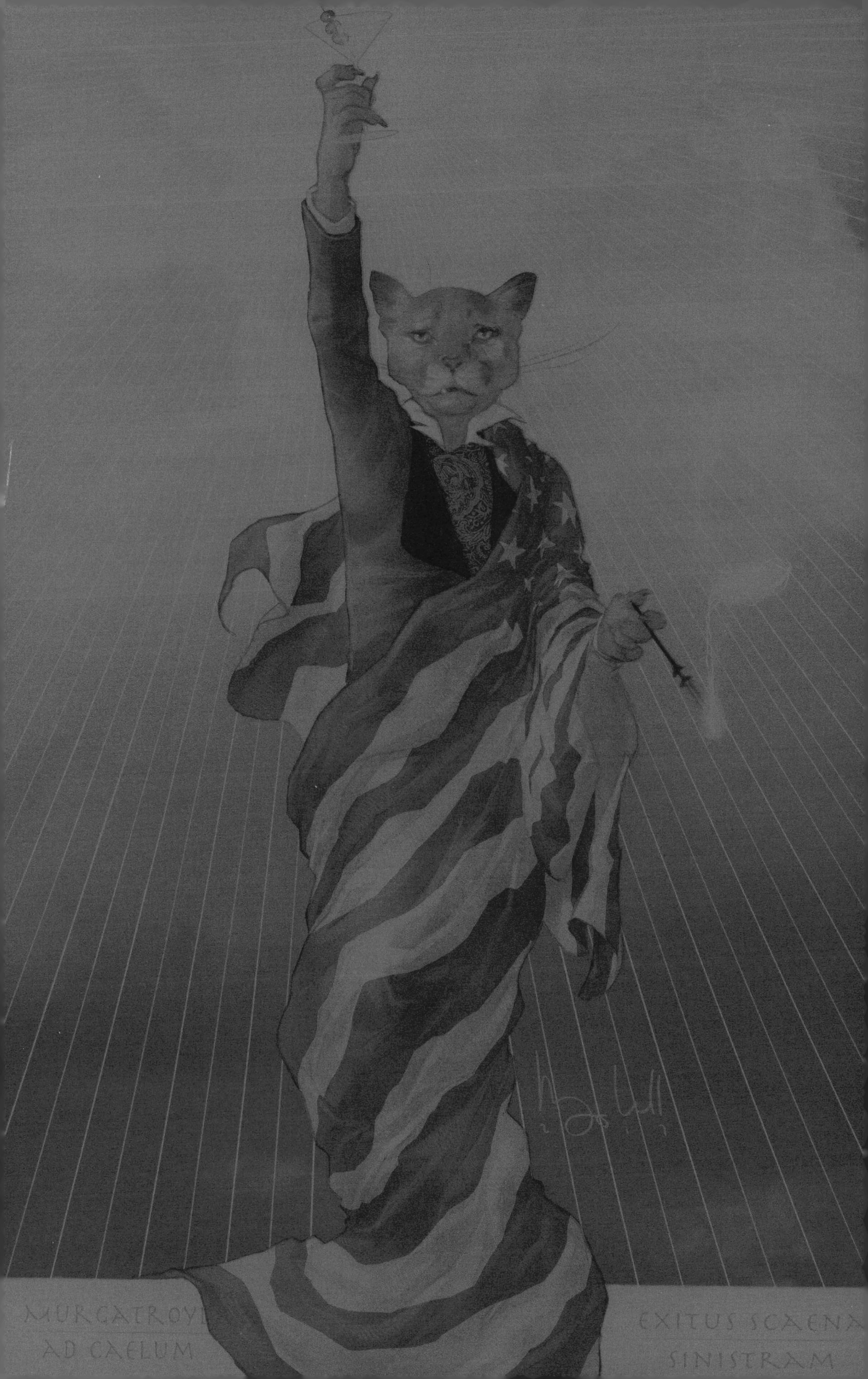
MURGATROY
AD CAELUM
EXITUS SCAENA
SINISTRAM

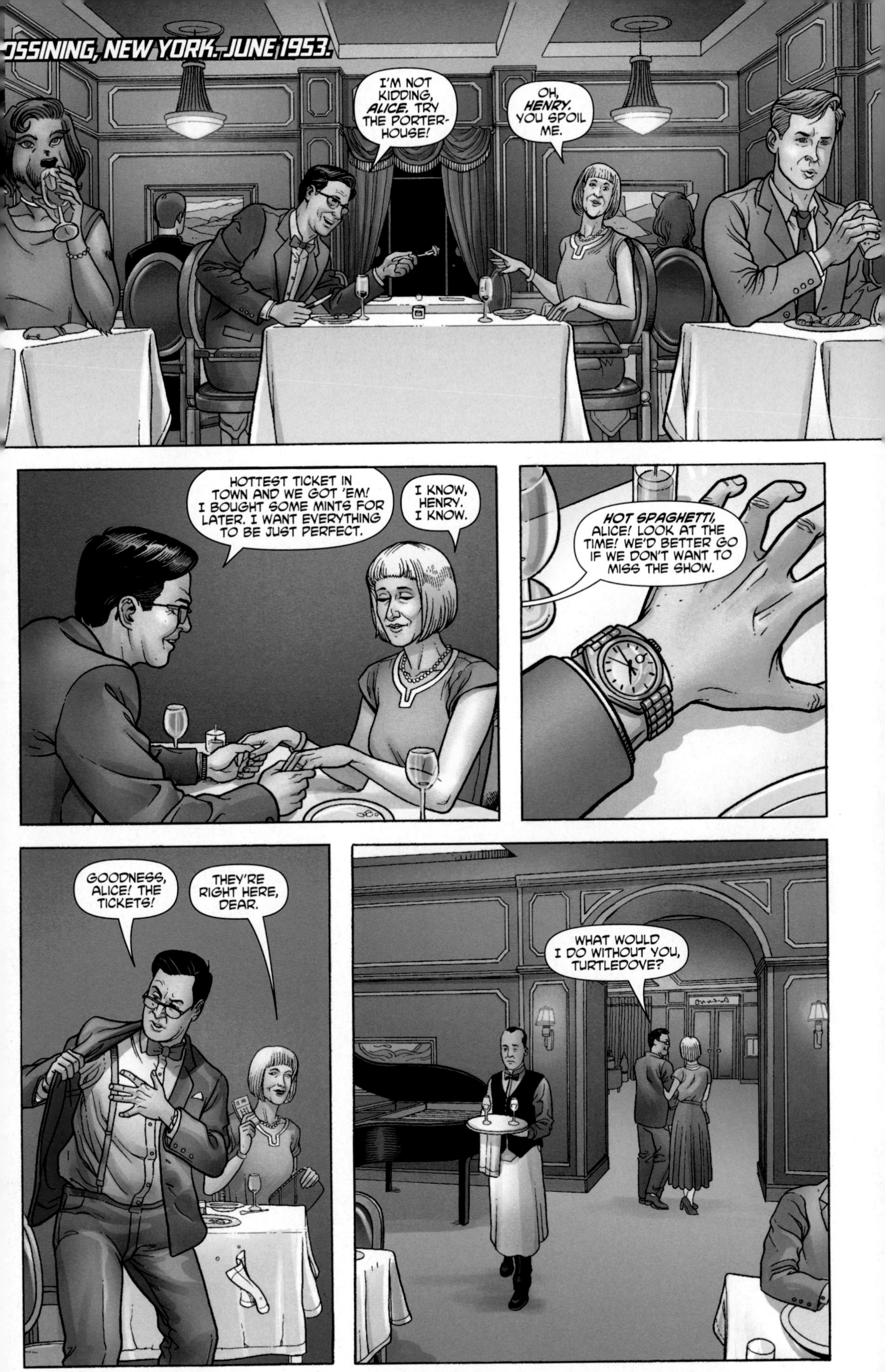
OSSINING, NEW YORK. JUNE 1953.
I'M NOT KIDDING, ALICE. TRY THE PORTERHOUSE!
OH, HENRY. YOU SPOIL ME.
HOTTEST TICKET IN TOWN AND WE GOT 'EM! I BOUGHT SOME MINTS FOR LATER. I WANT EVERYTHING TO BE JUST PERFECT.
I KNOW, HENRY. I KNOW.
HOT SPAGHETTI, ALICE! LOOK AT THE TIME! WE'D BETTER GO IF WE DON'T WANT TO MISS THE SHOW.
GOODNESS, ALICE! THE TICKETS!
THEY'RE RIGHT HERE, DEAR.
WHAT WOULD I DO WITHOUT YOU, TURTLEDOVE?

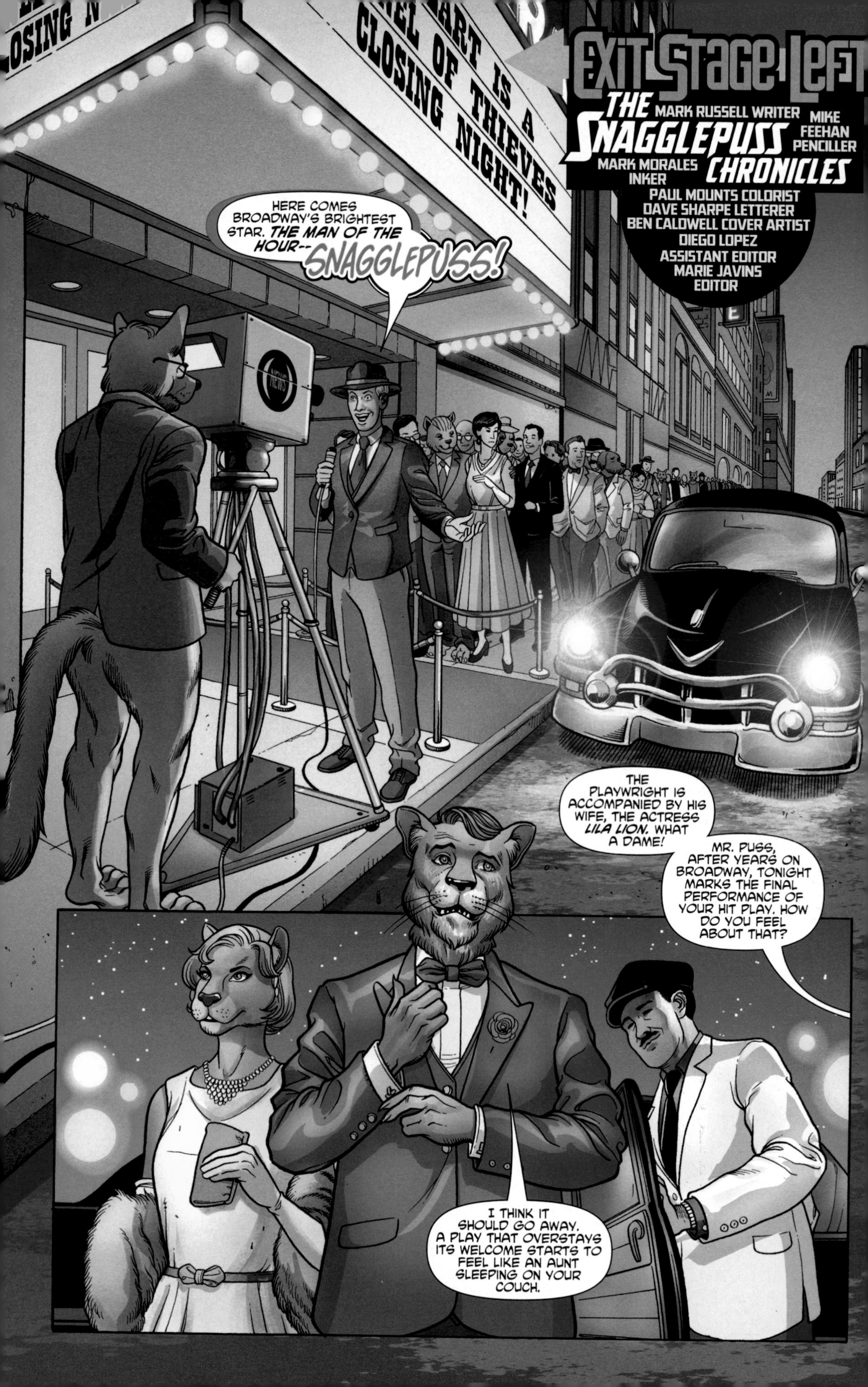

...NEL ART IS A
...OF THIEVES
CLOSING NIGHT!
...OSING N
EXIT STAGE LEFT
THE SNAGGLEPUSS CHRONICLES
MARK RUSSELL WRITER
MIKE FEEHAN PENCILLER
MARK MORALES INKER
PAUL MOUNTS COLORIST
DAVE SHARPE LETTERER
BEN CALDWELL COVER ARTIST
DIEGO LOPEZ ASSISTANT EDITOR
MARIE JAVINS EDITOR
HERE COMES BROADWAY'S BRIGHTEST STAR. *THE MAN OF THE HOUR--* SNAGGLEPUSS!
NEWS
THE PLAYWRIGHT IS ACCOMPANIED BY HIS WIFE, THE ACTRESS *LILA LION.* WHAT A DAME!
MR. PUSS, AFTER YEARS ON BROADWAY, TONIGHT MARKS THE FINAL PERFORMANCE OF YOUR HIT PLAY. HOW DO YOU FEEL ABOUT THAT?
I THINK IT SHOULD GO AWAY. A PLAY THAT OVERSTAYS ITS WELCOME STARTS TO FEEL LIKE AN AUNT SLEEPING ON YOUR COUCH.

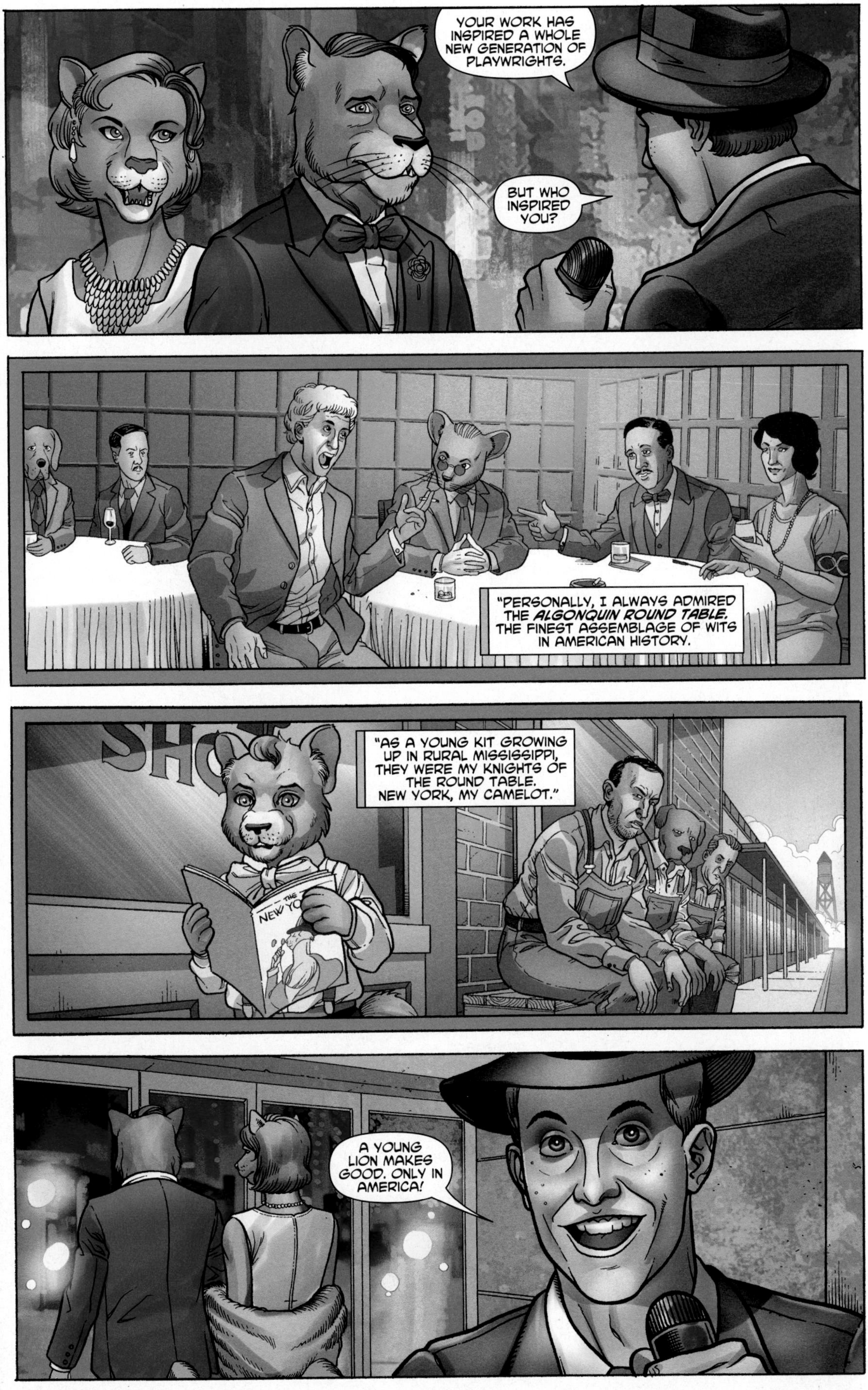
YOUR WORK HAS INSPIRED A WHOLE NEW GENERATION OF PLAYWRIGHTS.
BUT WHO INSPIRED YOU?
"PERSONALLY, I ALWAYS ADMIRED THE *ALGONQUIN ROUND TABLE.* THE FINEST ASSEMBLAGE OF WITS IN AMERICAN HISTORY.
"AS A YOUNG KIT GROWING UP IN RURAL MISSISSIPPI, THEY WERE MY KNIGHTS OF THE ROUND TABLE. NEW YORK, MY CAMELOT."
A YOUNG LION MAKES GOOD. ONLY IN AMERICA!

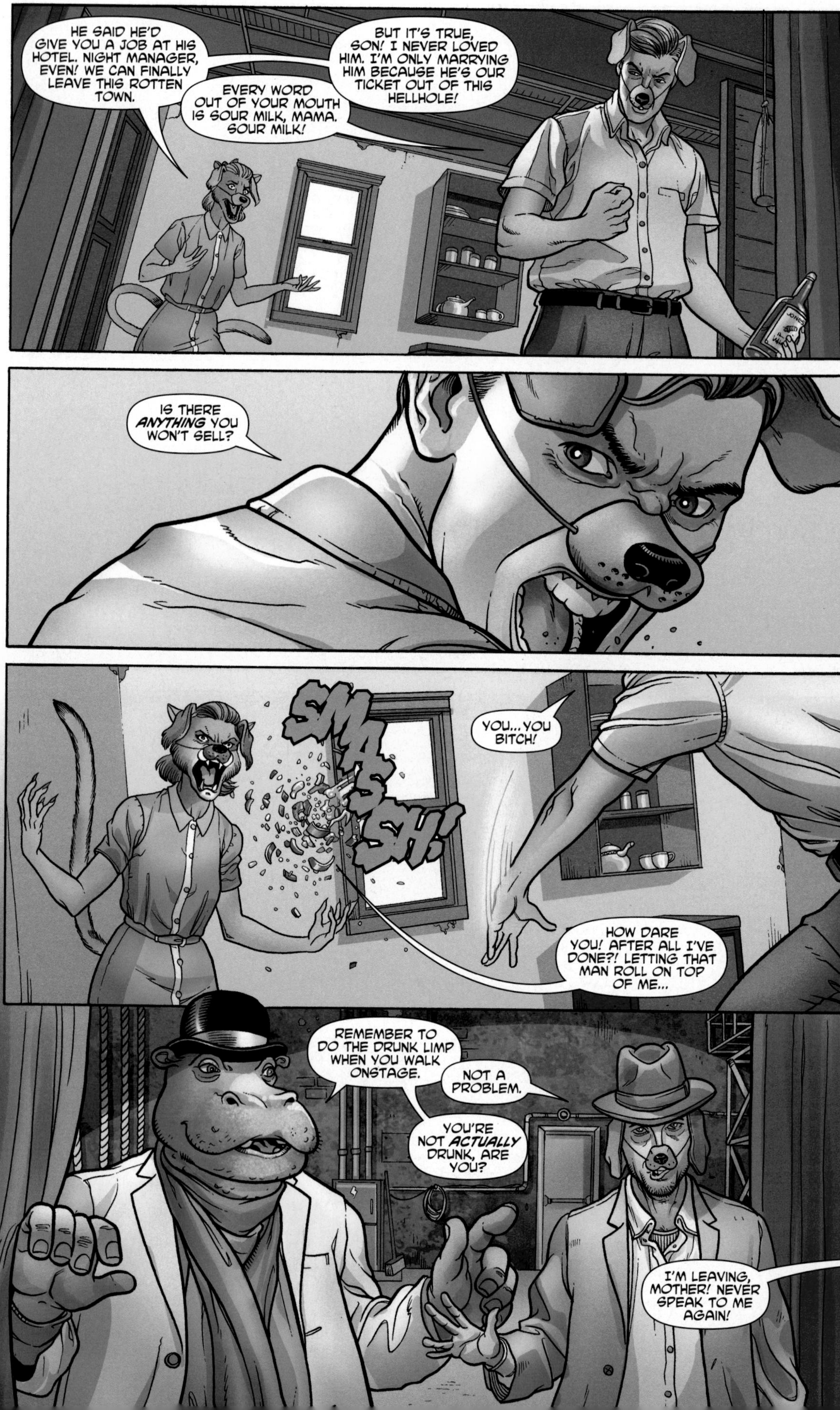

HE SAID HE'D GIVE YOU A JOB AT HIS HOTEL. NIGHT MANAGER, EVEN! WE CAN FINALLY LEAVE THIS ROTTEN TOWN.
EVERY WORD OUT OF YOUR MOUTH IS SOUR MILK, MAMA. SOUR MILK!
BUT IT'S TRUE, SON! I NEVER LOVED HIM. I'M ONLY MARRYING HIM BECAUSE HE'S OUR TICKET OUT OF THIS HELLHOLE!
IS THERE *ANYTHING* YOU WON'T SELL?
SMASSSH!
YOU...YOU BITCH!
HOW DARE YOU! AFTER ALL I'VE DONE?! LETTING THAT MAN ROLL ON TOP OF ME...
REMEMBER TO DO THE DRUNK LIMP WHEN YOU WALK ONSTAGE.
NOT A PROBLEM.
YOU'RE NOT *ACTUALLY* DRUNK, ARE YOU?
I'M LEAVING, MOTHER! NEVER SPEAK TO ME AGAIN!

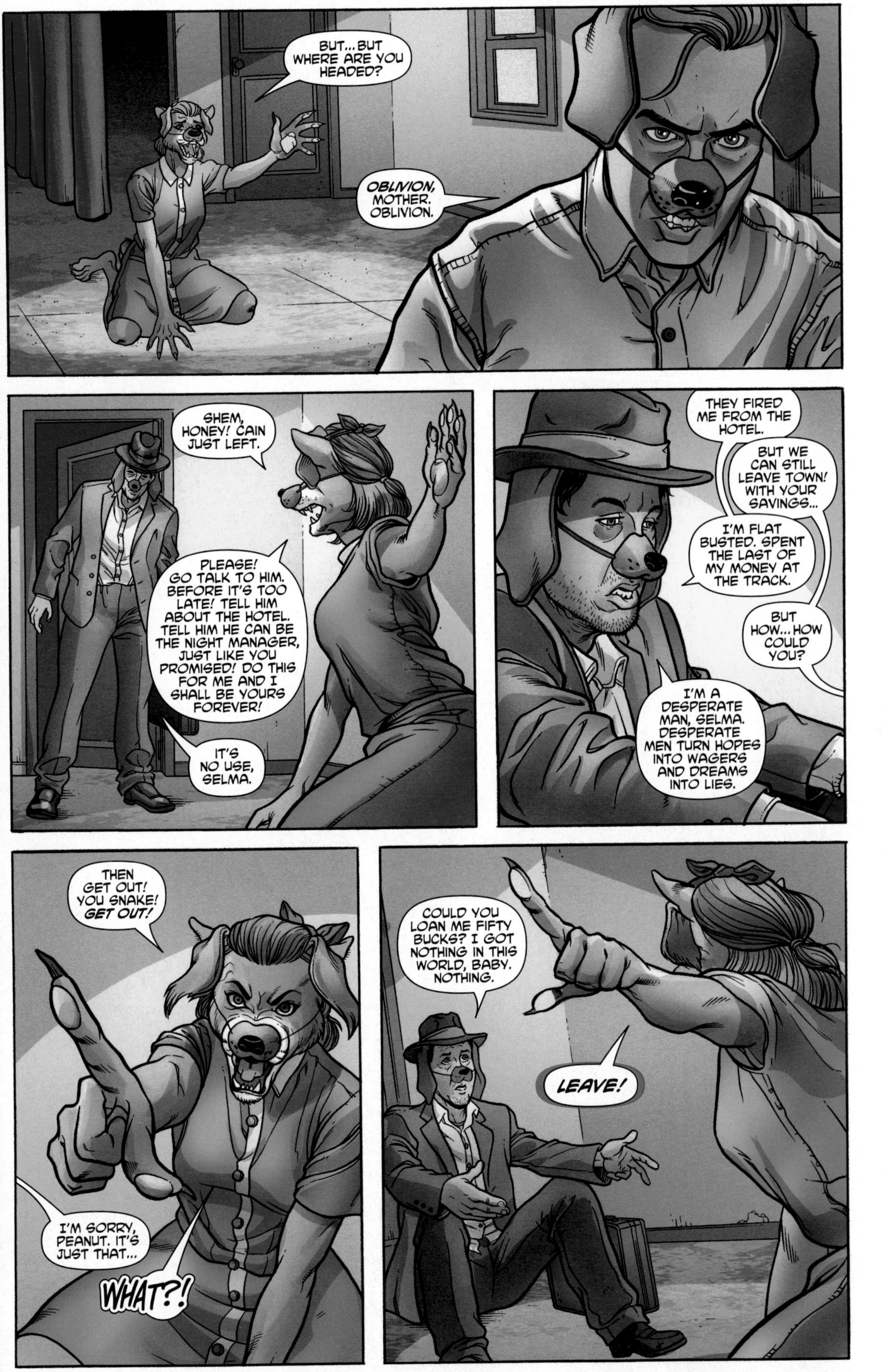
BUT... BUT WHERE ARE YOU HEADED?
OBLIVION, MOTHER. OBLIVION.
SHEM, HONEY! CAIN JUST LEFT.
PLEASE! GO TALK TO HIM. BEFORE IT'S TOO LATE! TELL HIM ABOUT THE HOTEL. TELL HIM HE CAN BE THE NIGHT MANAGER, JUST LIKE YOU PROMISED! DO THIS FOR ME AND I SHALL BE YOURS FOREVER!
IT'S NO USE, SELMA.
THEY FIRED ME FROM THE HOTEL.
BUT WE CAN STILL LEAVE TOWN! WITH YOUR SAVINGS...
I'M FLAT BUSTED. SPENT THE LAST OF MY MONEY AT THE TRACK.
BUT HOW... HOW COULD YOU?
I'M A DESPERATE MAN, SELMA. DESPERATE MEN TURN HOPES INTO WAGERS AND DREAMS INTO LIES.
THEN GET OUT! YOU SNAKE! *GET OUT!*
I'M SORRY, PEANUT. IT'S JUST THAT...
WHAT?!
COULD YOU LOAN ME FIFTY BUCKS? I GOT NOTHING IN THIS WORLD, BABY. NOTHING.
LEAVE!

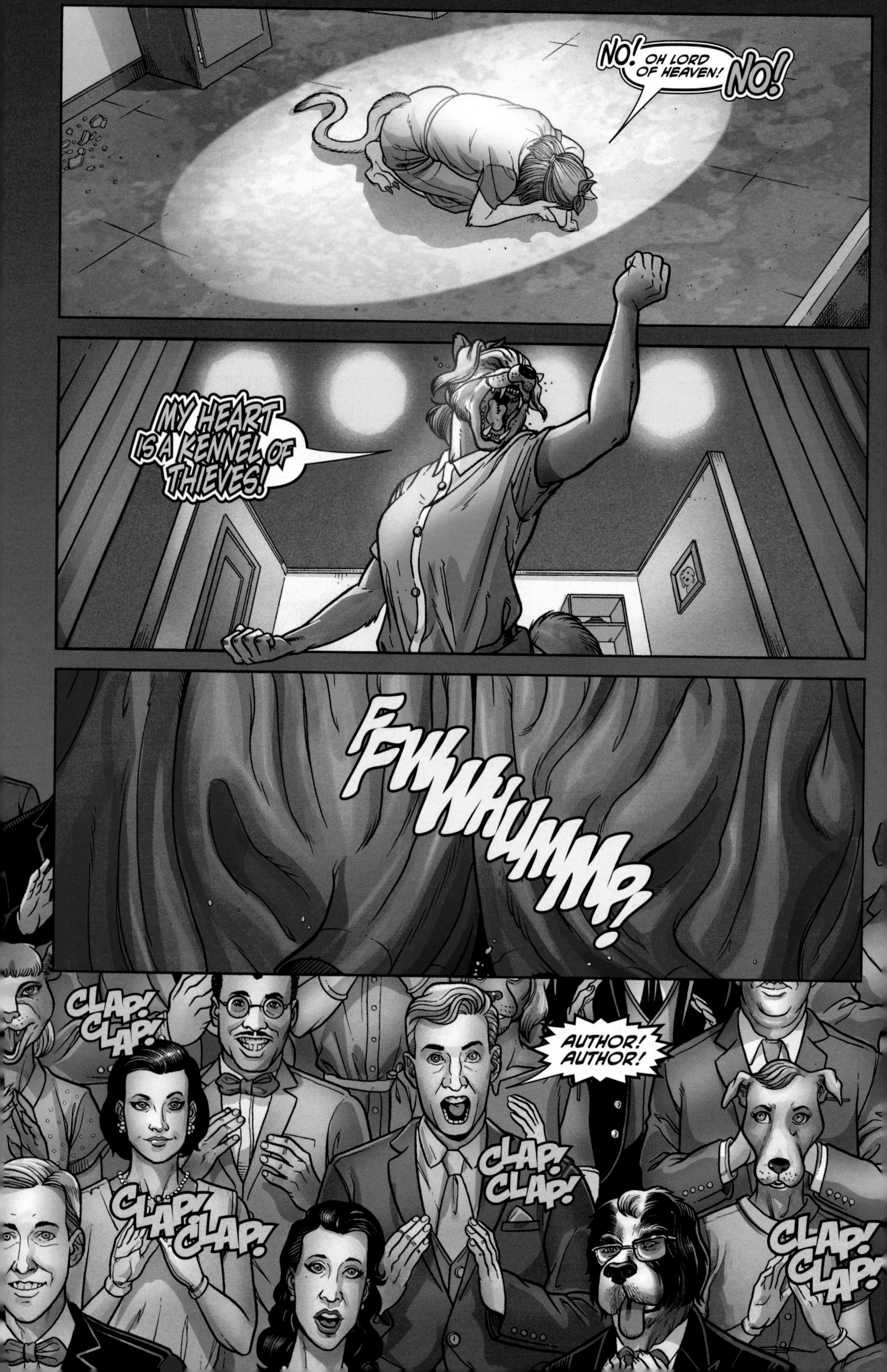
NO! OH LORD OF HEAVEN! NO!
MY HEART IS A KENNEL OF THIEVES!
FFWHUMMP!
CLAP! CLAP!
AUTHOR! AUTHOR!
CLAP! CLAP!
CLAP! CLAP!
CLAP! CLAP!

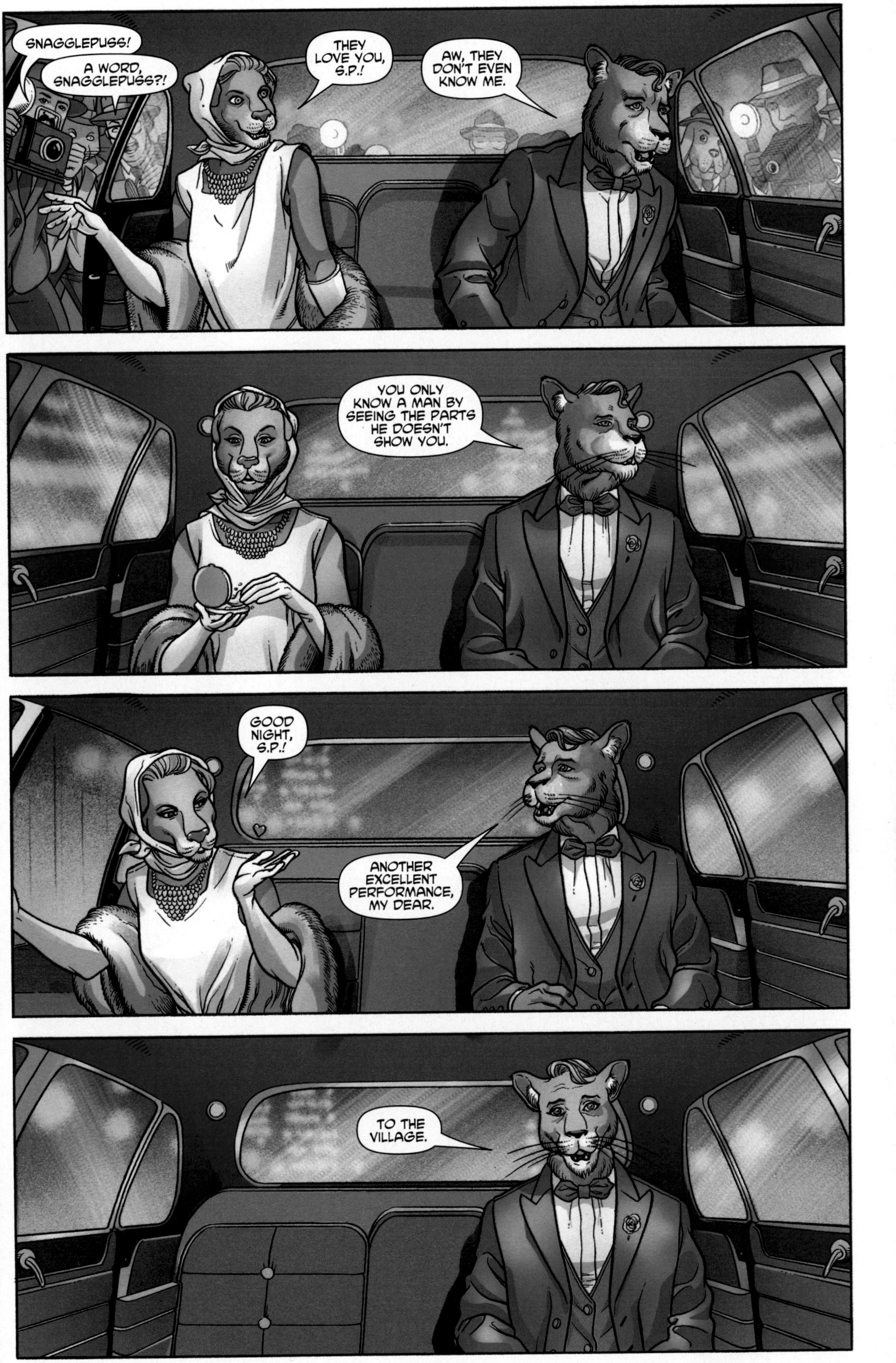
SNAGGLEPUSS!
A WORD, SNAGGLEPUSS?!
THEY LOVE YOU, S.P.!
AW, THEY DON'T EVEN KNOW ME.
YOU ONLY KNOW A MAN BY SEEING THE PARTS HE DOESN'T SHOW YOU.
GOOD NIGHT, S.P.!
ANOTHER EXCELLENT PERFORMANCE, MY DEAR.
TO THE VILLAGE.

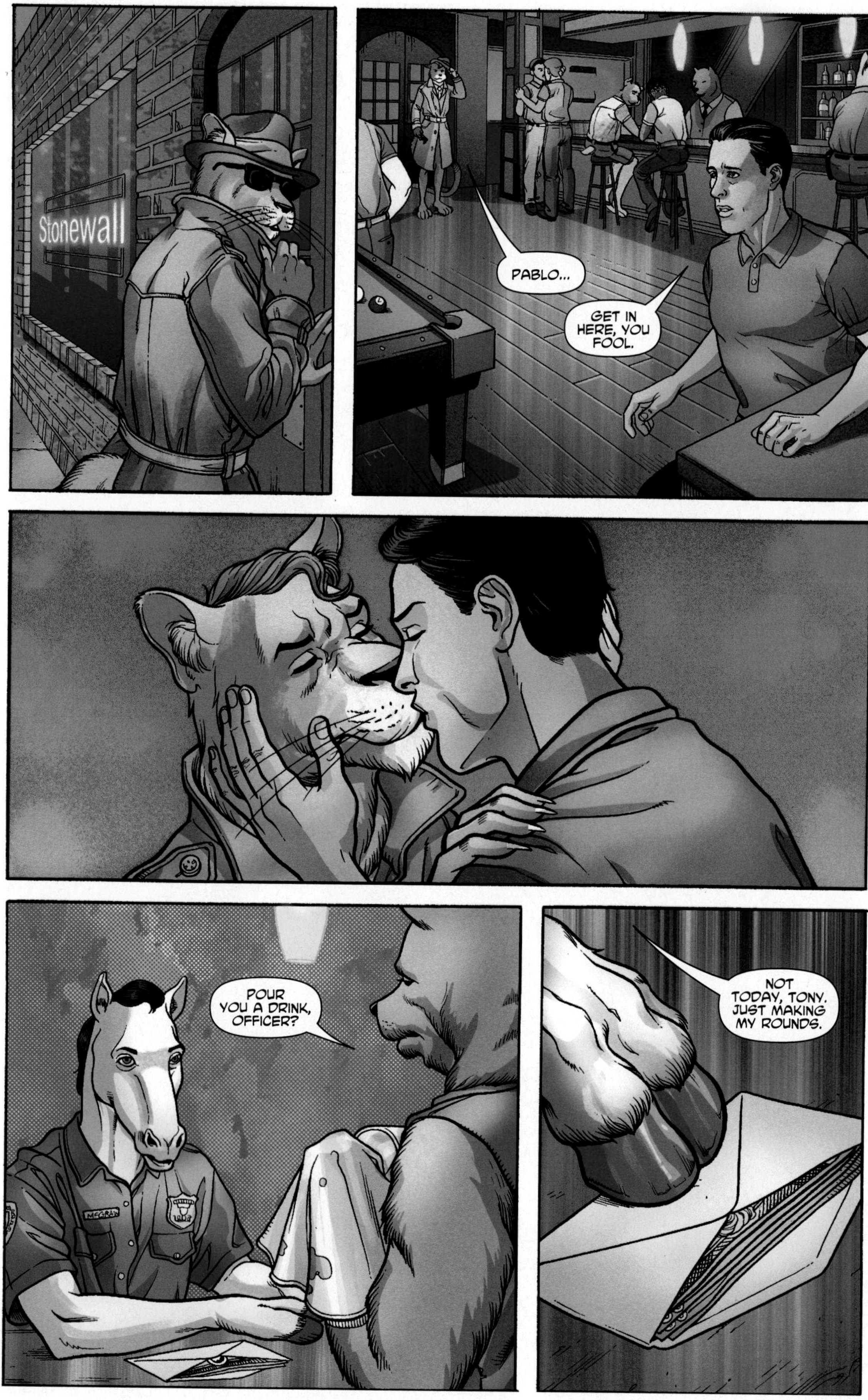
Stonewall
PABLO...
GET IN HERE, YOU FOOL.
POUR YOU A DRINK, OFFICER?
NOT TODAY, TONY. JUST MAKING MY ROUNDS.

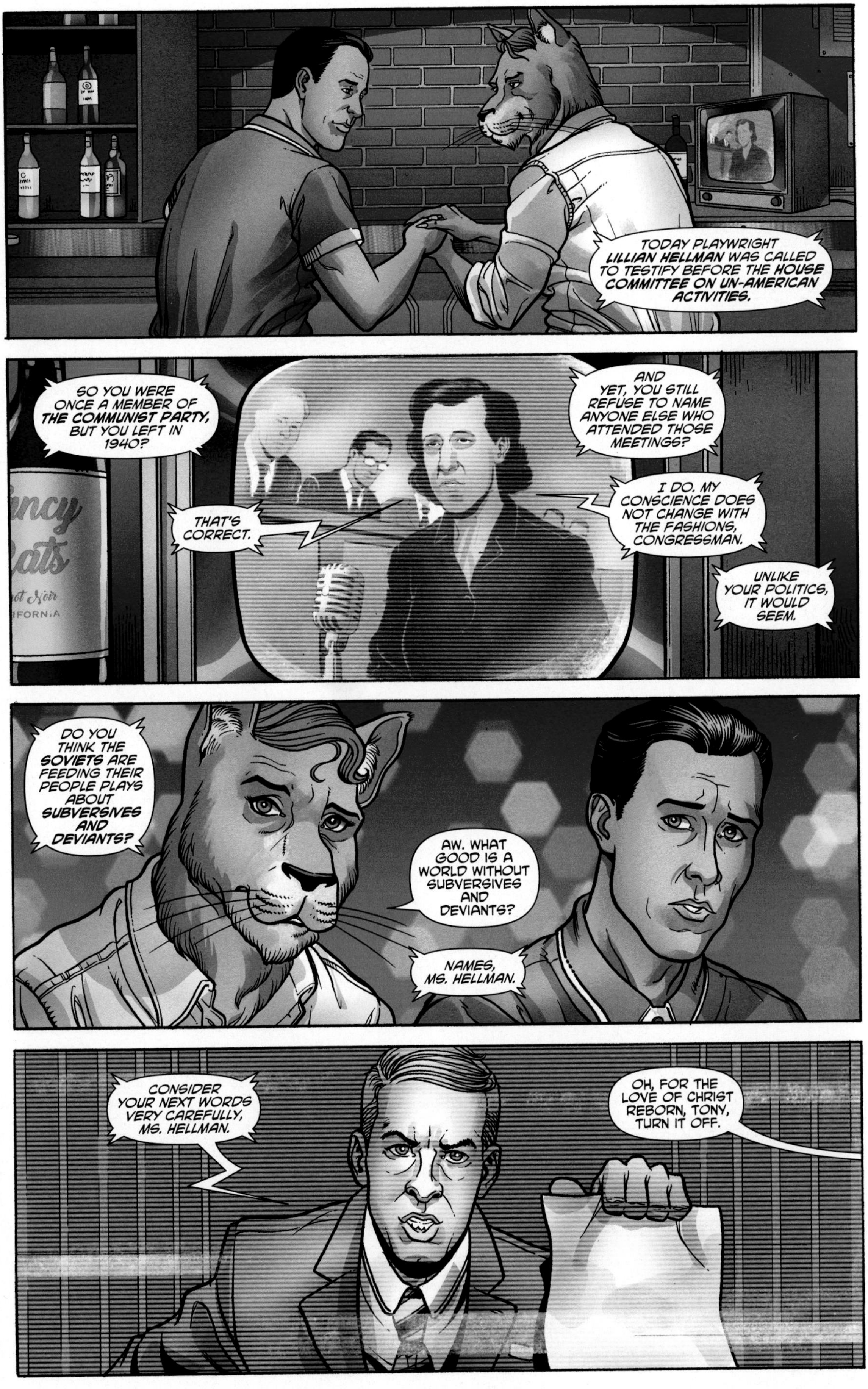
TODAY PLAYWRIGHT LILLIAN HELLMAN WAS CALLED TO TESTIFY BEFORE THE HOUSE COMMITTEE ON UN-AMERICAN ACTIVITIES.
SO YOU WERE ONCE A MEMBER OF THE COMMUNIST PARTY, BUT YOU LEFT IN 1940?
THAT'S CORRECT.
AND YET, YOU STILL REFUSE TO NAME ANYONE ELSE WHO ATTENDED THOSE MEETINGS?
I DO. MY CONSCIENCE DOES NOT CHANGE WITH THE FASHIONS, CONGRESSMAN.
UNLIKE YOUR POLITICS, IT WOULD SEEM.
DO YOU THINK THE SOVIETS ARE FEEDING THEIR PEOPLE PLAYS ABOUT SUBVERSIVES AND DEVIANTS?
AW. WHAT GOOD IS A WORLD WITHOUT SUBVERSIVES AND DEVIANTS?
NAMES, MS. HELLMAN.
CONSIDER YOUR NEXT WORDS VERY CAREFULLY, MS. HELLMAN.
OH, FOR THE LOVE OF CHRIST REBORN, TONY, TURN IT OFF.

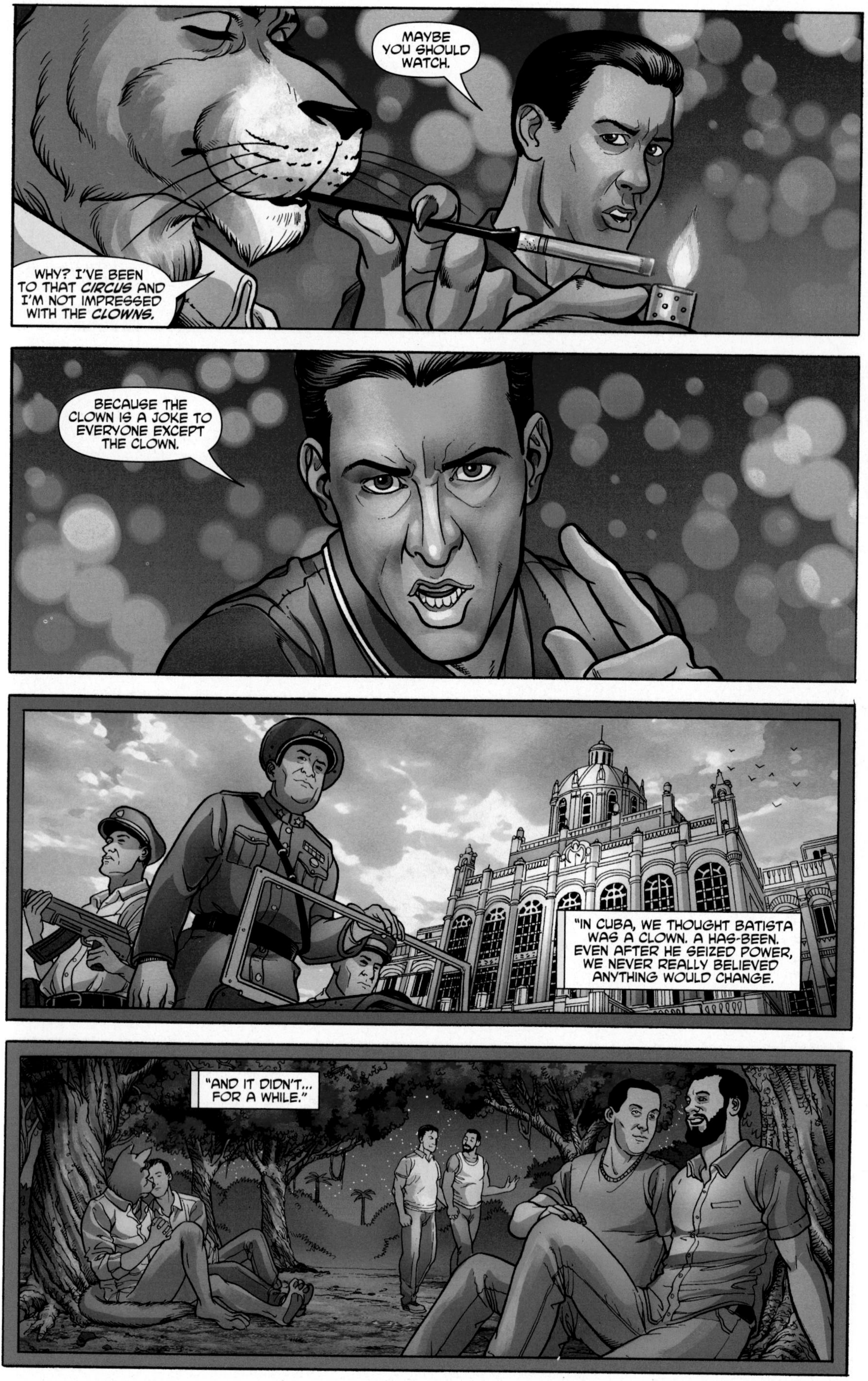
MAYBE YOU SHOULD WATCH.
WHY? I'VE BEEN TO THAT CIRCUS AND I'M NOT IMPRESSED WITH THE CLOWNS.
BECAUSE THE CLOWN IS A JOKE TO EVERYONE EXCEPT THE CLOWN.
"IN CUBA, WE THOUGHT BATISTA WAS A CLOWN. A HAS-BEEN. EVEN AFTER HE SEIZED POWER, WE NEVER REALLY BELIEVED ANYTHING WOULD CHANGE.
"AND IT DIDN'T... FOR A WHILE."

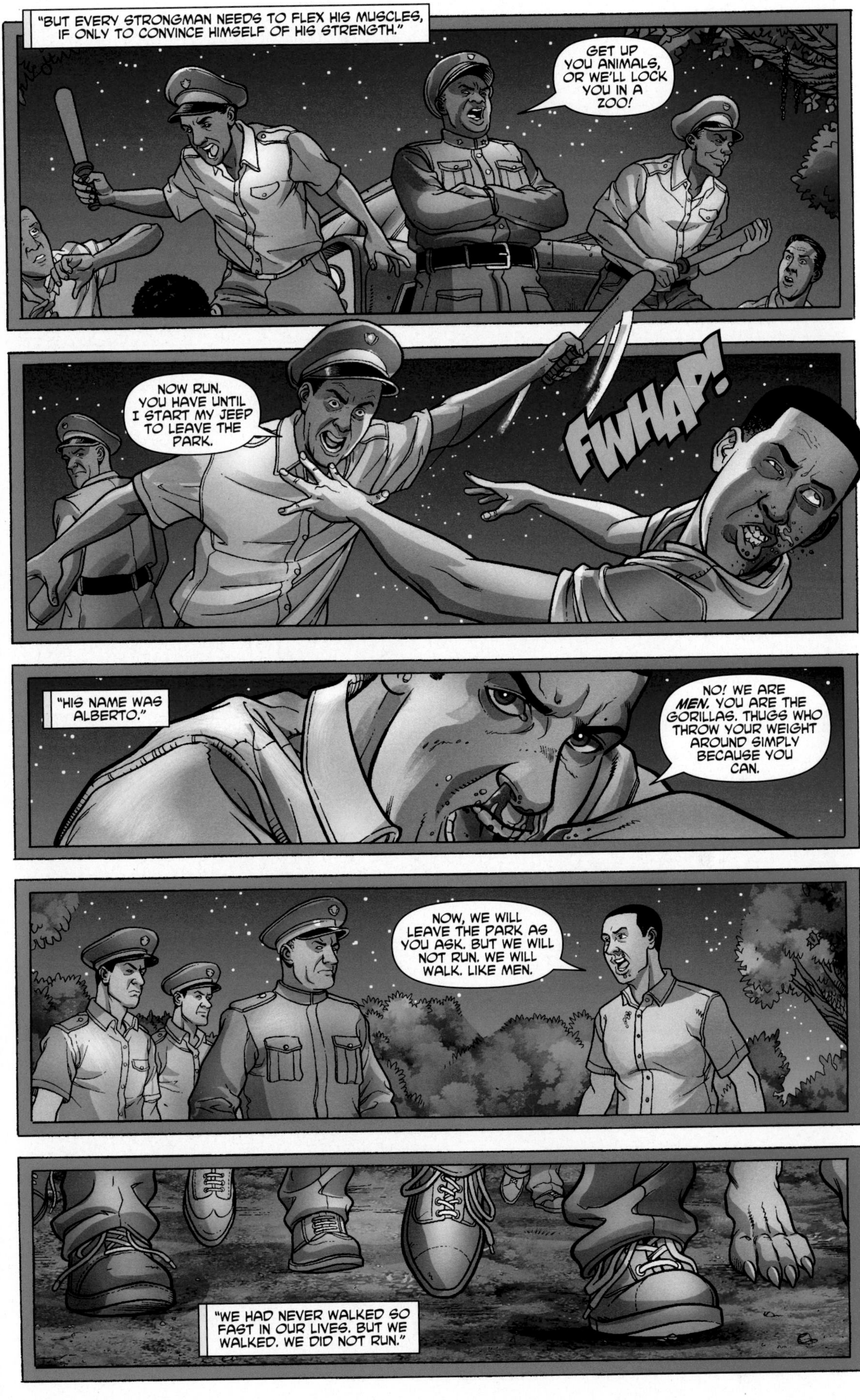
"BUT EVERY STRONGMAN NEEDS TO FLEX HIS MUSCLES, IF ONLY TO CONVINCE HIMSELF OF HIS STRENGTH."
GET UP YOU ANIMALS, OR WE'LL LOCK YOU IN A ZOO!
NOW RUN. YOU HAVE UNTIL I START MY JEEP TO LEAVE THE PARK.
FWHAP!
"HIS NAME WAS ALBERTO."
NO! WE ARE MEN. YOU ARE THE GORILLAS. THUGS WHO THROW YOUR WEIGHT AROUND SIMPLY BECAUSE YOU CAN.
NOW, WE WILL LEAVE THE PARK AS YOU ASK. BUT WE WILL NOT RUN. WE WILL WALK. LIKE MEN.
"WE HAD NEVER WALKED SO FAST IN OUR LIVES. BUT WE WALKED. WE DID NOT RUN."

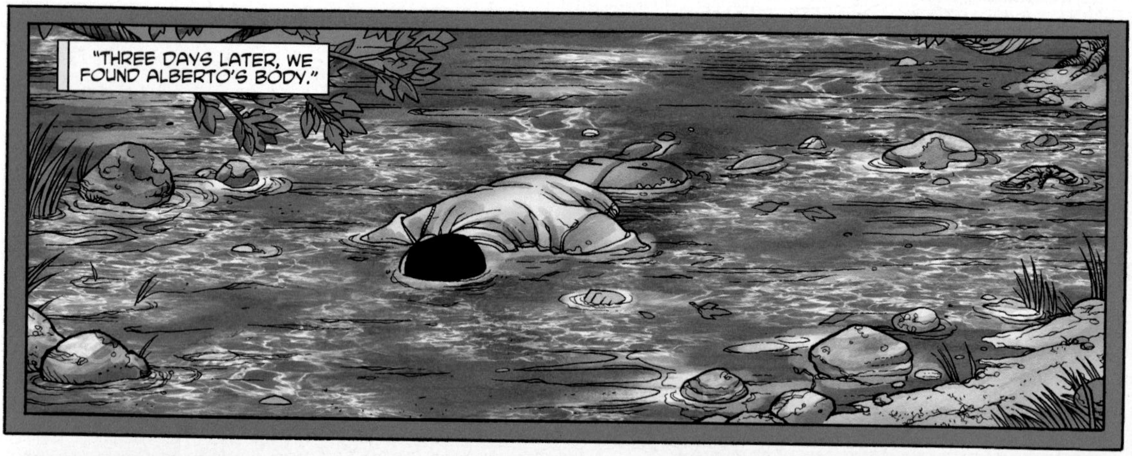
"THREE DAYS LATER, WE FOUND ALBERTO'S BODY."

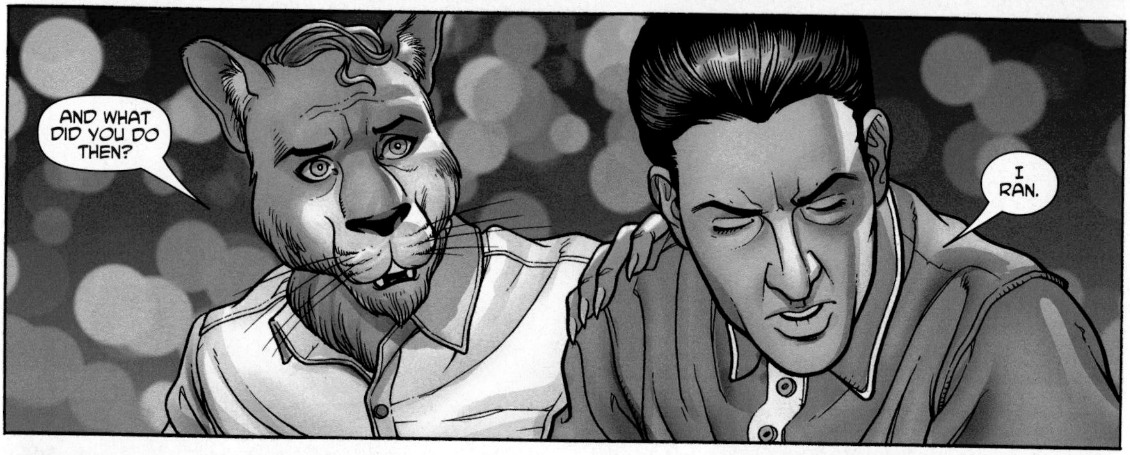
AND WHAT DID YOU DO THEN?
I RAN.

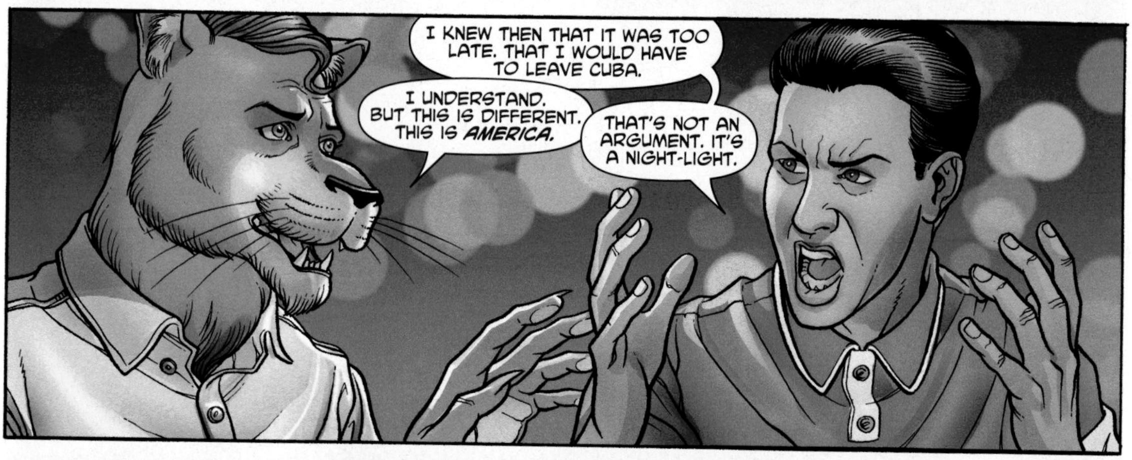
I KNEW THEN THAT IT WAS TOO LATE. THAT I WOULD HAVE TO LEAVE CUBA.
I UNDERSTAND. BUT THIS IS DIFFERENT. THIS IS *AMERICA.*
THAT'S NOT AN ARGUMENT. IT'S A NIGHT-LIGHT.

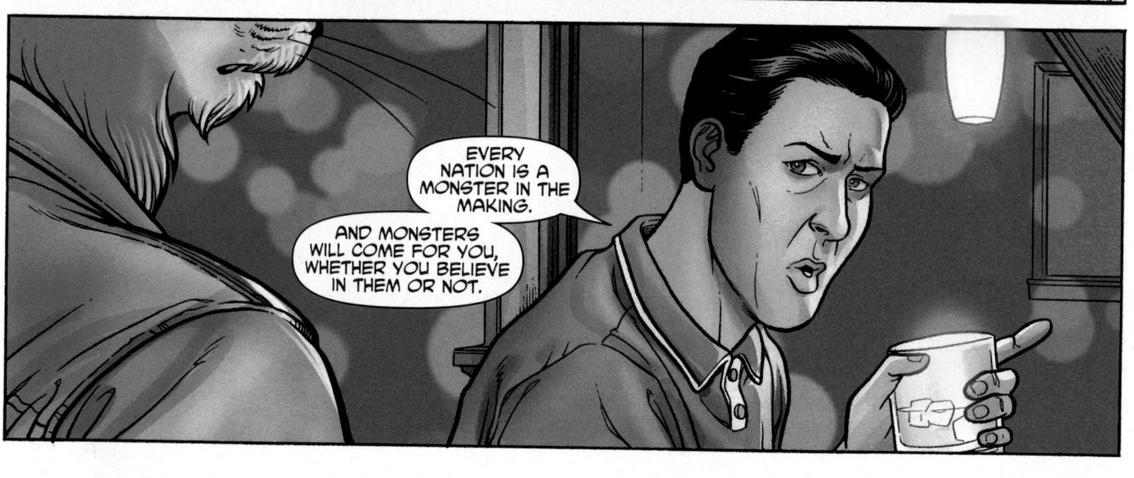
EVERY NATION IS A MONSTER IN THE MAKING.
AND MONSTERS WILL COME FOR YOU, WHETHER YOU BELIEVE IN THEM OR NOT.

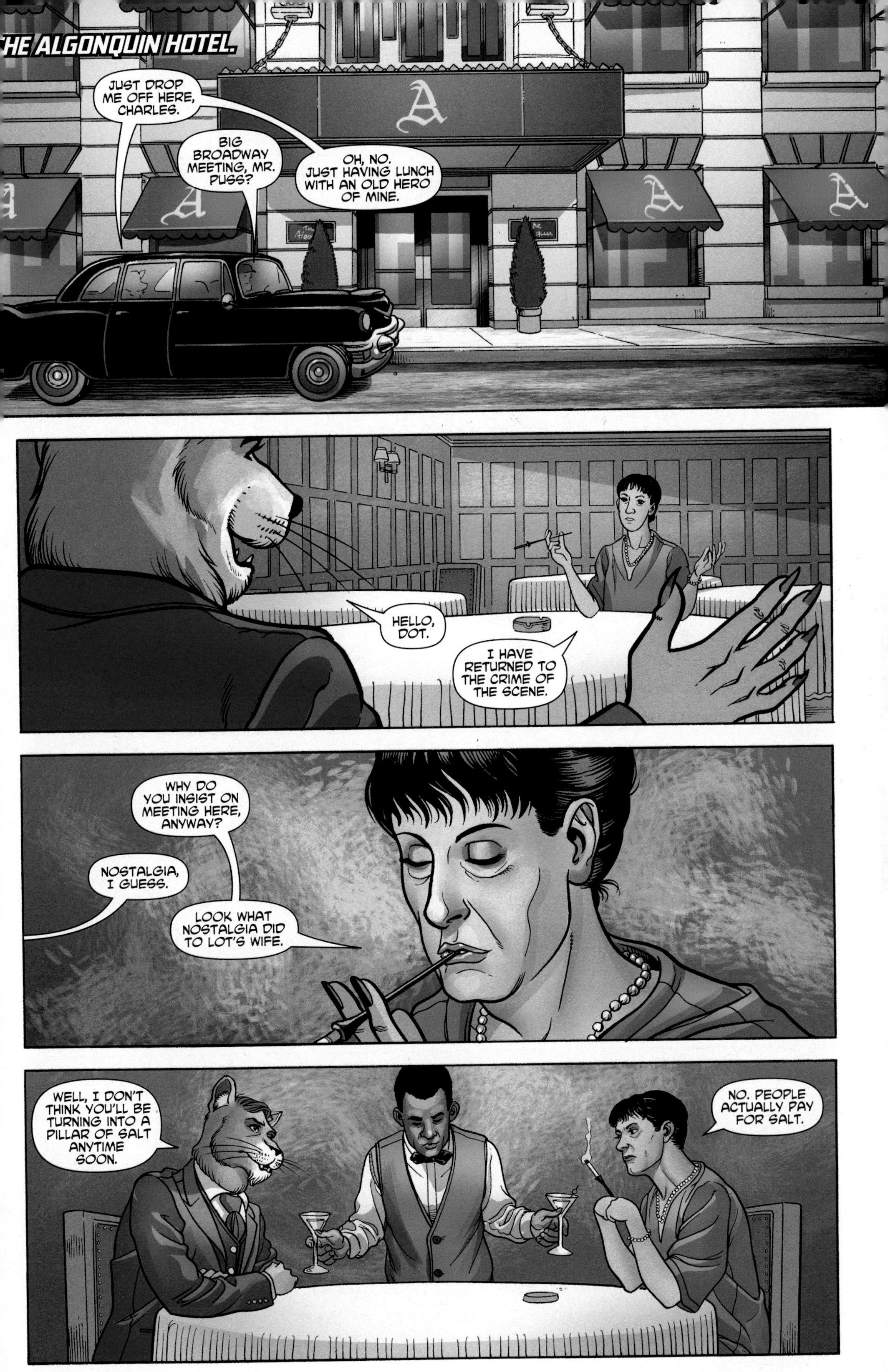
THE ALGONQUIN HOTEL.
JUST DROP ME OFF HERE, CHARLES.
BIG BROADWAY MEETING, MR. PUSS?
OH, NO. JUST HAVING LUNCH WITH AN OLD HERO OF MINE.
HELLO, DOT.
I HAVE RETURNED TO THE CRIME OF THE SCENE.
WHY DO YOU INSIST ON MEETING HERE, ANYWAY?
NOSTALGIA, I GUESS.
LOOK WHAT NOSTALGIA DID TO LOT'S WIFE.
WELL, I DON'T THINK YOU'LL BE TURNING INTO A PILLAR OF SALT ANYTIME SOON.
NO. PEOPLE ACTUALLY PAY FOR SALT.

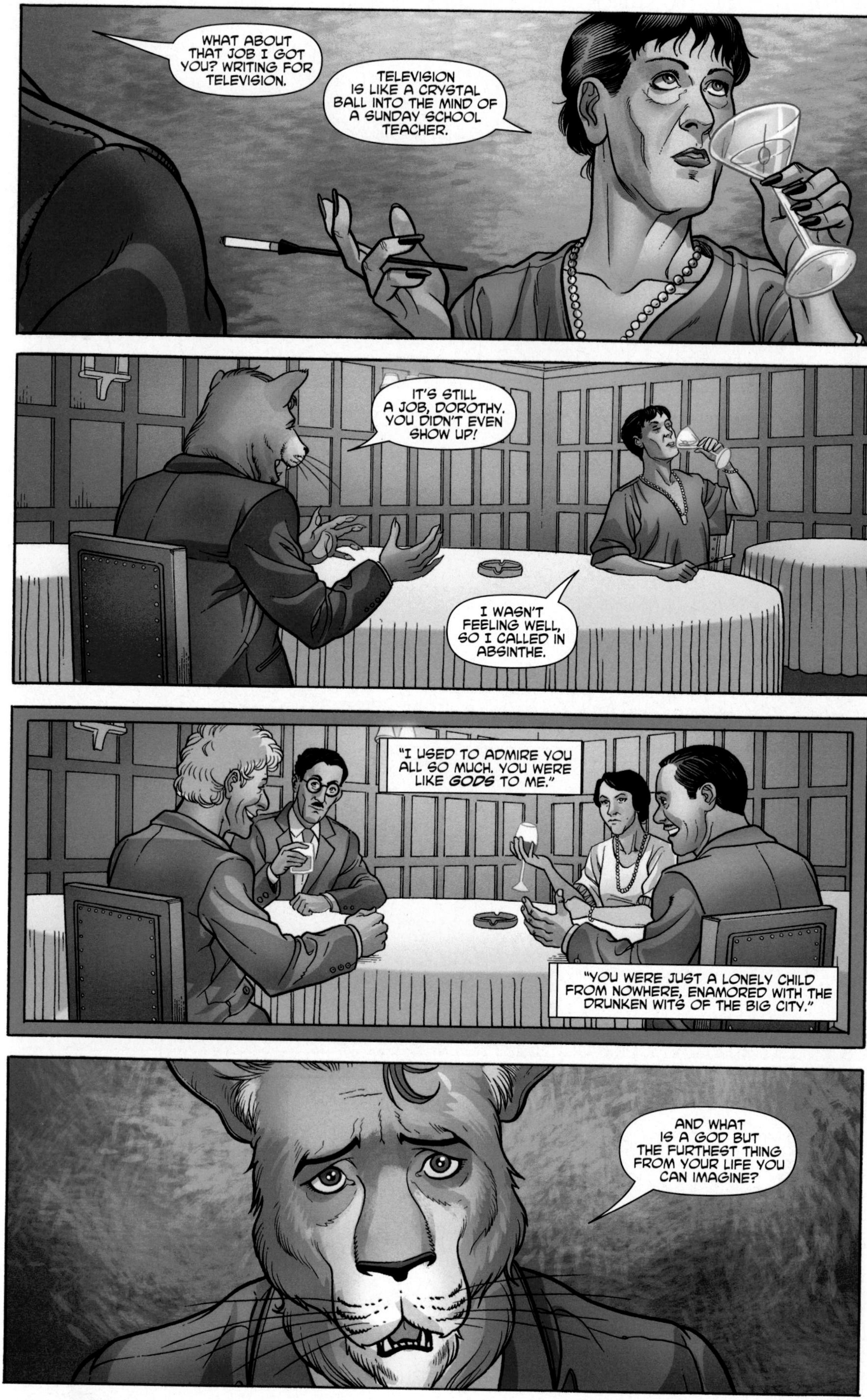
WHAT ABOUT THAT JOB I GOT YOU? WRITING FOR TELEVISION.
TELEVISION IS LIKE A CRYSTAL BALL INTO THE MIND OF A SUNDAY SCHOOL TEACHER.
IT'S STILL A JOB, DOROTHY. YOU DIDN'T EVEN SHOW UP!
I WASN'T FEELING WELL, SO I CALLED IN ABSINTHE.
"I USED TO ADMIRE YOU ALL SO MUCH. YOU WERE LIKE *GODS* TO ME."
"YOU WERE JUST A LONELY CHILD FROM NOWHERE, ENAMORED WITH THE DRUNKEN WITS OF THE BIG CITY."
AND WHAT IS A GOD BUT THE FURTHEST THING FROM YOUR LIFE YOU CAN IMAGINE?

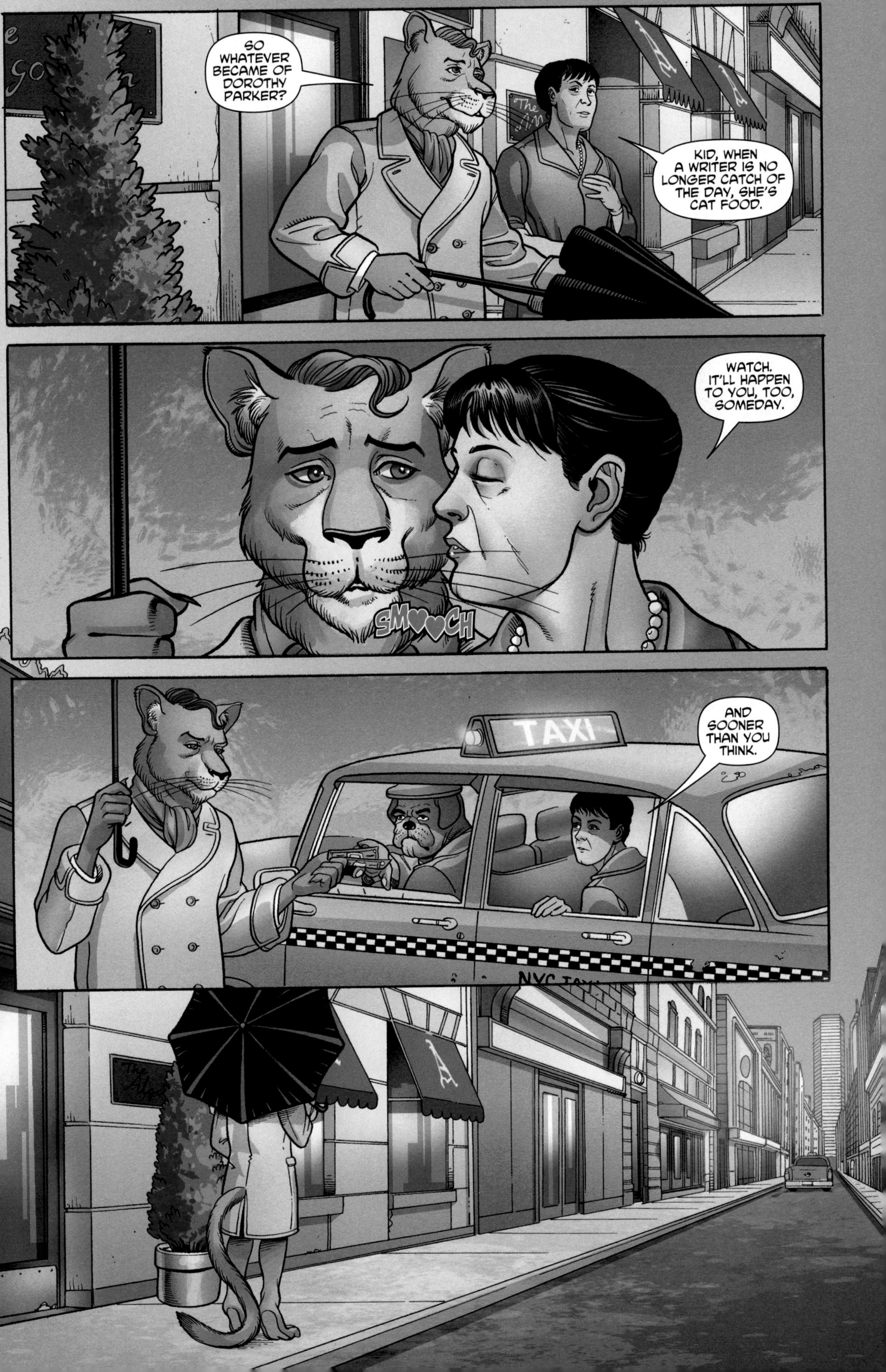
SO WHATEVER BECAME OF DOROTHY PARKER?
KID, WHEN A WRITER IS NO LONGER CATCH OF THE DAY, SHE'S CAT FOOD.
WATCH. IT'LL HAPPEN TO YOU, TOO, SOMEDAY.
SM♥♥CH
TAXI
AND SOONER THAN YOU THINK.

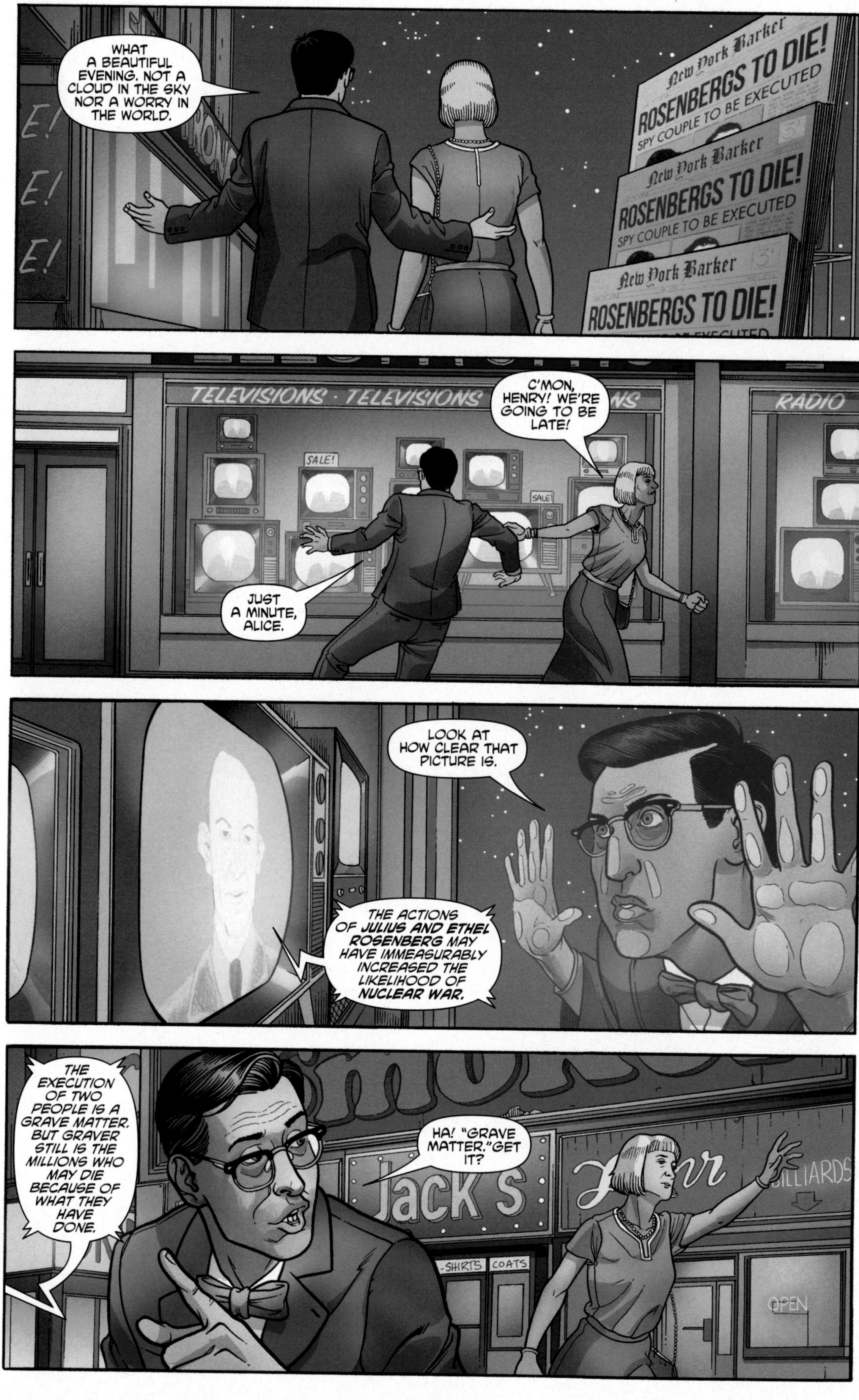
WHAT A BEAUTIFUL EVENING. NOT A CLOUD IN THE SKY NOR A WORRY IN THE WORLD.
New York Barker
ROSENBERGS TO DIE!
SPY COUPLE TO BE EXECUTED
New York Barker
ROSENBERGS TO DIE!
SPY COUPLE TO BE EXECUTED
New York Barker
ROSENBERGS TO DIE!
TELEVISIONS · TELEVISIONS
RADIO
SALE!
SALE!
C'MON, HENRY! WE'RE GOING TO BE LATE!
JUST A MINUTE, ALICE.
LOOK AT HOW CLEAR THAT PICTURE IS.
THE ACTIONS OF JULIUS AND ETHEL ROSENBERG MAY HAVE IMMEASURABLY INCREASED THE LIKELIHOOD OF NUCLEAR WAR.
THE EXECUTION OF TWO PEOPLE IS A GRAVE MATTER. BUT GRAVER STILL IS THE MILLIONS WHO MAY DIE BECAUSE OF WHAT THEY HAVE DONE.
HA! "GRAVE MATTER." GET IT?
Jack's
BILLIARDS
COATS
OPEN

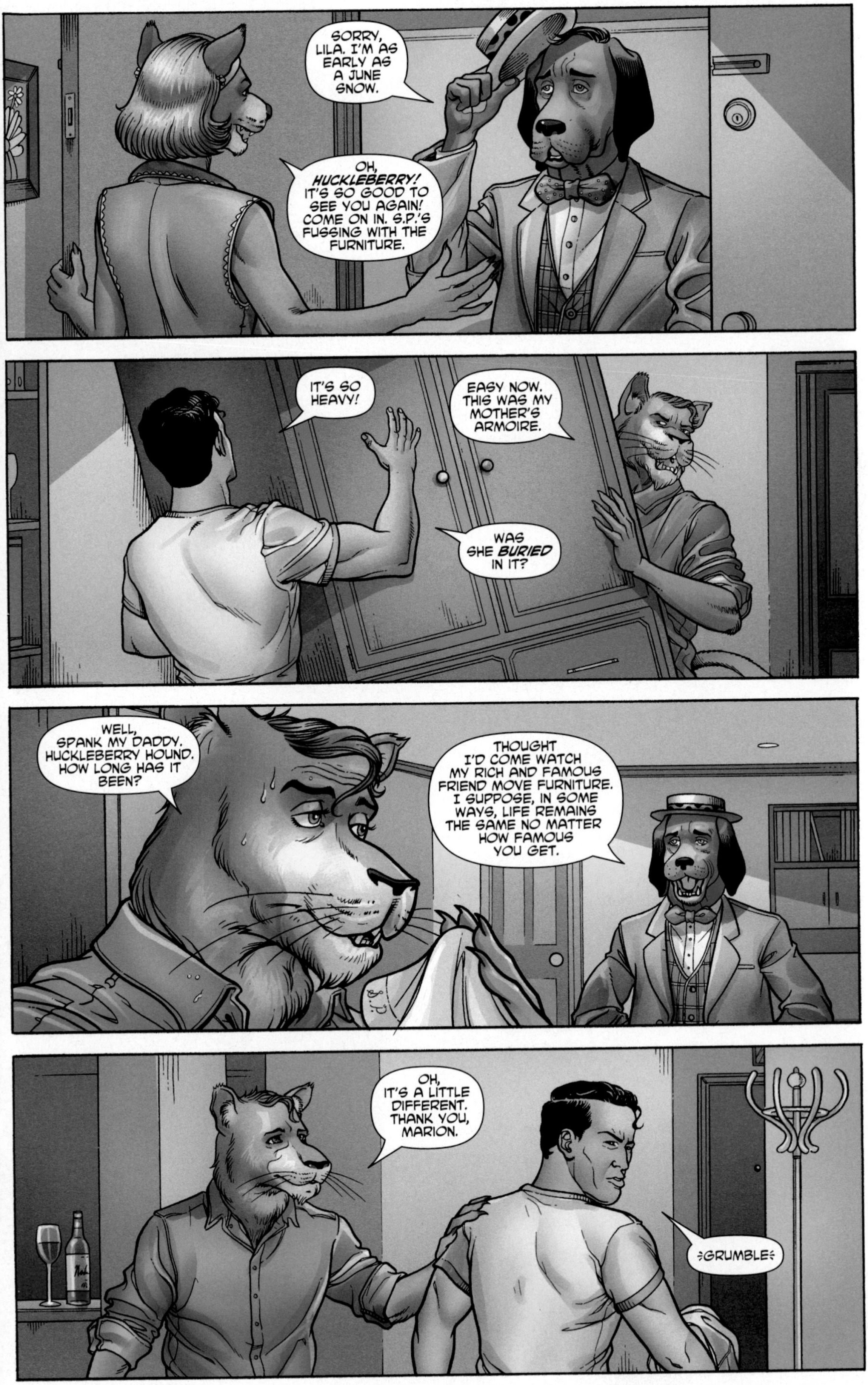
SORRY, LILA. I'M AS EARLY AS A JUNE SNOW.
OH, HUCKLEBERRY! IT'S SO GOOD TO SEE YOU AGAIN! COME ON IN. S.P.'S FUSSING WITH THE FURNITURE.
IT'S SO HEAVY!
EASY NOW. THIS WAS MY MOTHER'S ARMOIRE.
WAS SHE BURIED IN IT?
WELL, SPANK MY DADDY. HUCKLEBERRY HOUND. HOW LONG HAS IT BEEN?
THOUGHT I'D COME WATCH MY RICH AND FAMOUS FRIEND MOVE FURNITURE. I SUPPOSE, IN SOME WAYS, LIFE REMAINS THE SAME NO MATTER HOW FAMOUS YOU GET.
OH, IT'S A LITTLE DIFFERENT. THANK YOU, MARION.
GRUMBLE

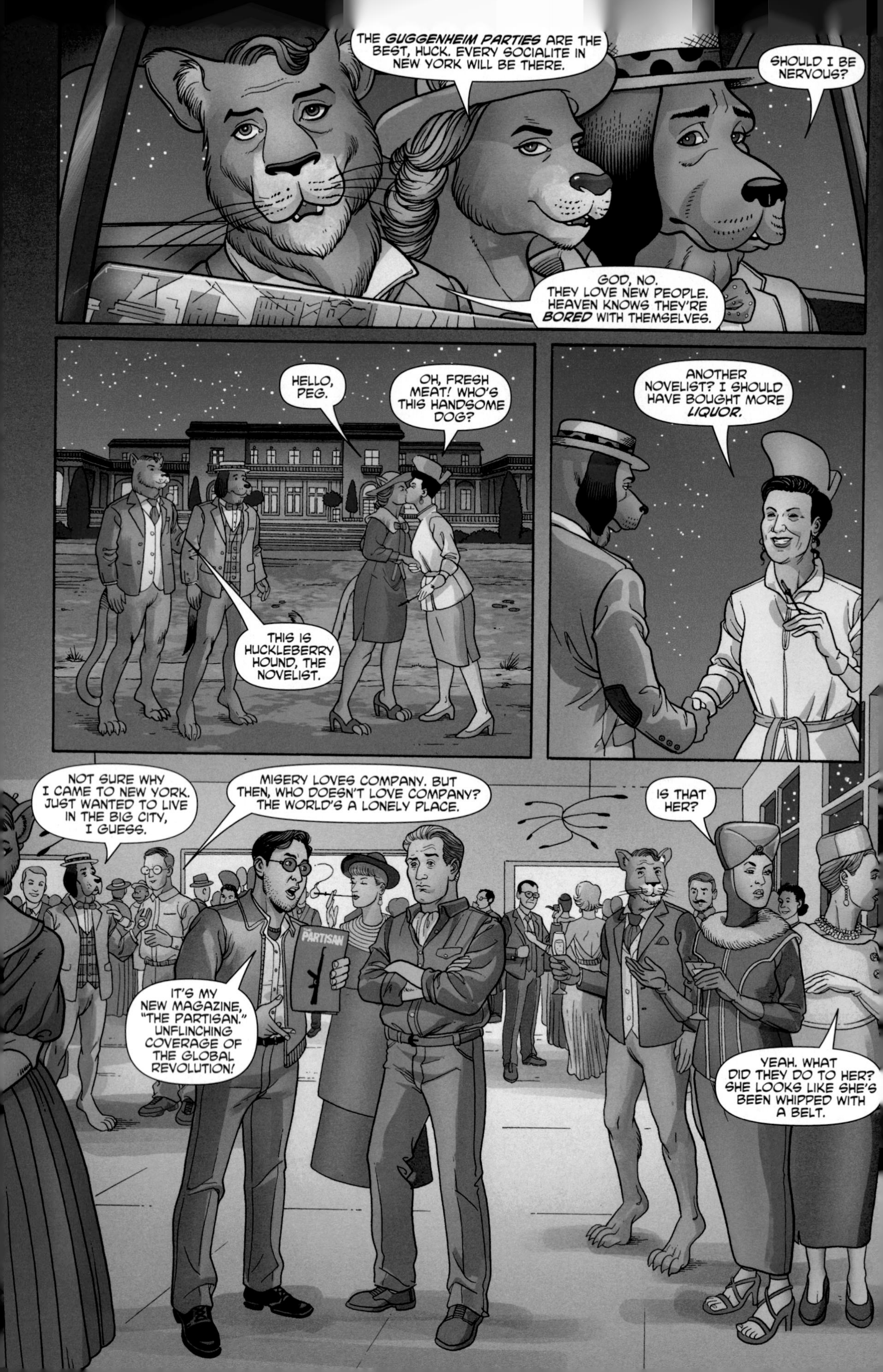
THE *GUGGENHEIM PARTIES* ARE THE BEST, HUCK. EVERY SOCIALITE IN NEW YORK WILL BE THERE.
SHOULD I BE NERVOUS?
GOD, NO. THEY LOVE NEW PEOPLE. HEAVEN KNOWS THEY'RE *BORED* WITH THEMSELVES.
HELLO, PEG.
OH, FRESH MEAT! WHO'S THIS HANDSOME DOG?
THIS IS HUCKLEBERRY HOUND, THE NOVELIST.
ANOTHER NOVELIST? I SHOULD HAVE BOUGHT MORE *LIQUOR*.
NOT SURE WHY I CAME TO NEW YORK. JUST WANTED TO LIVE IN THE BIG CITY, I GUESS.
MISERY LOVES COMPANY. BUT THEN, WHO DOESN'T LOVE COMPANY? THE WORLD'S A LONELY PLACE.
PARTISAN
IT'S MY NEW MAGAZINE, "THE PARTISAN." UNFLINCHING COVERAGE OF THE GLOBAL REVOLUTION!
IS THAT HER?
YEAH. WHAT DID THEY DO TO HER? SHE LOOKS LIKE SHE'S BEEN WHIPPED WITH A BELT.

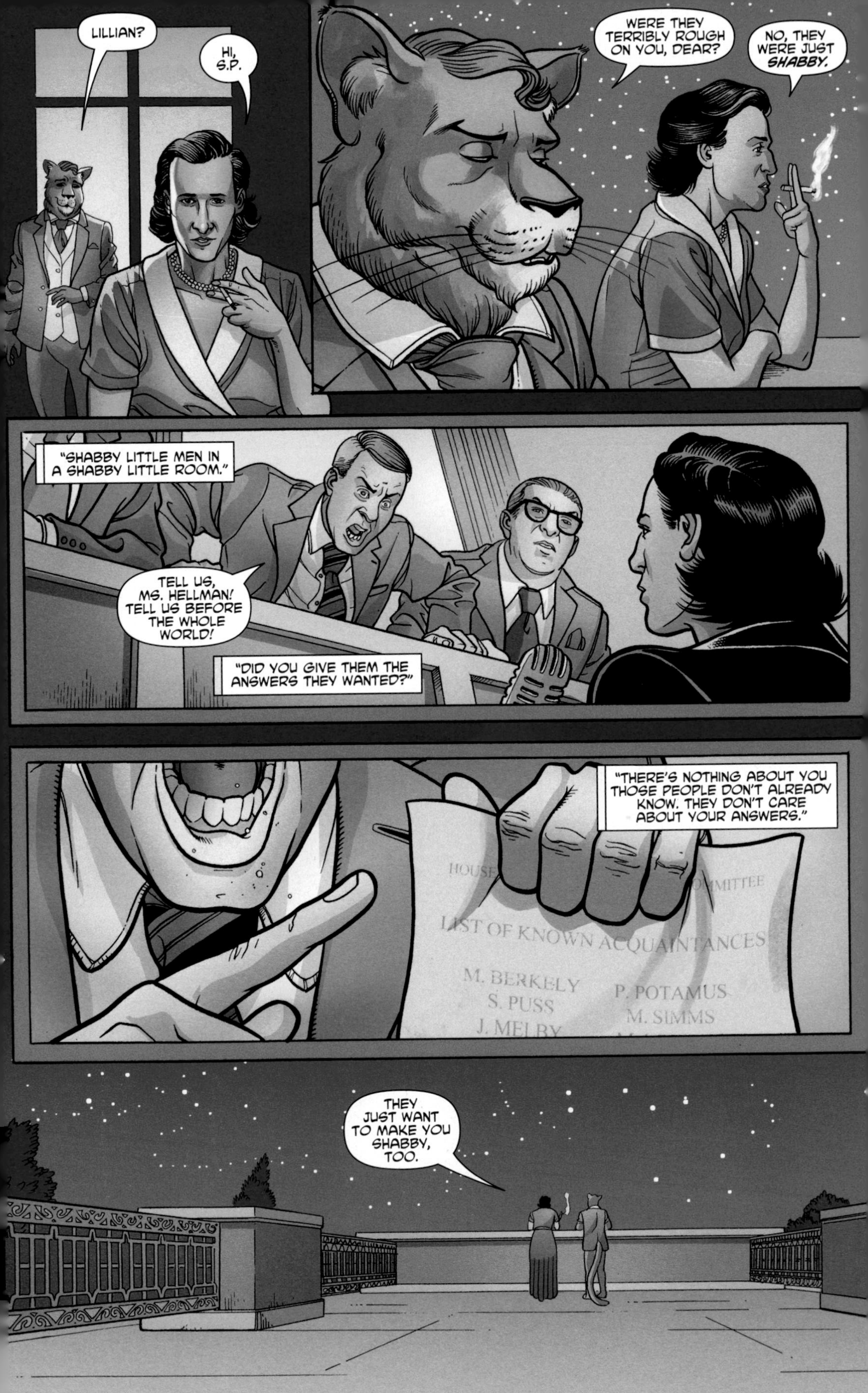

LILLIAN?
HI, S.P.
WERE THEY TERRIBLY ROUGH ON YOU, DEAR?
NO, THEY WERE JUST *SHABBY.*
"SHABBY LITTLE MEN IN A SHABBY LITTLE ROOM."
TELL US, MS. HELLMAN! TELL US BEFORE THE WHOLE WORLD!
"DID YOU GIVE THEM THE ANSWERS THEY WANTED?"
"THERE'S NOTHING ABOUT YOU THOSE PEOPLE DON'T ALREADY KNOW. THEY DON'T CARE ABOUT YOUR ANSWERS."
LIST OF KNOWN ACQUAINTANCES
M. BERKELY
S. PUSS
P. POTAMUS
M. SIMMS
THEY JUST WANT TO MAKE YOU SHABBY, TOO.

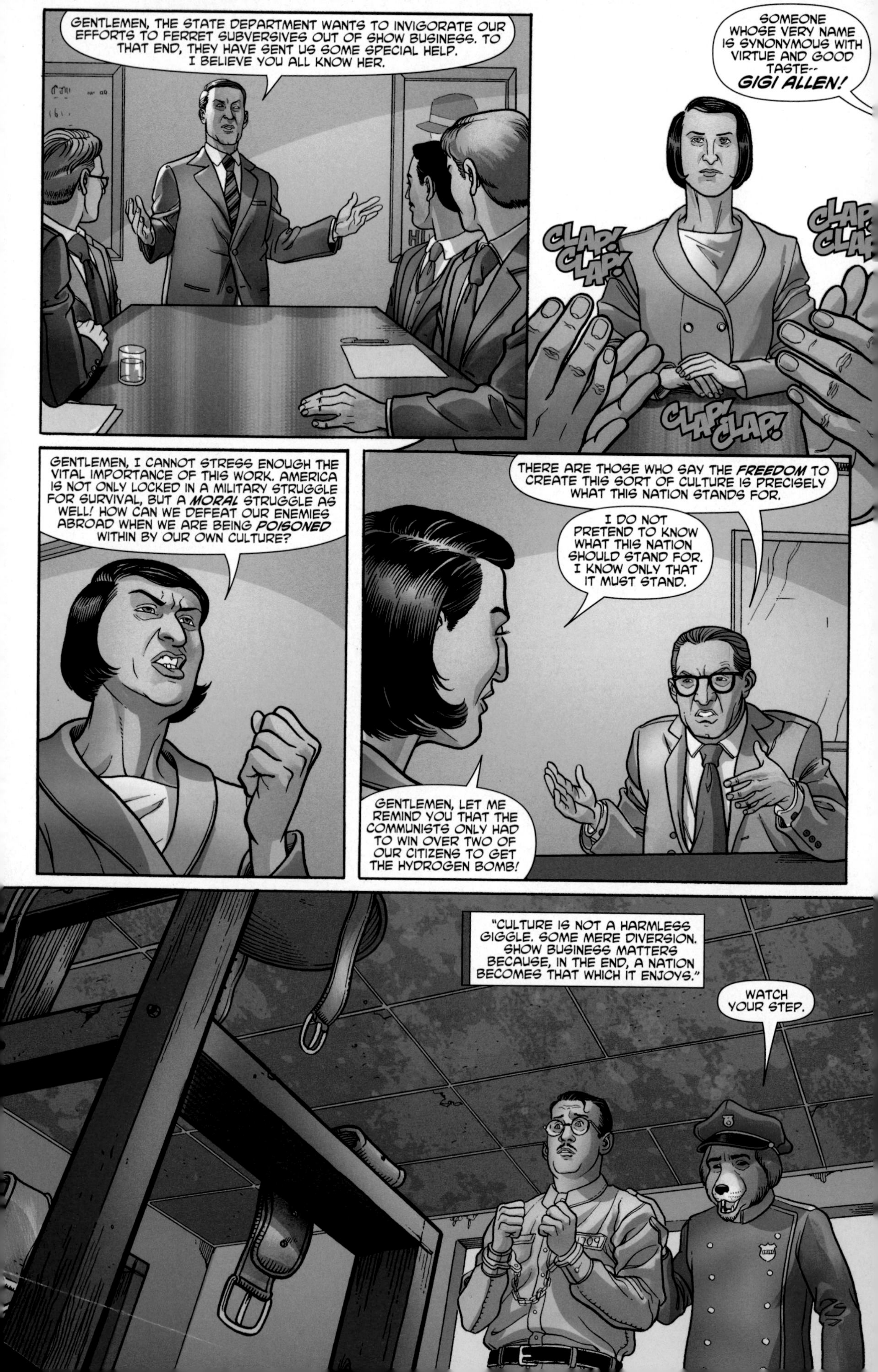
GENTLEMEN, THE STATE DEPARTMENT WANTS TO INVIGORATE OUR EFFORTS TO FERRET SUBVERSIVES OUT OF SHOW BUSINESS. TO THAT END, THEY HAVE SENT US SOME SPECIAL HELP. I BELIEVE YOU ALL KNOW HER.
SOMEONE WHOSE VERY NAME IS SYNONYMOUS WITH VIRTUE AND GOOD TASTE-- GIGI ALLEN!
CLAP! CLAP! CLAP!
CLAP! CLAP!
CLAP! CLAP!
GENTLEMEN, I CANNOT STRESS ENOUGH THE VITAL IMPORTANCE OF THIS WORK. AMERICA IS NOT ONLY LOCKED IN A MILITARY STRUGGLE FOR SURVIVAL, BUT A MORAL STRUGGLE AS WELL! HOW CAN WE DEFEAT OUR ENEMIES ABROAD WHEN WE ARE BEING POISONED WITHIN BY OUR OWN CULTURE?
THERE ARE THOSE WHO SAY THE FREEDOM TO CREATE THIS SORT OF CULTURE IS PRECISELY WHAT THIS NATION STANDS FOR.
I DO NOT PRETEND TO KNOW WHAT THIS NATION SHOULD STAND FOR. I KNOW ONLY THAT IT MUST STAND.
GENTLEMEN, LET ME REMIND YOU THAT THE COMMUNISTS ONLY HAD TO WIN OVER TWO OF OUR CITIZENS TO GET THE HYDROGEN BOMB!
"CULTURE IS NOT A HARMLESS GIGGLE. SOME MERE DIVERSION. SHOW BUSINESS MATTERS BECAUSE, IN THE END, A NATION BECOMES THAT WHICH IT ENJOYS."
WATCH YOUR STEP.

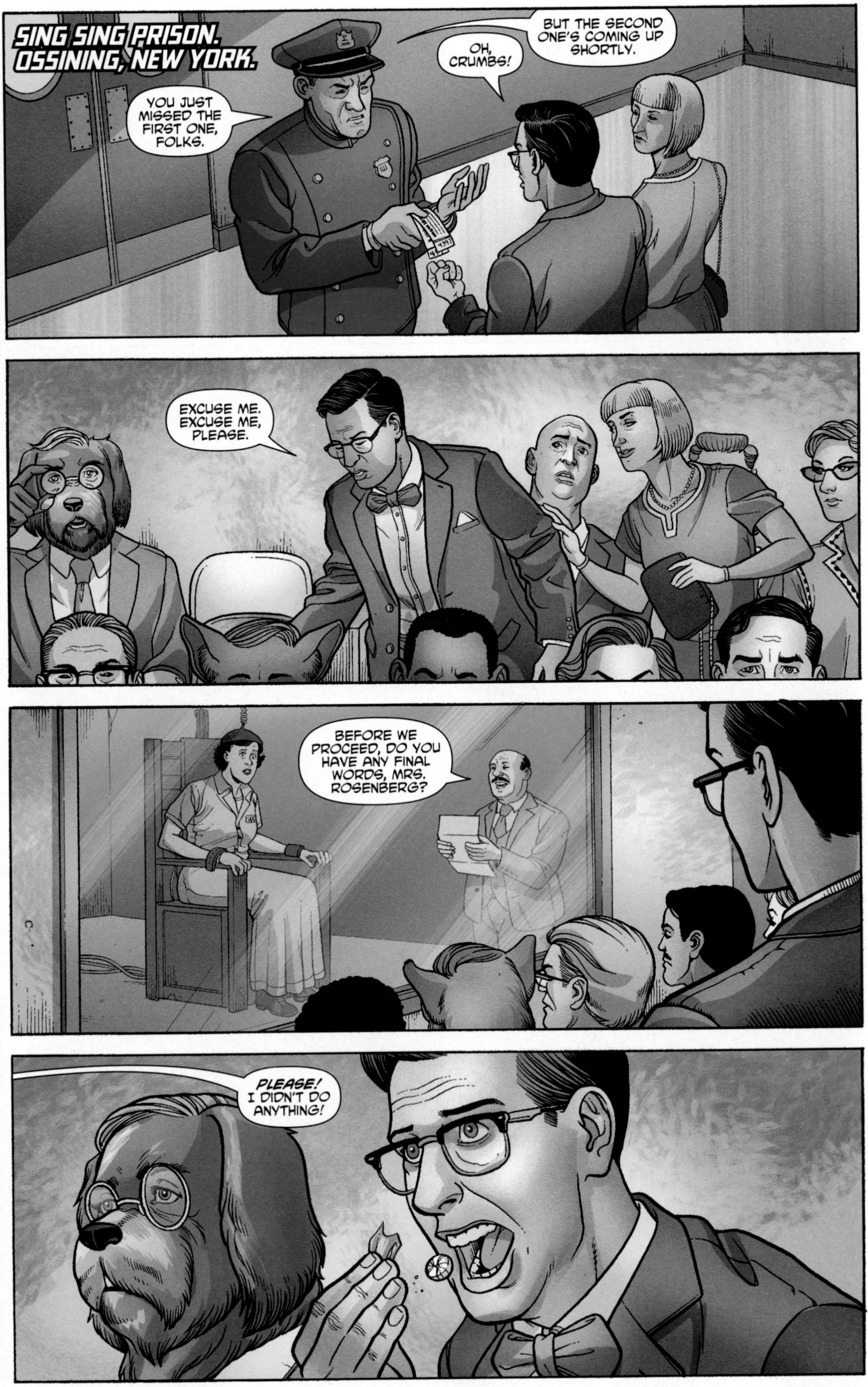
SING SING PRISON. OSSINING, NEW YORK.
YOU JUST MISSED THE FIRST ONE, FOLKS.
OH, CRUMBS!
BUT THE SECOND ONE'S COMING UP SHORTLY.
EXCUSE ME. EXCUSE ME, PLEASE.
BEFORE WE PROCEED, DO YOU HAVE ANY FINAL WORDS, MRS. ROSENBERG?
PLEASE! I DIDN'T DO ANYTHING!

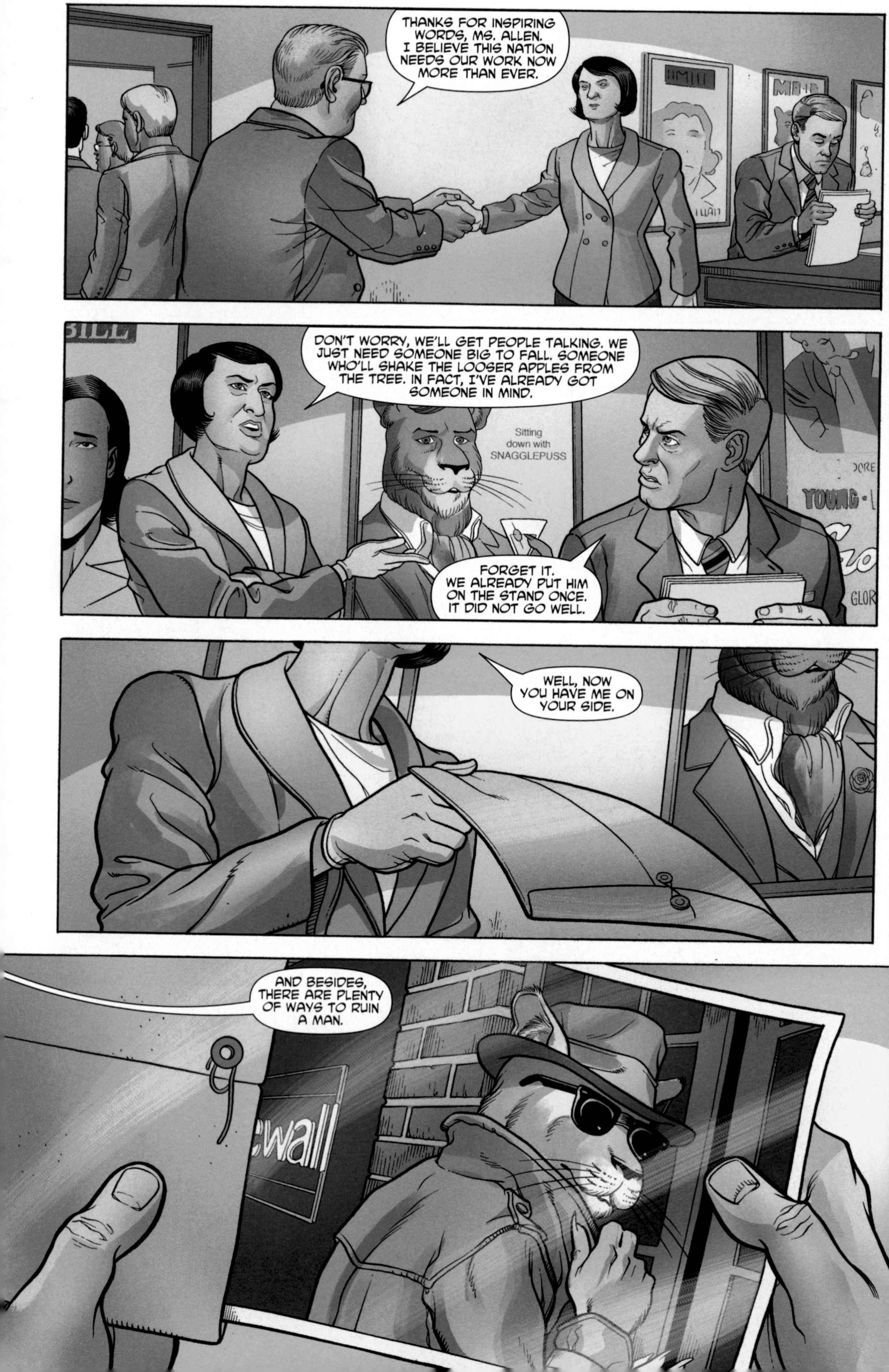
THANKS FOR INSPIRING WORDS, MS. ALLEN. I BELIEVE THIS NATION NEEDS OUR WORK NOW MORE THAN EVER.
DON'T WORRY, WE'LL GET PEOPLE TALKING. WE JUST NEED SOMEONE BIG TO FALL. SOMEONE WHO'LL SHAKE THE LOOSER APPLES FROM THE TREE. IN FACT, I'VE ALREADY GOT SOMEONE IN MIND.
Sitting down with SNAGGLEPUSS
FORGET IT. WE ALREADY PUT HIM ON THE STAND ONCE. IT DID NOT GO WELL.
WELL, NOW YOU HAVE ME ON YOUR SIDE.
AND BESIDES, THERE ARE PLENTY OF WAYS TO RUIN A MAN.

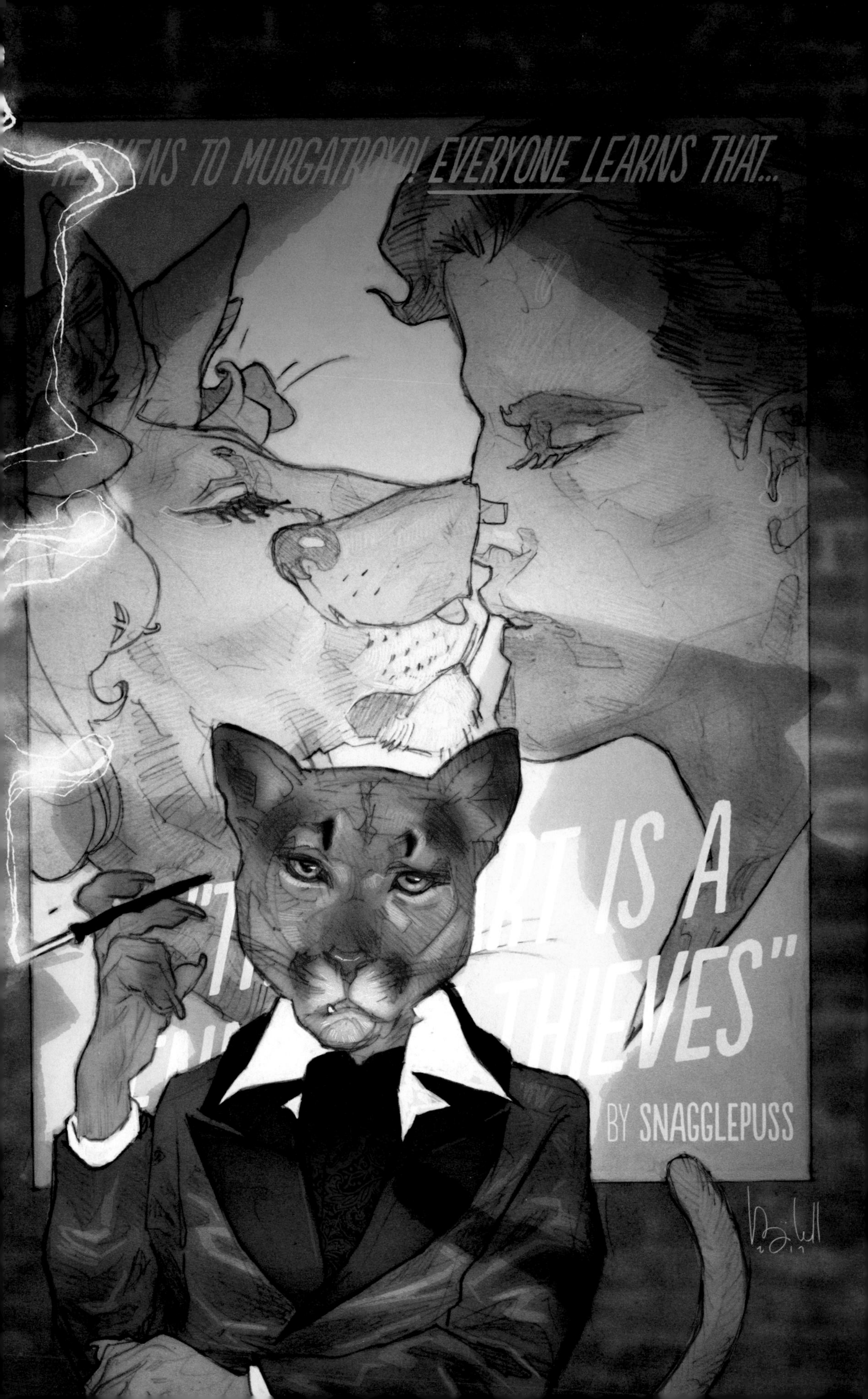
TO MURGATROYD! EVERYONE LEARNS THAT...
IS A
THIEVES"
BY SNAGGLEPUSS

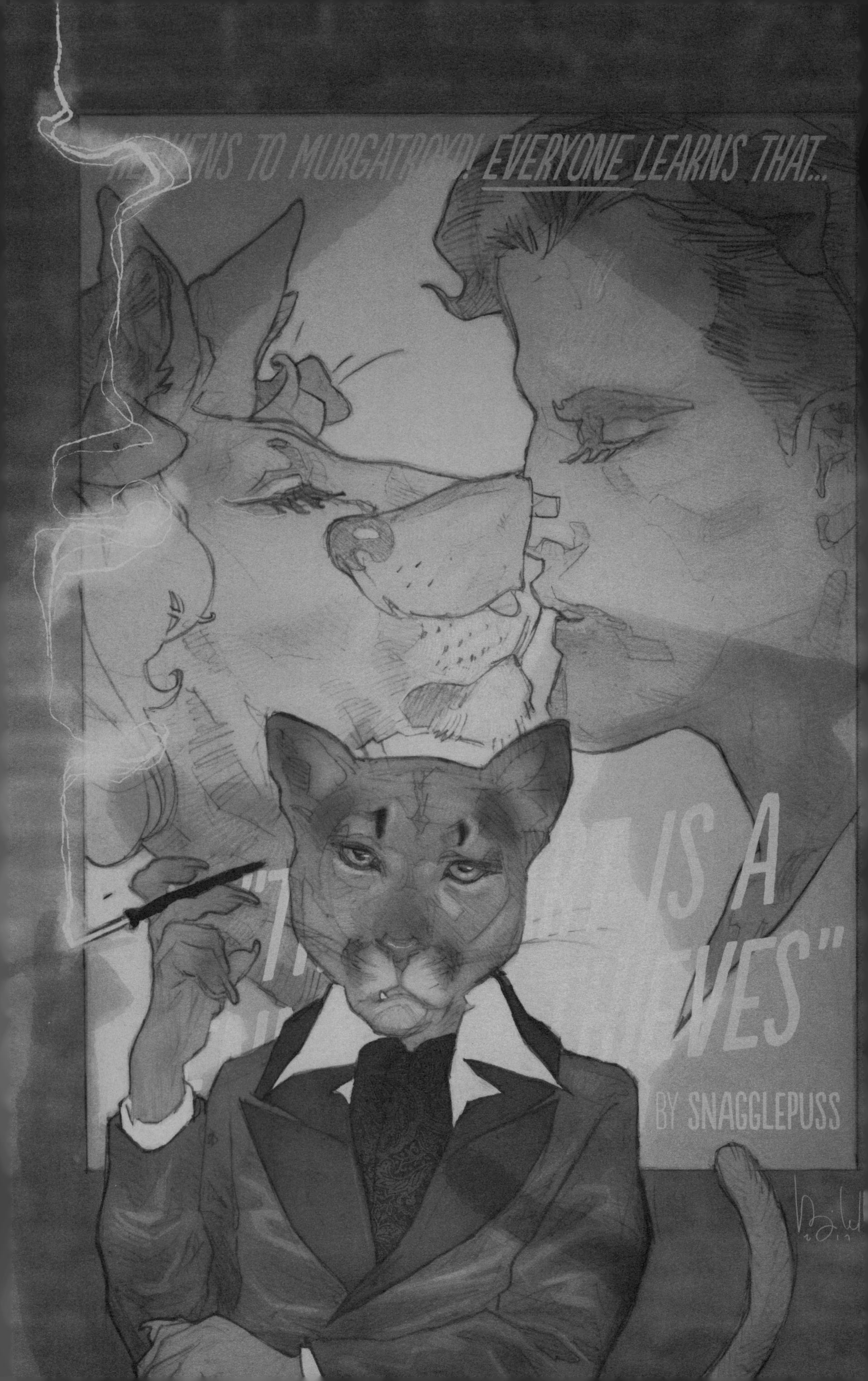
EVERYONE LEARNS THAT...
IS A
VES"
BY SNAGGLEPUSS

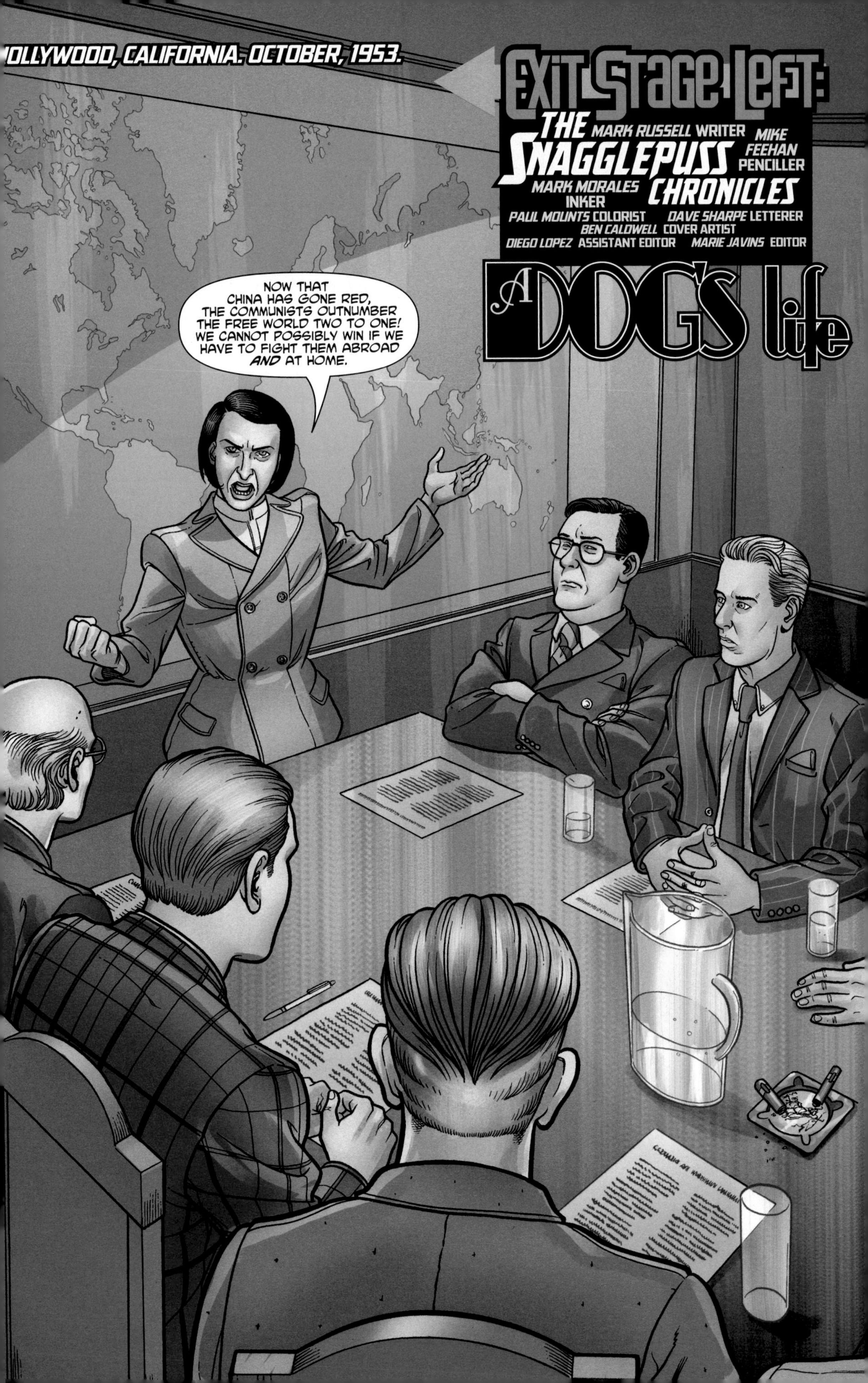

OLLYWOOD, CALIFORNIA. OCTOBER, 1953.
EXIT STAGE LEFT: THE SNAGGLEPUSS CHRONICLES
MARK RUSSELL WRITER
MIKE FEEHAN PENCILLER
MARK MORALES INKER
PAUL MOUNTS COLORIST
DAVE SHARPE LETTERER
BEN CALDWELL COVER ARTIST
DIEGO LOPEZ ASSISTANT EDITOR
MARIE JAVINS EDITOR
A DOG'S life
NOW THAT CHINA HAS GONE RED, THE COMMUNISTS OUTNUMBER THE FREE WORLD TWO TO ONE! WE CANNOT POSSIBLY WIN IF WE HAVE TO FIGHT THEM ABROAD AND AT HOME.

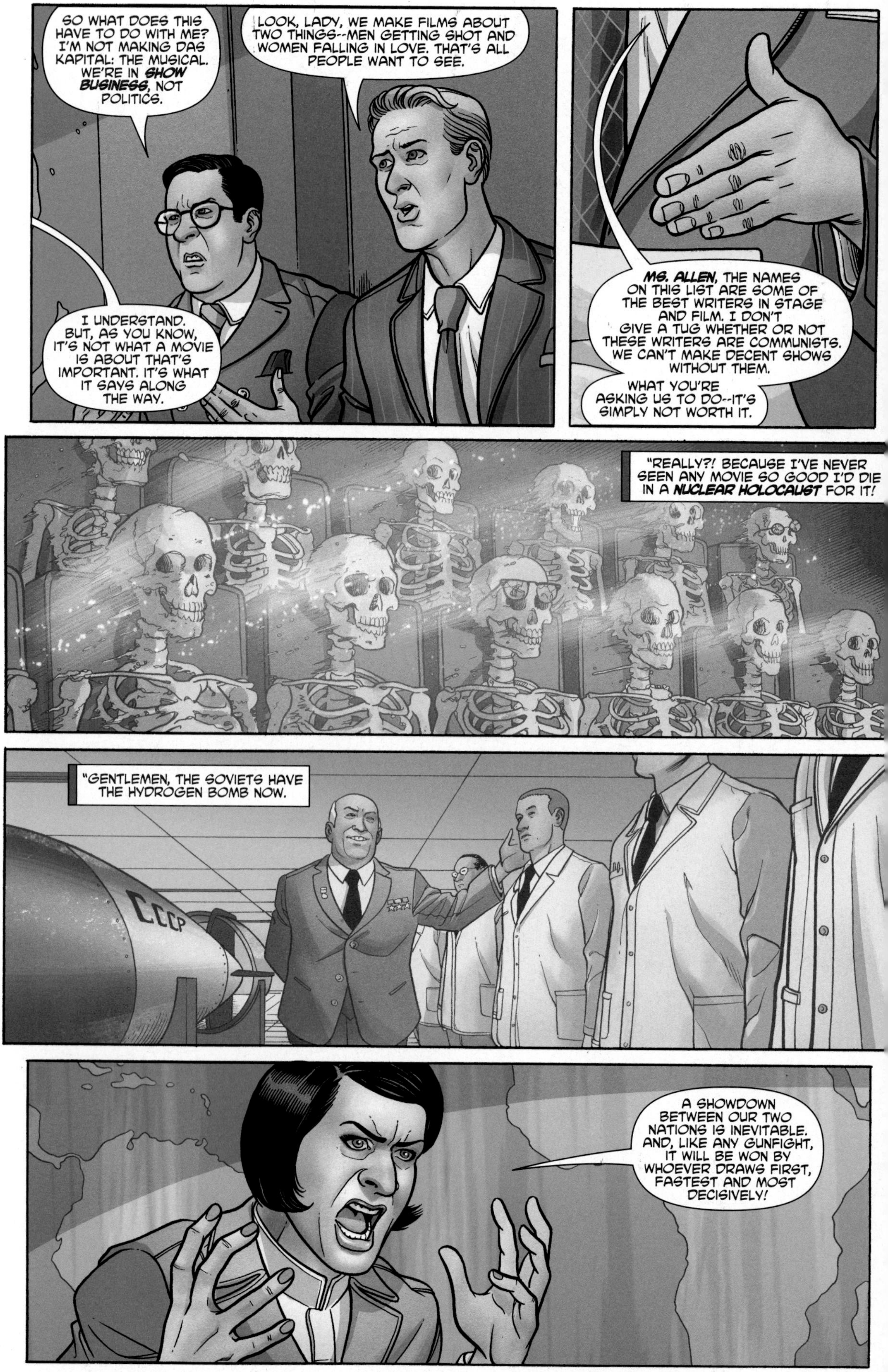
SO WHAT DOES THIS HAVE TO DO WITH ME? I'M NOT MAKING DAS KAPITAL: THE MUSICAL. WE'RE IN SHOW BUSINESS, NOT POLITICS.
LOOK, LADY, WE MAKE FILMS ABOUT TWO THINGS--MEN GETTING SHOT AND WOMEN FALLING IN LOVE. THAT'S ALL PEOPLE WANT TO SEE.
I UNDERSTAND. BUT, AS YOU KNOW, IT'S NOT WHAT A MOVIE IS ABOUT THAT'S IMPORTANT. IT'S WHAT IT SAYS ALONG THE WAY.
MS. ALLEN, THE NAMES ON THIS LIST ARE SOME OF THE BEST WRITERS IN STAGE AND FILM. I DON'T GIVE A TUG WHETHER OR NOT THESE WRITERS ARE COMMUNISTS. WE CAN'T MAKE DECENT SHOWS WITHOUT THEM.
WHAT YOU'RE ASKING US TO DO--IT'S SIMPLY NOT WORTH IT.
"REALLY?! BECAUSE I'VE NEVER SEEN ANY MOVIE SO GOOD I'D DIE IN A NUCLEAR HOLOCAUST FOR IT!
"GENTLEMEN, THE SOVIETS HAVE THE HYDROGEN BOMB NOW.
CCCP
A SHOWDOWN BETWEEN OUR TWO NATIONS IS INEVITABLE. AND, LIKE ANY GUNFIGHT, IT WILL BE WON BY WHOEVER DRAWS FIRST, FASTEST AND MOST DECISIVELY!

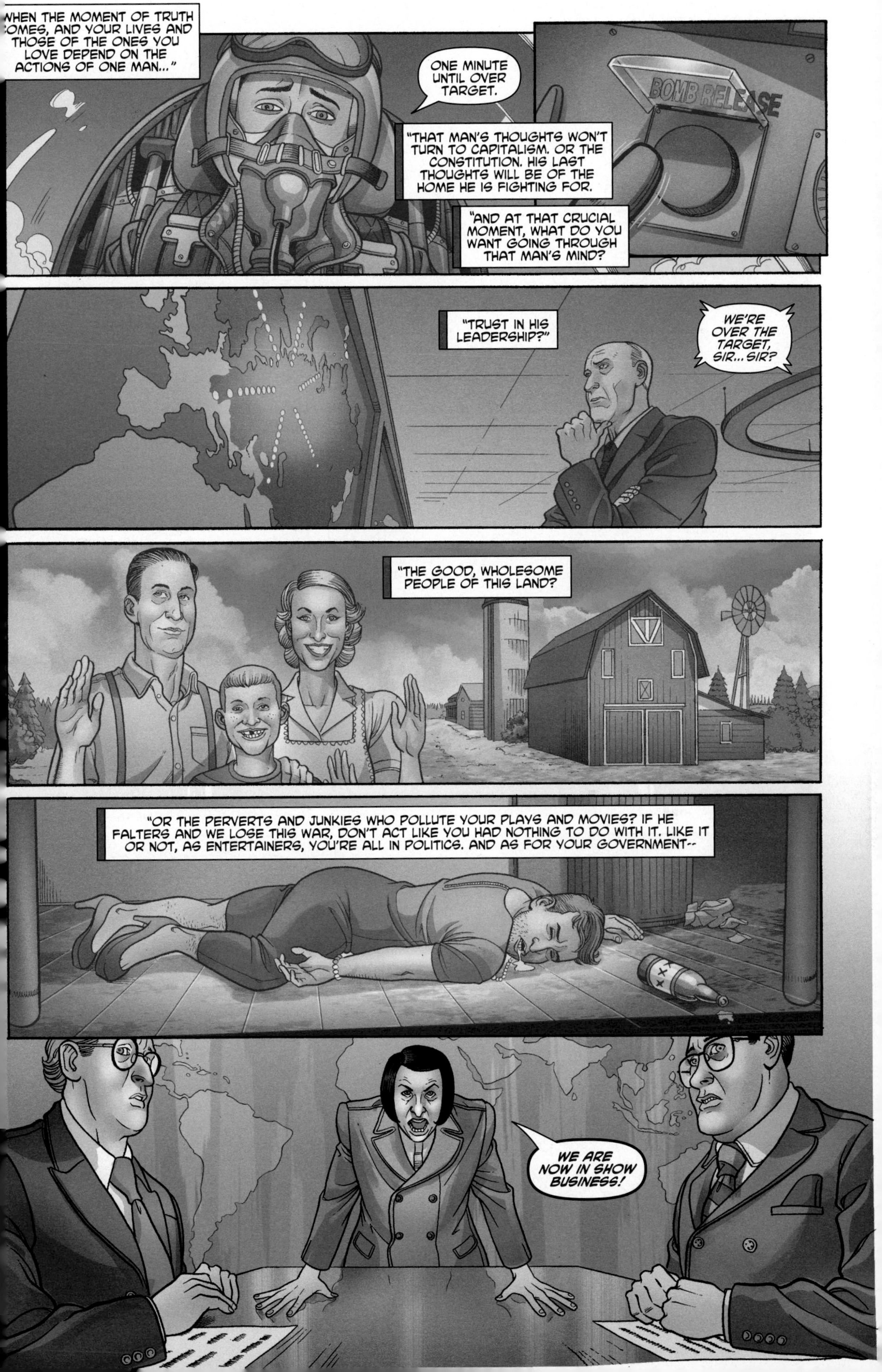

WHEN THE MOMENT OF TRUTH COMES, AND YOUR LIVES AND THOSE OF THE ONES YOU LOVE DEPEND ON THE ACTIONS OF ONE MAN..."
ONE MINUTE UNTIL OVER TARGET.
"THAT MAN'S THOUGHTS WON'T TURN TO CAPITALISM. OR THE CONSTITUTION. HIS LAST THOUGHTS WILL BE OF THE HOME HE IS FIGHTING FOR.
BOMB RELEASE
"AND AT THAT CRUCIAL MOMENT, WHAT DO YOU WANT GOING THROUGH THAT MAN'S MIND?
"TRUST IN HIS LEADERSHIP?"
WE'RE OVER THE TARGET, SIR... SIR?
"THE GOOD, WHOLESOME PEOPLE OF THIS LAND?
"OR THE PERVERTS AND JUNKIES WHO POLLUTE YOUR PLAYS AND MOVIES? IF HE FALTERS AND WE LOSE THIS WAR, DON'T ACT LIKE YOU HAD NOTHING TO DO WITH IT. LIKE IT OR NOT, AS ENTERTAINERS, YOU'RE ALL IN POLITICS. AND AS FOR YOUR GOVERNMENT--
WE ARE NOW IN SHOW BUSINESS!

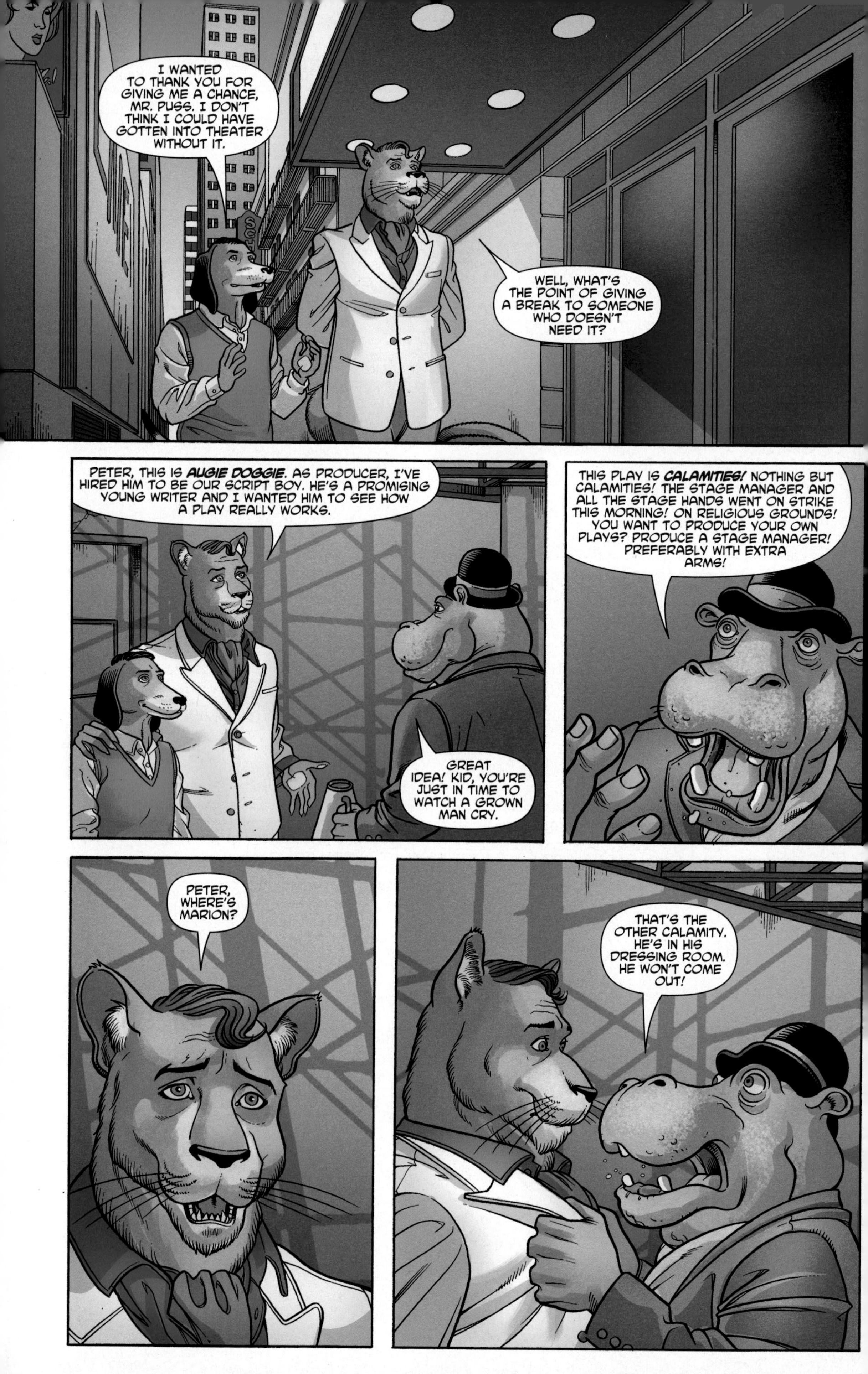
I WANTED TO THANK YOU FOR GIVING ME A CHANCE, MR. PUSS. I DON'T THINK I COULD HAVE GOTTEN INTO THEATER WITHOUT IT.
WELL, WHAT'S THE POINT OF GIVING A BREAK TO SOMEONE WHO DOESN'T NEED IT?
PETER, THIS IS AUGIE DOGGIE. AS PRODUCER, I'VE HIRED HIM TO BE OUR SCRIPT BOY. HE'S A PROMISING YOUNG WRITER AND I WANTED HIM TO SEE HOW A PLAY REALLY WORKS.
GREAT IDEA! KID, YOU'RE JUST IN TIME TO WATCH A GROWN MAN CRY.
THIS PLAY IS CALAMITIES! NOTHING BUT CALAMITIES! THE STAGE MANAGER AND ALL THE STAGE HANDS WENT ON STRIKE THIS MORNING! ON RELIGIOUS GROUNDS! YOU WANT TO PRODUCE YOUR OWN PLAYS? PRODUCE A STAGE MANAGER! PREFERABLY WITH EXTRA ARMS!
PETER, WHERE'S MARION?
THAT'S THE OTHER CALAMITY. HE'S IN HIS DRESSING ROOM. HE WON'T COME OUT!

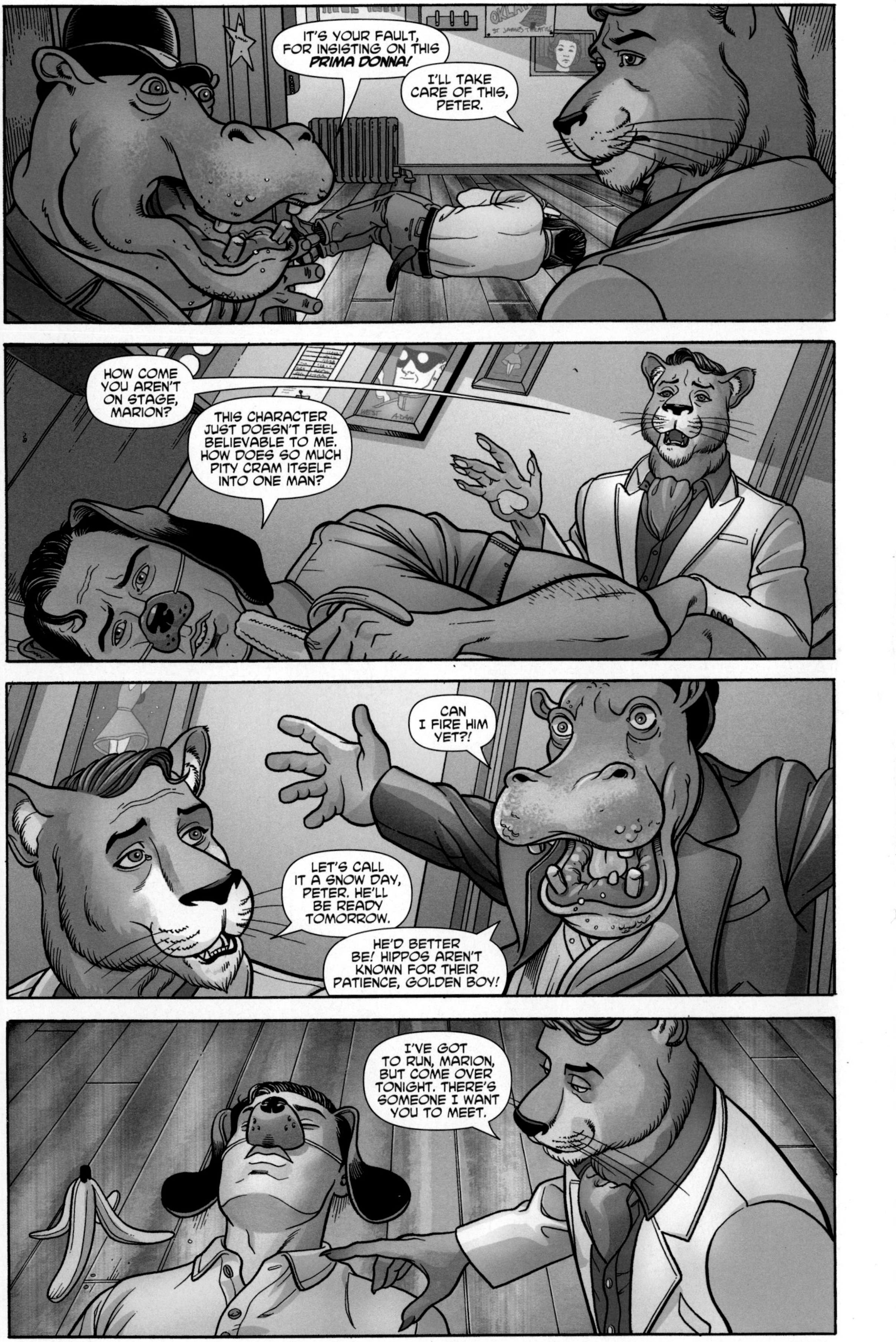

IT'S YOUR FAULT, FOR INSISTING ON THIS PRIMA DONNA!
I'LL TAKE CARE OF THIS, PETER.
HOW COME YOU AREN'T ON STAGE, MARION?
THIS CHARACTER JUST DOESN'T FEEL BELIEVABLE TO ME. HOW DOES SO MUCH PITY CRAM ITSELF INTO ONE MAN?
CAN I FIRE HIM YET?!
LET'S CALL IT A SNOW DAY, PETER. HE'LL BE READY TOMORROW.
HE'D BETTER BE! HIPPOS AREN'T KNOWN FOR THEIR PATIENCE, GOLDEN BOY!
I'VE GOT TO RUN, MARION, BUT COME OVER TONIGHT. THERE'S SOMEONE I WANT YOU TO MEET.

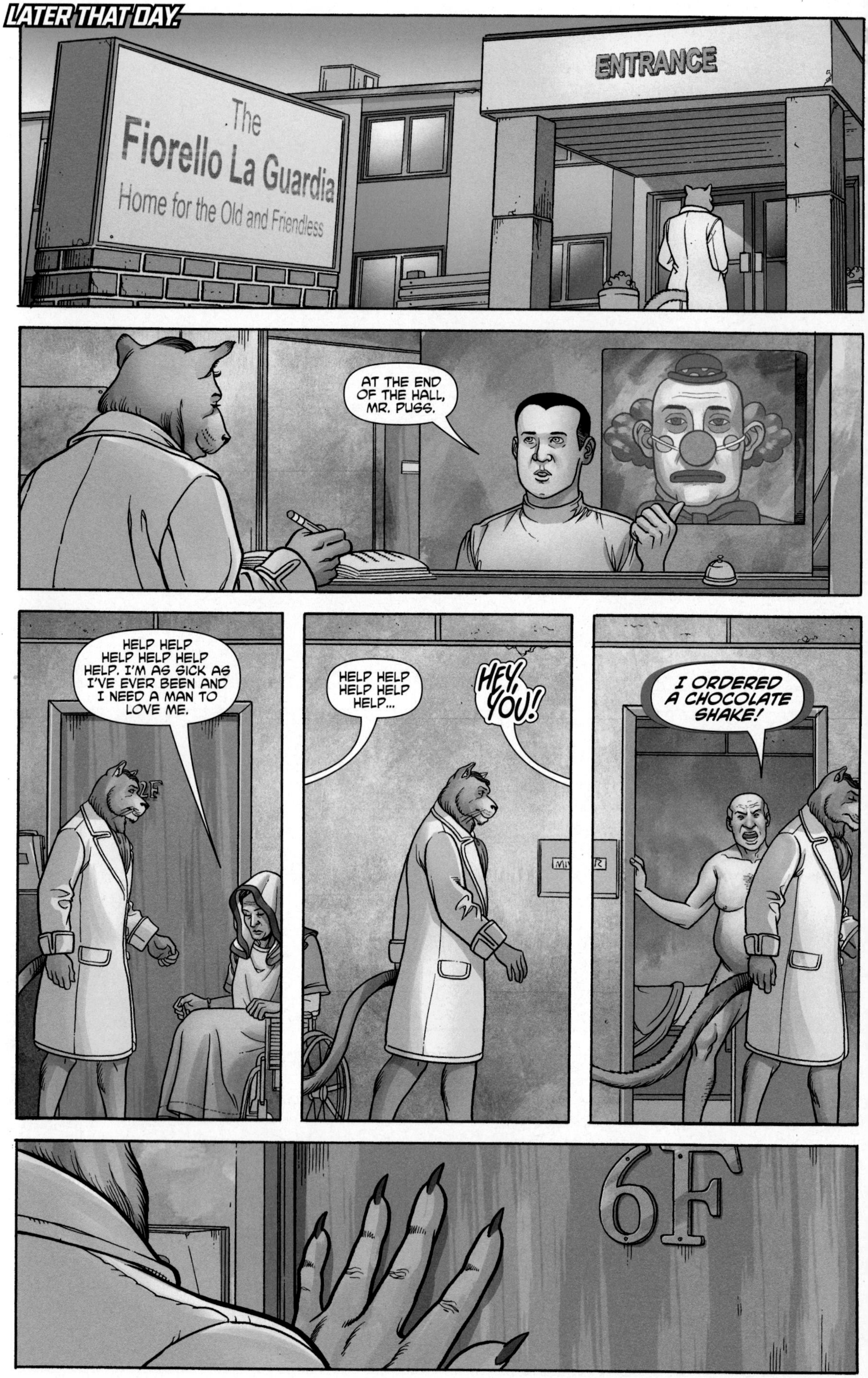
LATER THAT DAY.
ENTRANCE
The Fiorello La Guardia Home for the Old and Friendless
AT THE END OF THE HALL, MR. PUSS.
HELP HELP HELP HELP HELP HELP. I'M AS SICK AS I'VE EVER BEEN AND I NEED A MAN TO LOVE ME.
HELP HELP HELP HELP HELP...
HEY, YOU!
I ORDERED A CHOCOLATE SHAKE!
6F

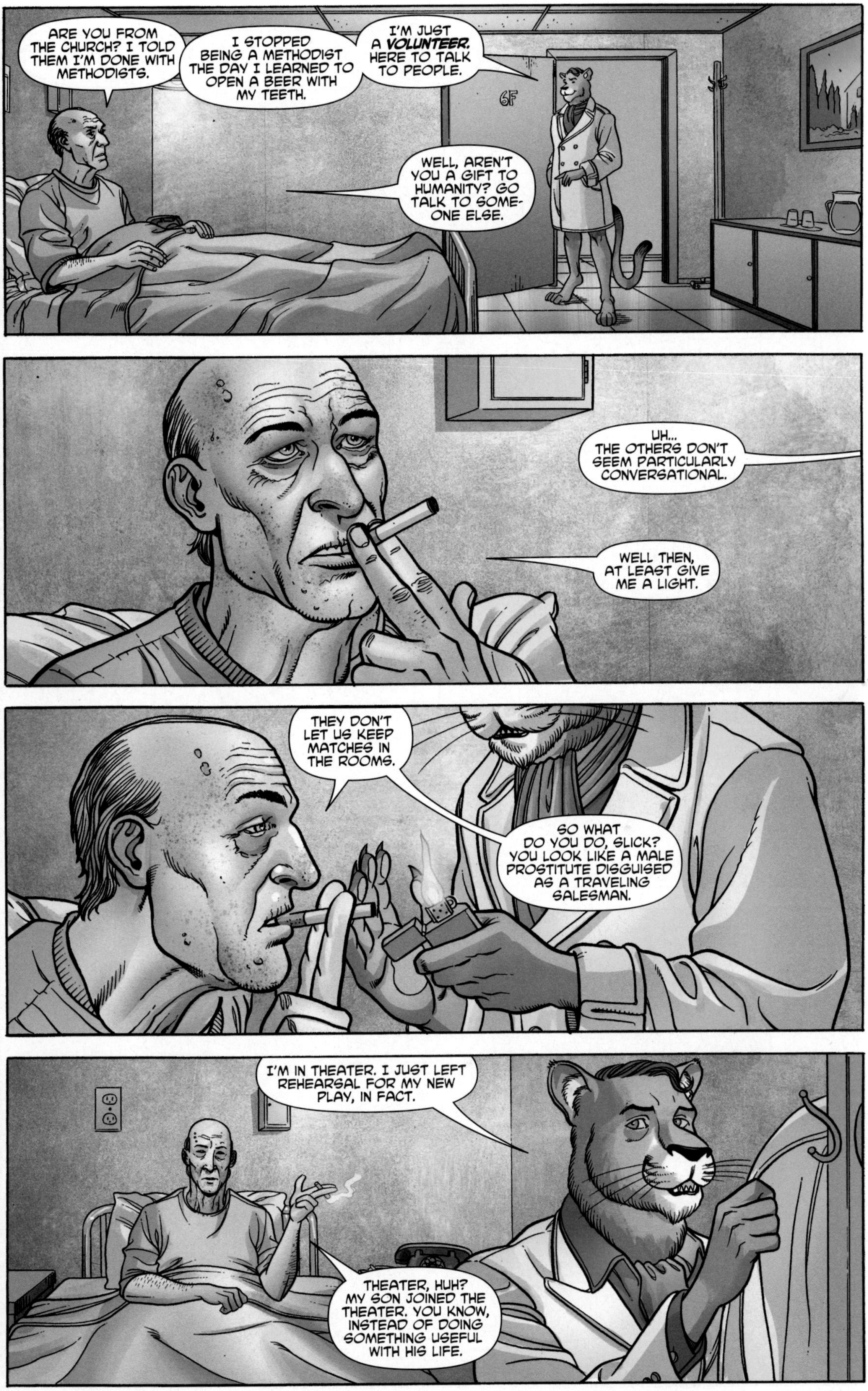
ARE YOU FROM THE CHURCH? I TOLD THEM I'M DONE WITH METHODISTS.
I STOPPED BEING A METHODIST THE DAY I LEARNED TO OPEN A BEER WITH MY TEETH.
I'M JUST A VOLUNTEER. HERE TO TALK TO PEOPLE.
6F
WELL, AREN'T YOU A GIFT TO HUMANITY? GO TALK TO SOME-ONE ELSE.
UH... THE OTHERS DON'T SEEM PARTICULARLY CONVERSATIONAL.
WELL THEN, AT LEAST GIVE ME A LIGHT.
THEY DON'T LET US KEEP MATCHES IN THE ROOMS.
SO WHAT DO YOU DO, SLICK? YOU LOOK LIKE A MALE PROSTITUTE DISGUISED AS A TRAVELING SALESMAN.
I'M IN THEATER. I JUST LEFT REHEARSAL FOR MY NEW PLAY, IN FACT.
THEATER, HUH? MY SON JOINED THE THEATER. YOU KNOW, INSTEAD OF DOING SOMETHING USEFUL WITH HIS LIFE.

WELL, IT KEEPS ME IN LOAFERS AND CIGARETTES.

SO WHAT'S YOUR PLAY ABOUT?

WHAT'S ANY GOOD PLAY ABOUT? FAILURE *AND LOSS.*

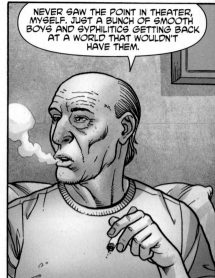

NEVER SAW THE POINT IN THEATER, MYSELF. JUST A BUNCH OF SMOOTH BOYS AND SYPHILITICS GETTING BACK AT A WORLD THAT WOULDN'T HAVE THEM.

SO WHAT DID YOU DO, BACK WHEN YOU DID THINGS?

HAPPY RETIREMENT!

I WAS A JUDGE.

YOU DON'T SAY.

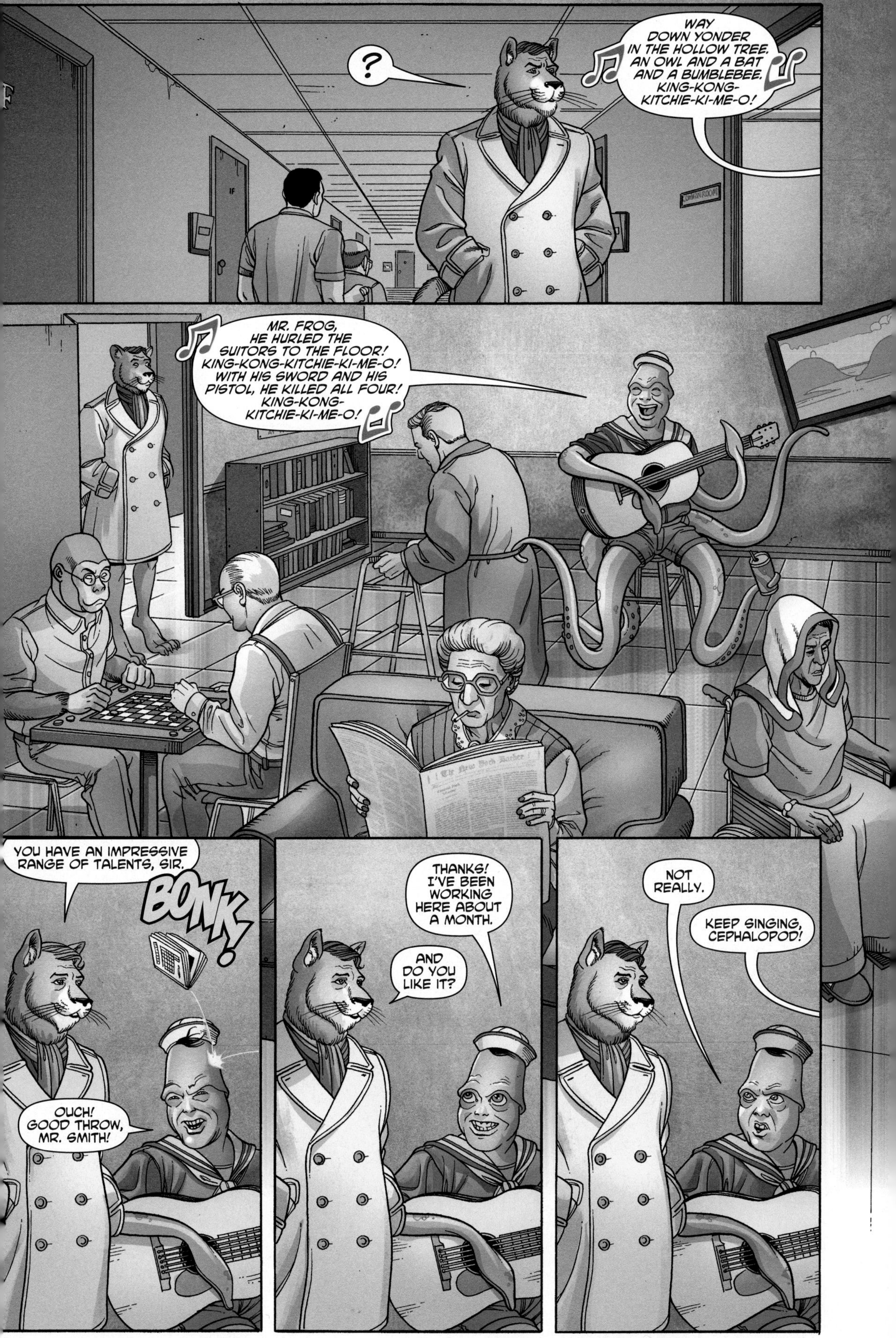
?
WAY DOWN YONDER IN THE HOLLOW TREE. AN OWL AND A BAT AND A BUMBLEBEE. KING-KONG-KITCHIE-KI-ME-O!
MR. FROG, HE HURLED THE SUITORS TO THE FLOOR! KING-KONG-KITCHIE-KI-ME-O! WITH HIS SWORD AND HIS PISTOL, HE KILLED ALL FOUR! KING-KONG-KITCHIE-KI-ME-O!
YOU HAVE AN IMPRESSIVE RANGE OF TALENTS, SIR.
BONK!
OUCH! GOOD THROW, MR. SMITH!
THANKS! I'VE BEEN WORKING HERE ABOUT A MONTH.
AND DO YOU LIKE IT?
NOT REALLY.
KEEP SINGING, CEPHALOPOD!

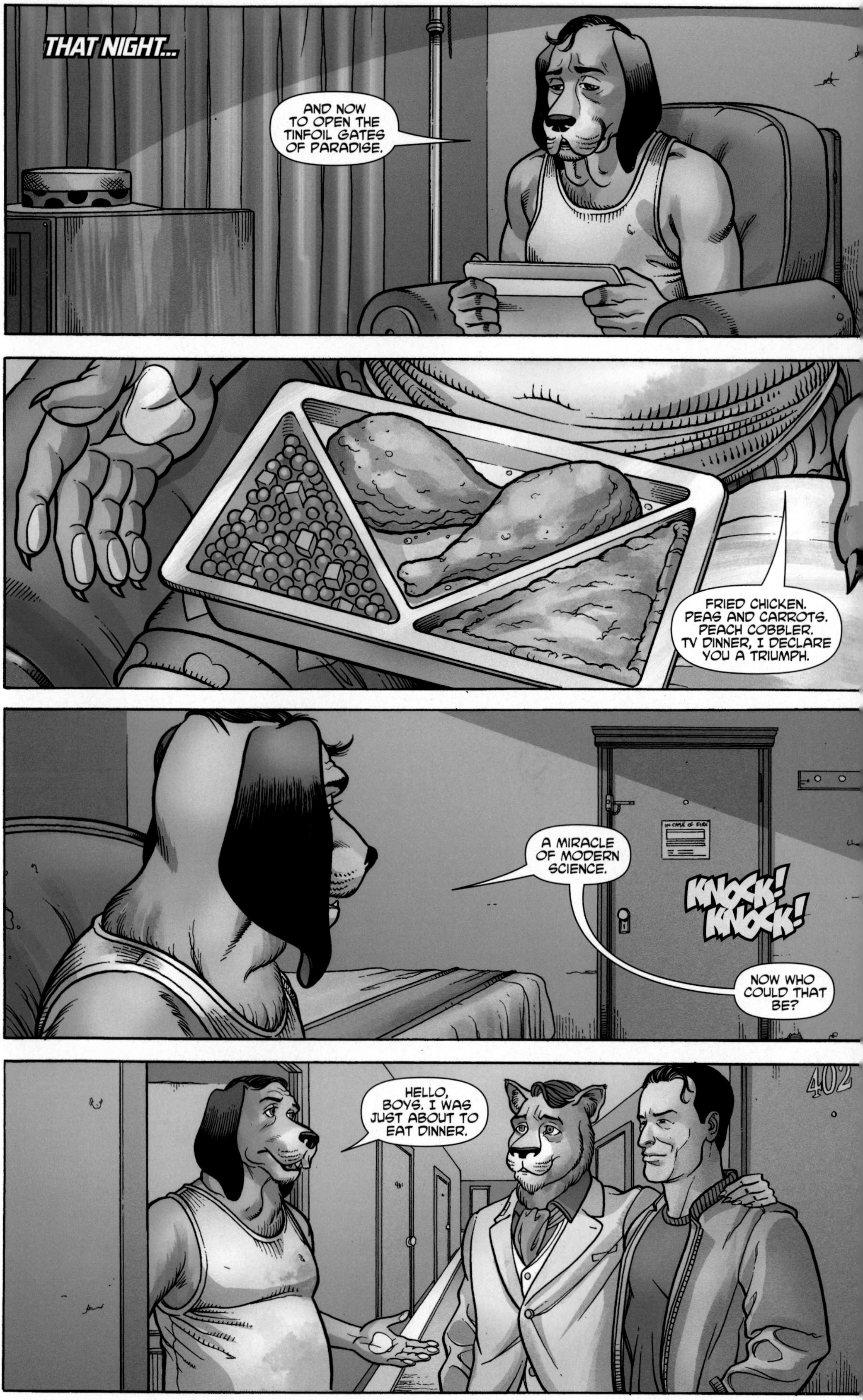
THAT NIGHT...
AND NOW TO OPEN THE TINFOIL GATES OF PARADISE.
FRIED CHICKEN. PEAS AND CARROTS. PEACH COBBLER. TV DINNER, I DECLARE YOU A TRIUMPH.
A MIRACLE OF MODERN SCIENCE.
KNOCK! KNOCK!
NOW WHO COULD THAT BE?
402
HELLO, BOYS. I WAS JUST ABOUT TO EAT DINNER.

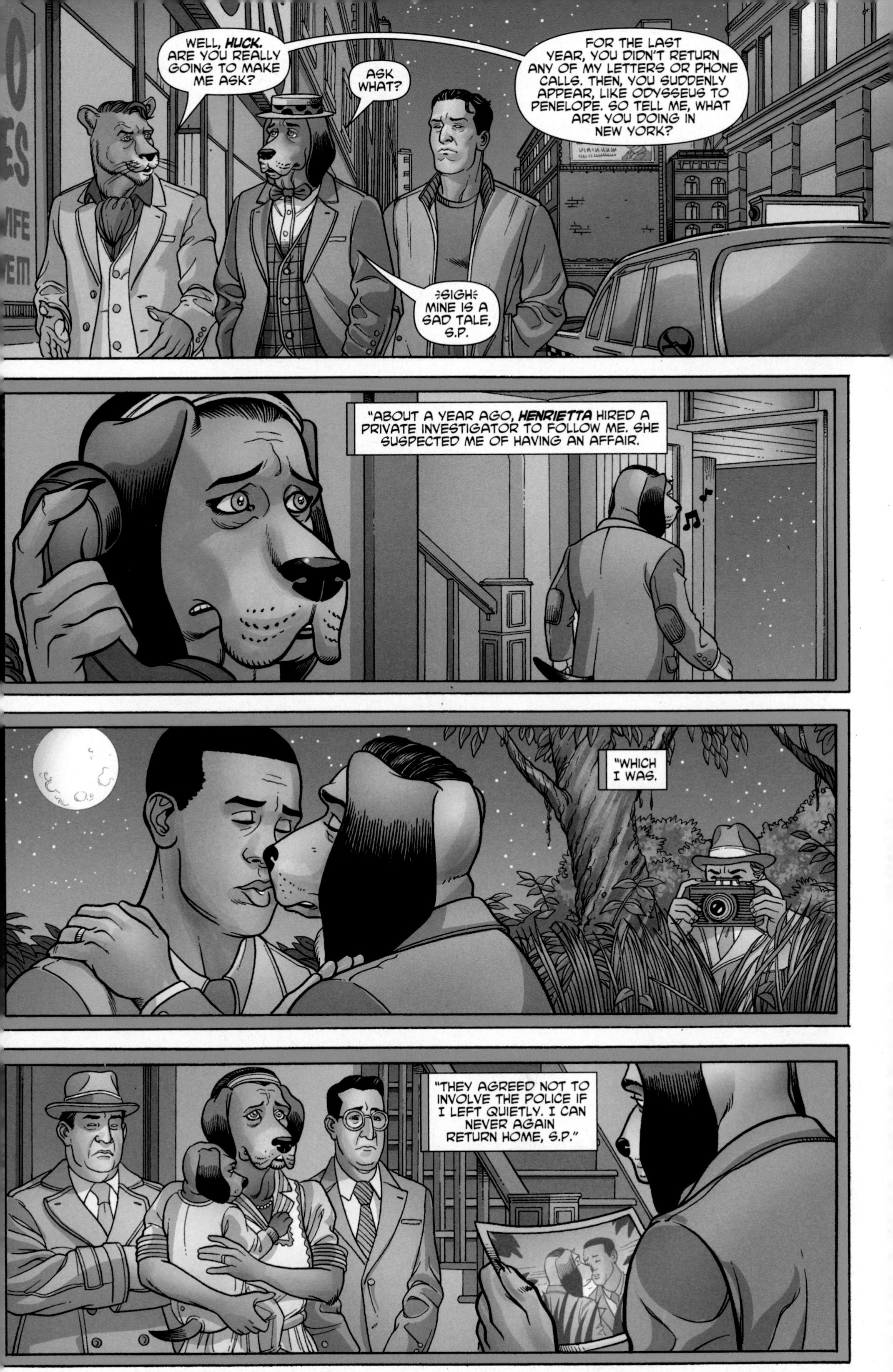
WELL, HUCK. ARE YOU REALLY GOING TO MAKE ME ASK?
ASK WHAT?
FOR THE LAST YEAR, YOU DIDN'T RETURN ANY OF MY LETTERS OR PHONE CALLS. THEN, YOU SUDDENLY APPEAR, LIKE ODYSSEUS TO PENELOPE. SO TELL ME, WHAT ARE YOU DOING IN NEW YORK?
SIGH MINE IS A SAD TALE, S.P.
"ABOUT A YEAR AGO, HENRIETTA HIRED A PRIVATE INVESTIGATOR TO FOLLOW ME. SHE SUSPECTED ME OF HAVING AN AFFAIR.
"WHICH I WAS.
"THEY AGREED NOT TO INVOLVE THE POLICE IF I LEFT QUIETLY. I CAN NEVER AGAIN RETURN HOME, S.P."

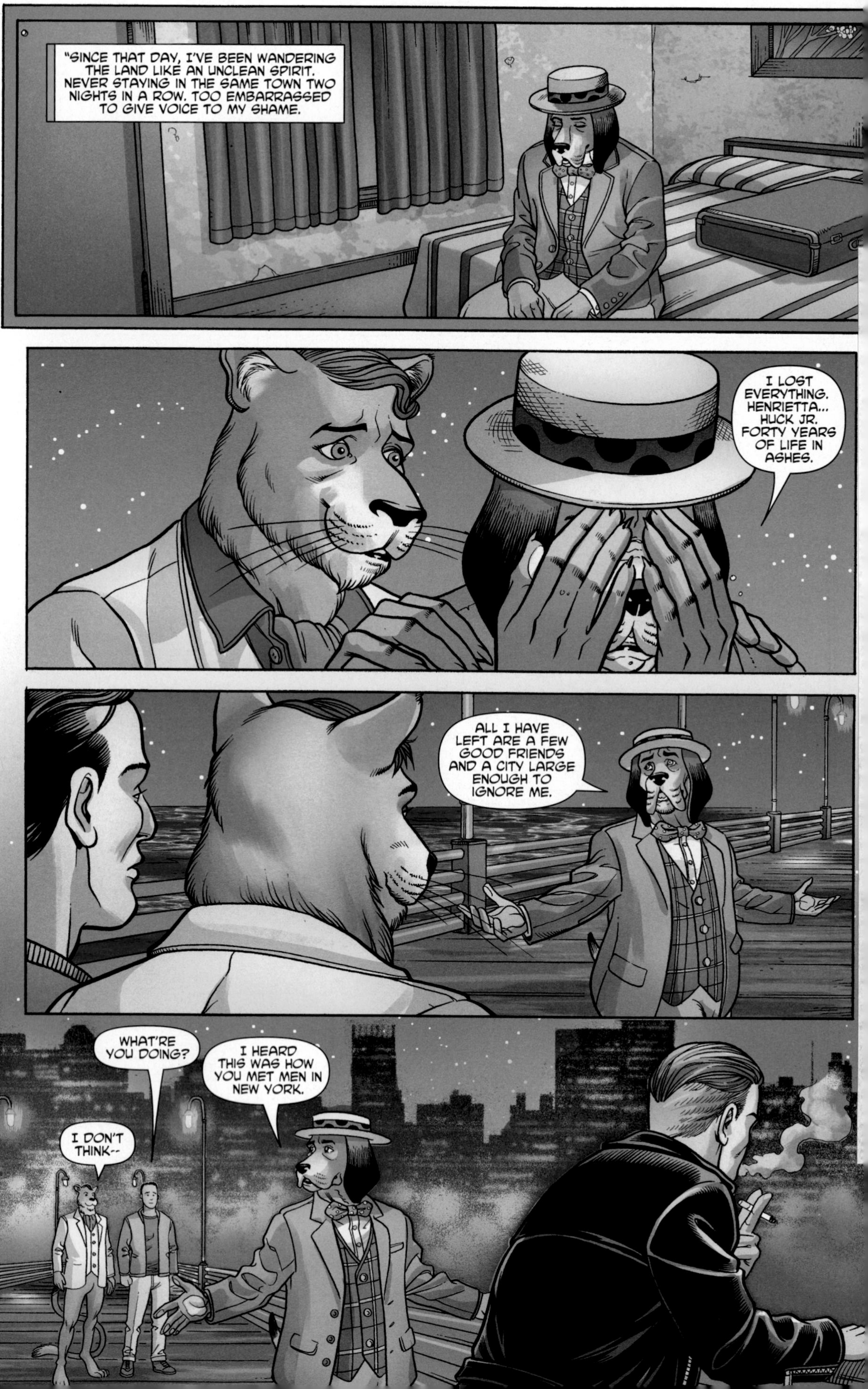

"SINCE THAT DAY, I'VE BEEN WANDERING THE LAND LIKE AN UNCLEAN SPIRIT. NEVER STAYING IN THE SAME TOWN TWO NIGHTS IN A ROW. TOO EMBARRASSED TO GIVE VOICE TO MY SHAME.
I LOST EVERYTHING. HENRIETTA... HUCK JR. FORTY YEARS OF LIFE IN ASHES.
ALL I HAVE LEFT ARE A FEW GOOD FRIENDS AND A CITY LARGE ENOUGH TO IGNORE ME.
WHAT'RE YOU DOING?
I HEARD THIS WAS HOW YOU MET MEN IN NEW YORK.
I DON'T THINK--

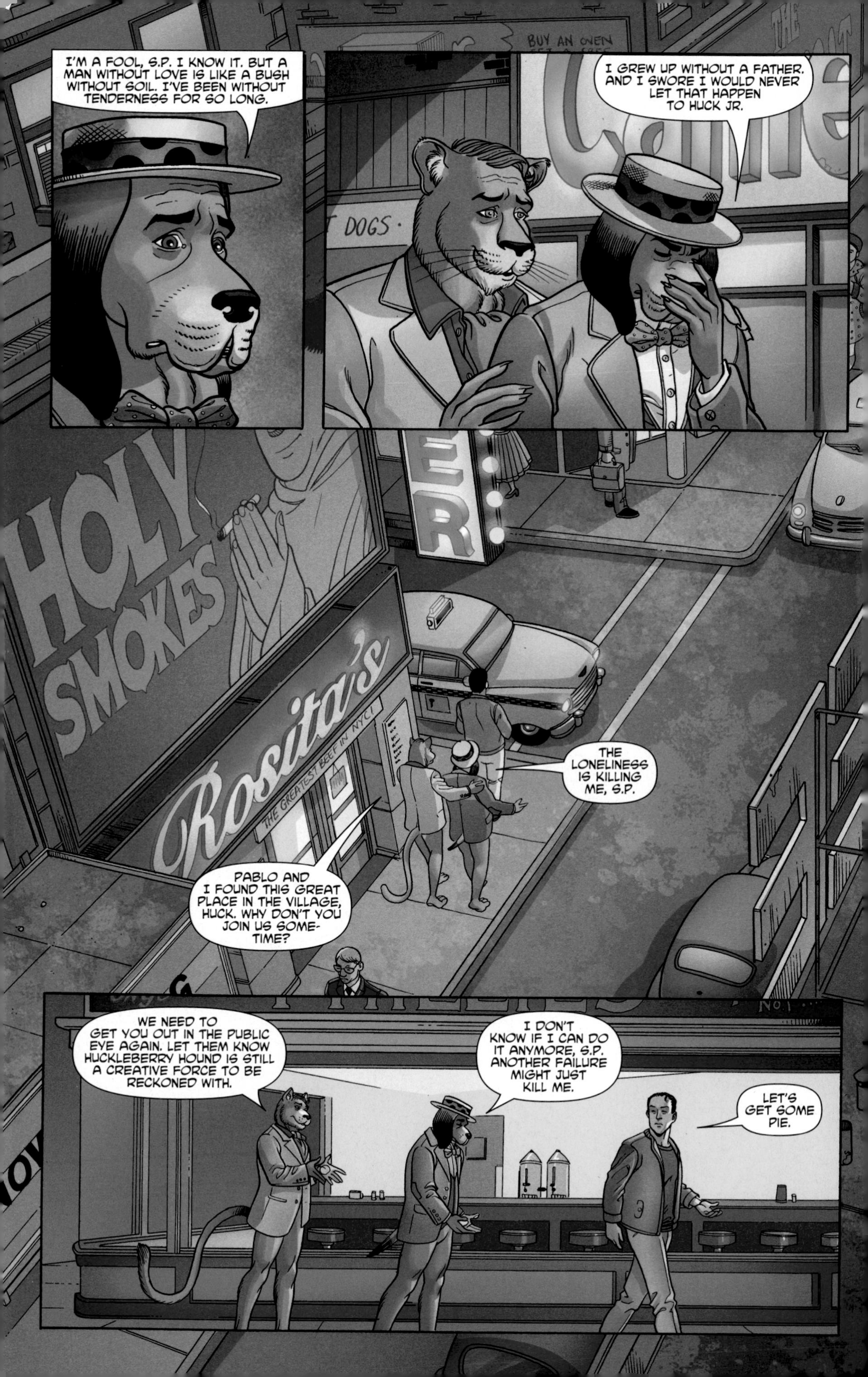
I'M A FOOL, S.P. I KNOW IT. BUT A MAN WITHOUT LOVE IS LIKE A BUSH WITHOUT SOIL. I'VE BEEN WITHOUT TENDERNESS FOR SO LONG.
BUY AN OVEN
I GREW UP WITHOUT A FATHER. AND I SWORE I WOULD NEVER LET THAT HAPPEN TO HUCK JR.
DOGS
HOLY SMOKES
Rosita's
THE GREATEST BEEF IN NYC!
THE LONELINESS IS KILLING ME, S.P.
PABLO AND I FOUND THIS GREAT PLACE IN THE VILLAGE, HUCK. WHY DON'T YOU JOIN US SOME-TIME?
WE NEED TO GET YOU OUT IN THE PUBLIC EYE AGAIN. LET THEM KNOW HUCKLEBERRY HOUND IS STILL A CREATIVE FORCE TO BE RECKONED WITH.
I DON'T KNOW IF I CAN DO IT ANYMORE, S.P. ANOTHER FAILURE MIGHT JUST KILL ME.
LET'S GET SOME PIE.

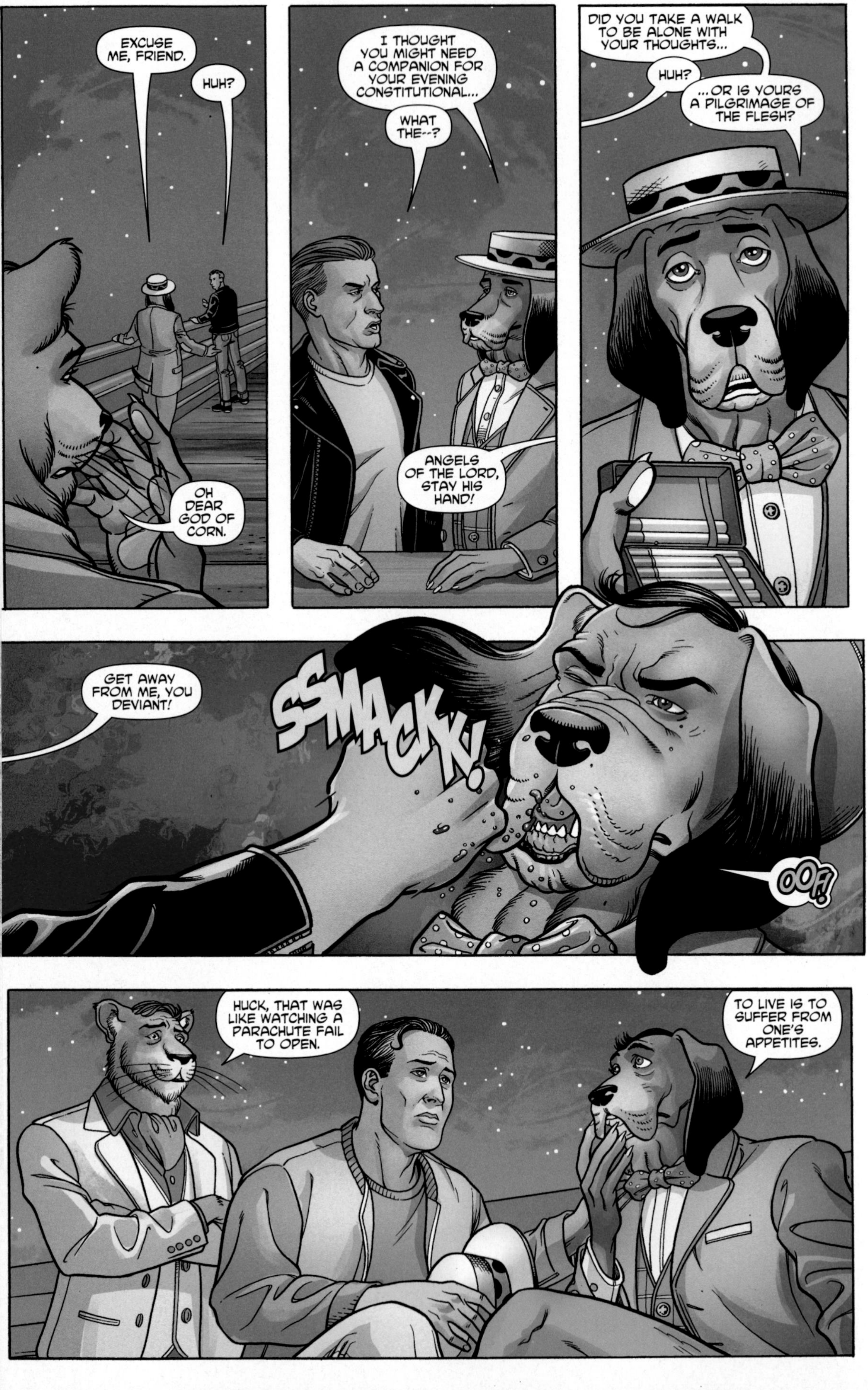
EXCUSE ME, FRIEND.
HUH?
OH DEAR GOD OF CORN.
I THOUGHT YOU MIGHT NEED A COMPANION FOR YOUR EVENING CONSTITUTIONAL...
WHAT THE--?
ANGELS OF THE LORD, STAY HIS HAND!
DID YOU TAKE A WALK TO BE ALONE WITH YOUR THOUGHTS...
HUH?
...OR IS YOURS A PILGRIMAGE OF THE FLESH?
GET AWAY FROM ME, YOU DEVIANT!
SSMACKK!
OOF!
HUCK, THAT WAS LIKE WATCHING A PARACHUTE FAIL TO OPEN.
TO LIVE IS TO SUFFER FROM ONE'S APPETITES.

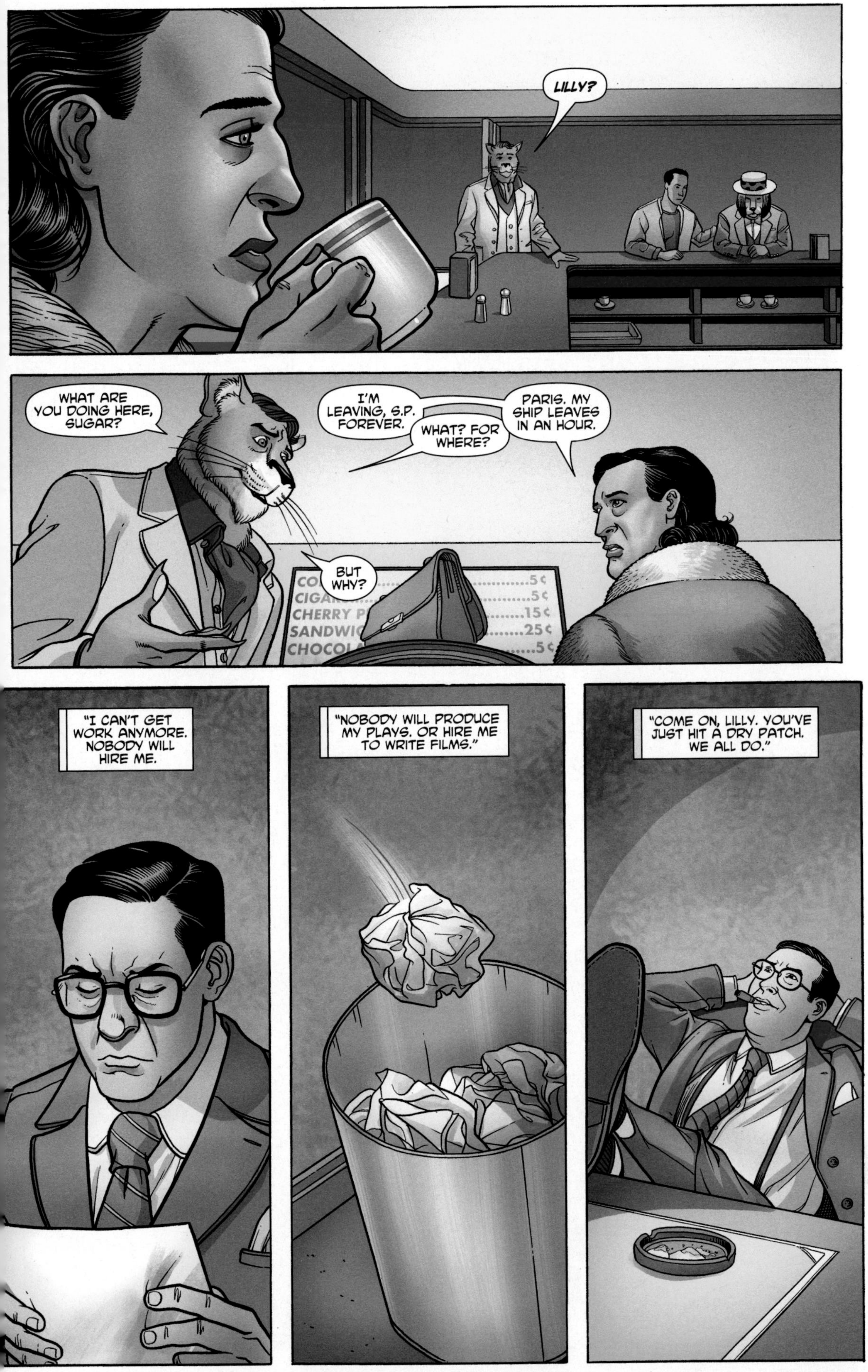
LILLY?
WHAT ARE YOU DOING HERE, SUGAR?
I'M LEAVING, S.P. FOREVER.
WHAT? FOR WHERE?
PARIS. MY SHIP LEAVES IN AN HOUR.
BUT WHY?
"I CAN'T GET WORK ANYMORE. NOBODY WILL HIRE ME.
"NOBODY WILL PRODUCE MY PLAYS. OR HIRE ME TO WRITE FILMS."
"COME ON, LILLY. YOU'VE JUST HIT A DRY PATCH. WE ALL DO."

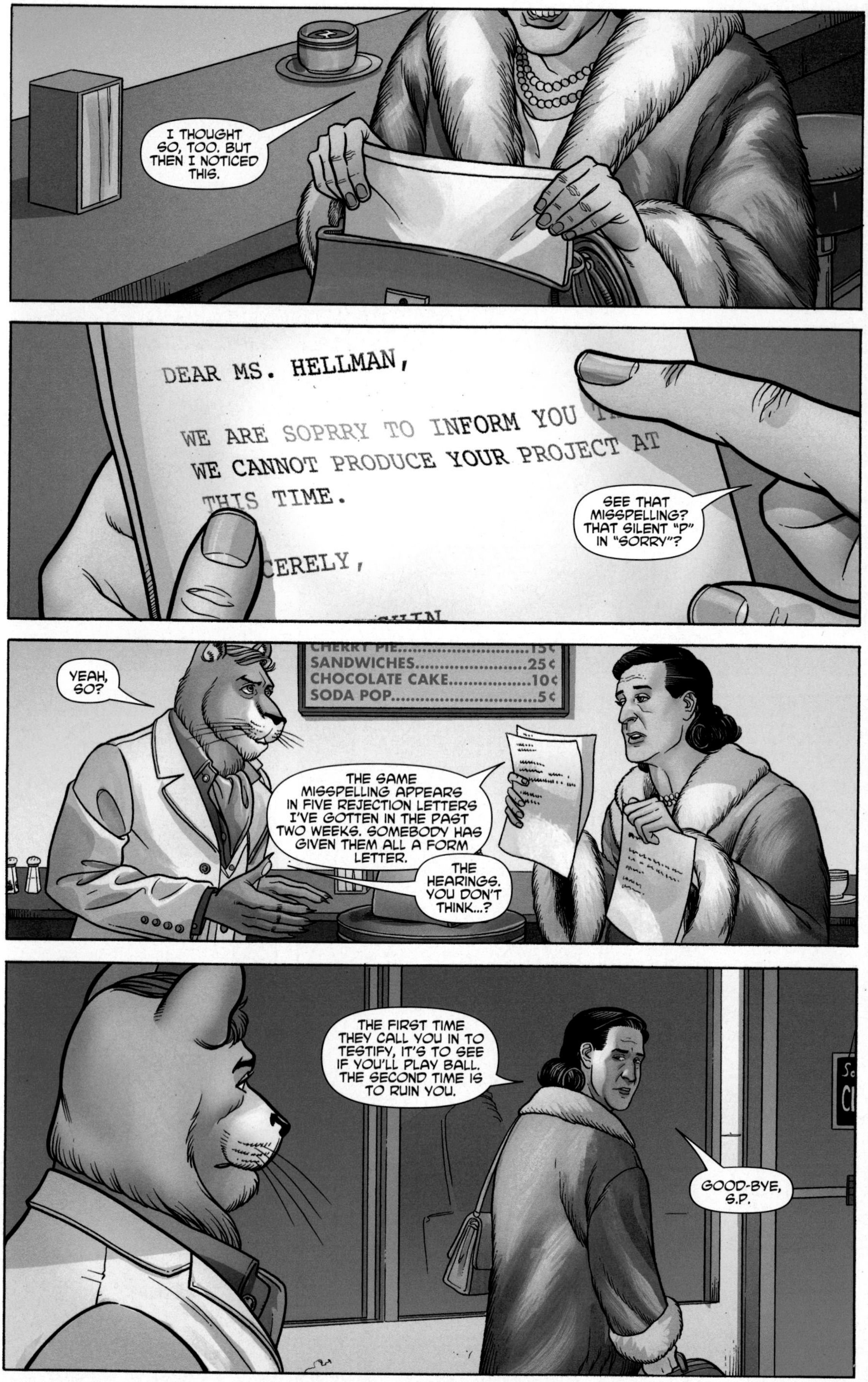
I THOUGHT SO, TOO. BUT THEN I NOTICED THIS.
DEAR MS. HELLMAN,
WE ARE SOPRRY TO INFORM YOU
WE CANNOT PRODUCE YOUR PROJECT AT
THIS TIME.
SEE THAT MISSPELLING? THAT SILENT "P" IN "SORRY"?
SANDWICHES........25¢
CHOCOLATE CAKE........10¢
SODA POP........5¢
YEAH, SO?
THE SAME MISSPELLING APPEARS IN FIVE REJECTION LETTERS I'VE GOTTEN IN THE PAST TWO WEEKS. SOMEBODY HAS GIVEN THEM ALL A FORM LETTER.
THE HEARINGS. YOU DON'T THINK...?
THE FIRST TIME THEY CALL YOU IN TO TESTIFY, IT'S TO SEE IF YOU'LL PLAY BALL. THE SECOND TIME IS TO RUIN YOU.
GOOD-BYE, S.P.

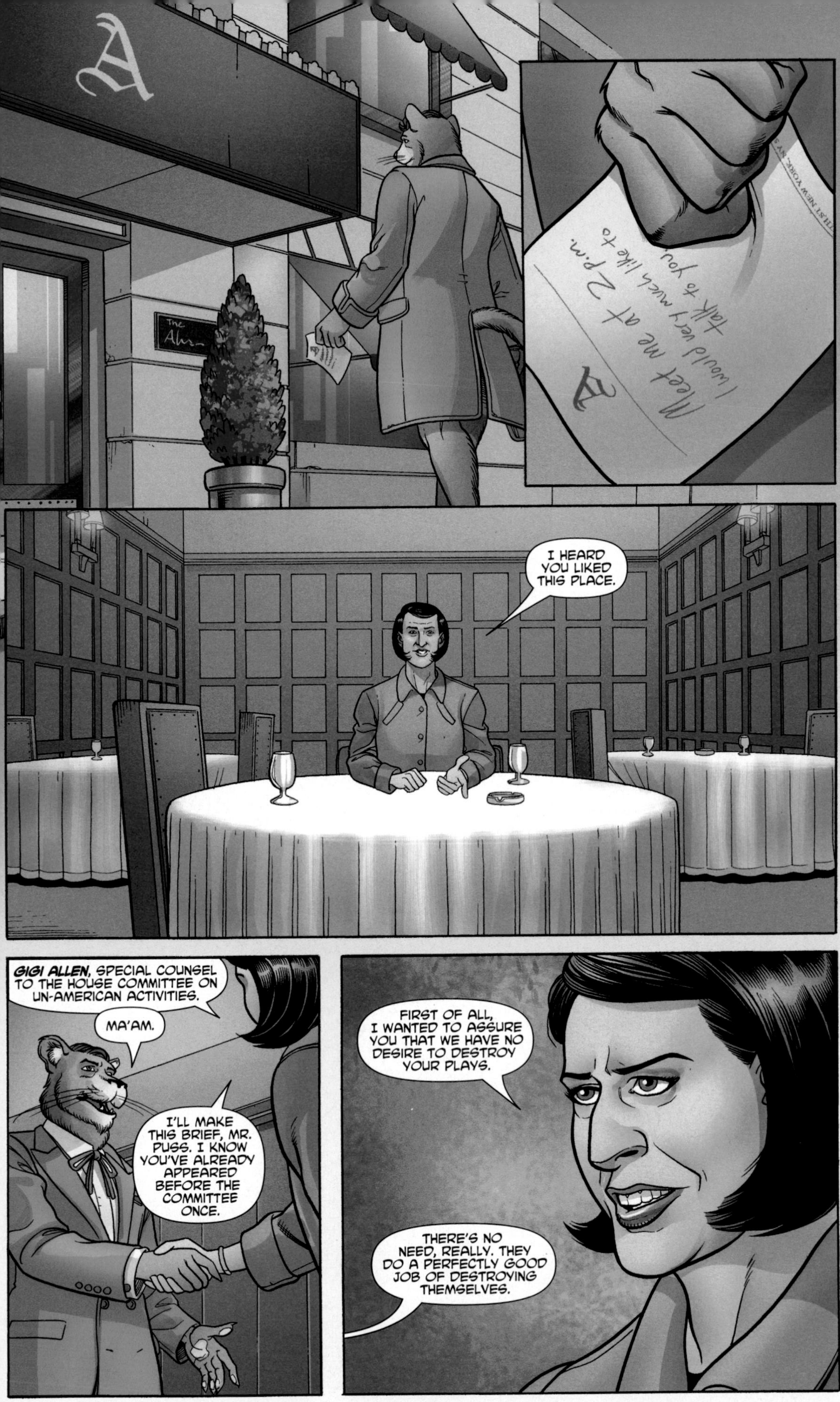

Meet me at 2 p.m.
I would very much like to talk to you
I HEARD YOU LIKED THIS PLACE.
GIGI ALLEN, SPECIAL COUNSEL TO THE HOUSE COMMITTEE ON UN-AMERICAN ACTIVITIES.
MA'AM.
I'LL MAKE THIS BRIEF, MR. PUSS. I KNOW YOU'VE ALREADY APPEARED BEFORE THE COMMITTEE ONCE.
FIRST OF ALL, I WANTED TO ASSURE YOU THAT WE HAVE NO DESIRE TO DESTROY YOUR PLAYS.
THERE'S NO NEED, REALLY. THEY DO A PERFECTLY GOOD JOB OF DESTROYING THEMSELVES.

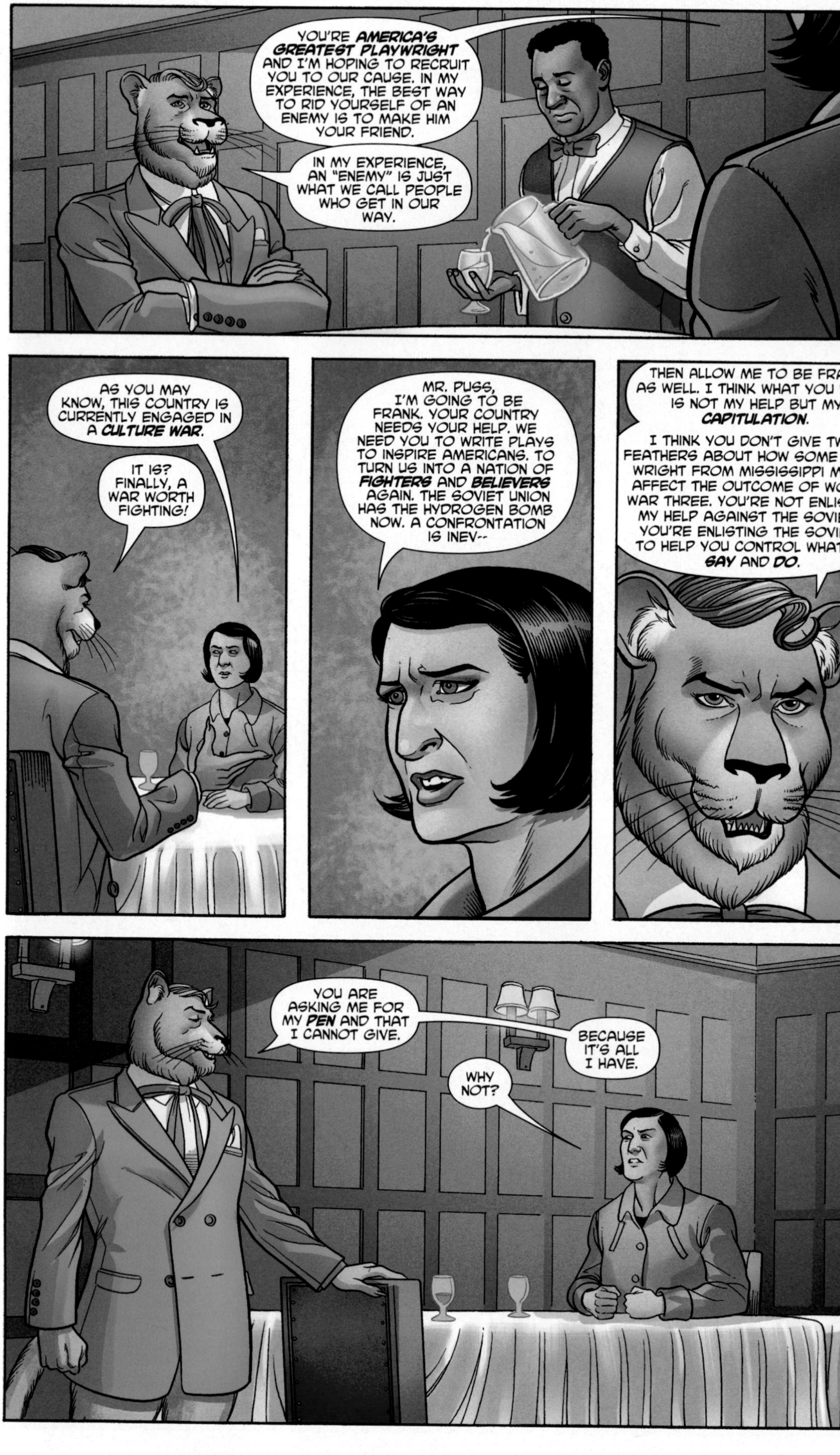
YOU'RE AMERICA'S GREATEST PLAYWRIGHT AND I'M HOPING TO RECRUIT YOU TO OUR CAUSE. IN MY EXPERIENCE, THE BEST WAY TO RID YOURSELF OF AN ENEMY IS TO MAKE HIM YOUR FRIEND.
IN MY EXPERIENCE, AN "ENEMY" IS JUST WHAT WE CALL PEOPLE WHO GET IN OUR WAY.
AS YOU MAY KNOW, THIS COUNTRY IS CURRENTLY ENGAGED IN A CULTURE WAR.
IT IS? FINALLY, A WAR WORTH FIGHTING!
MR. PUSS, I'M GOING TO BE FRANK. YOUR COUNTRY NEEDS YOUR HELP. WE NEED YOU TO WRITE PLAYS TO INSPIRE AMERICANS. TO TURN US INTO A NATION OF FIGHTERS AND BELIEVERS AGAIN. THE SOVIET UNION HAS THE HYDROGEN BOMB NOW. A CONFRONTATION IS INEV--
THEN ALLOW ME TO BE FRANK AS WELL. I THINK WHAT YOU WANT IS NOT MY HELP BUT MY CAPITULATION.
I THINK YOU DON'T GIVE TWO FEATHERS ABOUT HOW SOME PLAY-WRIGHT FROM MISSISSIPPI MIGHT AFFECT THE OUTCOME OF WORLD WAR THREE. YOU'RE NOT ENLISTING MY HELP AGAINST THE SOVIETS. YOU'RE ENLISTING THE SOVIETS TO HELP YOU CONTROL WHAT WE SAY AND DO.
YOU ARE ASKING ME FOR MY PEN AND THAT I CANNOT GIVE.
WHY NOT?
BECAUSE IT'S ALL I HAVE.

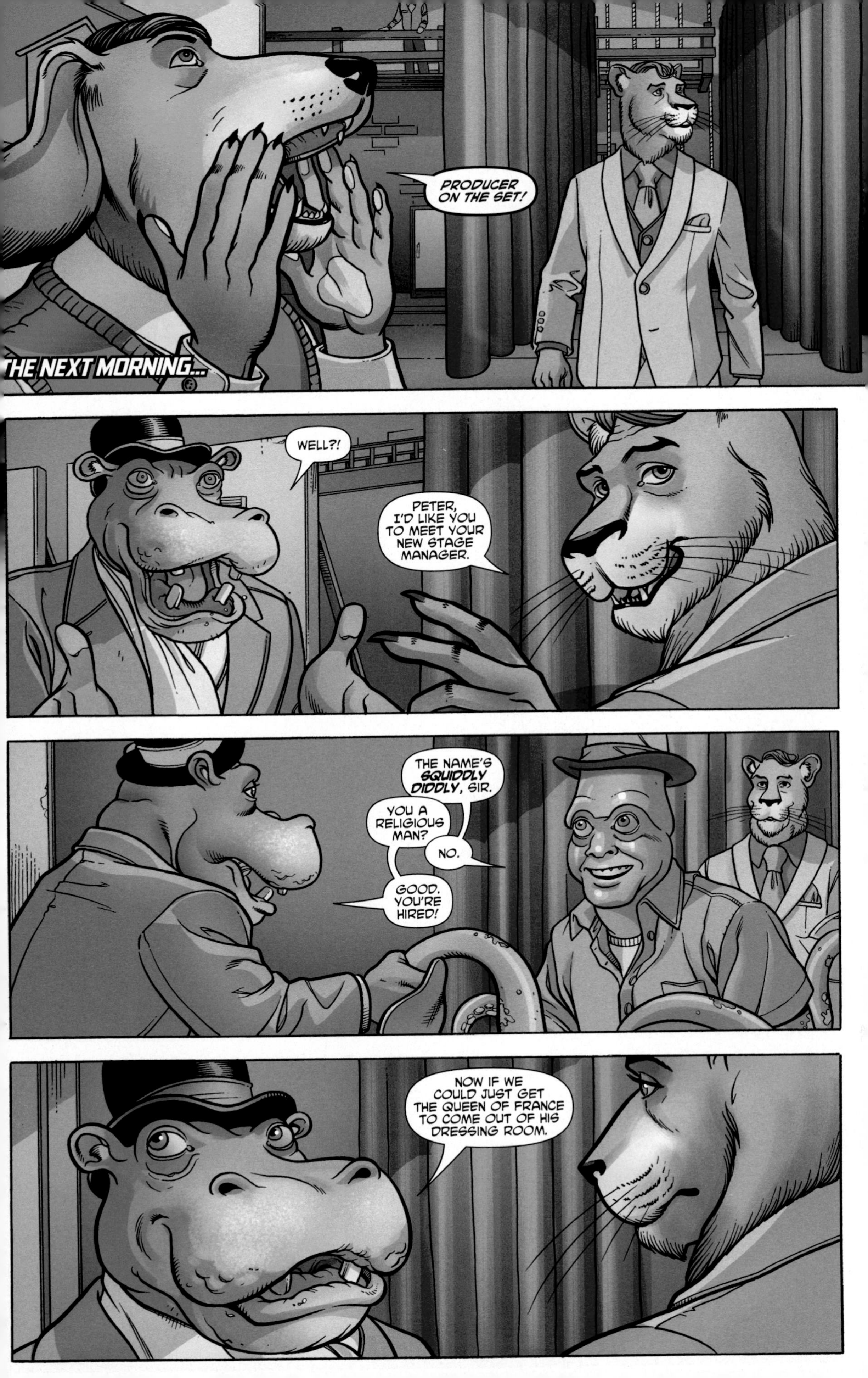
THE NEXT MORNING...
PRODUCER ON THE SET!
WELL?!
PETER, I'D LIKE YOU TO MEET YOUR NEW STAGE MANAGER.
THE NAME'S SQUIDDLY DIDDLY, SIR.
YOU A RELIGIOUS MAN?
NO.
GOOD. YOU'RE HIRED!
NOW IF WE COULD JUST GET THE QUEEN OF FRANCE TO COME OUT OF HIS DRESSING ROOM.

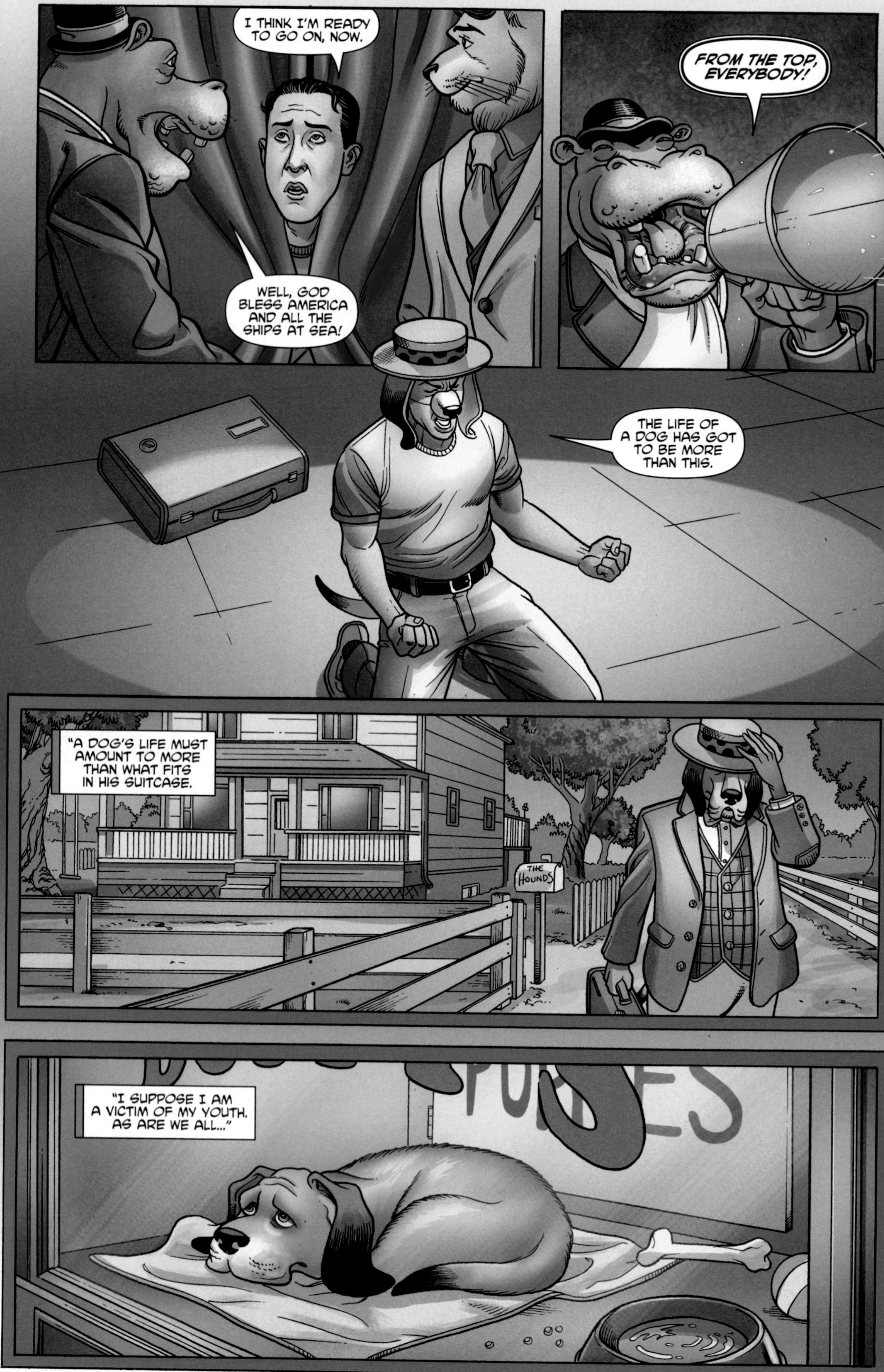
I THINK I'M READY TO GO ON, NOW.
WELL, GOD BLESS AMERICA AND ALL THE SHIPS AT SEA!
FROM THE TOP, EVERYBODY!
THE LIFE OF A DOG HAS GOT TO BE MORE THAN THIS.
"A DOG'S LIFE MUST AMOUNT TO MORE THAN WHAT FITS IN HIS SUITCASE.
THE HOUNDS
"I SUPPOSE I AM A VICTIM OF MY YOUTH. AS ARE WE ALL..."

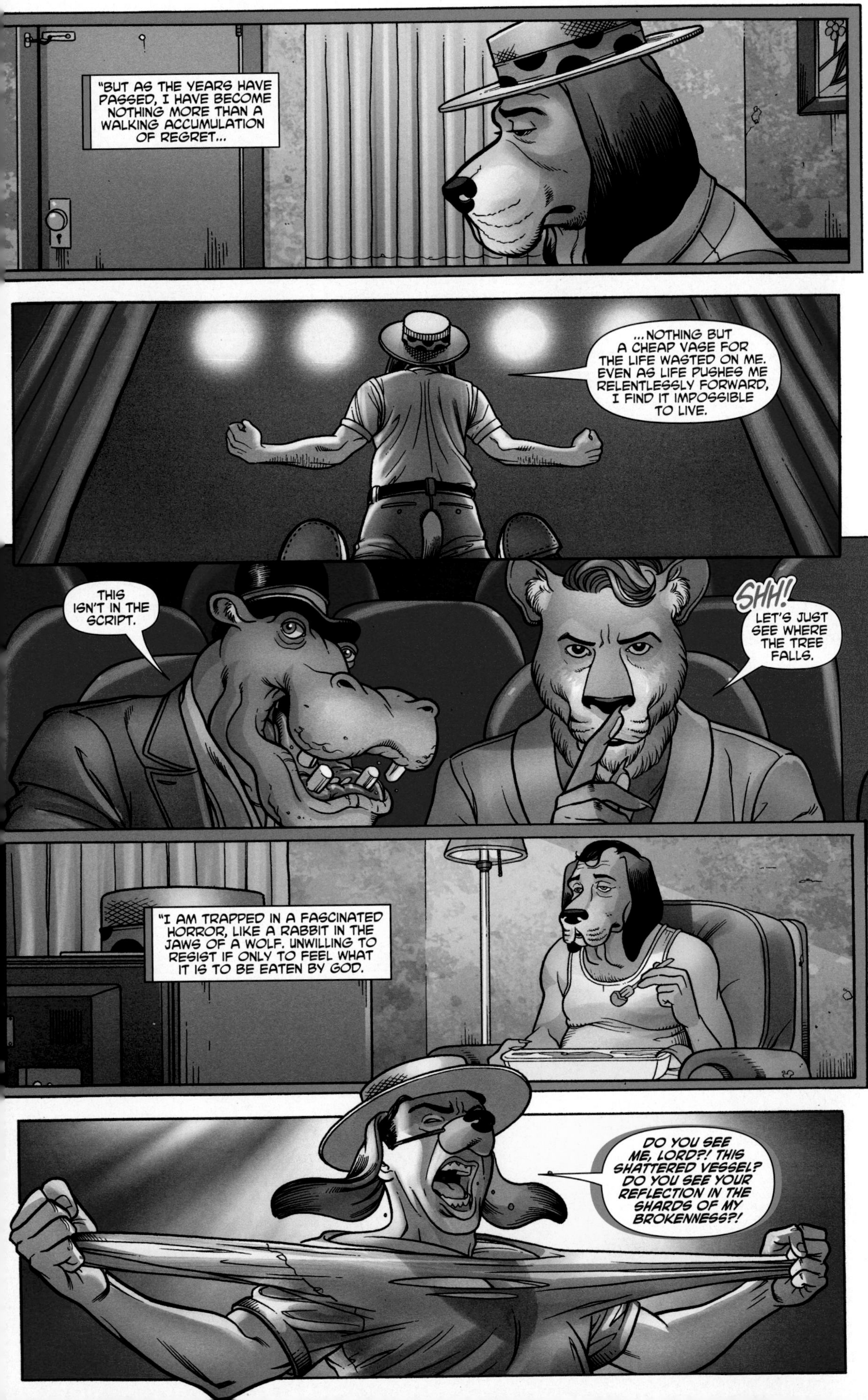
"BUT AS THE YEARS HAVE PASSED, I HAVE BECOME NOTHING MORE THAN A WALKING ACCUMULATION OF REGRET...
...NOTHING BUT A CHEAP VASE FOR THE LIFE WASTED ON ME. EVEN AS LIFE PUSHES ME RELENTLESSLY FORWARD, I FIND IT IMPOSSIBLE TO LIVE.
THIS ISN'T IN THE SCRIPT.
SHH! LET'S JUST SEE WHERE THE TREE FALLS.
"I AM TRAPPED IN A FASCINATED HORROR, LIKE A RABBIT IN THE JAWS OF A WOLF. UNWILLING TO RESIST IF ONLY TO FEEL WHAT IT IS TO BE EATEN BY GOD.
DO YOU SEE ME, LORD?! THIS SHATTERED VESSEL? DO YOU SEE YOUR REFLECTION IN THE SHARDS OF MY BROKENNESS?!

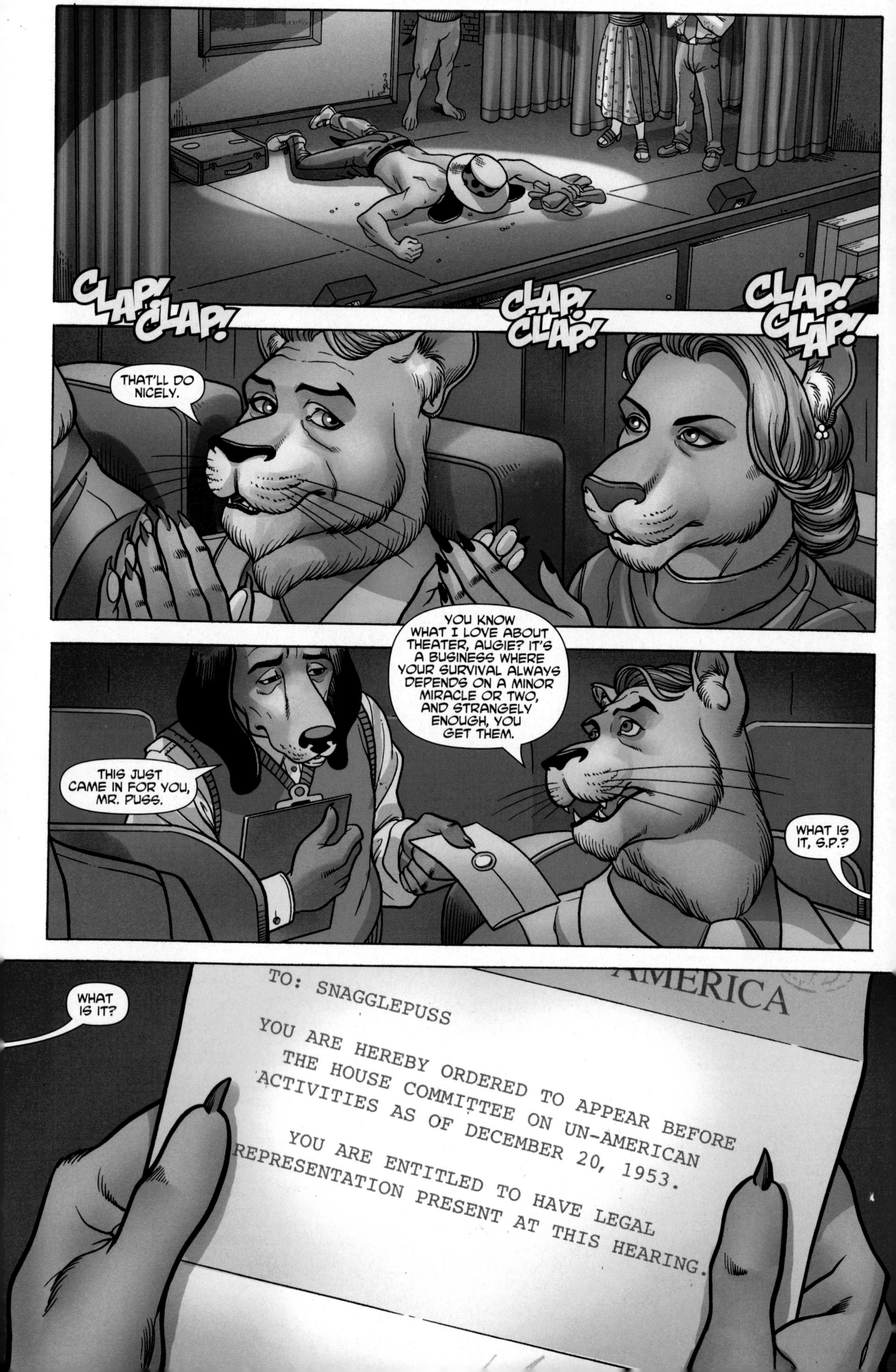
CLAP! CLAP!
CLAP! CLAP!
CLAP! CLAP!
THAT'LL DO NICELY.
YOU KNOW WHAT I LOVE ABOUT THEATER, AUGIE? IT'S A BUSINESS WHERE YOUR SURVIVAL ALWAYS DEPENDS ON A MINOR MIRACLE OR TWO, AND STRANGELY ENOUGH, YOU GET THEM.
THIS JUST CAME IN FOR YOU, MR. PUSS.
WHAT IS IT, S.P.?
WHAT IS IT?
AMERICA
TO: SNAGGLEPUSS
YOU ARE HEREBY ORDERED TO APPEAR BEFORE THE HOUSE COMMITTEE ON UN-AMERICAN ACTIVITIES AS OF DECEMBER 20, 1953.
YOU ARE ENTITLED TO HAVE LEGAL REPRESENTATION PRESENT AT THIS HEARING.

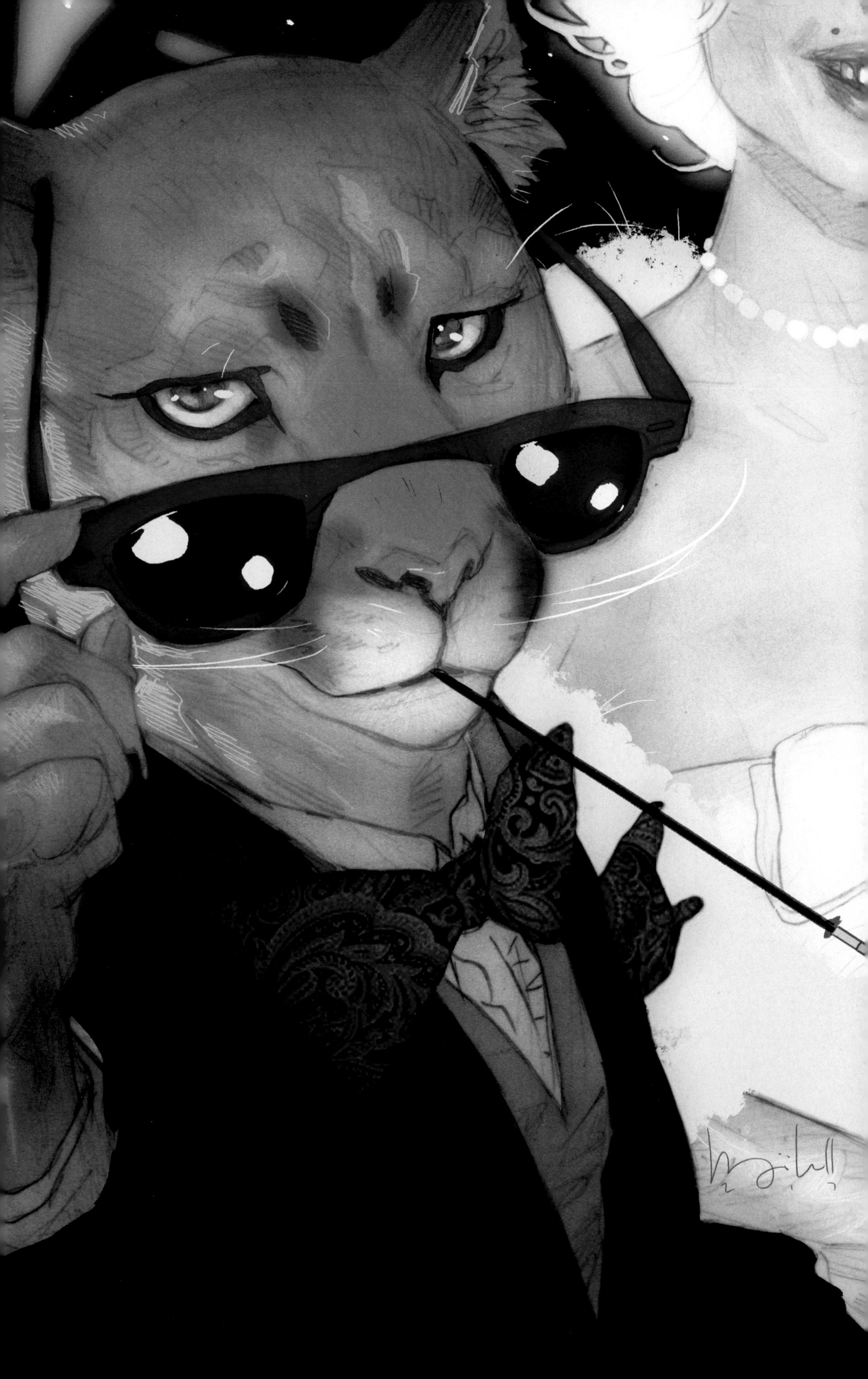

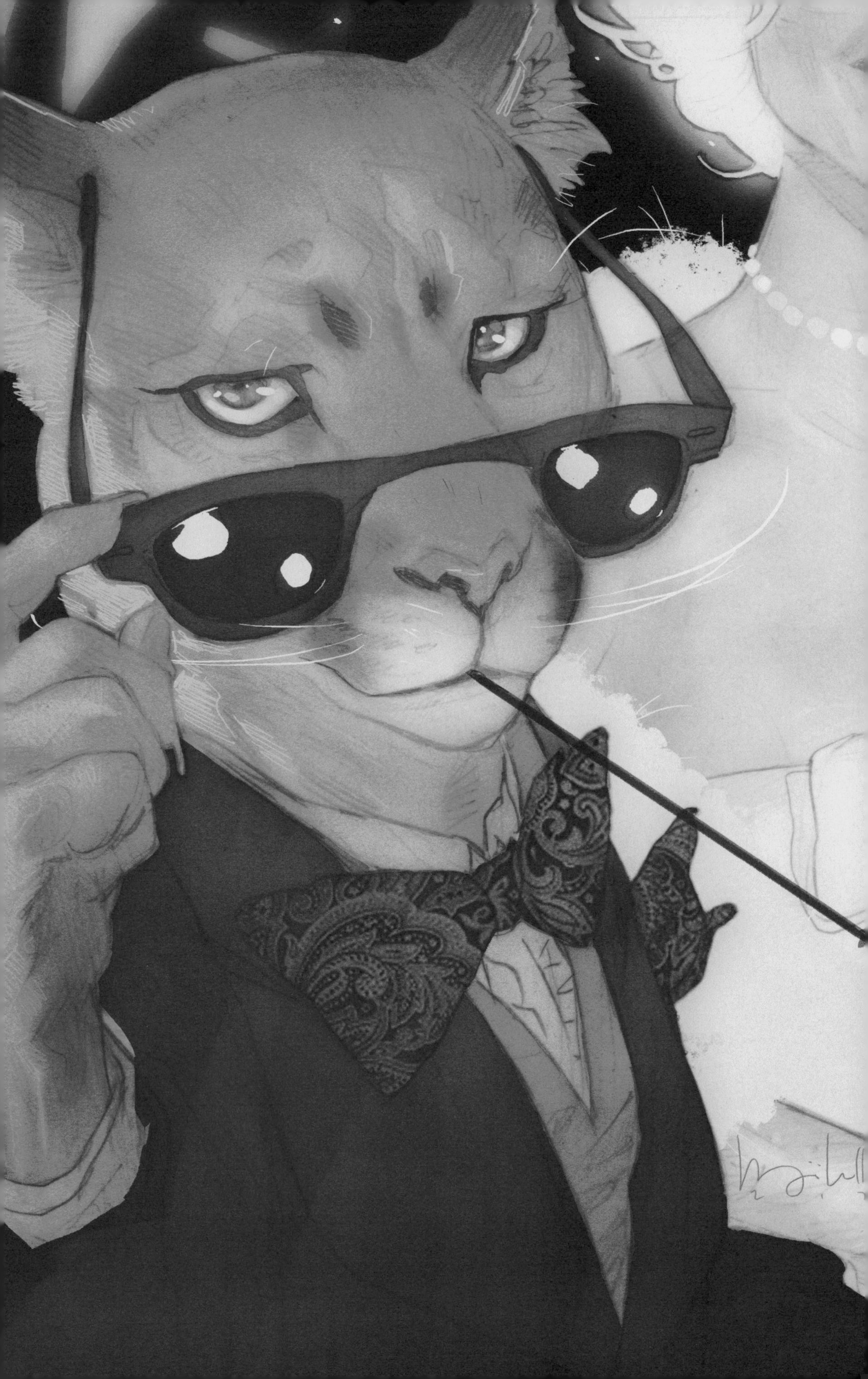

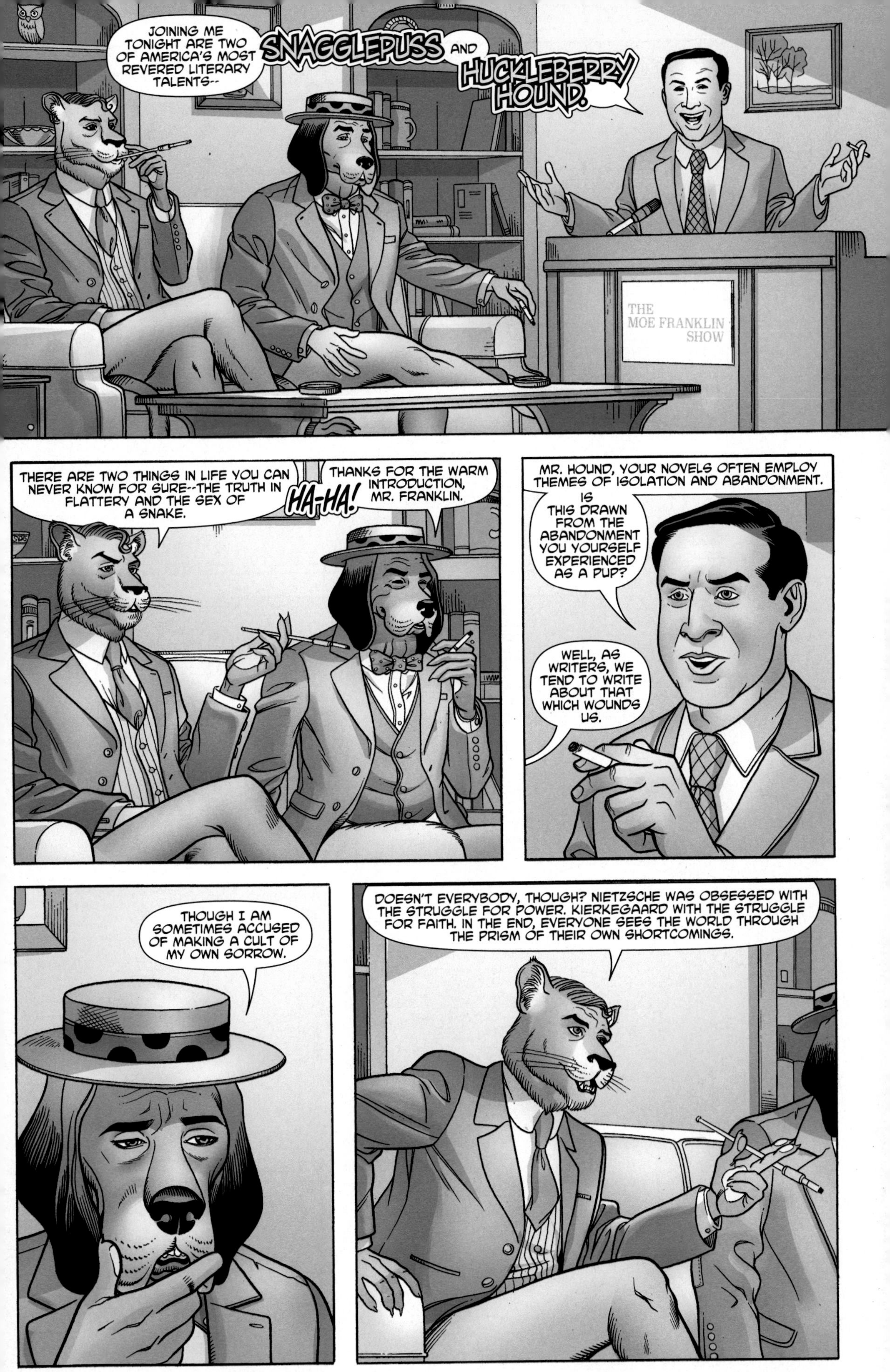
JOINING ME TONIGHT ARE TWO OF AMERICA'S MOST REVERED LITERARY TALENTS-- SNAGGLEPUSS AND HUCKLEBERRY HOUND.
THE MOE FRANKLIN SHOW
THERE ARE TWO THINGS IN LIFE YOU CAN NEVER KNOW FOR SURE--THE TRUTH IN FLATTERY AND THE SEX OF A SNAKE.
HA-HA!
THANKS FOR THE WARM INTRODUCTION, MR. FRANKLIN.
MR. HOUND, YOUR NOVELS OFTEN EMPLOY THEMES OF ISOLATION AND ABANDONMENT.
IS THIS DRAWN FROM THE ABANDONMENT YOU YOURSELF EXPERIENCED AS A PUP?
WELL, AS WRITERS, WE TEND TO WRITE ABOUT THAT WHICH WOUNDS US.
THOUGH I AM SOMETIMES ACCUSED OF MAKING A CULT OF MY OWN SORROW.
DOESN'T EVERYBODY, THOUGH? NIETZSCHE WAS OBSESSED WITH THE STRUGGLE FOR POWER. KIERKEGAARD WITH THE STRUGGLE FOR FAITH. IN THE END, EVERYONE SEES THE WORLD THROUGH THE PRISM OF THEIR OWN SHORTCOMINGS.

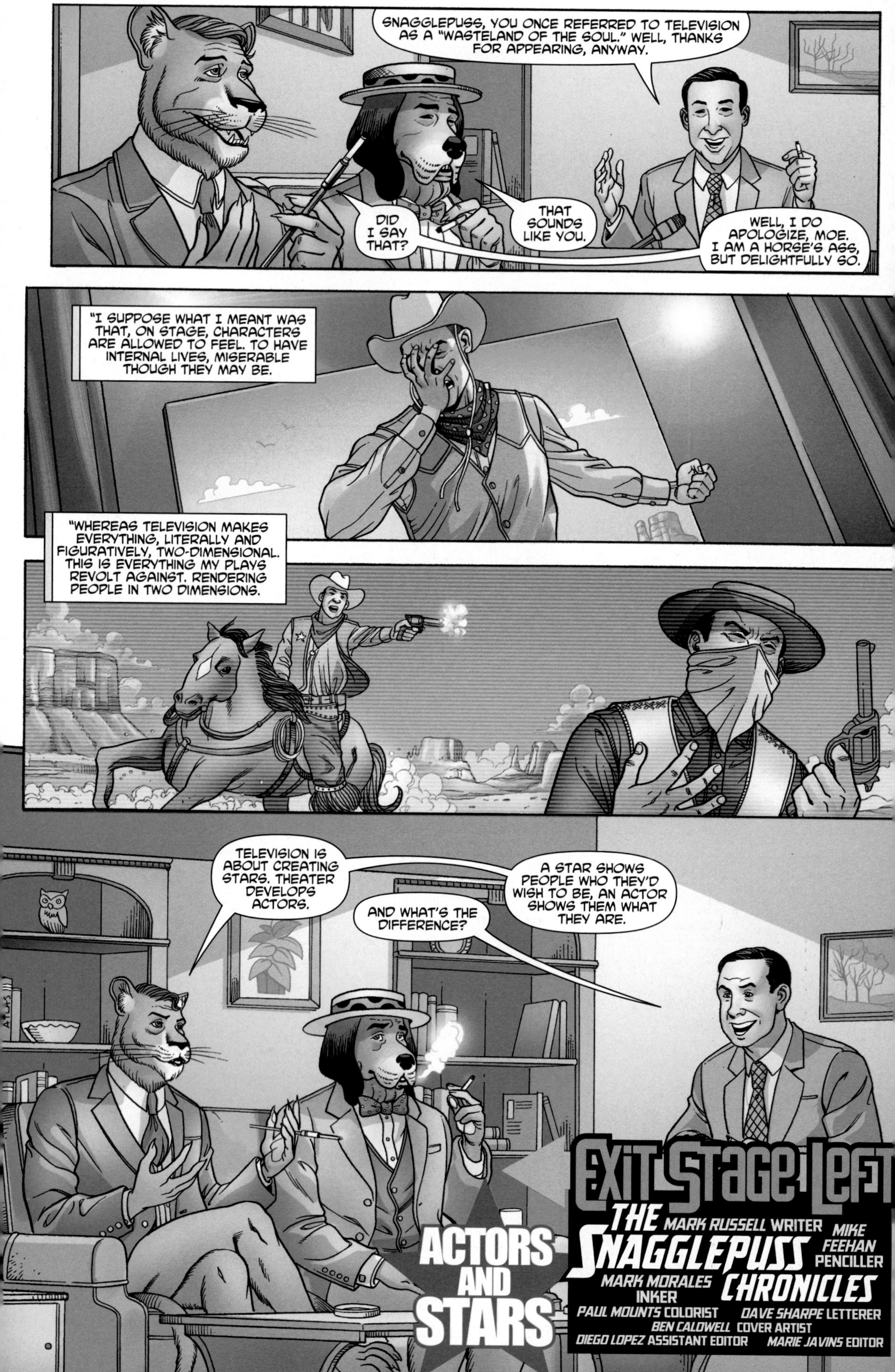
SNAGGLEPUSS, YOU ONCE REFERRED TO TELEVISION AS A "WASTELAND OF THE SOUL." WELL, THANKS FOR APPEARING, ANYWAY.
DID I SAY THAT?
THAT SOUNDS LIKE YOU.
WELL, I DO APOLOGIZE, MOE. I AM A HORSE'S ASS, BUT DELIGHTFULLY SO.
"I SUPPOSE WHAT I MEANT WAS THAT, ON STAGE, CHARACTERS ARE ALLOWED TO FEEL. TO HAVE INTERNAL LIVES, MISERABLE THOUGH THEY MAY BE.
"WHEREAS TELEVISION MAKES EVERYTHING, LITERALLY AND FIGURATIVELY, TWO-DIMENSIONAL. THIS IS EVERYTHING MY PLAYS REVOLT AGAINST. RENDERING PEOPLE IN TWO DIMENSIONS.
TELEVISION IS ABOUT CREATING STARS. THEATER DEVELOPS ACTORS.
AND WHAT'S THE DIFFERENCE?
A STAR SHOWS PEOPLE WHO THEY'D WISH TO BE, AN ACTOR SHOWS THEM WHAT THEY ARE.
ACTORS AND STARS
EXIT STAGE LEFT
THE SNAGGLEPUSS CHRONICLES
MARK RUSSELL WRITER
MIKE FEEHAN PENCILLER
MARK MORALES INKER
PAUL MOUNTS COLORIST
DAVE SHARPE LETTERER
BEN CALDWELL COVER ARTIST
DIEGO LOPEZ ASSISTANT EDITOR
MARIE JAVINS EDITOR

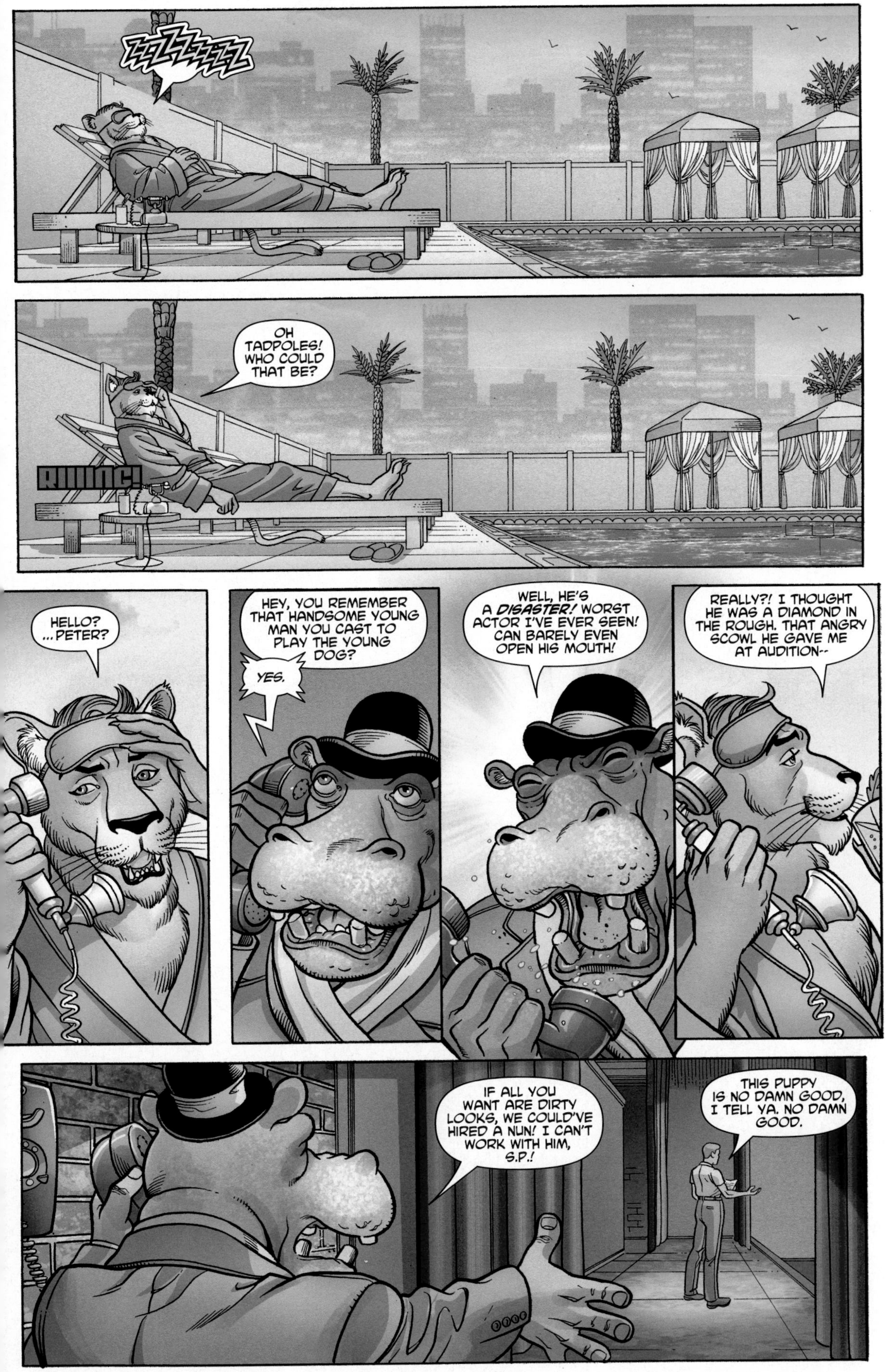
ZZZZZZZZ
OH TADPOLES! WHO COULD THAT BE?
RIIIING!
HELLO? ...PETER?
HEY, YOU REMEMBER THAT HANDSOME YOUNG MAN YOU CAST TO PLAY THE YOUNG DOG?
YES.
WELL, HE'S A *DISASTER!* WORST ACTOR I'VE EVER SEEN! CAN BARELY EVEN OPEN HIS MOUTH!
REALLY?! I THOUGHT HE WAS A DIAMOND IN THE ROUGH. THAT ANGRY SCOWL HE GAVE ME AT AUDITION--
IF ALL YOU WANT ARE DIRTY LOOKS, WE COULD'VE HIRED A NUN! I CAN'T WORK WITH HIM, S.P.!
THIS PUPPY IS NO DAMN GOOD, I TELL YA. NO DAMN GOOD.

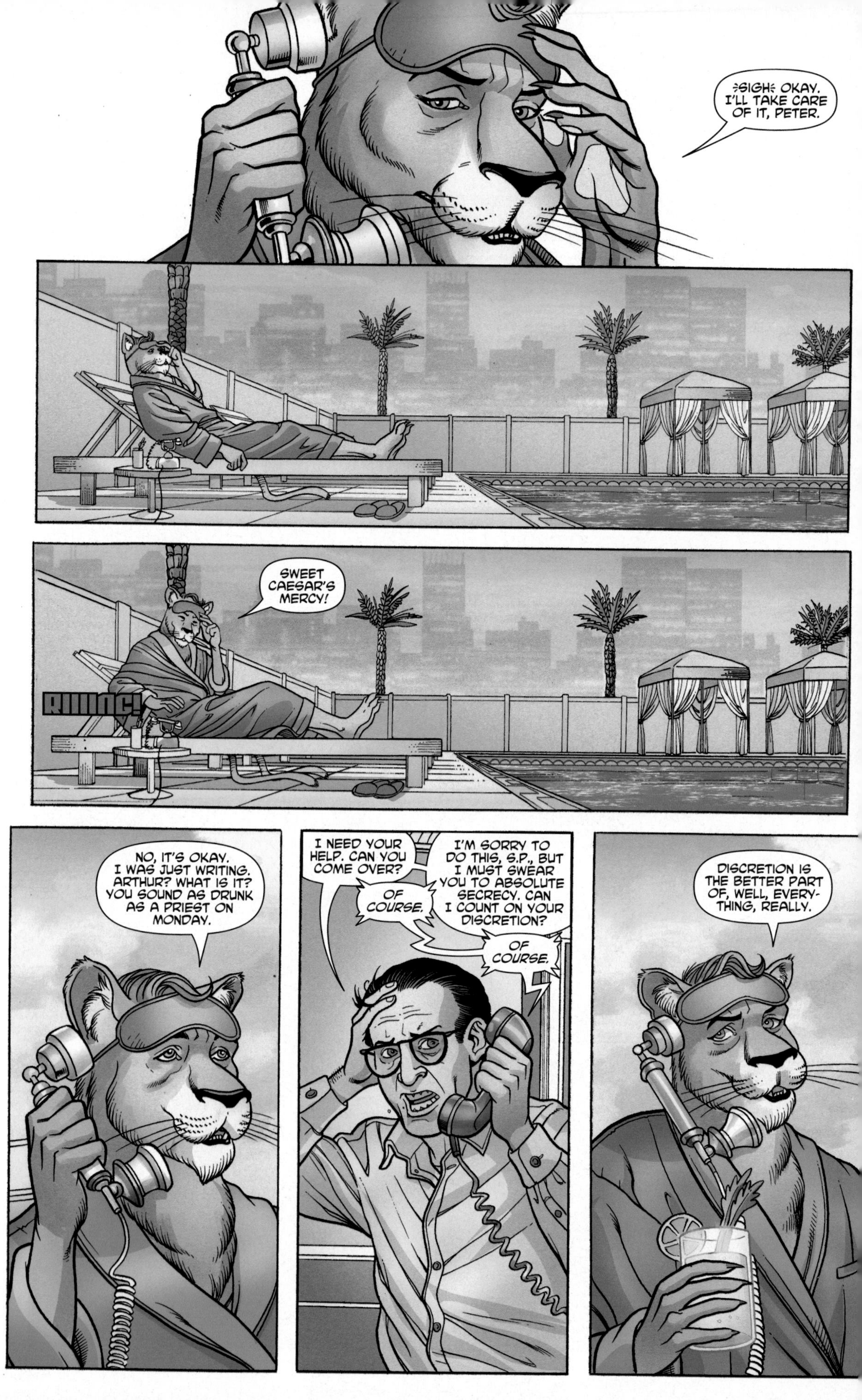

≠SIGH≠ OKAY. I'LL TAKE CARE OF IT, PETER.
RIIING!
SWEET CAESAR'S MERCY!
NO, IT'S OKAY. I WAS JUST WRITING. ARTHUR? WHAT IS IT? YOU SOUND AS DRUNK AS A PRIEST ON MONDAY.
I NEED YOUR HELP. CAN YOU COME OVER?
OF COURSE.
I'M SORRY TO DO THIS, S.P., BUT I MUST SWEAR YOU TO ABSOLUTE SECRECY. CAN I COUNT ON YOUR DISCRETION?
OF COURSE.
DISCRETION IS THE BETTER PART OF, WELL, EVERY-THING, REALLY.

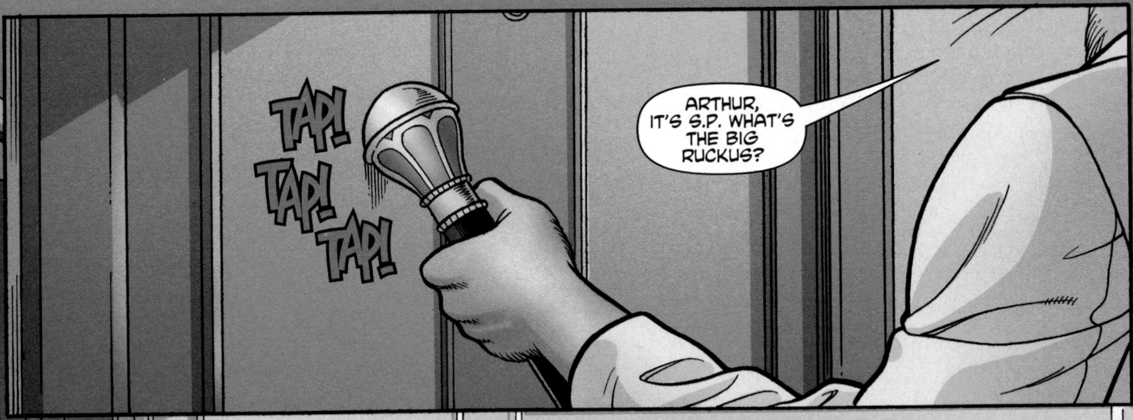
TAP! TAP! TAP!
ARTHUR, IT'S S.P. WHAT'S THE BIG RUCKUS?
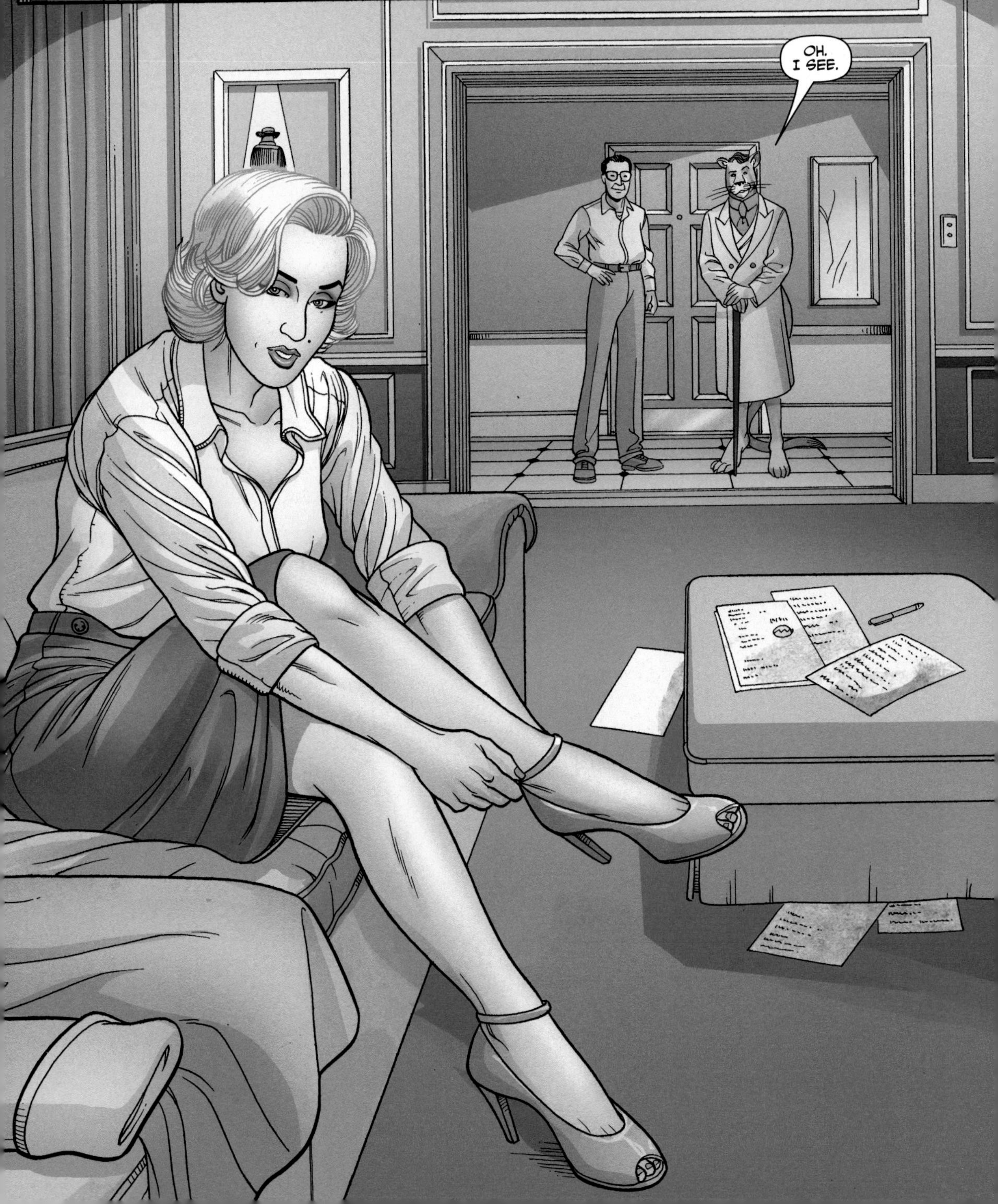
OH. I SEE.

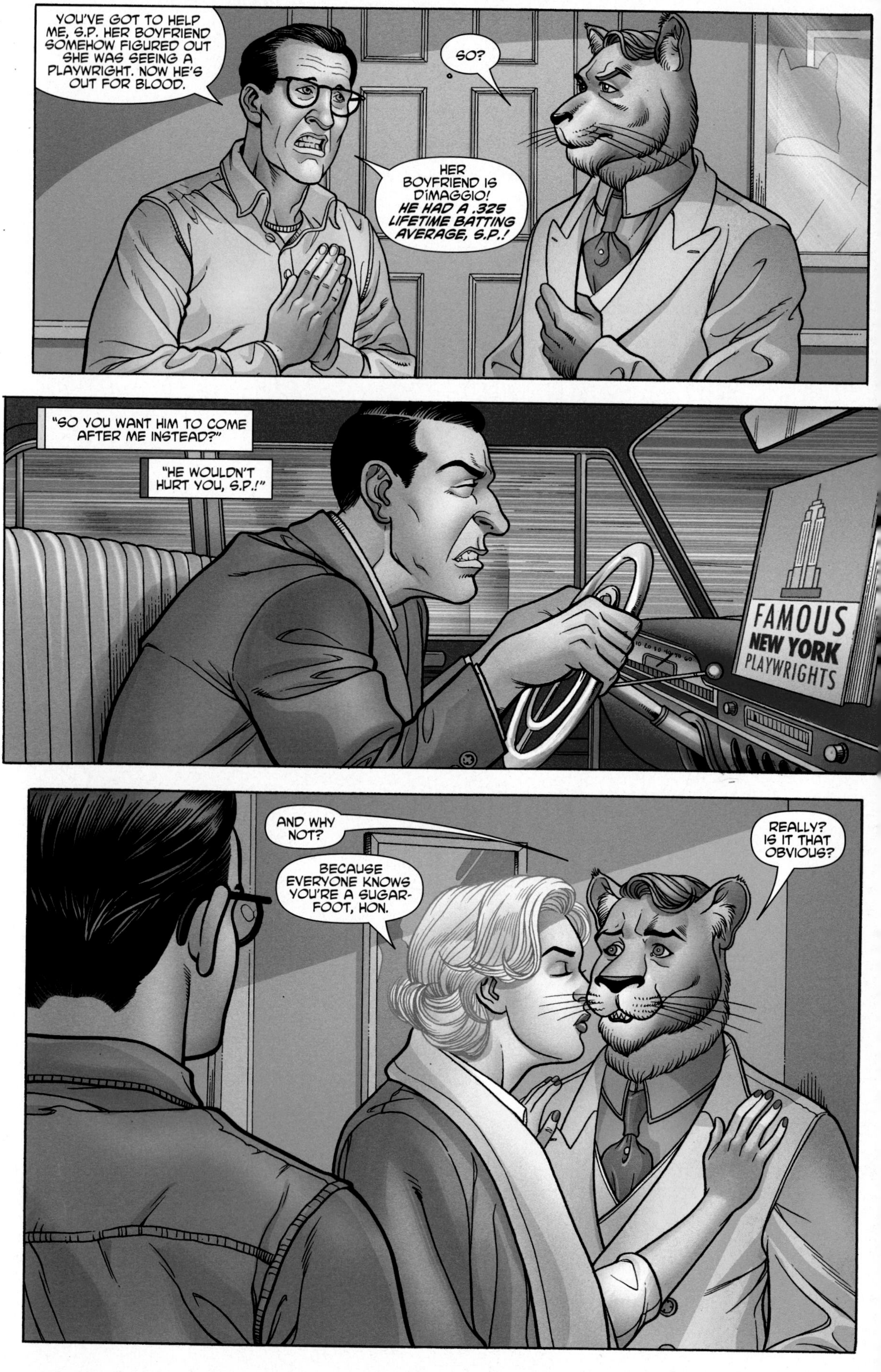

YOU'VE GOT TO HELP ME, S.P. HER BOYFRIEND SOMEHOW FIGURED OUT SHE WAS SEEING A PLAYWRIGHT. NOW HE'S OUT FOR BLOOD.
SO?
HER BOYFRIEND IS DiMAGGIO! HE HAD A .325 LIFETIME BATTING AVERAGE, S.P.!
"SO YOU WANT HIM TO COME AFTER ME INSTEAD?"
"HE WOULDN'T HURT YOU, S.P.!"
FAMOUS NEW YORK PLAYWRIGHTS
AND WHY NOT?
BECAUSE EVERYONE KNOWS YOU'RE A SUGAR-FOOT, HON.
REALLY? IS IT THAT OBVIOUS?

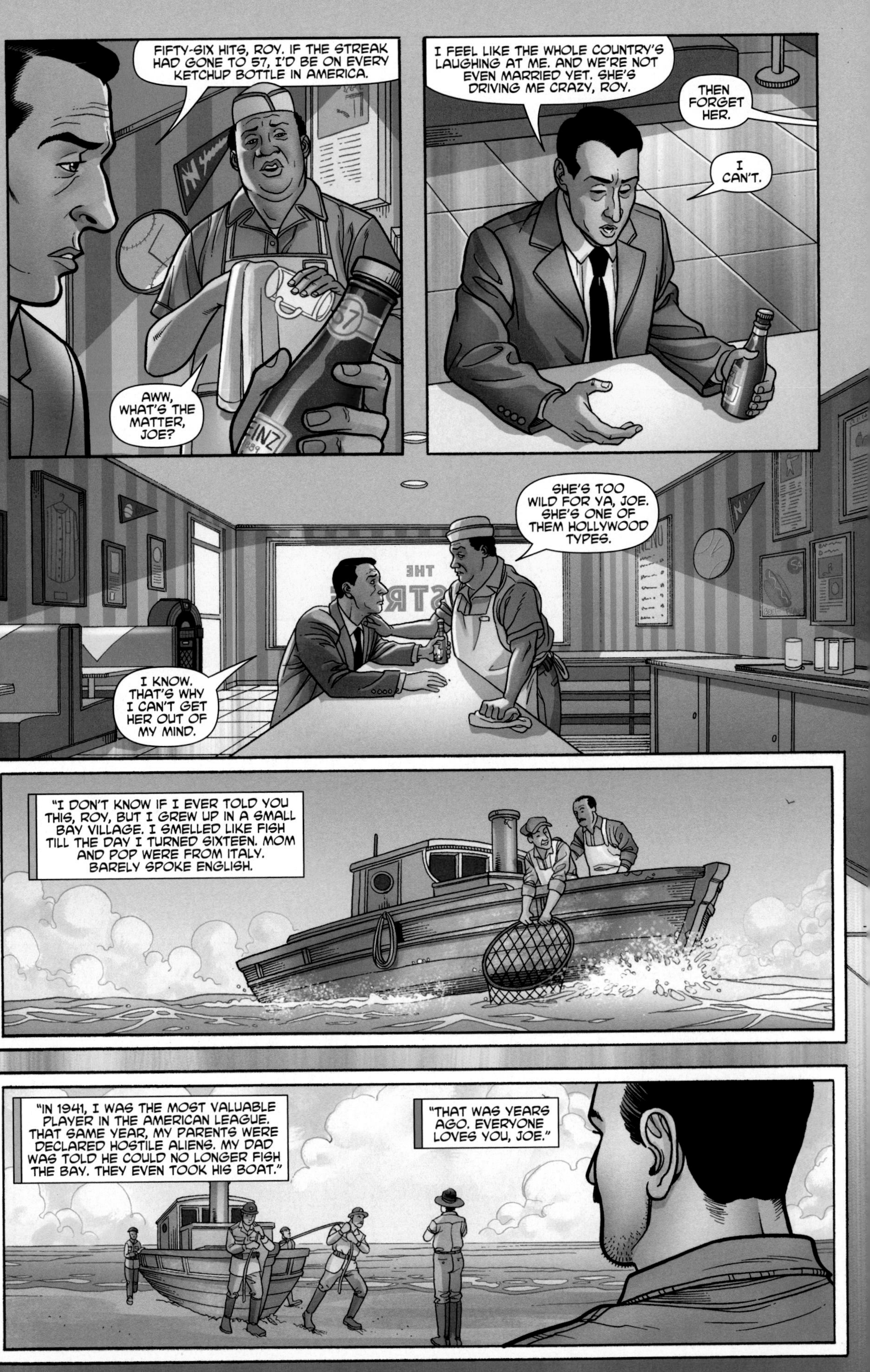
FIFTY-SIX HITS, ROY. IF THE STREAK HAD GONE TO 57, I'D BE ON EVERY KETCHUP BOTTLE IN AMERICA.
AWW, WHAT'S THE MATTER, JOE?
I FEEL LIKE THE WHOLE COUNTRY'S LAUGHING AT ME. AND WE'RE NOT EVEN MARRIED YET. SHE'S DRIVING ME CRAZY, ROY.
THEN FORGET HER.
I CAN'T.
SHE'S TOO WILD FOR YA, JOE. SHE'S ONE OF THEM HOLLYWOOD TYPES.
I KNOW. THAT'S WHY I CAN'T GET HER OUT OF MY MIND.
"I DON'T KNOW IF I EVER TOLD YOU THIS, ROY, BUT I GREW UP IN A SMALL BAY VILLAGE. I SMELLED LIKE FISH TILL THE DAY I TURNED SIXTEEN. MOM AND POP WERE FROM ITALY. BARELY SPOKE ENGLISH.
"IN 1941, I WAS THE MOST VALUABLE PLAYER IN THE AMERICAN LEAGUE. THAT SAME YEAR, MY PARENTS WERE DECLARED HOSTILE ALIENS. MY DAD WAS TOLD HE COULD NO LONGER FISH THE BAY. THEY EVEN TOOK HIS BOAT."
"THAT WAS YEARS AGO. EVERYONE LOVES YOU, JOE."

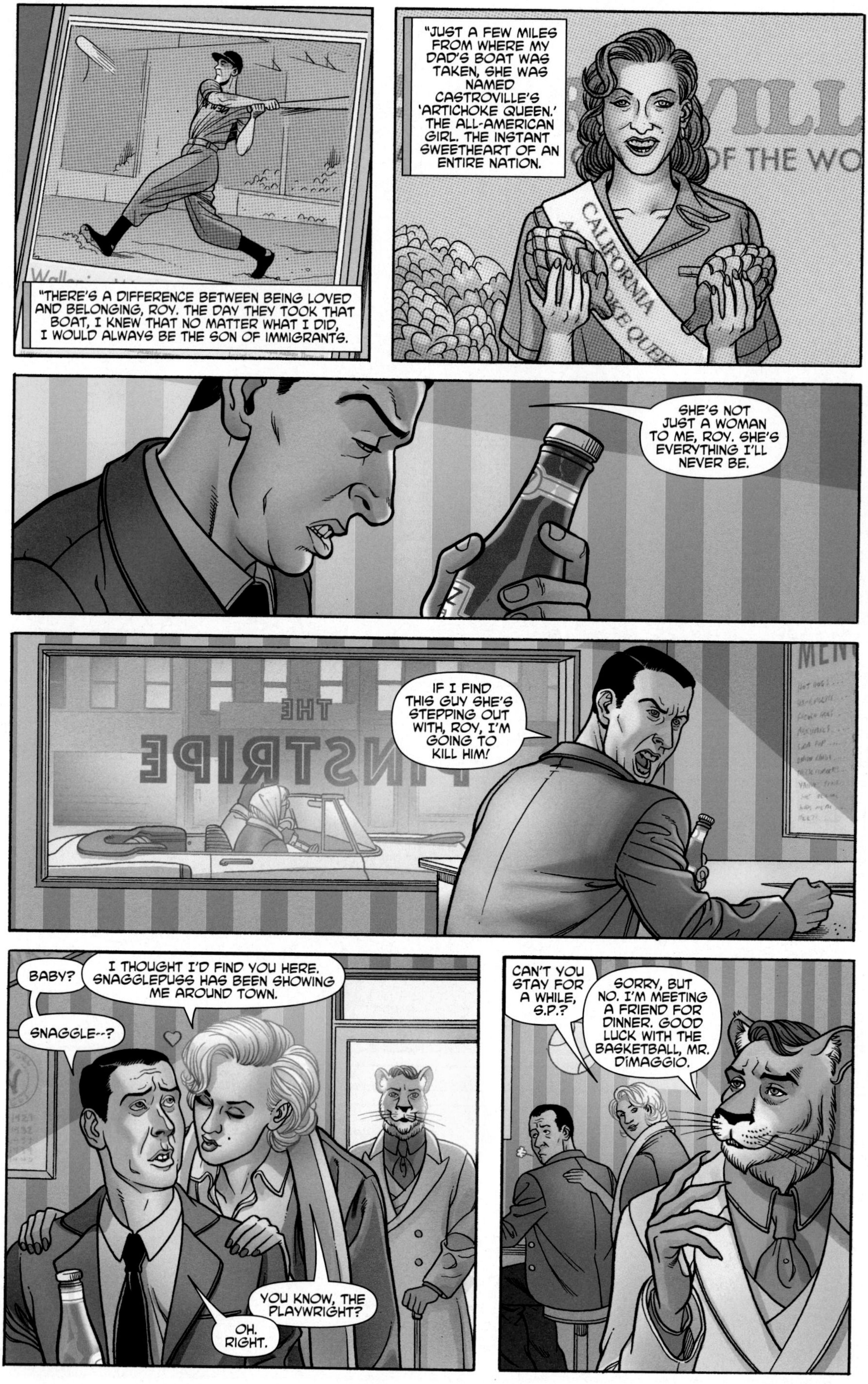
"THERE'S A DIFFERENCE BETWEEN BEING LOVED AND BELONGING, ROY. THE DAY THEY TOOK THAT BOAT, I KNEW THAT NO MATTER WHAT I DID, I WOULD ALWAYS BE THE SON OF IMMIGRANTS.
"JUST A FEW MILES FROM WHERE MY DAD'S BOAT WAS TAKEN, SHE WAS NAMED CASTROVILLE'S 'ARTICHOKE QUEEN.' THE ALL-AMERICAN GIRL. THE INSTANT SWEETHEART OF AN ENTIRE NATION.
CALIFORNIA
SHE'S NOT JUST A WOMAN TO ME, ROY. SHE'S EVERYTHING I'LL NEVER BE.
THE
PINSTRIPE
IF I FIND THIS GUY SHE'S STEPPING OUT WITH, ROY, I'M GOING TO KILL HIM!
BABY?
I THOUGHT I'D FIND YOU HERE. SNAGGLEPUSS HAS BEEN SHOWING ME AROUND TOWN.
SNAGGLE--?
YOU KNOW, THE PLAYWRIGHT?
OH. RIGHT.
CAN'T YOU STAY FOR A WHILE, S.P.?
SORRY, BUT NO. I'M MEETING A FRIEND FOR DINNER. GOOD LUCK WITH THE BASKETBALL, MR. DiMAGGIO.

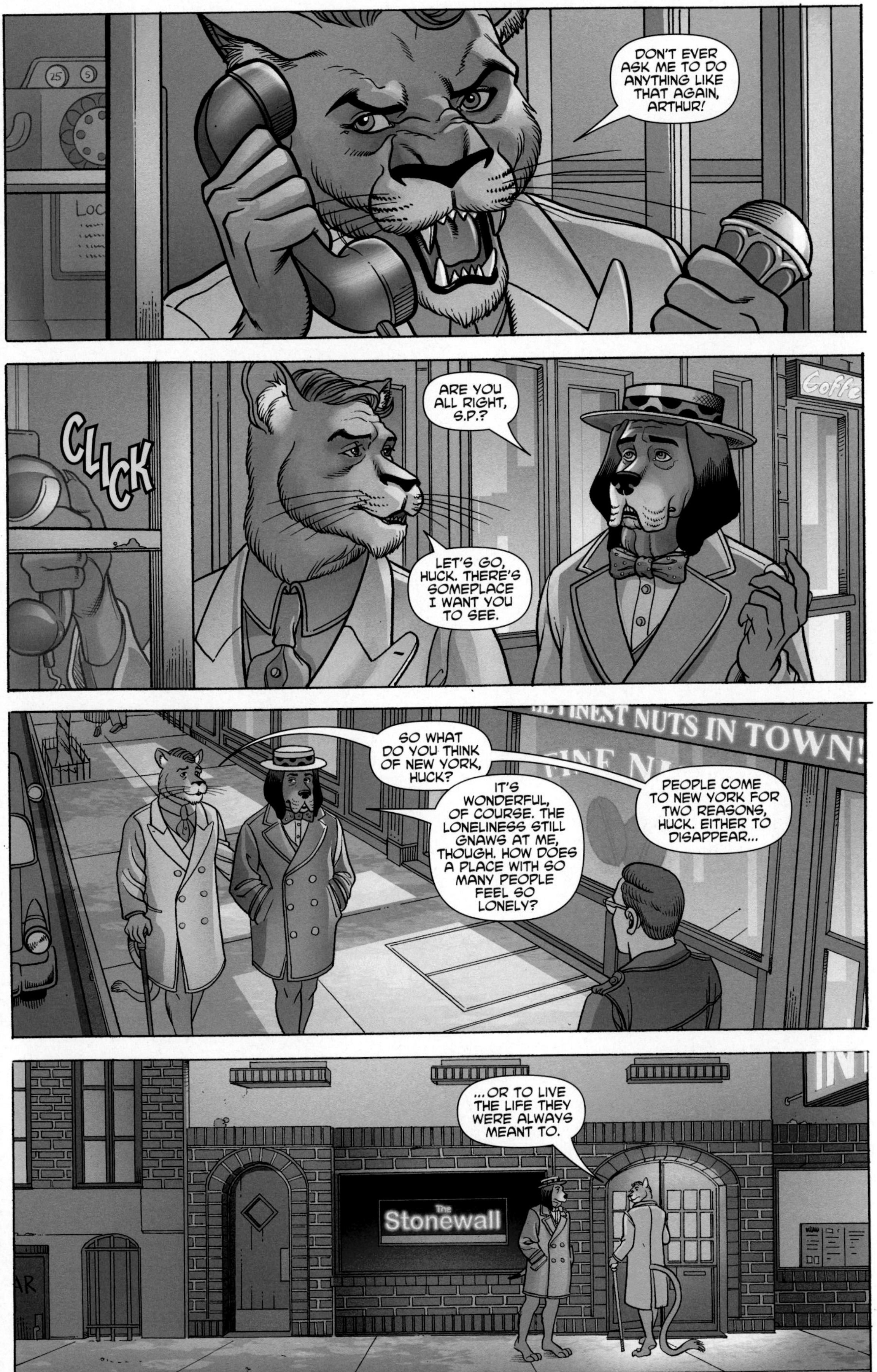
DON'T EVER ASK ME TO DO ANYTHING LIKE THAT AGAIN, ARTHUR!
CLICK
ARE YOU ALL RIGHT, S.P.?
LET'S GO, HUCK. THERE'S SOMEPLACE I WANT YOU TO SEE.
FINEST NUTS IN TOWN!
SO WHAT DO YOU THINK OF NEW YORK, HUCK?
IT'S WONDERFUL, OF COURSE. THE LONELINESS STILL GNAWS AT ME, THOUGH. HOW DOES A PLACE WITH SO MANY PEOPLE FEEL SO LONELY?
PEOPLE COME TO NEW YORK FOR TWO REASONS, HUCK. EITHER TO DISAPPEAR...
...OR TO LIVE THE LIFE THEY WERE ALWAYS MEANT TO.
The Stonewall

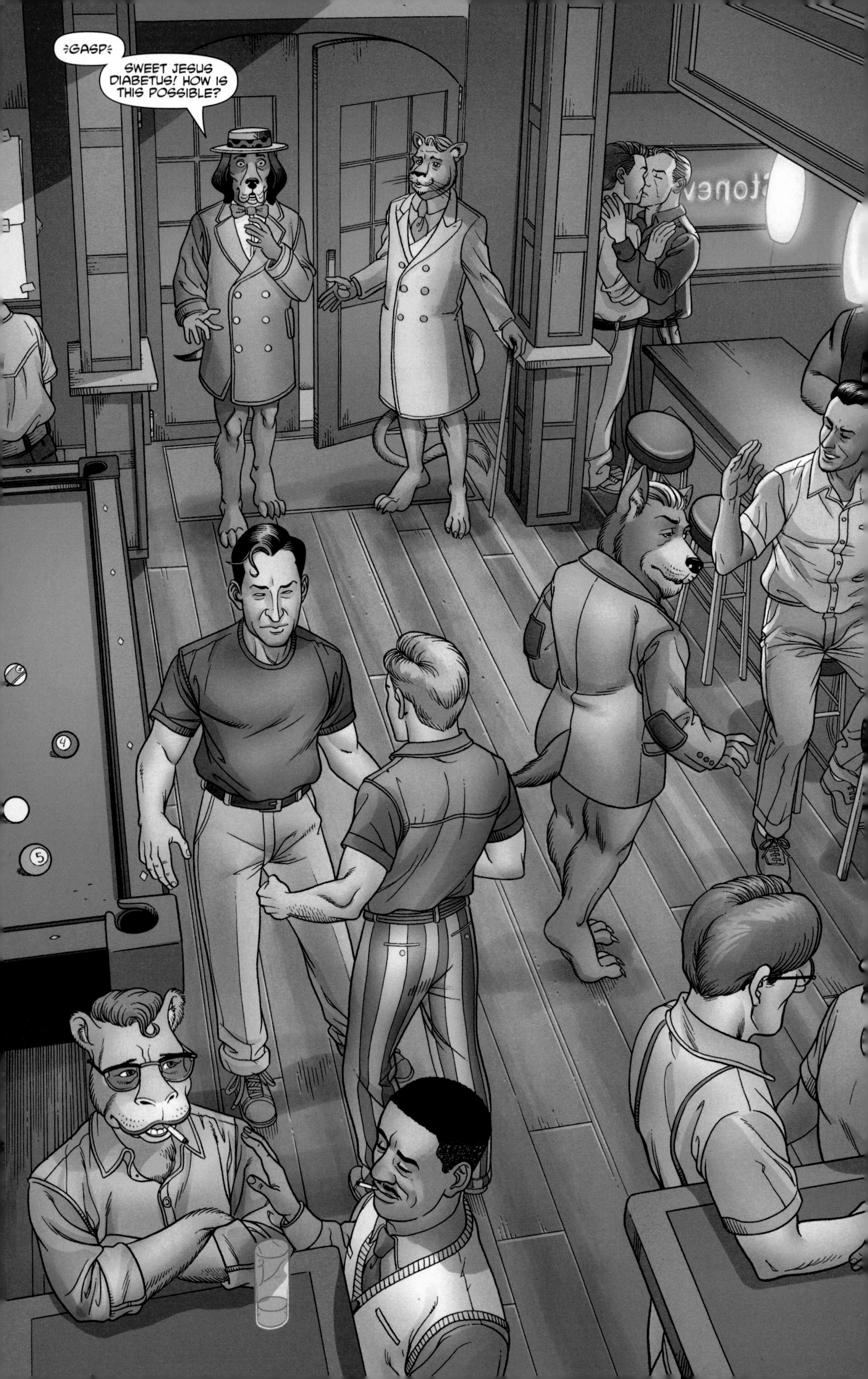
GASP
SWEET JESUS DIABETUS! HOW IS THIS POSSIBLE?
Stonew

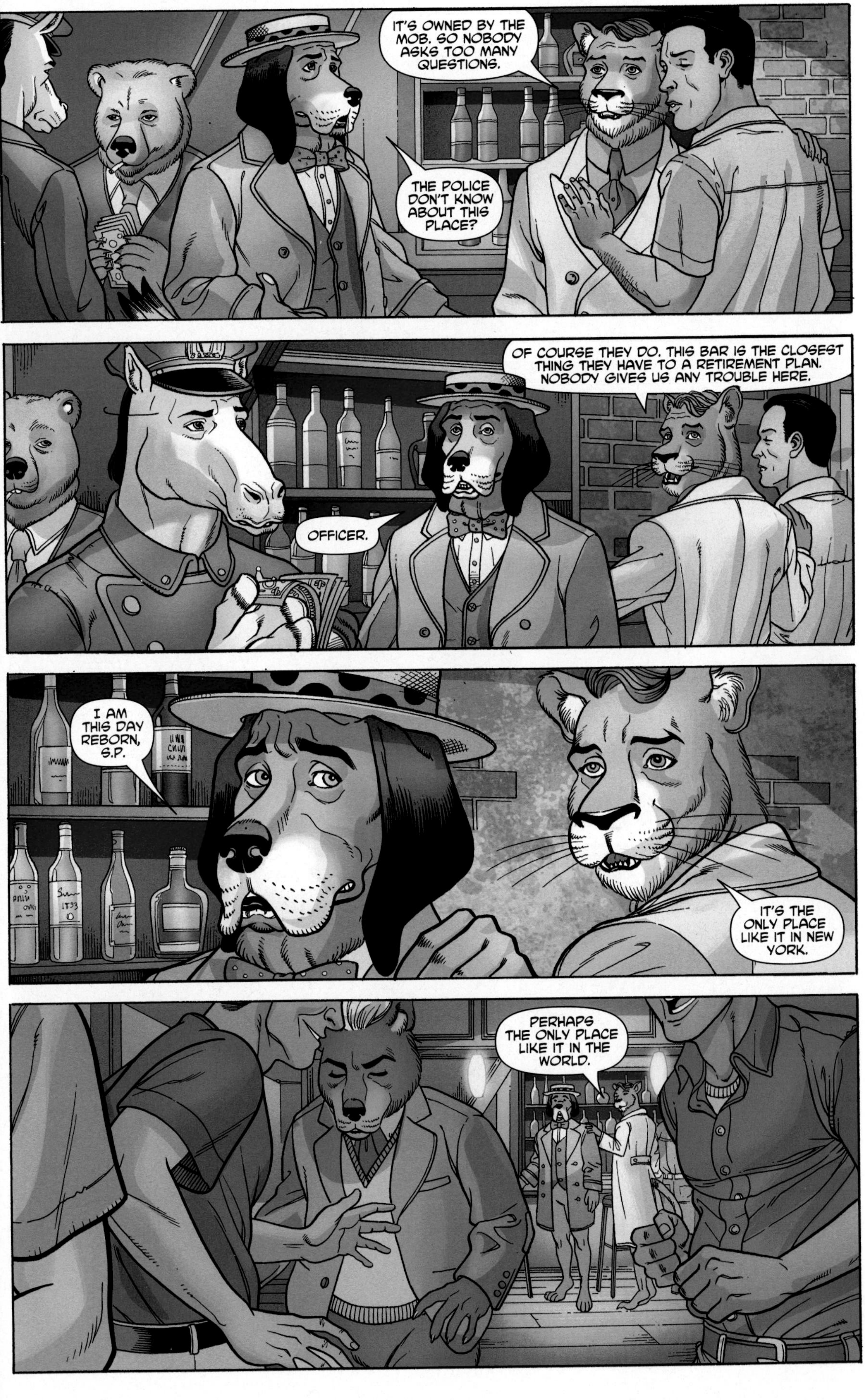
IT'S OWNED BY THE MOB. SO NOBODY ASKS TOO MANY QUESTIONS.
THE POLICE DON'T KNOW ABOUT THIS PLACE?
OF COURSE THEY DO. THIS BAR IS THE CLOSEST THING THEY HAVE TO A RETIREMENT PLAN. NOBODY GIVES US ANY TROUBLE HERE.
OFFICER.
I AM THIS DAY REBORN, S.P.
IT'S THE ONLY PLACE LIKE IT IN NEW YORK.
PERHAPS THE ONLY PLACE LIKE IT IN THE WORLD.

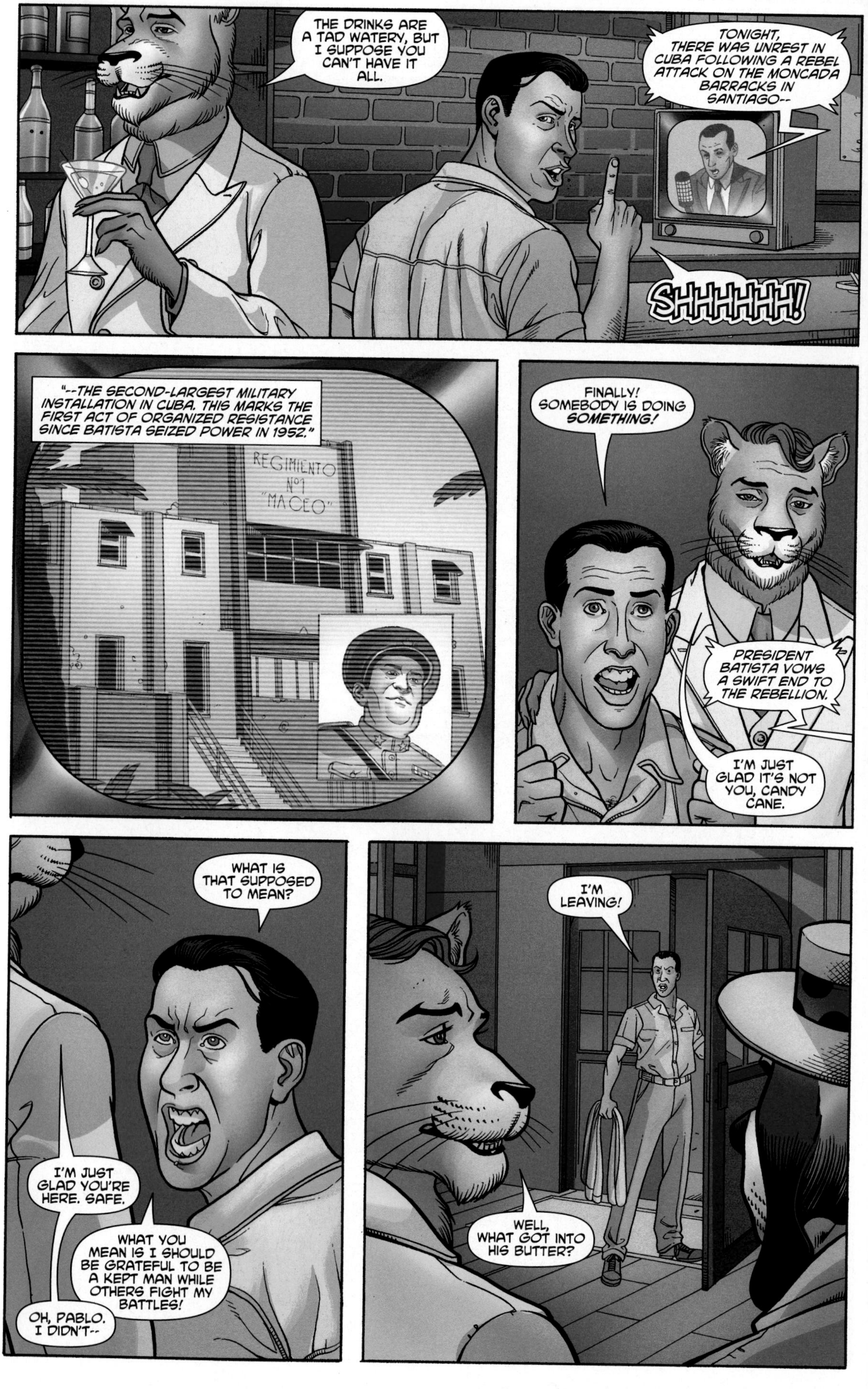
THE DRINKS ARE A TAD WATERY, BUT I SUPPOSE YOU CAN'T HAVE IT ALL.
TONIGHT, THERE WAS UNREST IN CUBA FOLLOWING A REBEL ATTACK ON THE MONCADA BARRACKS IN SANTIAGO--
SHHHHHH!
"--THE SECOND-LARGEST MILITARY INSTALLATION IN CUBA. THIS MARKS THE FIRST ACT OF ORGANIZED RESISTANCE SINCE BATISTA SEIZED POWER IN 1952."
REGIMIENTO Nº1 "MACEO"
FINALLY! SOMEBODY IS DOING SOMETHING!
PRESIDENT BATISTA VOWS A SWIFT END TO THE REBELLION.
I'M JUST GLAD IT'S NOT YOU, CANDY CANE.
WHAT IS THAT SUPPOSED TO MEAN?
I'M JUST GLAD YOU'RE HERE. SAFE.
WHAT YOU MEAN IS I SHOULD BE GRATEFUL TO BE A KEPT MAN WHILE OTHERS FIGHT MY BATTLES!
OH, PABLO. I DIDN'T--
I'M LEAVING!
WELL, WHAT GOT INTO HIS BUTTER?

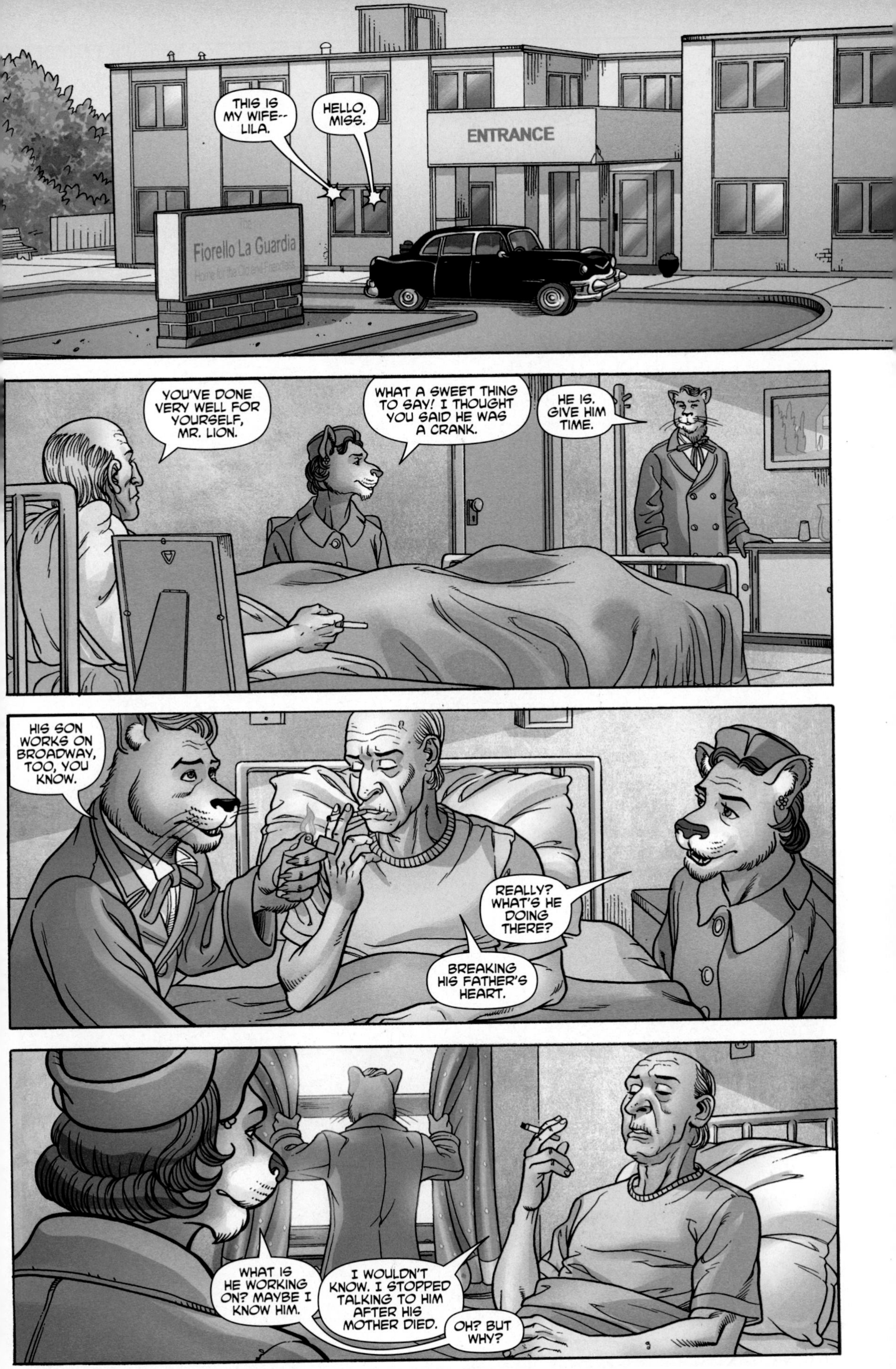
THIS IS MY WIFE-- LILA.
HELLO, MISS.
ENTRANCE
Fiorello La Guardia
YOU'VE DONE VERY WELL FOR YOURSELF, MR. LION.
WHAT A SWEET THING TO SAY! I THOUGHT YOU SAID HE WAS A CRANK.
HE IS. GIVE HIM TIME.
HIS SON WORKS ON BROADWAY, TOO, YOU KNOW.
REALLY? WHAT'S HE DOING THERE?
BREAKING HIS FATHER'S HEART.
WHAT IS HE WORKING ON? MAYBE I KNOW HIM.
I WOULDN'T KNOW. I STOPPED TALKING TO HIM AFTER HIS MOTHER DIED.
OH? BUT WHY?

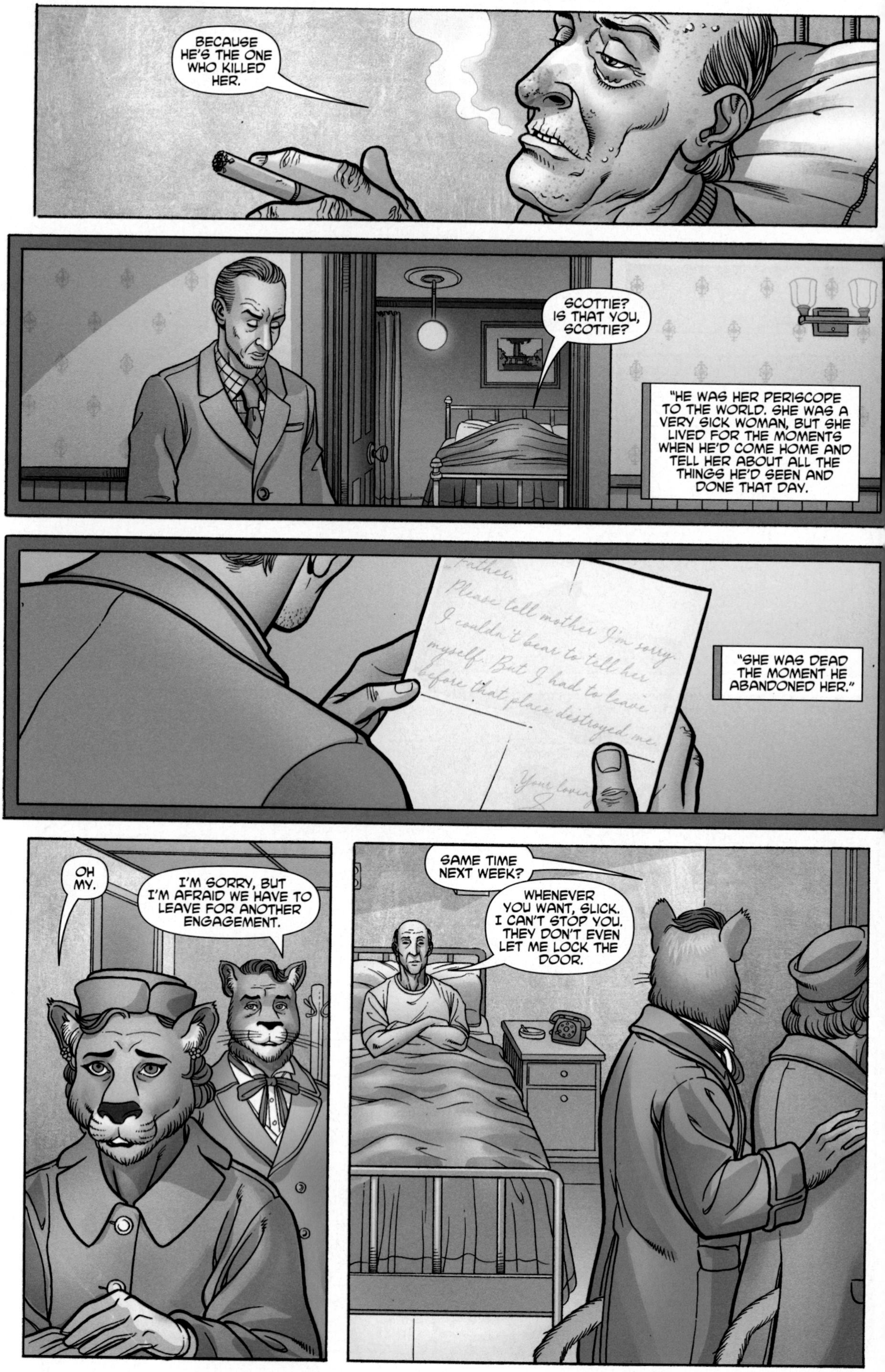
BECAUSE HE'S THE ONE WHO KILLED HER.
SCOTTIE? IS THAT YOU, SCOTTIE?
"HE WAS HER PERISCOPE TO THE WORLD. SHE WAS A VERY SICK WOMAN, BUT SHE LIVED FOR THE MOMENTS WHEN HE'D COME HOME AND TELL HER ABOUT ALL THE THINGS HE'D SEEN AND DONE THAT DAY.
Father,
Please tell mother I'm sorry.
I couldn't bear to tell her
myself. But I had to leave
before that place destroyed me.
"SHE WAS DEAD THE MOMENT HE ABANDONED HER."
OH MY.
I'M SORRY, BUT I'M AFRAID WE HAVE TO LEAVE FOR ANOTHER ENGAGEMENT.
SAME TIME NEXT WEEK?
WHENEVER YOU WANT, SLICK. I CAN'T STOP YOU. THEY DON'T EVEN LET ME LOCK THE DOOR.

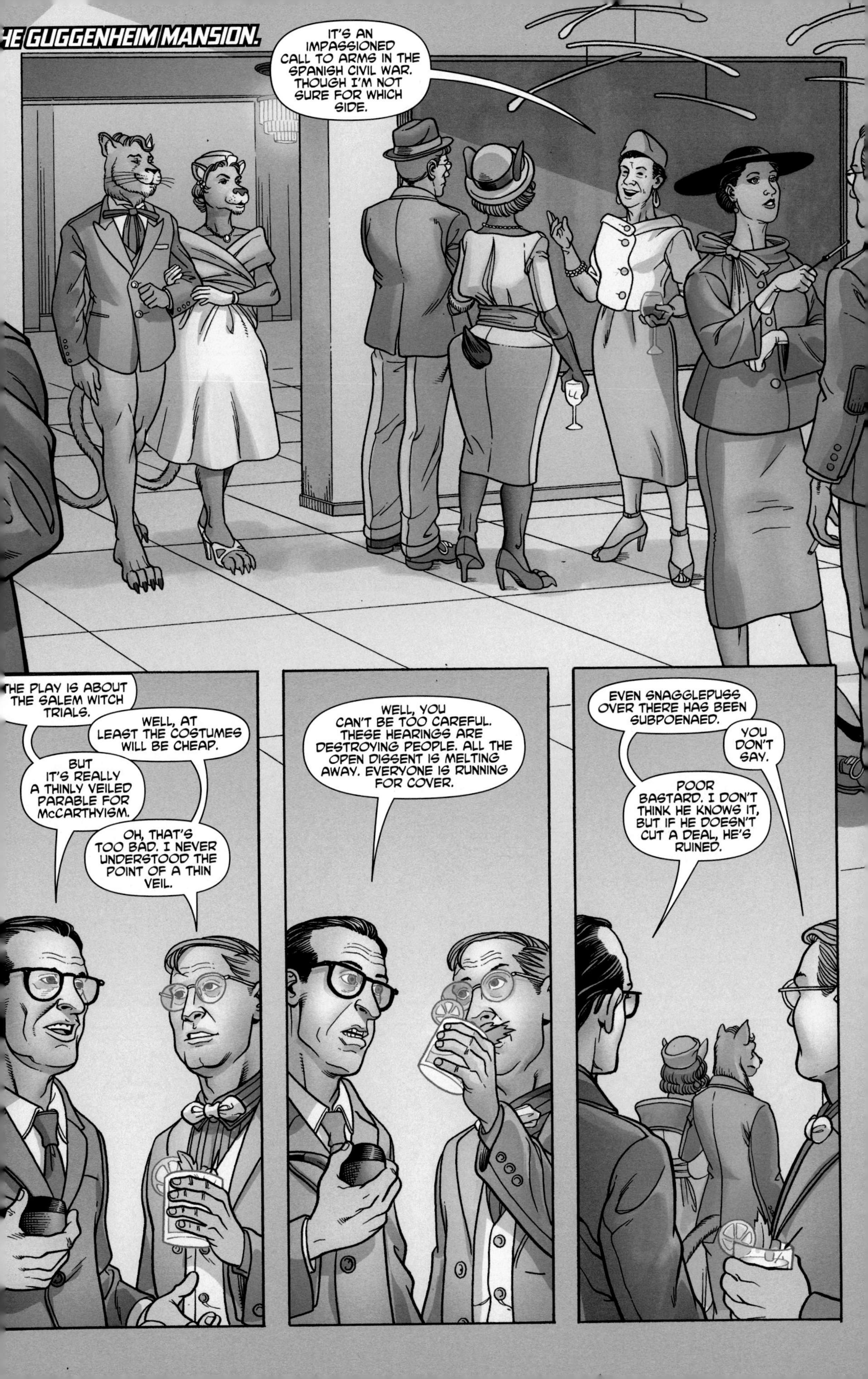
HE GUGGENHEIM MANSION.
IT'S AN IMPASSIONED CALL TO ARMS IN THE SPANISH CIVIL WAR. THOUGH I'M NOT SURE FOR WHICH SIDE.
HE PLAY IS ABOUT THE SALEM WITCH TRIALS.
WELL, AT LEAST THE COSTUMES WILL BE CHEAP.
BUT IT'S REALLY A THINLY VEILED PARABLE FOR McCARTHYISM.
OH, THAT'S TOO BAD. I NEVER UNDERSTOOD THE POINT OF A THIN VEIL.
WELL, YOU CAN'T BE TOO CAREFUL. THESE HEARINGS ARE DESTROYING PEOPLE. ALL THE OPEN DISSENT IS MELTING AWAY. EVERYONE IS RUNNING FOR COVER.
EVEN SNAGGLEPUSS OVER THERE HAS BEEN SUBPOENAED.
YOU DON'T SAY.
POOR BASTARD. I DON'T THINK HE KNOWS IT, BUT IF HE DOESN'T CUT A DEAL, HE'S RUINED.

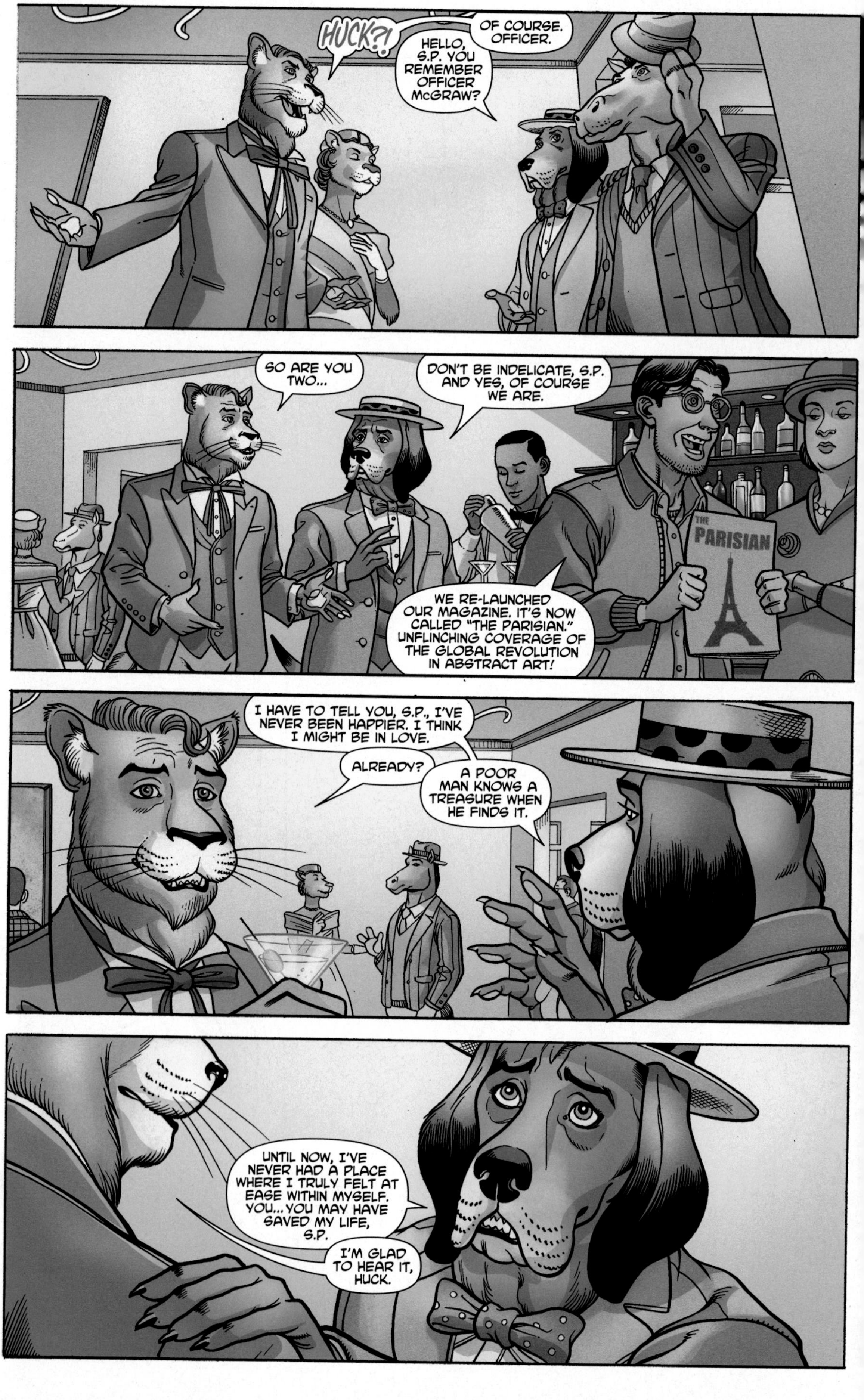
HUCK?!
OF COURSE. OFFICER.
HELLO, S.P. YOU REMEMBER OFFICER McGRAW?
SO ARE YOU TWO...
DON'T BE INDELICATE, S.P. AND YES, OF COURSE WE ARE.
THE PARISIAN
WE RE-LAUNCHED OUR MAGAZINE. IT'S NOW CALLED "THE PARISIAN." UNFLINCHING COVERAGE OF THE GLOBAL REVOLUTION IN ABSTRACT ART!
I HAVE TO TELL YOU, S.P., I'VE NEVER BEEN HAPPIER. I THINK I MIGHT BE IN LOVE.
ALREADY?
A POOR MAN KNOWS A TREASURE WHEN HE FINDS IT.
UNTIL NOW, I'VE NEVER HAD A PLACE WHERE I TRULY FELT AT EASE WITHIN MYSELF. YOU...YOU MAY HAVE SAVED MY LIFE, S.P.
I'M GLAD TO HEAR IT, HUCK.

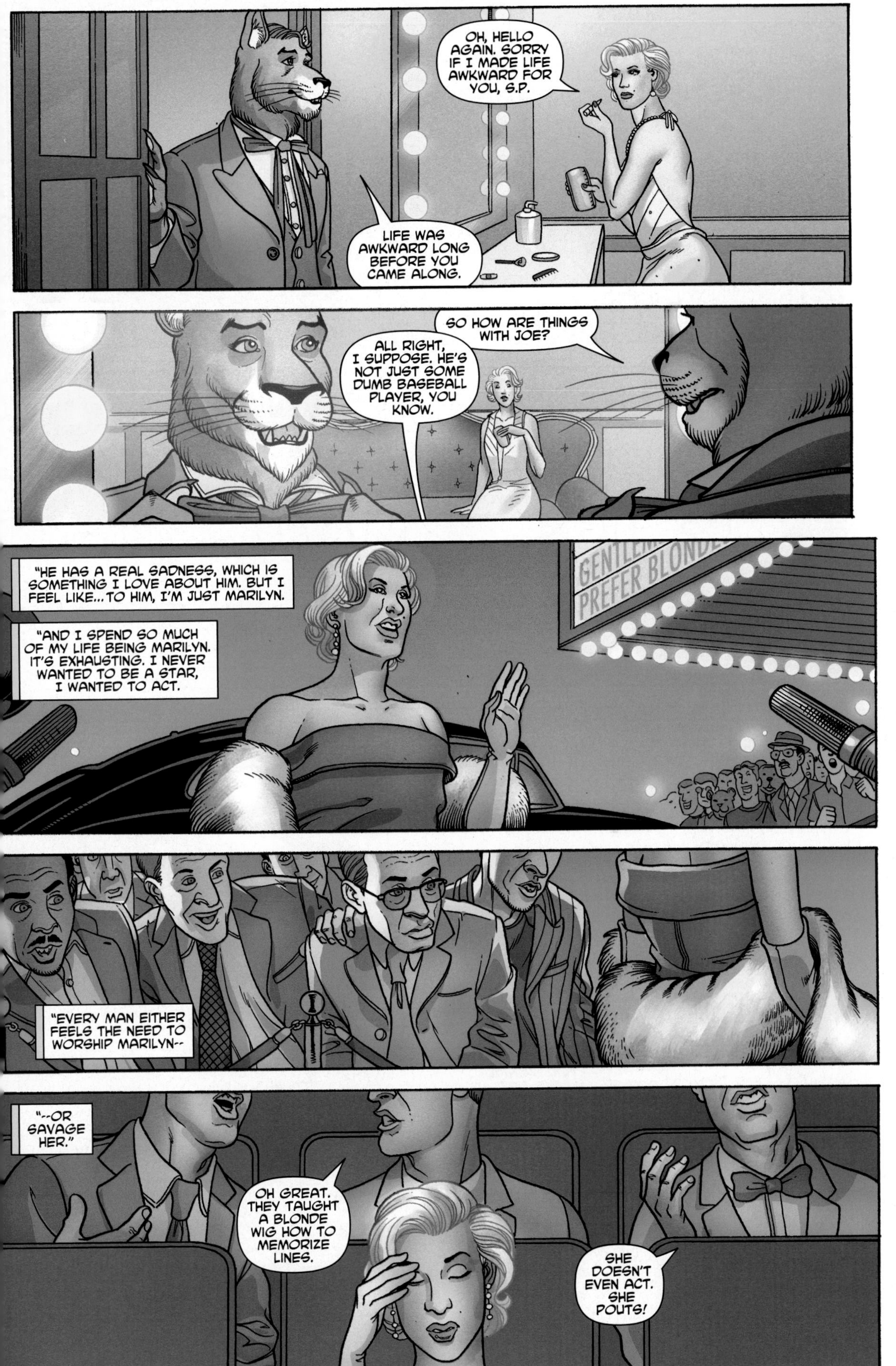

OH, HELLO AGAIN. SORRY IF I MADE LIFE AWKWARD FOR YOU, S.P.
LIFE WAS AWKWARD LONG BEFORE YOU CAME ALONG.
SO HOW ARE THINGS WITH JOE?
ALL RIGHT, I SUPPOSE. HE'S NOT JUST SOME DUMB BASEBALL PLAYER, YOU KNOW.
"HE HAS A REAL SADNESS, WHICH IS SOMETHING I LOVE ABOUT HIM. BUT I FEEL LIKE... TO HIM, I'M JUST MARILYN.
"AND I SPEND SO MUCH OF MY LIFE BEING MARILYN. IT'S EXHAUSTING. I NEVER WANTED TO BE A STAR, I WANTED TO ACT.
"EVERY MAN EITHER FEELS THE NEED TO WORSHIP MARILYN--
"--OR SAVAGE HER."
OH GREAT. THEY TAUGHT A BLONDE WIG HOW TO MEMORIZE LINES.
SHE DOESN'T EVEN ACT. SHE POUTS!

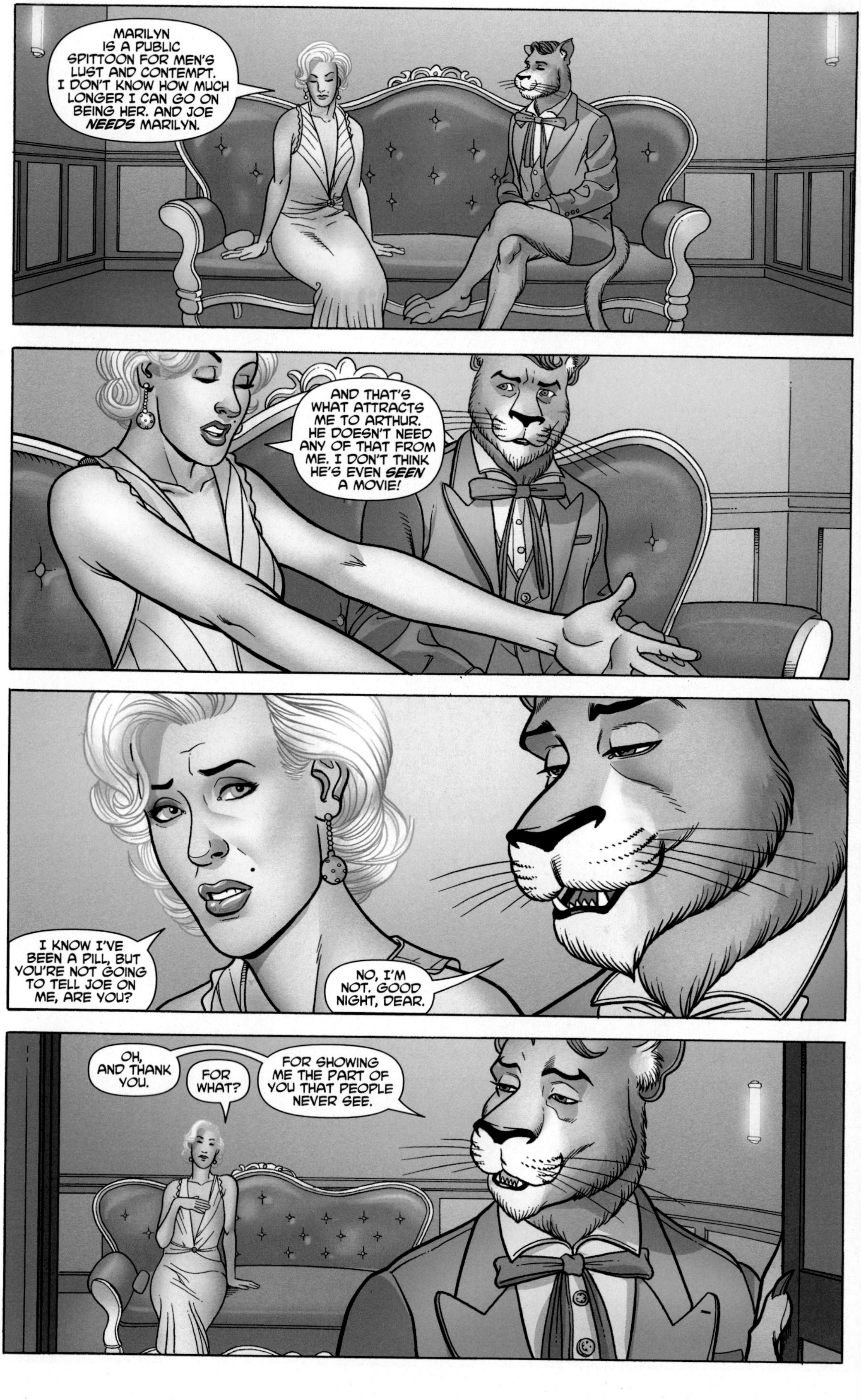
MARILYN IS A PUBLIC SPITTOON FOR MEN'S LUST AND CONTEMPT. I DON'T KNOW HOW MUCH LONGER I CAN GO ON BEING HER. AND JOE *NEEDS* MARILYN.
AND THAT'S WHAT ATTRACTS ME TO ARTHUR. HE DOESN'T NEED ANY OF THAT FROM ME. I DON'T THINK HE'S EVEN *SEEN* A MOVIE!
I KNOW I'VE BEEN A PILL, BUT YOU'RE NOT GOING TO TELL JOE ON ME, ARE YOU?
NO, I'M NOT. GOOD NIGHT, DEAR.
OH, AND THANK YOU.
FOR WHAT?
FOR SHOWING ME THE PART OF YOU THAT PEOPLE NEVER SEE.

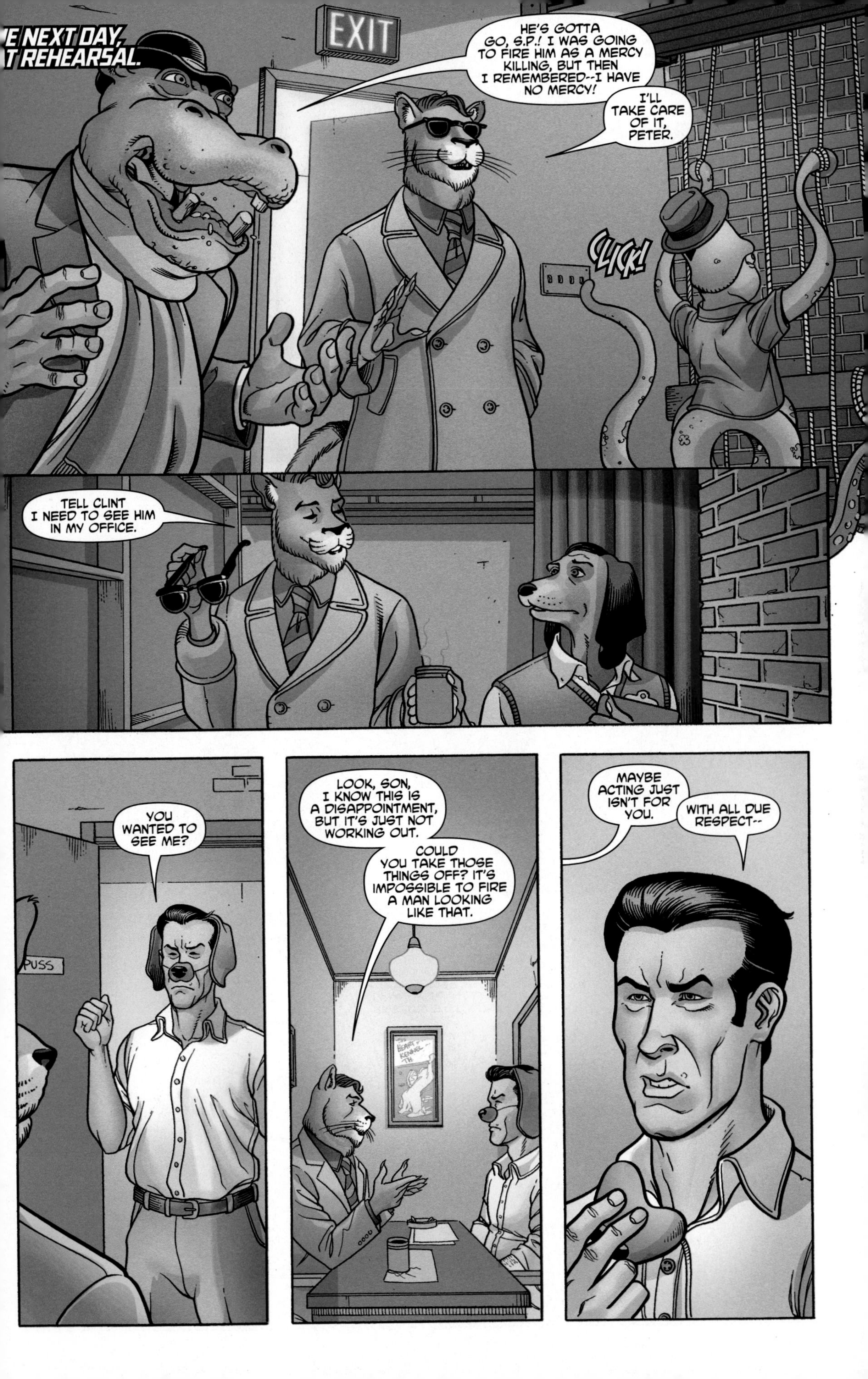
E NEXT DAY,
T REHEARSAL.
EXIT
HE'S GOTTA GO, S.P.! I WAS GOING TO FIRE HIM AS A MERCY KILLING, BUT THEN I REMEMBERED--I HAVE NO MERCY!
I'LL TAKE CARE OF IT, PETER.
CLICK!
TELL CLINT I NEED TO SEE HIM IN MY OFFICE.
YOU WANTED TO SEE ME?
PUSS
LOOK, SON, I KNOW THIS IS A DISAPPOINTMENT, BUT IT'S JUST NOT WORKING OUT.
COULD YOU TAKE THOSE THINGS OFF? IT'S IMPOSSIBLE TO FIRE A MAN LOOKING LIKE THAT.
MAYBE ACTING JUST ISN'T FOR YOU.
WITH ALL DUE RESPECT--

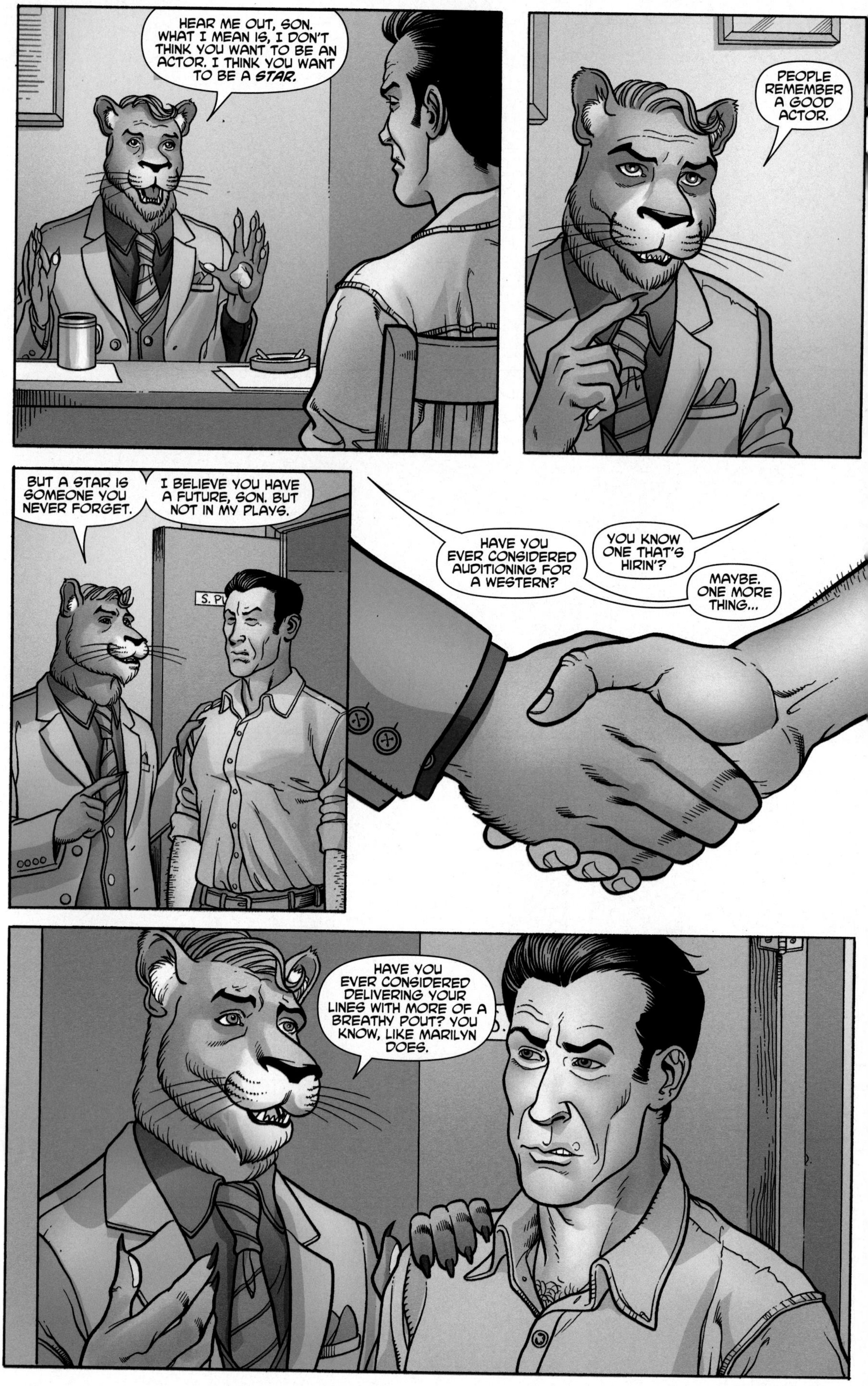
HEAR ME OUT, SON. WHAT I MEAN IS, I DON'T THINK YOU WANT TO BE AN ACTOR. I THINK YOU WANT TO BE A *STAR.*
PEOPLE REMEMBER A GOOD ACTOR.
BUT A STAR IS SOMEONE YOU NEVER FORGET.
I BELIEVE YOU HAVE A FUTURE, SON. BUT NOT IN MY PLAYS.
S. P
HAVE YOU EVER CONSIDERED AUDITIONING FOR A WESTERN?
YOU KNOW ONE THAT'S HIRIN'?
MAYBE. ONE MORE THING...
HAVE YOU EVER CONSIDERED DELIVERING YOUR LINES WITH MORE OF A BREATHY POUT? YOU KNOW, LIKE MARILYN DOES.

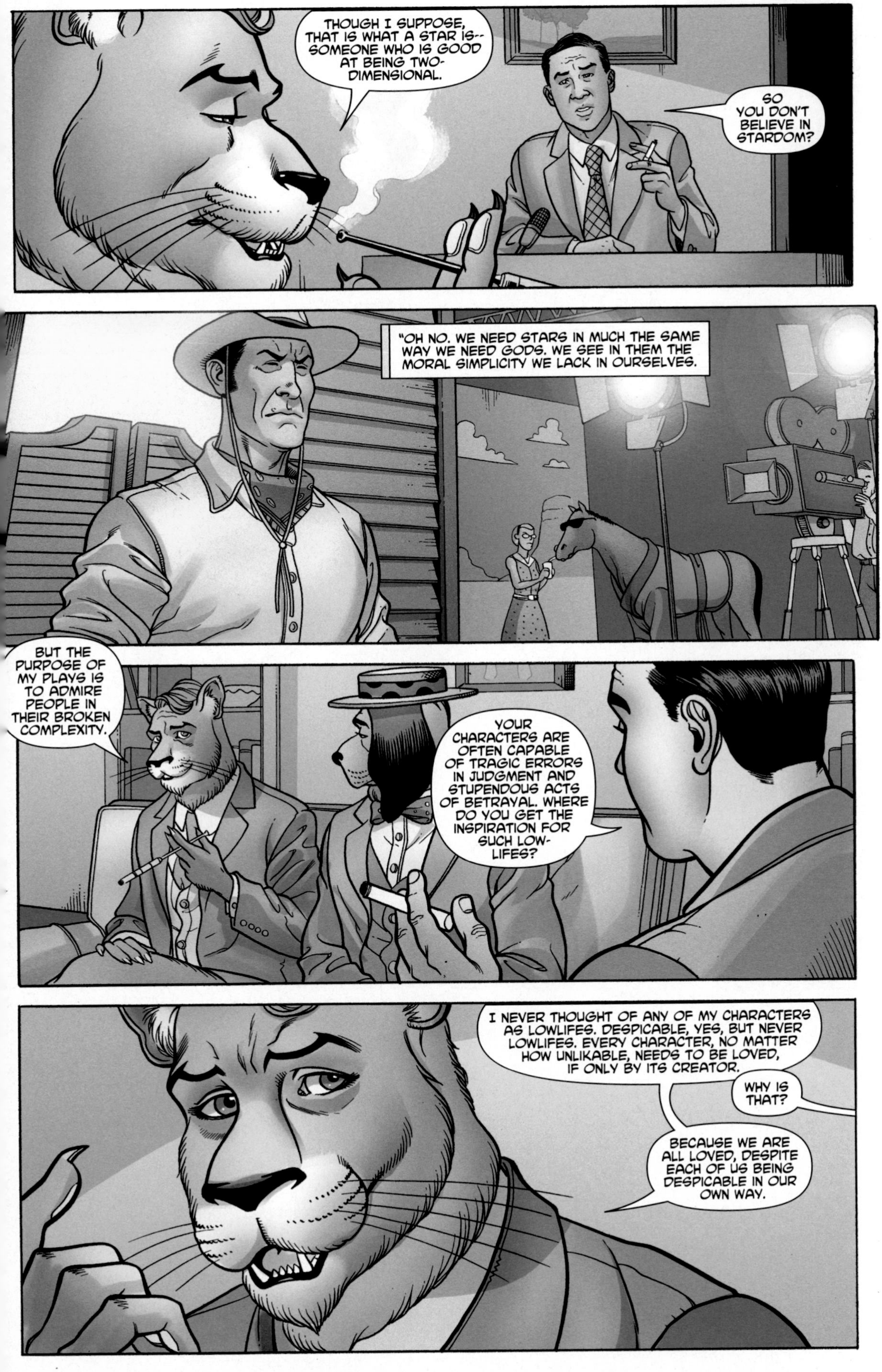
THOUGH I SUPPOSE, THAT IS WHAT A STAR IS-- SOMEONE WHO IS GOOD AT BEING TWO-DIMENSIONAL.
SO YOU DON'T BELIEVE IN STARDOM?
"OH NO. WE NEED STARS IN MUCH THE SAME WAY WE NEED GODS. WE SEE IN THEM THE MORAL SIMPLICITY WE LACK IN OURSELVES.
BUT THE PURPOSE OF MY PLAYS IS TO ADMIRE PEOPLE IN THEIR BROKEN COMPLEXITY.
YOUR CHARACTERS ARE OFTEN CAPABLE OF TRAGIC ERRORS IN JUDGMENT AND STUPENDOUS ACTS OF BETRAYAL. WHERE DO YOU GET THE INSPIRATION FOR SUCH LOW-LIFES?
I NEVER THOUGHT OF ANY OF MY CHARACTERS AS LOWLIFES. DESPICABLE, YES, BUT NEVER LOWLIFES. EVERY CHARACTER, NO MATTER HOW UNLIKABLE, NEEDS TO BE LOVED, IF ONLY BY ITS CREATOR.
WHY IS THAT?
BECAUSE WE ARE ALL LOVED, DESPITE EACH OF US BEING DESPICABLE IN OUR OWN WAY.

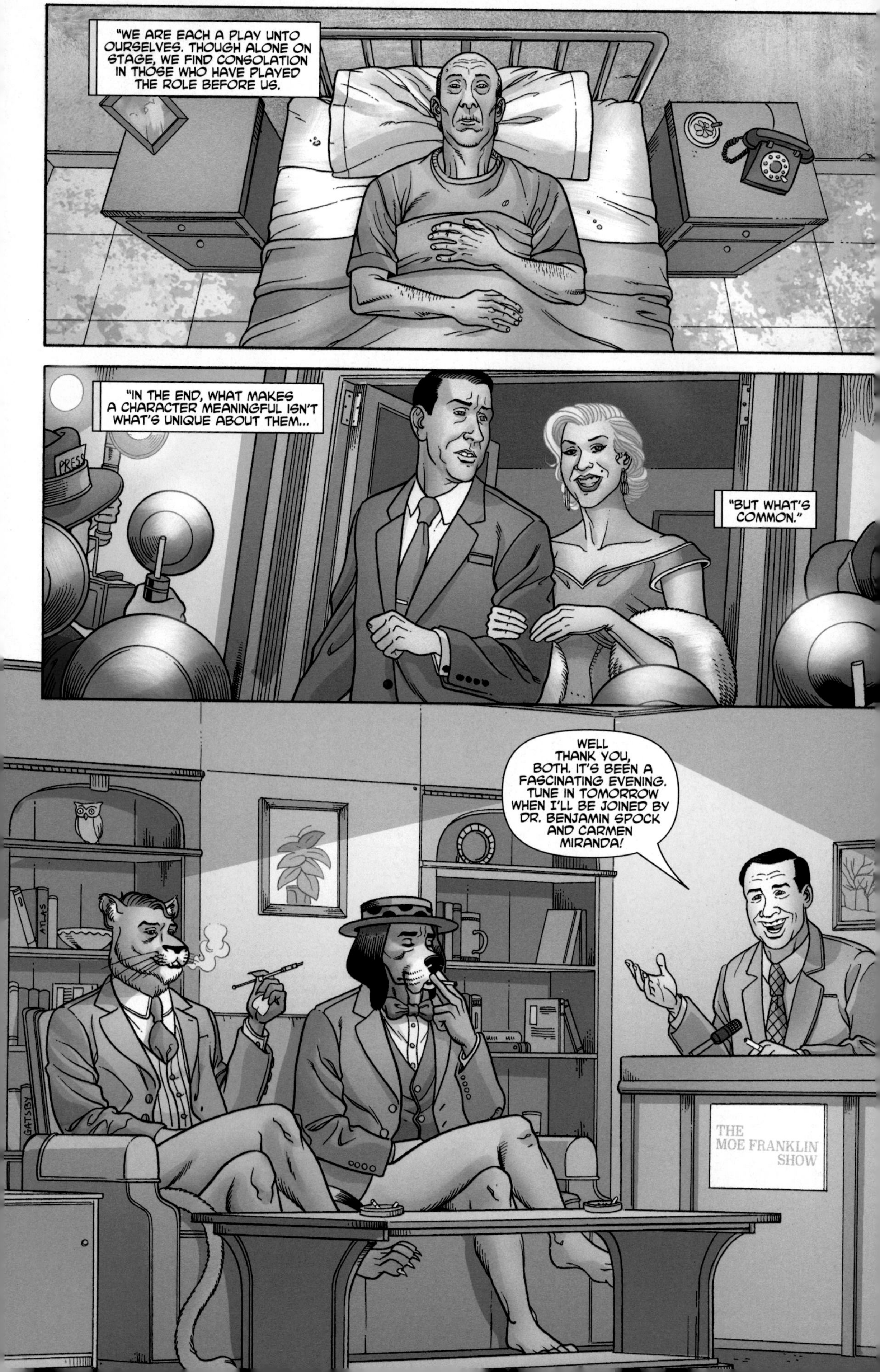
"WE ARE EACH A PLAY UNTO OURSELVES. THOUGH ALONE ON STAGE, WE FIND CONSOLATION IN THOSE WHO HAVE PLAYED THE ROLE BEFORE US.
"IN THE END, WHAT MAKES A CHARACTER MEANINGFUL ISN'T WHAT'S UNIQUE ABOUT THEM...
PRESS
"BUT WHAT'S COMMON."
WELL THANK YOU, BOTH. IT'S BEEN A FASCINATING EVENING. TUNE IN TOMORROW WHEN I'LL BE JOINED BY DR. BENJAMIN SPOCK AND CARMEN MIRANDA!
ATLAS
GATSBY
THE MOE FRANKLIN SHOW

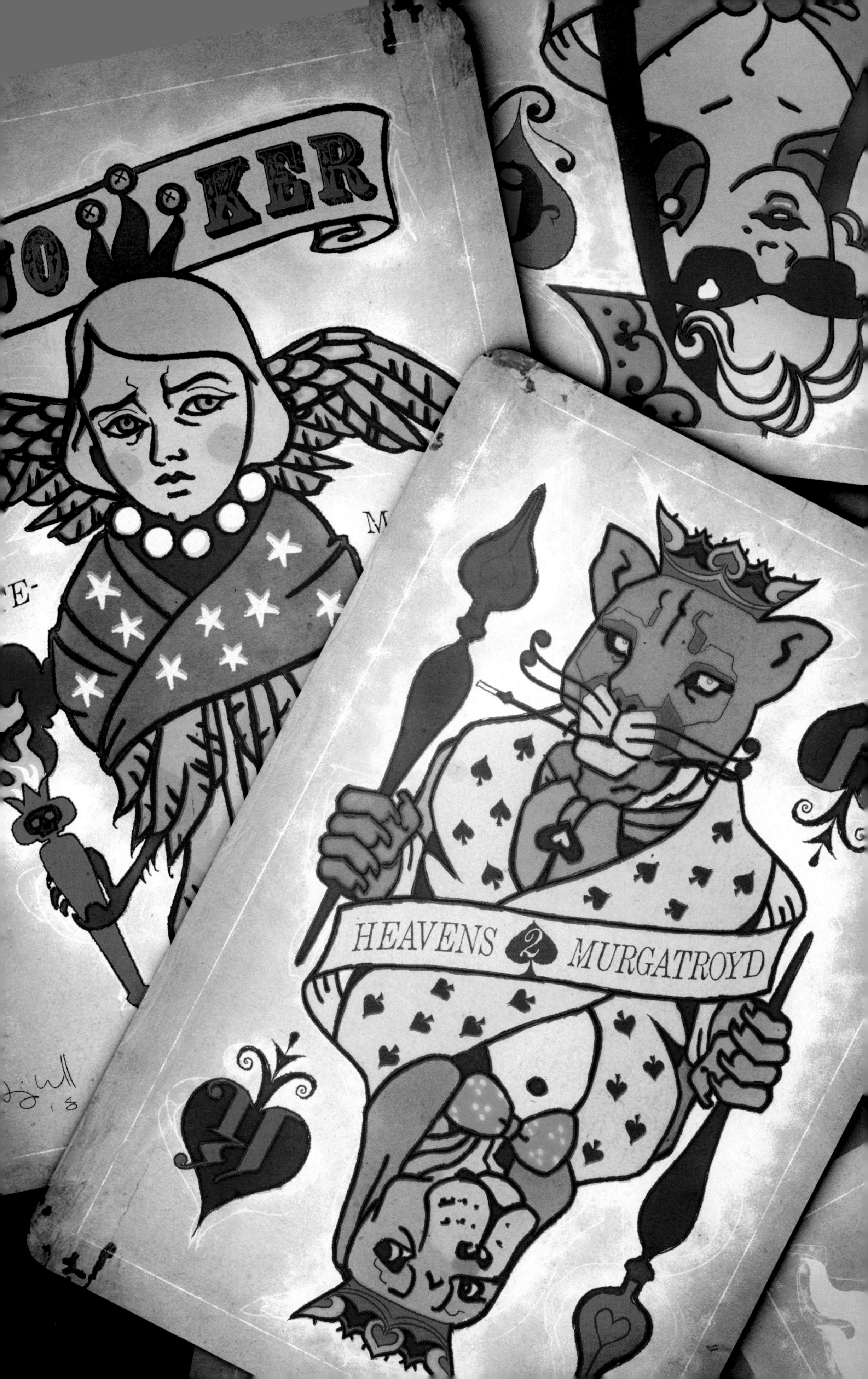
JO KER
HEAVENS 2 MURGATROYD

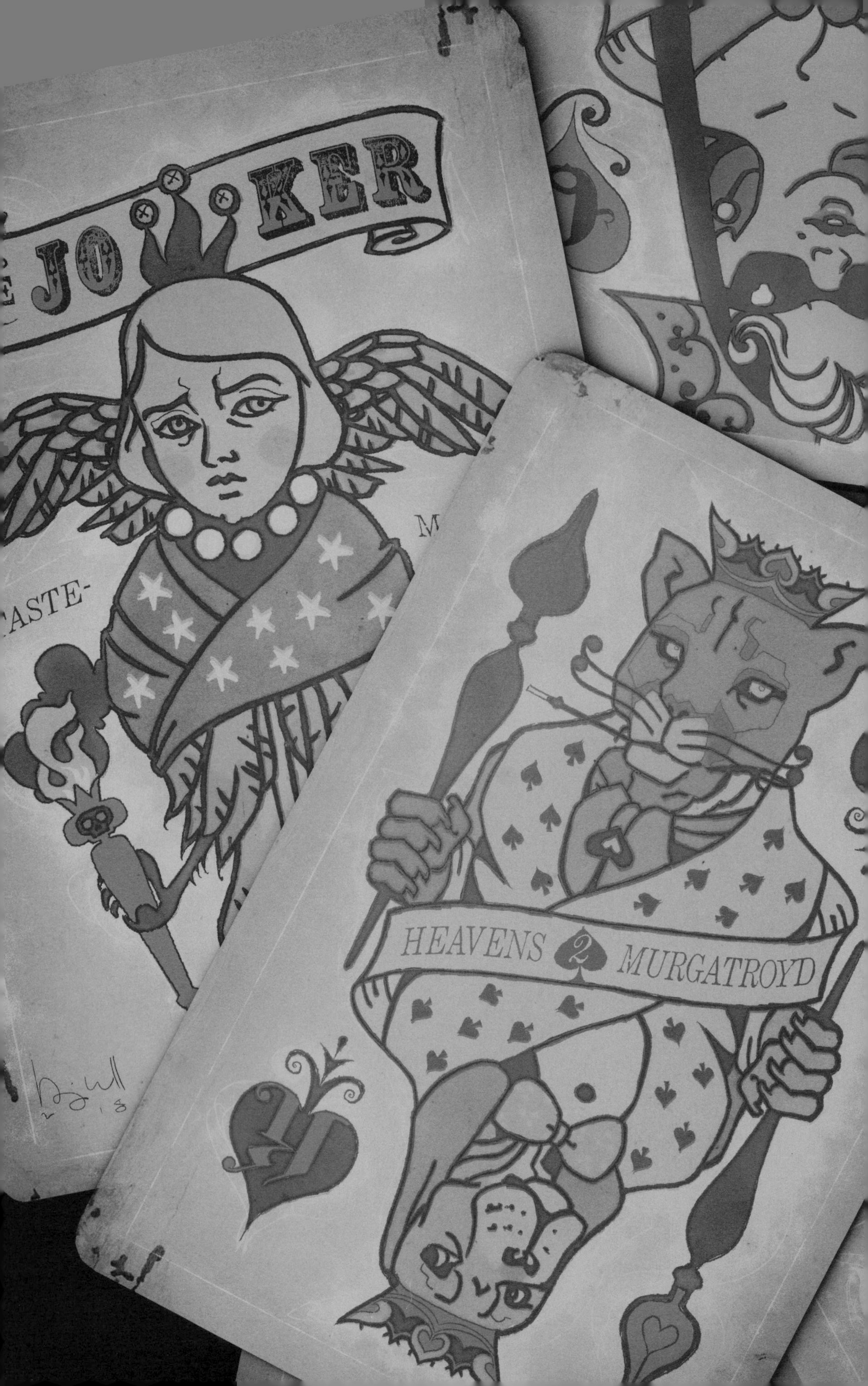
JOKER
CASTE-
HEAVENS
2
MURGATROYD

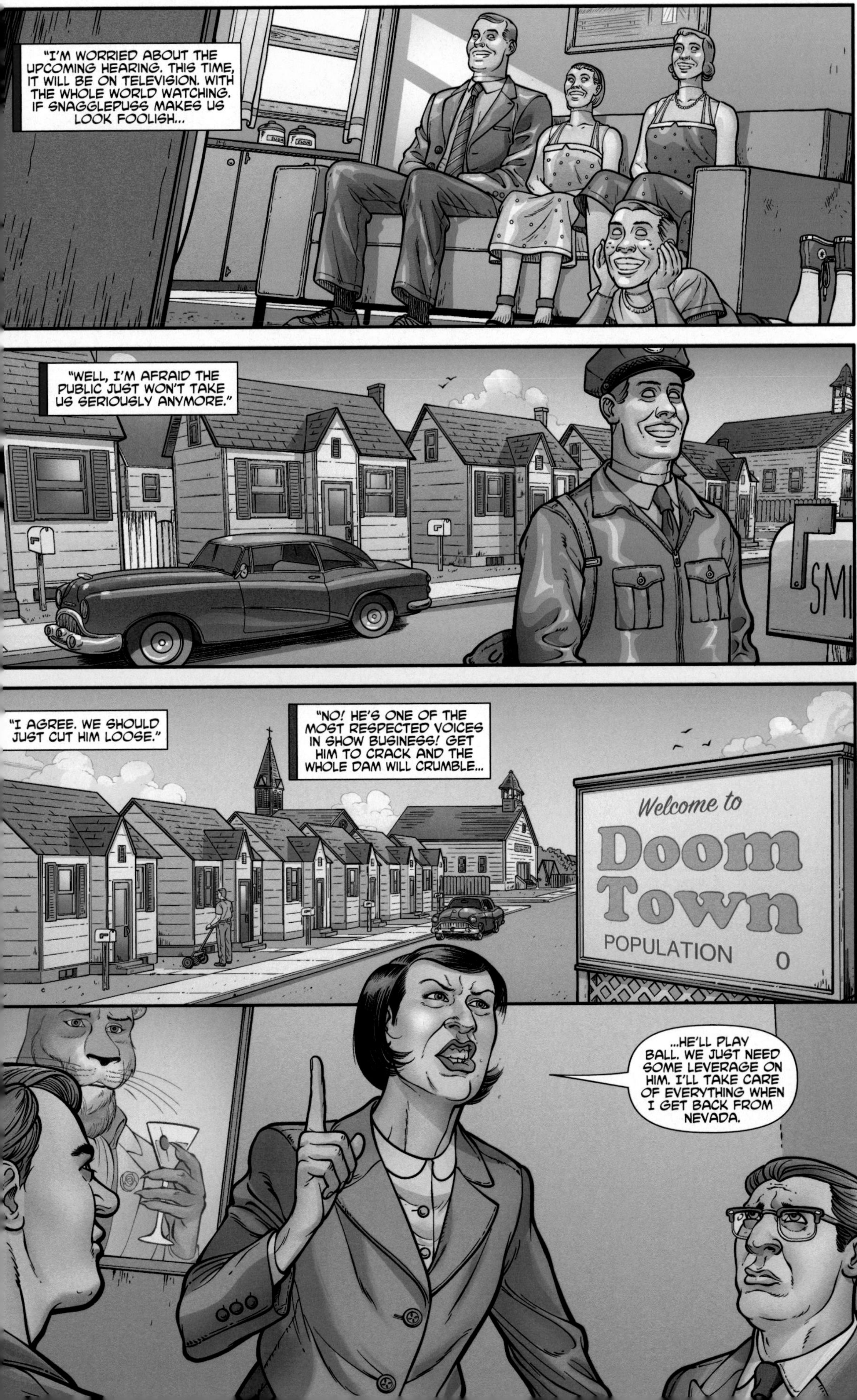
"I'M WORRIED ABOUT THE UPCOMING HEARING. THIS TIME, IT WILL BE ON TELEVISION. WITH THE WHOLE WORLD WATCHING, IF SNAGGLEPUSS MAKES US LOOK FOOLISH...
"WELL, I'M AFRAID THE PUBLIC JUST WON'T TAKE US SERIOUSLY ANYMORE."
SMI
"I AGREE. WE SHOULD JUST CUT HIM LOOSE."
"NO! HE'S ONE OF THE MOST RESPECTED VOICES IN SHOW BUSINESS! GET HIM TO CRACK AND THE WHOLE DAM WILL CRUMBLE...
Welcome to
Doom Town
POPULATION 0
...HE'LL PLAY BALL. WE JUST NEED SOME LEVERAGE ON HIM. I'LL TAKE CARE OF EVERYTHING WHEN I GET BACK FROM NEVADA.

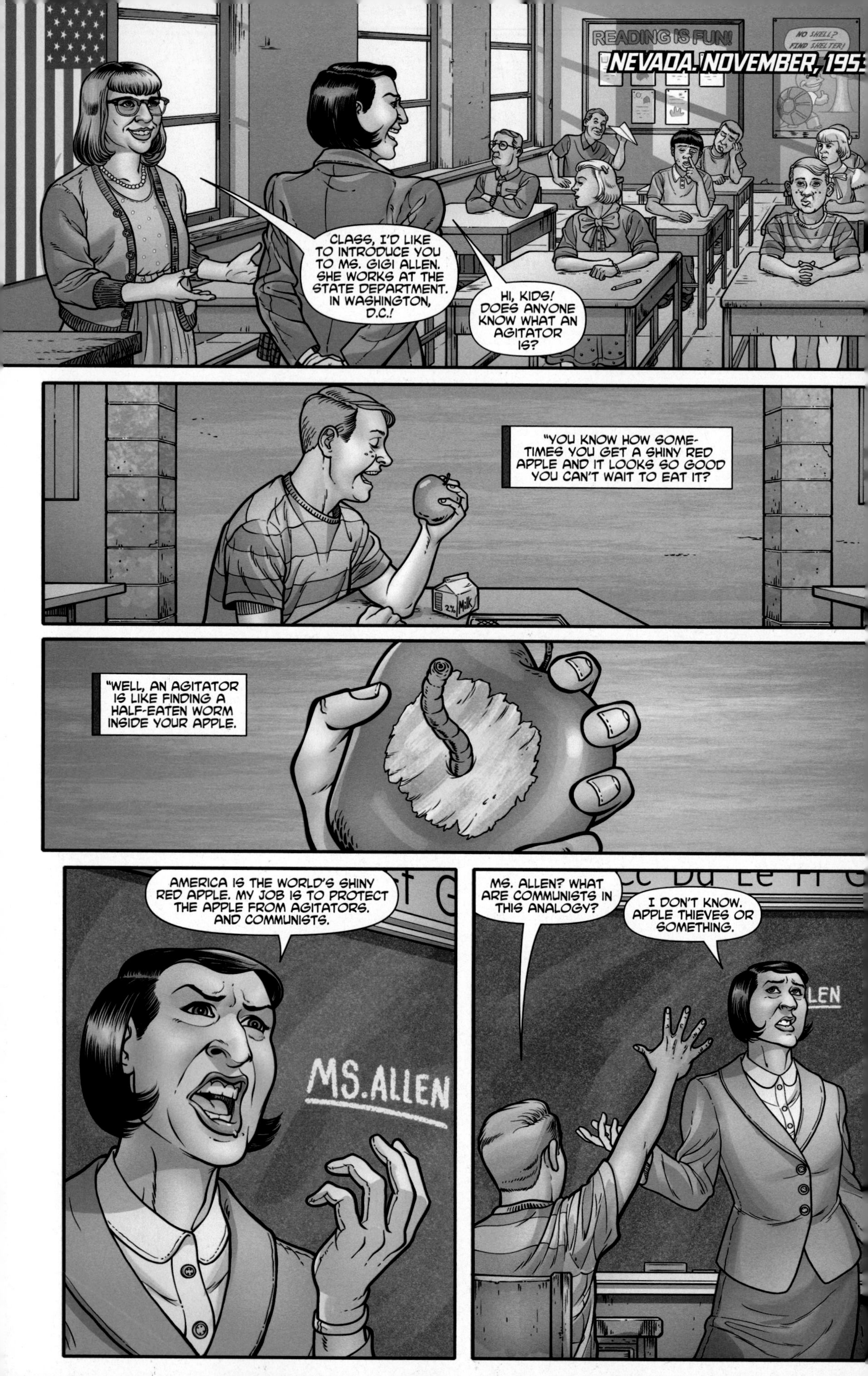
NEVADA. NOVEMBER, 195
READING IS FUN!
NO SHELL? FIND SHELTER!
CLASS, I'D LIKE TO INTRODUCE YOU TO MS. GIGI ALLEN. SHE WORKS AT THE STATE DEPARTMENT. IN WASHINGTON, D.C.!
HI, KIDS! DOES ANYONE KNOW WHAT AN AGITATOR IS?
"YOU KNOW HOW SOMETIMES YOU GET A SHINY RED APPLE AND IT LOOKS SO GOOD YOU CAN'T WAIT TO EAT IT?
2% Milk
"WELL, AN AGITATOR IS LIKE FINDING A HALF-EATEN WORM INSIDE YOUR APPLE.
AMERICA IS THE WORLD'S SHINY RED APPLE. MY JOB IS TO PROTECT THE APPLE FROM AGITATORS. AND COMMUNISTS.
MS. ALLEN
MS. ALLEN? WHAT ARE COMMUNISTS IN THIS ANALOGY?
I DON'T KNOW. APPLE THIEVES OR SOMETHING.
LEN

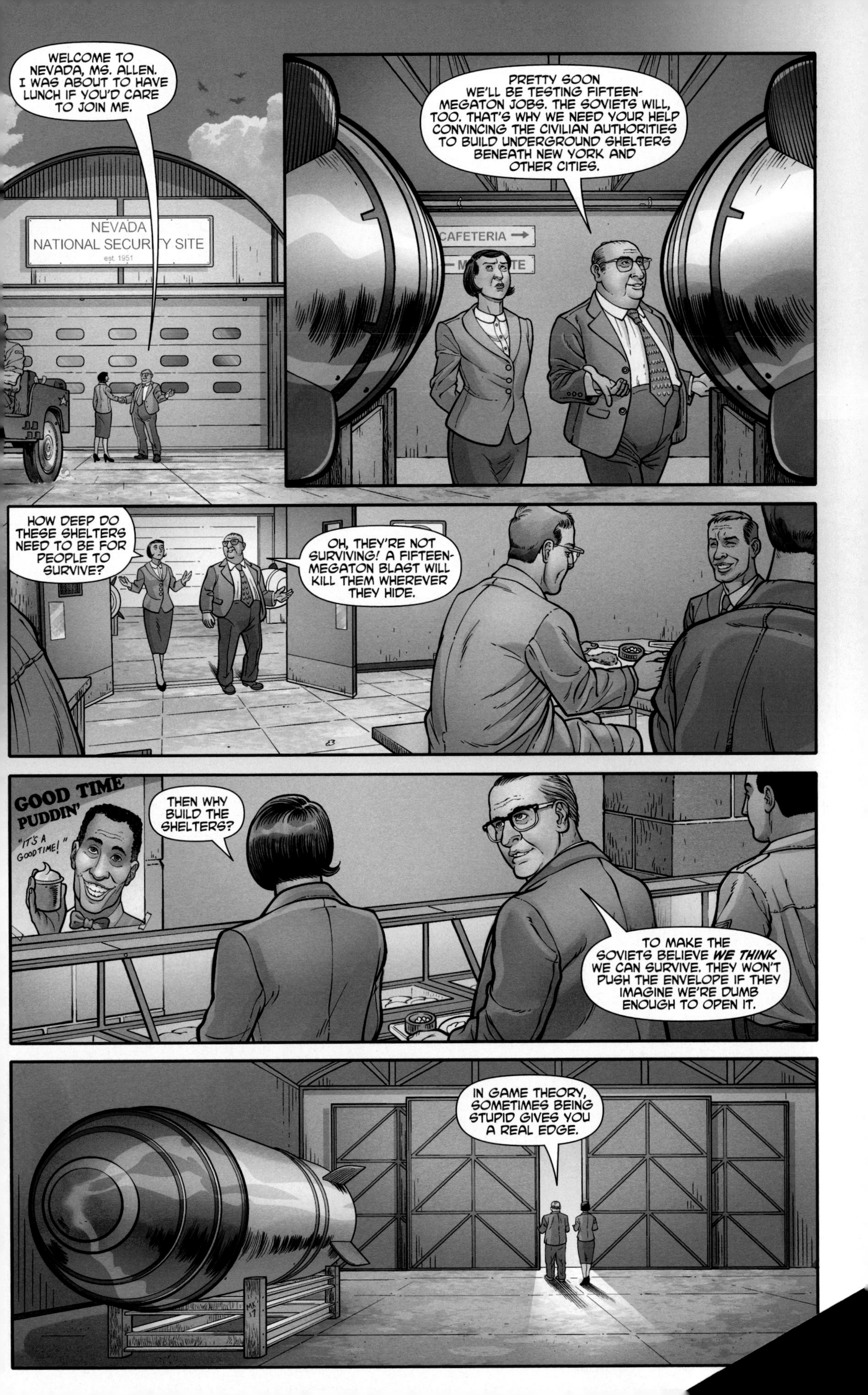
WELCOME TO NEVADA, MS. ALLEN. I WAS ABOUT TO HAVE LUNCH IF YOU'D CARE TO JOIN ME.
NEVADA NATIONAL SECURITY SITE est. 1951
PRETTY SOON WE'LL BE TESTING FIFTEEN-MEGATON JOBS. THE SOVIETS WILL, TOO. THAT'S WHY WE NEED YOUR HELP CONVINCING THE CIVILIAN AUTHORITIES TO BUILD UNDERGROUND SHELTERS BENEATH NEW YORK AND OTHER CITIES.
CAFETERIA
HOW DEEP DO THESE SHELTERS NEED TO BE FOR PEOPLE TO SURVIVE?
OH, THEY'RE NOT SURVIVING! A FIFTEEN-MEGATON BLAST WILL KILL THEM WHEREVER THEY HIDE.
GOOD TIME PUDDIN'
"IT'S A GOOD TIME!"
THEN WHY BUILD THE SHELTERS?
TO MAKE THE SOVIETS BELIEVE WE THINK WE CAN SURVIVE. THEY WON'T PUSH THE ENVELOPE IF THEY IMAGINE WE'RE DUMB ENOUGH TO OPEN IT.
IN GAME THEORY, SOMETIMES BEING STUPID GIVES YOU A REAL EDGE.

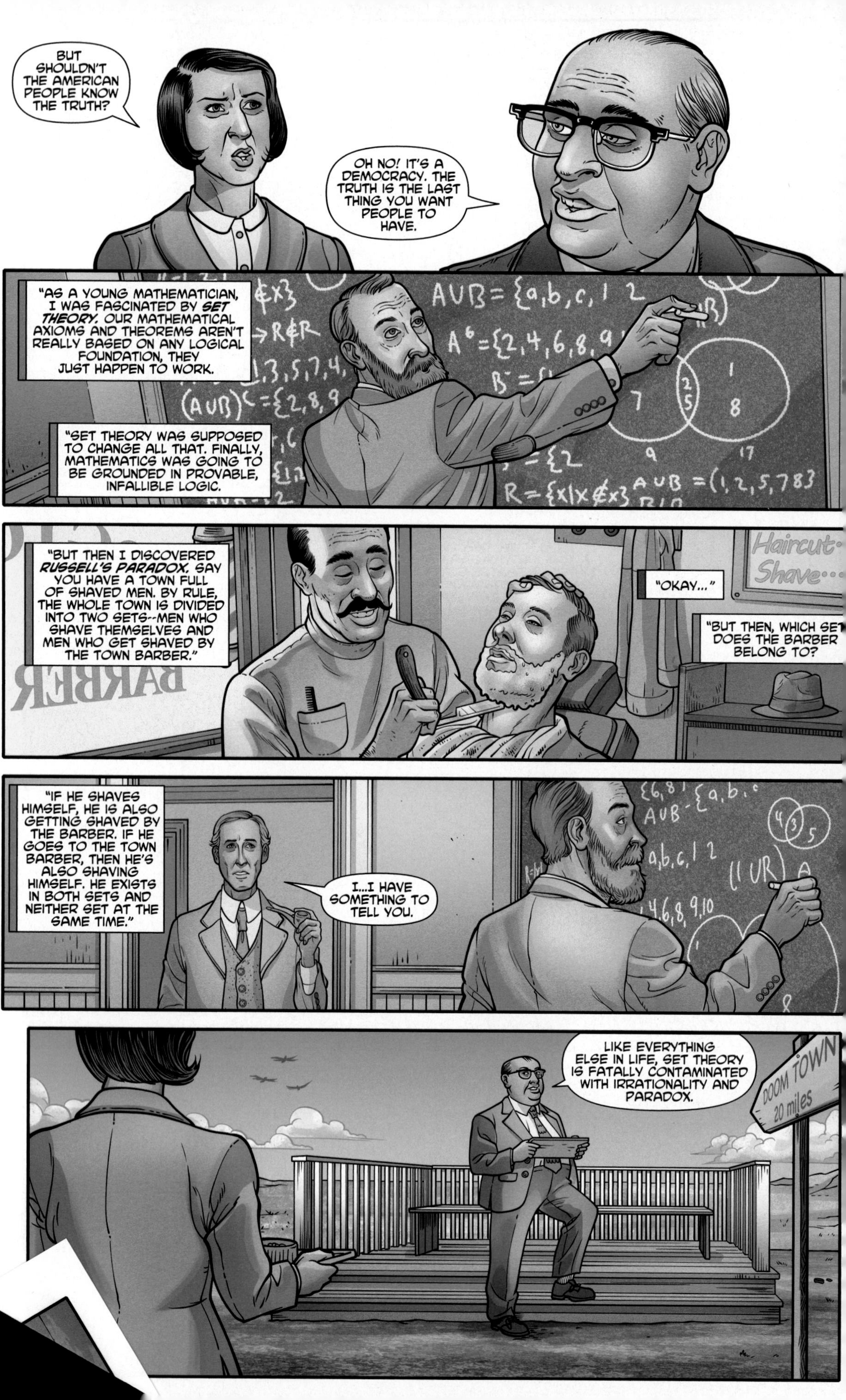
BUT SHOULDN'T THE AMERICAN PEOPLE KNOW THE TRUTH?
OH NO! IT'S A DEMOCRACY. THE TRUTH IS THE LAST THING YOU WANT PEOPLE TO HAVE.
"AS A YOUNG MATHEMATICIAN, I WAS FASCINATED BY SET THEORY. OUR MATHEMATICAL AXIOMS AND THEOREMS AREN'T REALLY BASED ON ANY LOGICAL FOUNDATION, THEY JUST HAPPEN TO WORK.
"SET THEORY WAS SUPPOSED TO CHANGE ALL THAT. FINALLY, MATHEMATICS WAS GOING TO BE GROUNDED IN PROVABLE, INFALLIBLE LOGIC.
"BUT THEN I DISCOVERED RUSSELL'S PARADOX. SAY YOU HAVE A TOWN FULL OF SHAVED MEN. BY RULE, THE WHOLE TOWN IS DIVIDED INTO TWO SETS--MEN WHO SHAVE THEMSELVES AND MEN WHO GET SHAVED BY THE TOWN BARBER."
BARBER
Haircut Shave...
"OKAY..."
"BUT THEN, WHICH SET DOES THE BARBER BELONG TO?
"IF HE SHAVES HIMSELF, HE IS ALSO GETTING SHAVED BY THE BARBER. IF HE GOES TO THE TOWN BARBER, THEN HE'S ALSO SHAVING HIMSELF. HE EXISTS IN BOTH SETS AND NEITHER SET AT THE SAME TIME."
I...I HAVE SOMETHING TO TELL YOU.
LIKE EVERYTHING ELSE IN LIFE, SET THEORY IS FATALLY CONTAMINATED WITH IRRATIONALITY AND PARADOX.
DOOM TOWN 20 miles

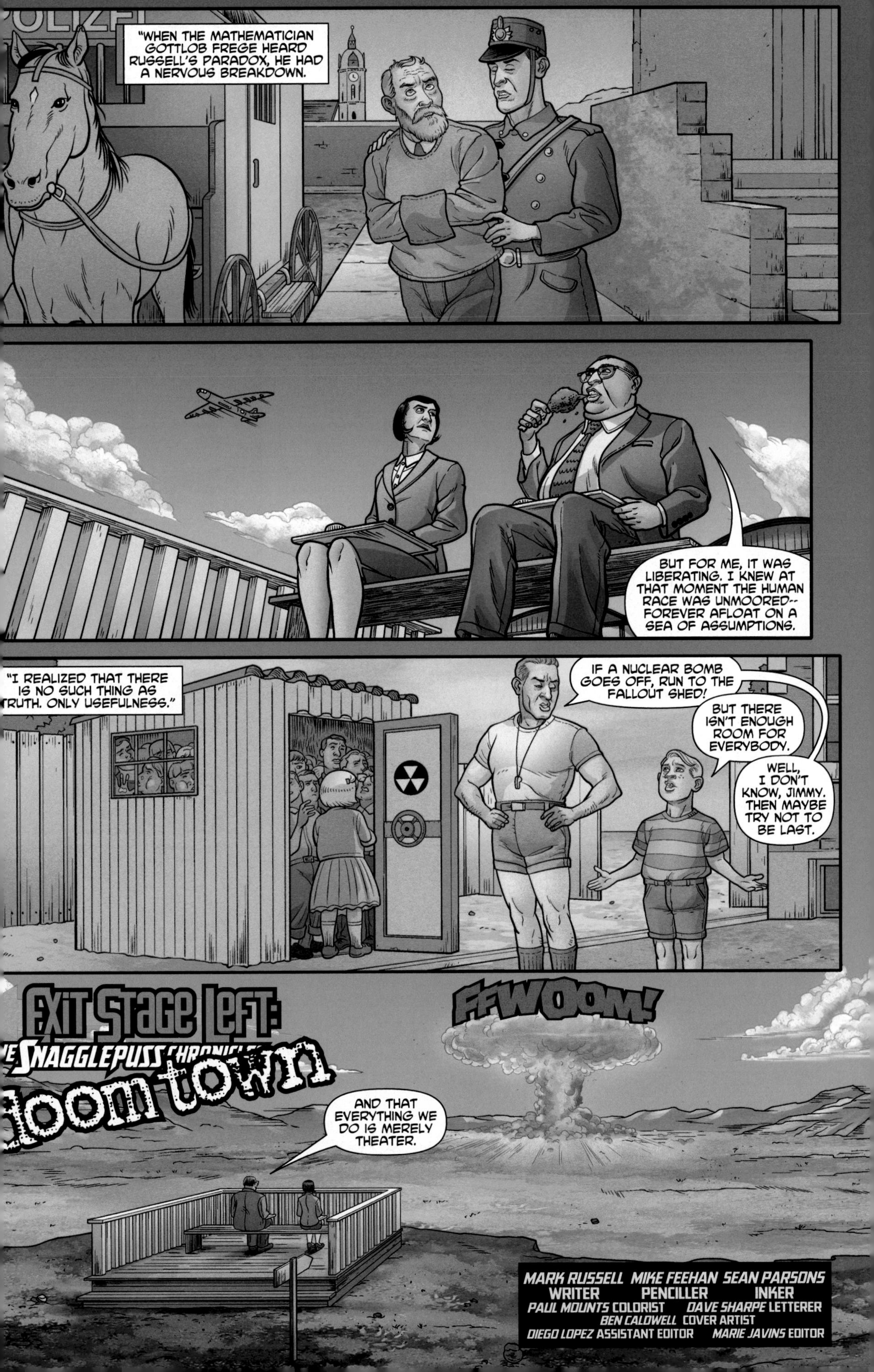
OLIZEI
"WHEN THE MATHEMATICIAN GOTTLOB FREGE HEARD RUSSELL'S PARADOX, HE HAD A NERVOUS BREAKDOWN.
BUT FOR ME, IT WAS LIBERATING. I KNEW AT THAT MOMENT THE HUMAN RACE WAS UNMOORED-- FOREVER AFLOAT ON A SEA OF ASSUMPTIONS.
"I REALIZED THAT THERE IS NO SUCH THING AS TRUTH. ONLY USEFULNESS."
IF A NUCLEAR BOMB GOES OFF, RUN TO THE FALLOUT SHED!
BUT THERE ISN'T ENOUGH ROOM FOR EVERYBODY.
WELL, I DON'T KNOW, JIMMY. THEN MAYBE TRY NOT TO BE LAST.
EXIT STAGE LEFT:
SNAGGLEPUSS
oom town
FFWOOM!
AND THAT EVERYTHING WE DO IS MERELY THEATER.
MARK RUSSELL WRITER
MIKE FEEHAN PENCILLER
SEAN PARSONS INKER
PAUL MOUNTS COLORIST
DAVE SHARPE LETTERER
BEN CALDWELL COVER ARTIST
DIEGO LOPEZ ASSISTANT EDITOR
MARIE JAVINS EDITOR

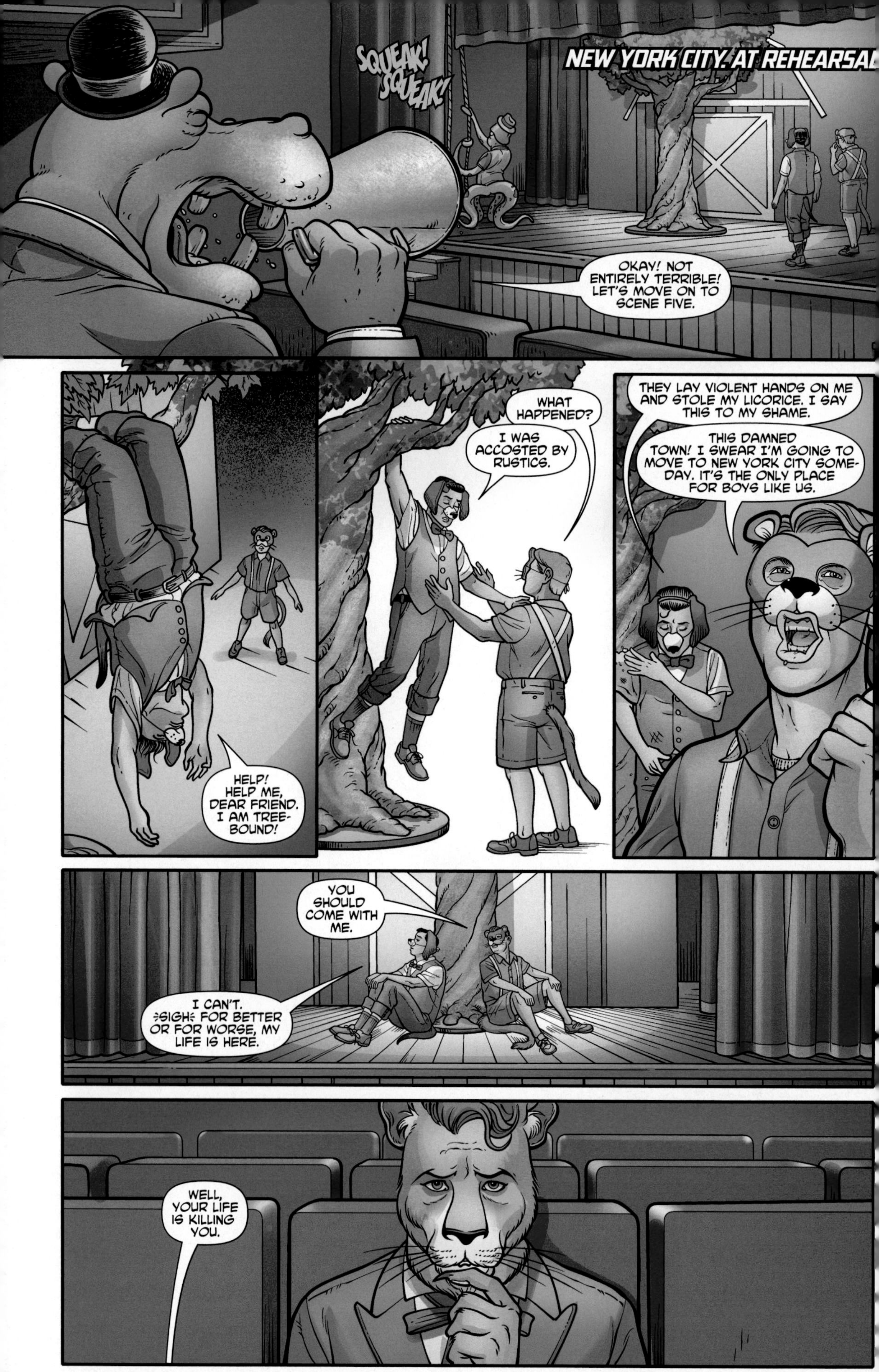
NEW YORK CITY. AT REHEARSAL
SQUEAK! SQUEAK!
OKAY! NOT ENTIRELY TERRIBLE! LET'S MOVE ON TO SCENE FIVE.
HELP! HELP ME, DEAR FRIEND. I AM TREE-BOUND!
WHAT HAPPENED?
I WAS ACCOSTED BY RUSTICS.
THEY LAY VIOLENT HANDS ON ME AND STOLE MY LICORICE. I SAY THIS TO MY SHAME.
THIS DAMNED TOWN! I SWEAR I'M GOING TO MOVE TO NEW YORK CITY SOME-DAY. IT'S THE ONLY PLACE FOR BOYS LIKE US.
YOU SHOULD COME WITH ME.
I CAN'T. *SIGH* FOR BETTER OR FOR WORSE, MY LIFE IS HERE.
WELL, YOUR LIFE IS KILLING YOU.

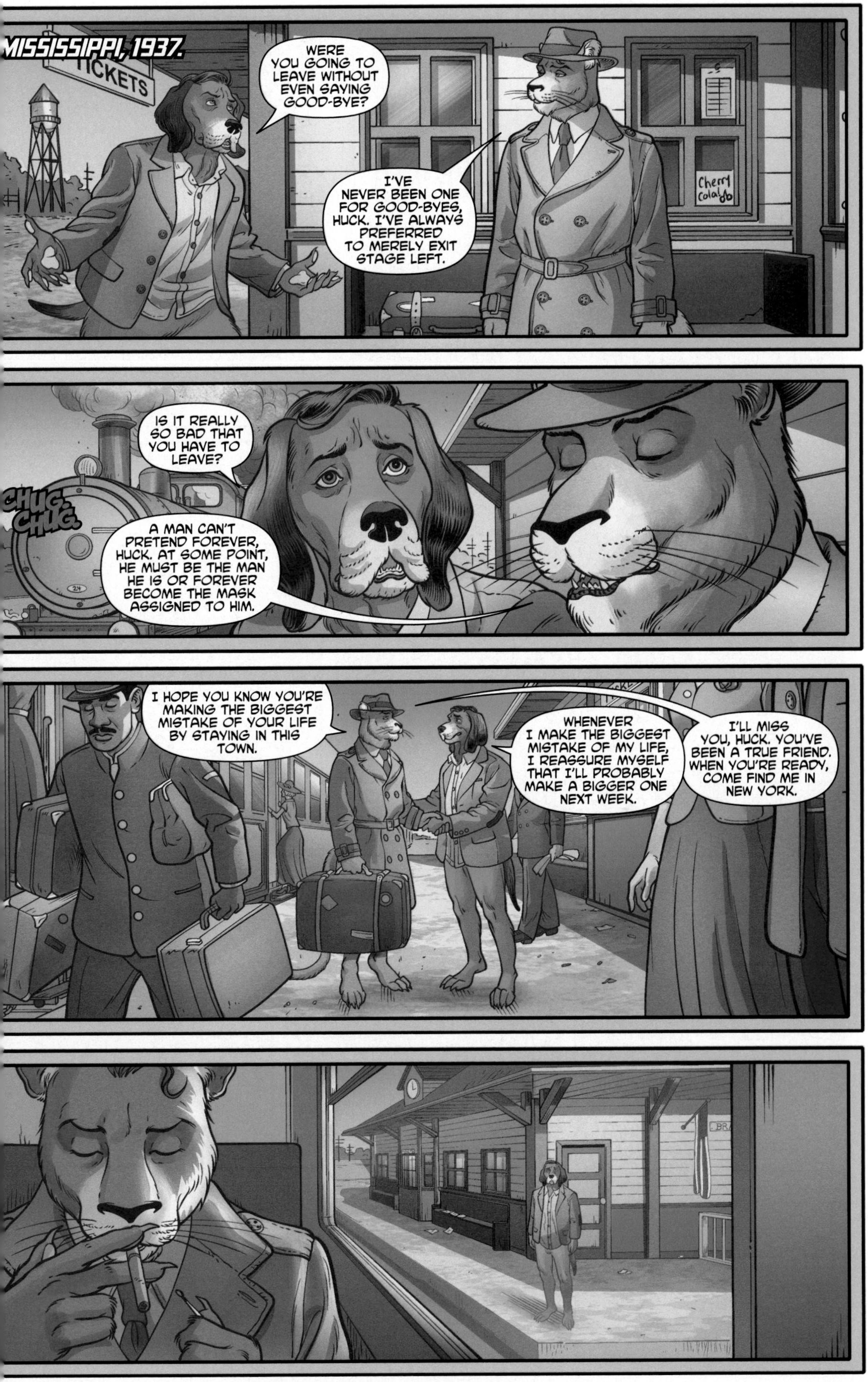
MISSISSIPPI, 1937.
TICKETS
WERE YOU GOING TO LEAVE WITHOUT EVEN SAYING GOOD-BYE?
I'VE NEVER BEEN ONE FOR GOOD-BYES, HUCK. I'VE ALWAYS PREFERRED TO MERELY EXIT STAGE LEFT.
Cherry Cola
IS IT REALLY SO BAD THAT YOU HAVE TO LEAVE?
CHUG CHUG
A MAN CAN'T PRETEND FOREVER, HUCK. AT SOME POINT, HE MUST BE THE MAN HE IS OR FOREVER BECOME THE MASK ASSIGNED TO HIM.
I HOPE YOU KNOW YOU'RE MAKING THE BIGGEST MISTAKE OF YOUR LIFE BY STAYING IN THIS TOWN.
WHENEVER I MAKE THE BIGGEST MISTAKE OF MY LIFE, I REASSURE MYSELF THAT I'LL PROBABLY MAKE A BIGGER ONE NEXT WEEK.
I'LL MISS YOU, HUCK. YOU'VE BEEN A TRUE FRIEND. WHEN YOU'RE READY, COME FIND ME IN NEW YORK.

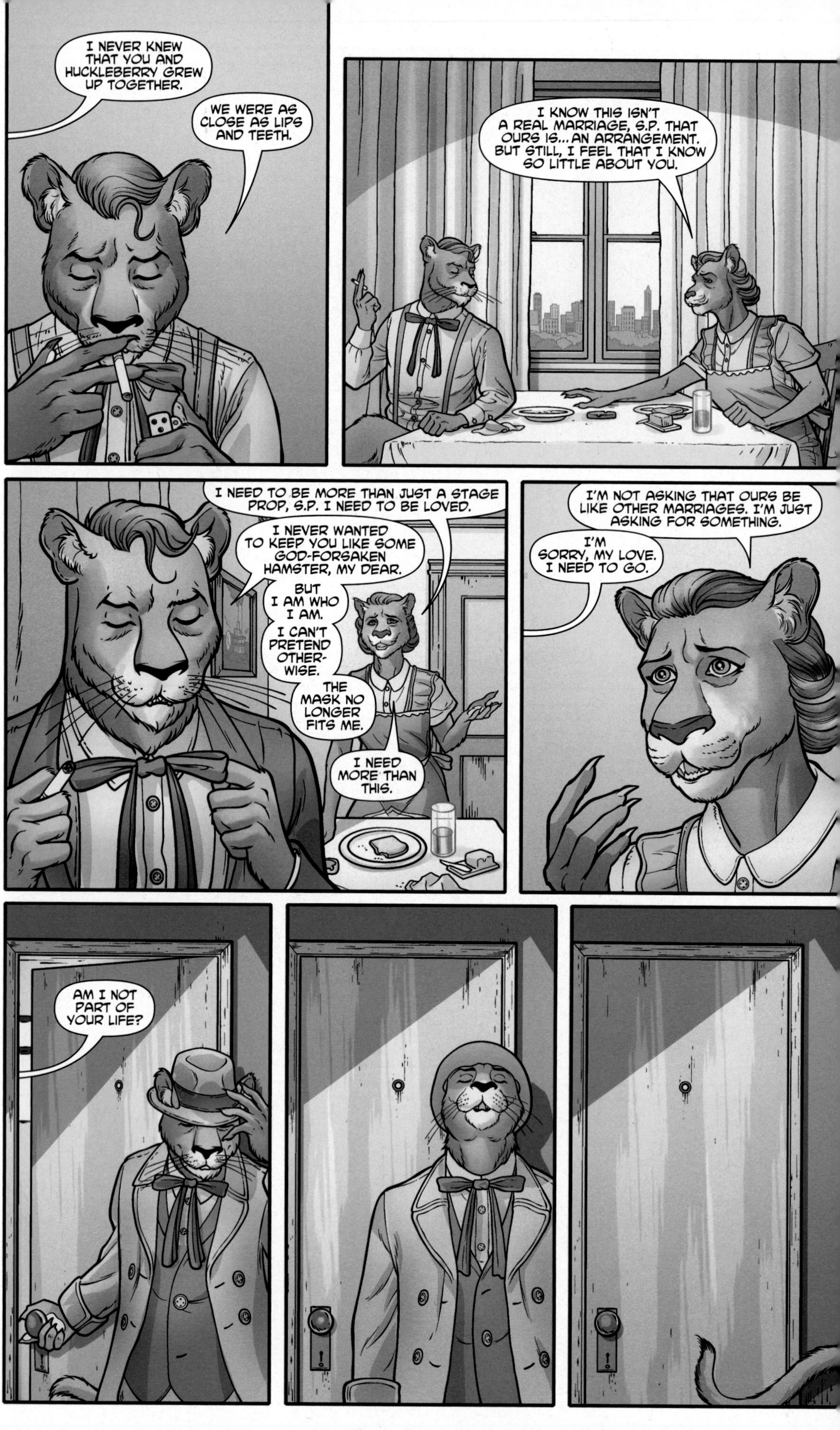
I NEVER KNEW THAT YOU AND HUCKLEBERRY GREW UP TOGETHER.
WE WERE AS CLOSE AS LIPS AND TEETH.
I KNOW THIS ISN'T A REAL MARRIAGE, S.P. THAT OURS IS... AN ARRANGEMENT. BUT STILL, I FEEL THAT I KNOW SO LITTLE ABOUT YOU.
I NEED TO BE MORE THAN JUST A STAGE PROP, S.P. I NEED TO BE LOVED.
I NEVER WANTED TO KEEP YOU LIKE SOME GOD-FORSAKEN HAMSTER, MY DEAR.
BUT I AM WHO I AM.
I CAN'T PRETEND OTHER-WISE.
THE MASK NO LONGER FITS ME.
I NEED MORE THAN THIS.
I'M NOT ASKING THAT OURS BE LIKE OTHER MARRIAGES. I'M JUST ASKING FOR SOMETHING.
I'M SORRY, MY LOVE. I NEED TO GO.
AM I NOT PART OF YOUR LIFE?

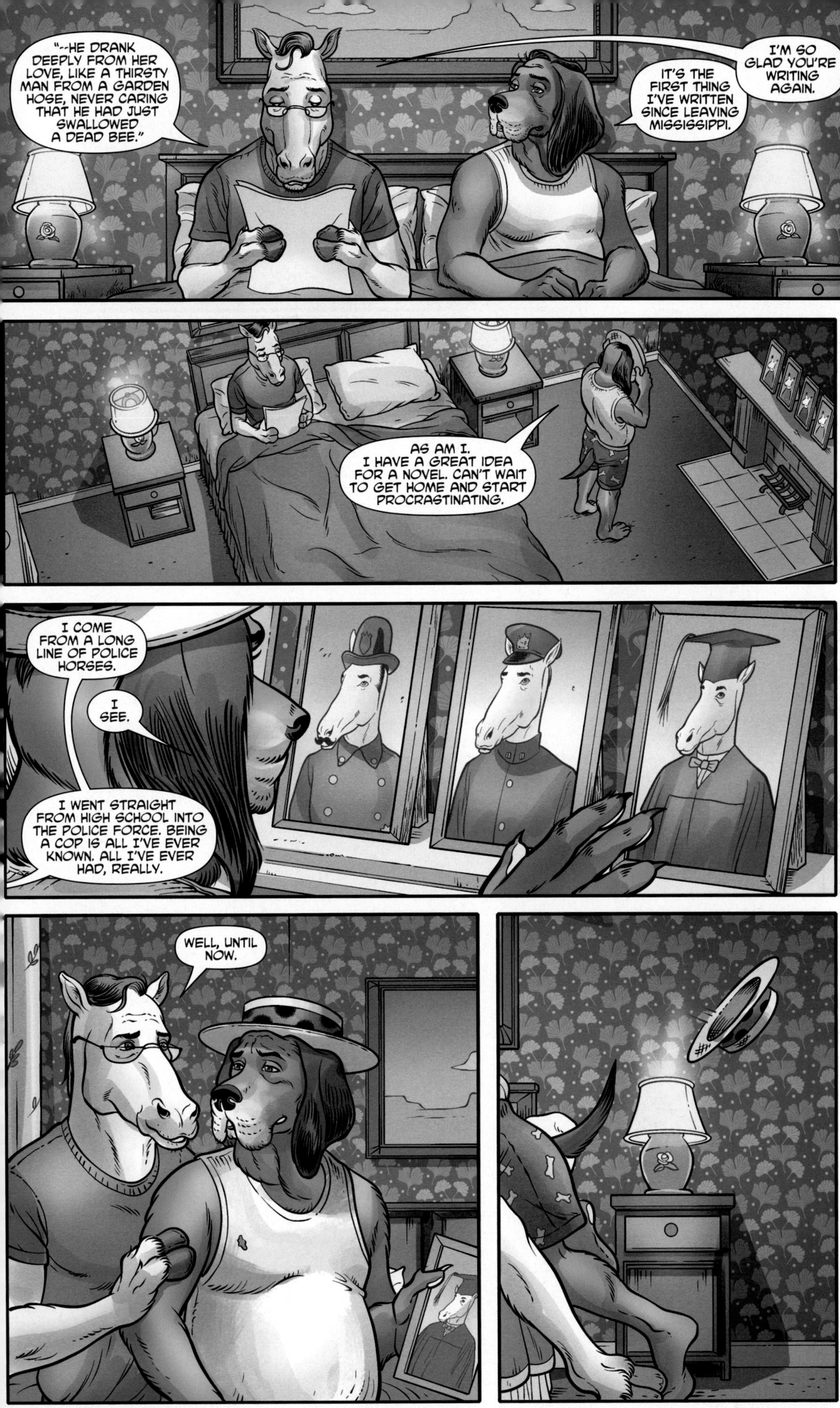
"--HE DRANK DEEPLY FROM HER LOVE, LIKE A THIRSTY MAN FROM A GARDEN HOSE, NEVER CARING THAT HE HAD JUST SWALLOWED A DEAD BEE."
I'M SO GLAD YOU'RE WRITING AGAIN.
IT'S THE FIRST THING I'VE WRITTEN SINCE LEAVING MISSISSIPPI.
AS AM I. I HAVE A GREAT IDEA FOR A NOVEL. CAN'T WAIT TO GET HOME AND START PROCRASTINATING.
I COME FROM A LONG LINE OF POLICE HORSES.
I SEE.
I WENT STRAIGHT FROM HIGH SCHOOL INTO THE POLICE FORCE. BEING A COP IS ALL I'VE EVER KNOWN. ALL I'VE EVER HAD, REALLY.
WELL, UNTIL NOW.

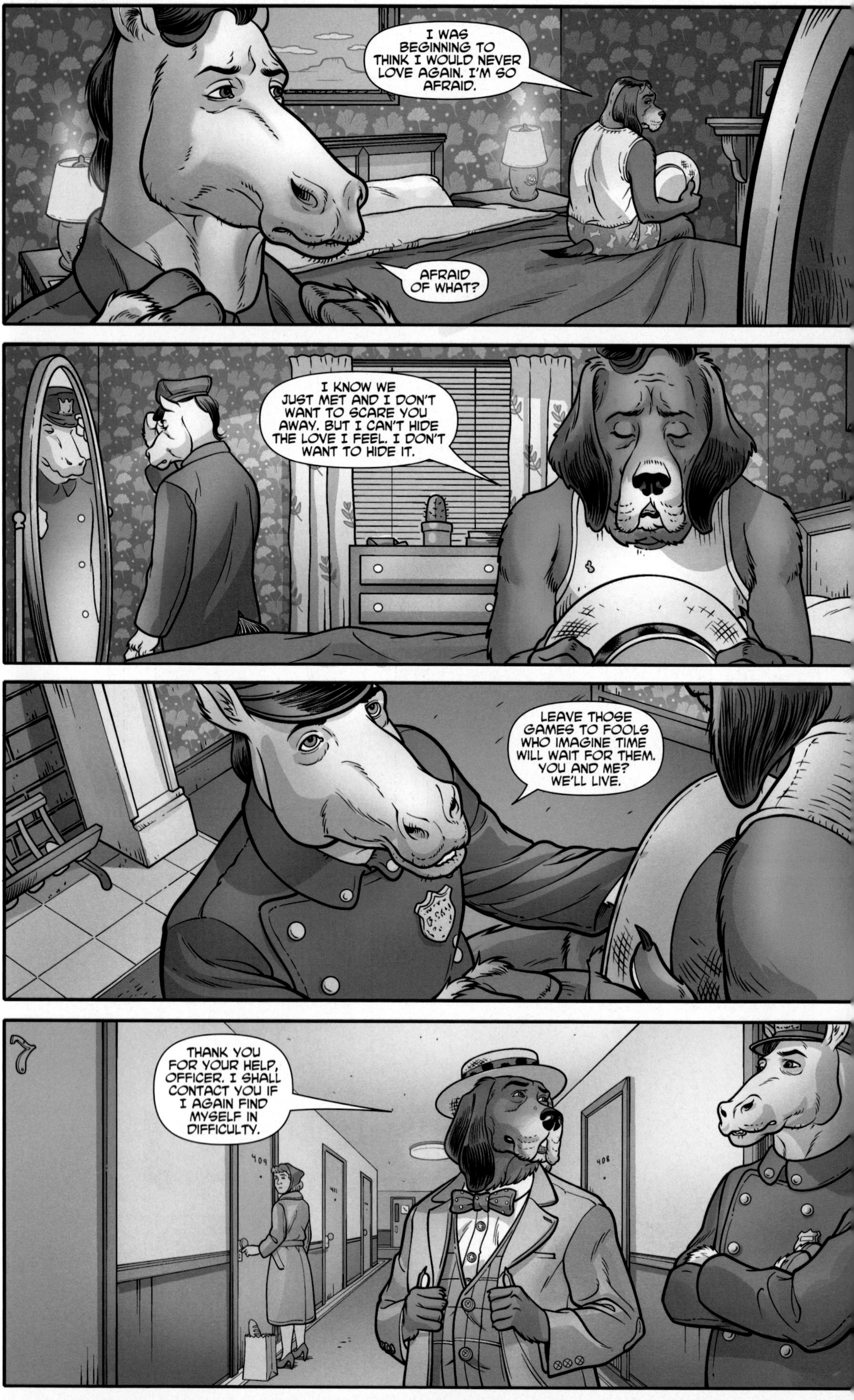
I WAS BEGINNING TO THINK I WOULD NEVER LOVE AGAIN. I'M SO AFRAID.
AFRAID OF WHAT?
I KNOW WE JUST MET AND I DON'T WANT TO SCARE YOU AWAY. BUT I CAN'T HIDE THE LOVE I FEEL. I DON'T WANT TO HIDE IT.
LEAVE THOSE GAMES TO FOOLS WHO IMAGINE TIME WILL WAIT FOR THEM. YOU AND ME? WE'LL LIVE.
THANK YOU FOR YOUR HELP, OFFICER. I SHALL CONTACT YOU IF I AGAIN FIND MYSELF IN DIFFICULTY.

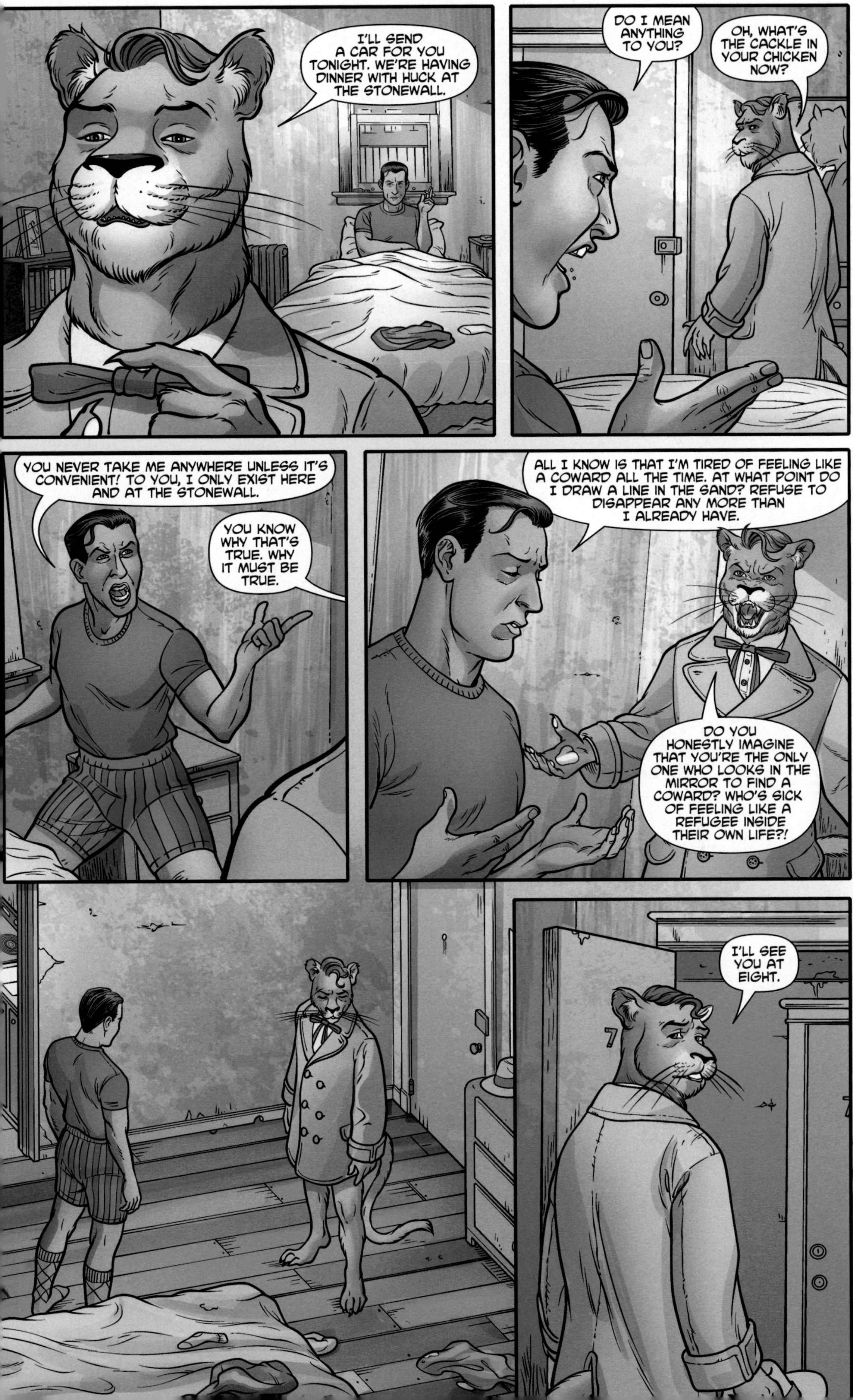
I'LL SEND A CAR FOR YOU TONIGHT. WE'RE HAVING DINNER WITH HUCK AT THE STONEWALL.
DO I MEAN ANYTHING TO YOU?
OH, WHAT'S THE CACKLE IN YOUR CHICKEN NOW?
YOU NEVER TAKE ME ANYWHERE UNLESS IT'S CONVENIENT! TO YOU, I ONLY EXIST HERE AND AT THE STONEWALL.
YOU KNOW WHY THAT'S TRUE. WHY IT MUST BE TRUE.
ALL I KNOW IS THAT I'M TIRED OF FEELING LIKE A COWARD ALL THE TIME. AT WHAT POINT DO I DRAW A LINE IN THE SAND? REFUSE TO DISAPPEAR ANY MORE THAN I ALREADY HAVE.
DO YOU HONESTLY IMAGINE THAT YOU'RE THE ONLY ONE WHO LOOKS IN THE MIRROR TO FIND A COWARD? WHO'S SICK OF FEELING LIKE A REFUGEE INSIDE THEIR OWN LIFE?!
I'LL SEE YOU AT EIGHT.
7

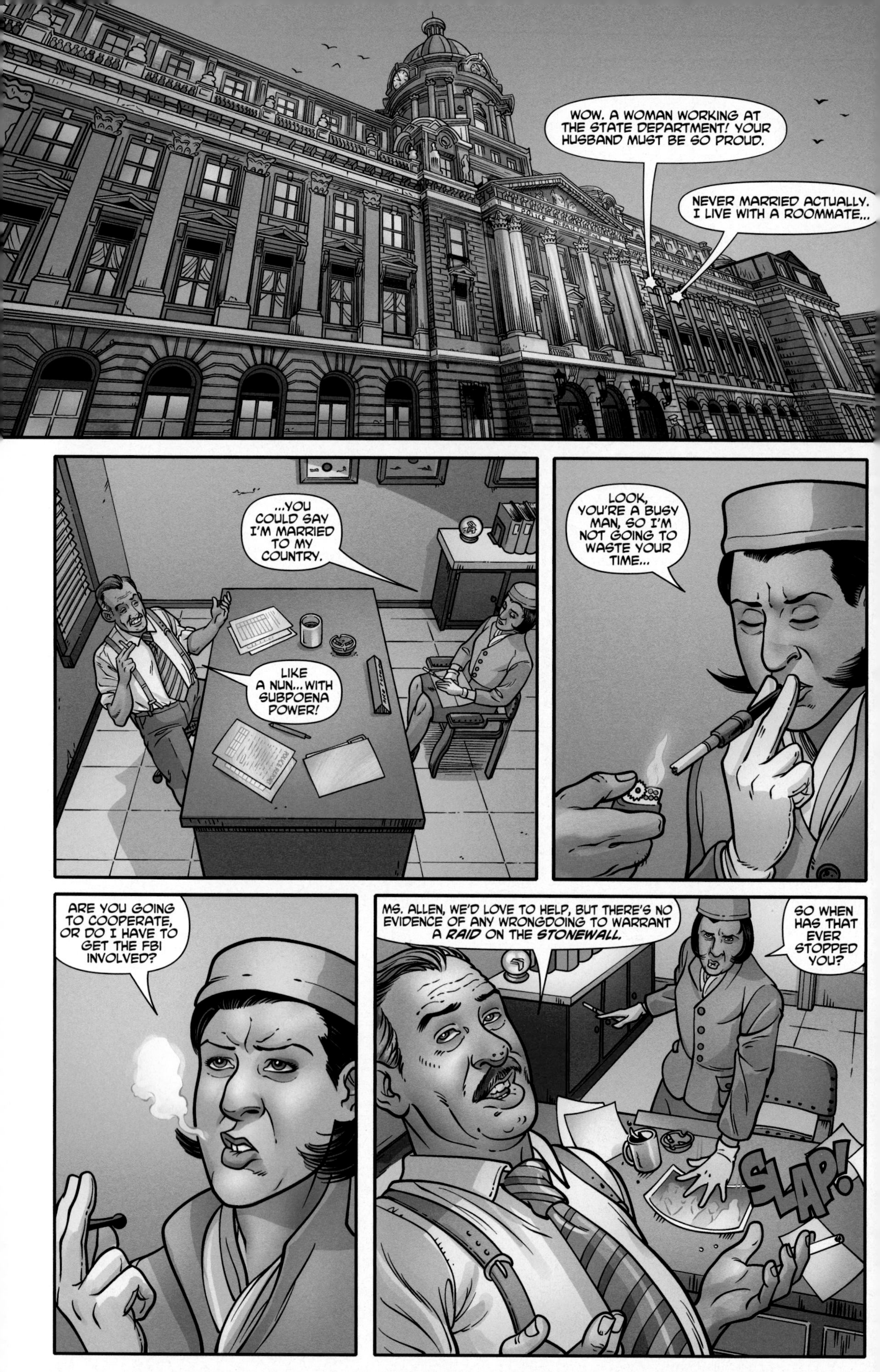
WOW. A WOMAN WORKING AT THE STATE DEPARTMENT! YOUR HUSBAND MUST BE SO PROUD.
NEVER MARRIED ACTUALLY. I LIVE WITH A ROOMMATE...
...YOU COULD SAY I'M MARRIED TO MY COUNTRY.
LIKE A NUN...WITH SUBPOENA POWER!
LOOK, YOU'RE A BUSY MAN, SO I'M NOT GOING TO WASTE YOUR TIME...
ARE YOU GOING TO COOPERATE, OR DO I HAVE TO GET THE FBI INVOLVED?
MS. ALLEN, WE'D LOVE TO HELP, BUT THERE'S NO EVIDENCE OF ANY WRONGDOING TO WARRANT A RAID ON THE STONEWALL.
SO WHEN HAS THAT EVER STOPPED YOU?
SLAP!

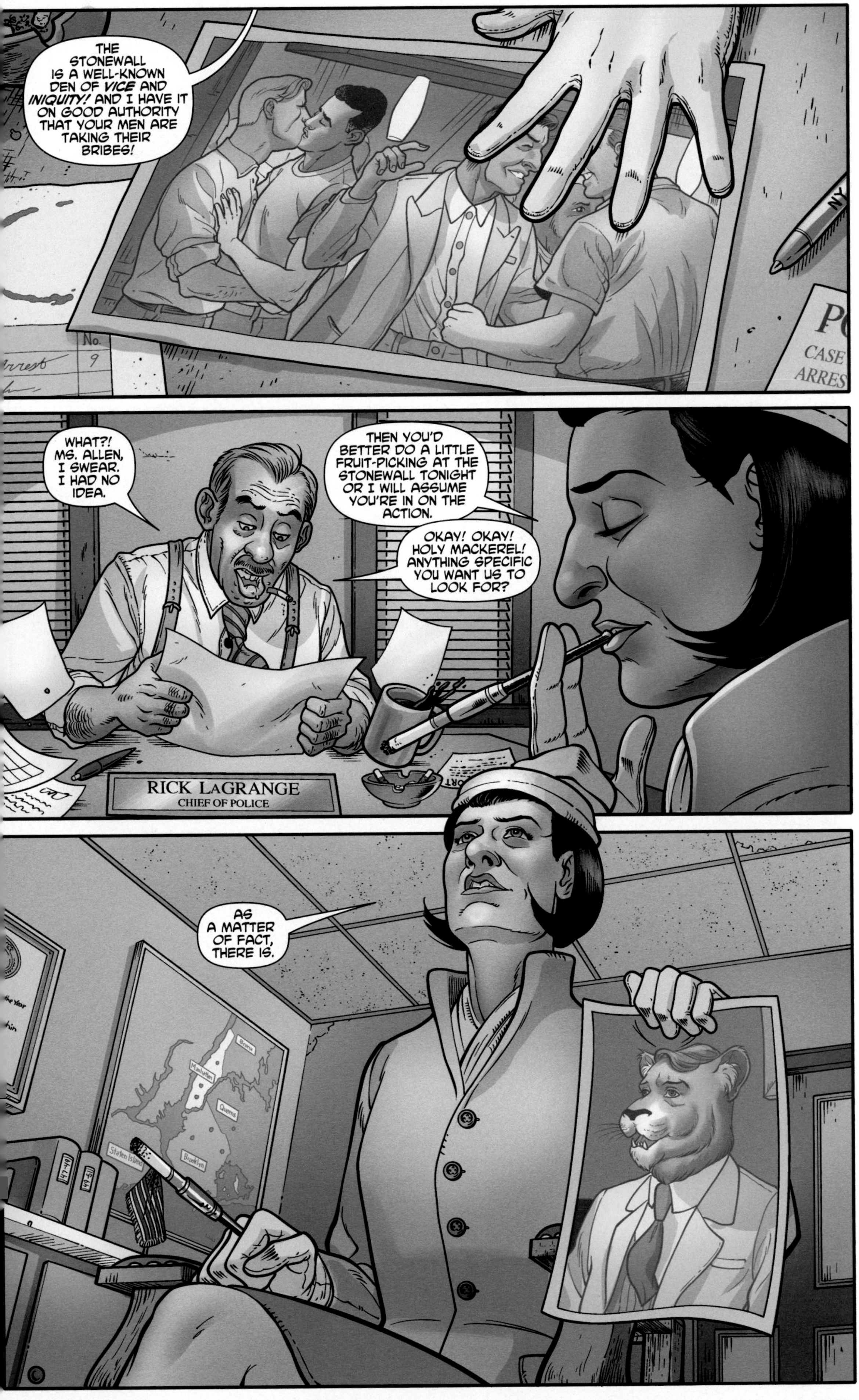
THE STONEWALL IS A WELL-KNOWN DEN OF *VICE* AND *INIQUITY!* AND I HAVE IT ON GOOD AUTHORITY THAT YOUR MEN ARE TAKING THEIR BRIBES!
WHAT?! MS. ALLEN, I SWEAR. I HAD NO IDEA.
THEN YOU'D BETTER DO A LITTLE FRUIT-PICKING AT THE STONEWALL TONIGHT OR I WILL ASSUME YOU'RE IN ON THE ACTION.
OKAY! OKAY! HOLY MACKEREL! ANYTHING SPECIFIC YOU WANT US TO LOOK FOR?
RICK LaGRANGE
CHIEF OF POLICE
AS A MATTER OF FACT, THERE IS.
Bronx
Manhattan
Queens
Brooklyn
Staten Island

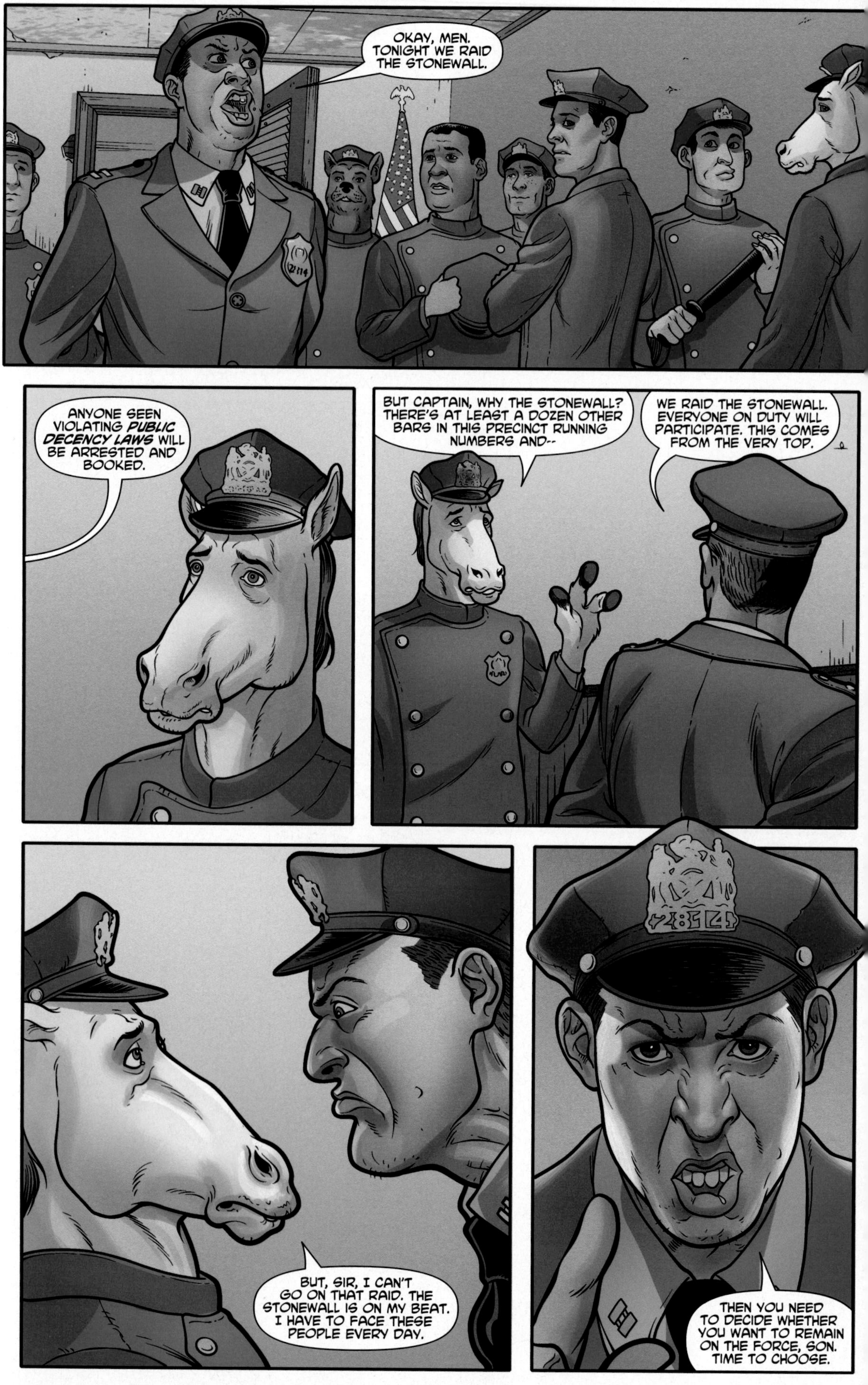

OKAY, MEN. TONIGHT WE RAID THE STONEWALL.
ANYONE SEEN VIOLATING *PUBLIC DECENCY LAWS* WILL BE ARRESTED AND BOOKED.
BUT CAPTAIN, WHY THE STONEWALL? THERE'S AT LEAST A DOZEN OTHER BARS IN THIS PRECINCT RUNNING NUMBERS AND--
WE RAID THE STONEWALL. EVERYONE ON DUTY WILL PARTICIPATE. THIS COMES FROM THE VERY TOP.
BUT, SIR, I CAN'T GO ON THAT RAID. THE STONEWALL IS ON MY BEAT. I HAVE TO FACE THESE PEOPLE EVERY DAY.
THEN YOU NEED TO DECIDE WHETHER YOU WANT TO REMAIN ON THE FORCE, SON. TIME TO CHOOSE.

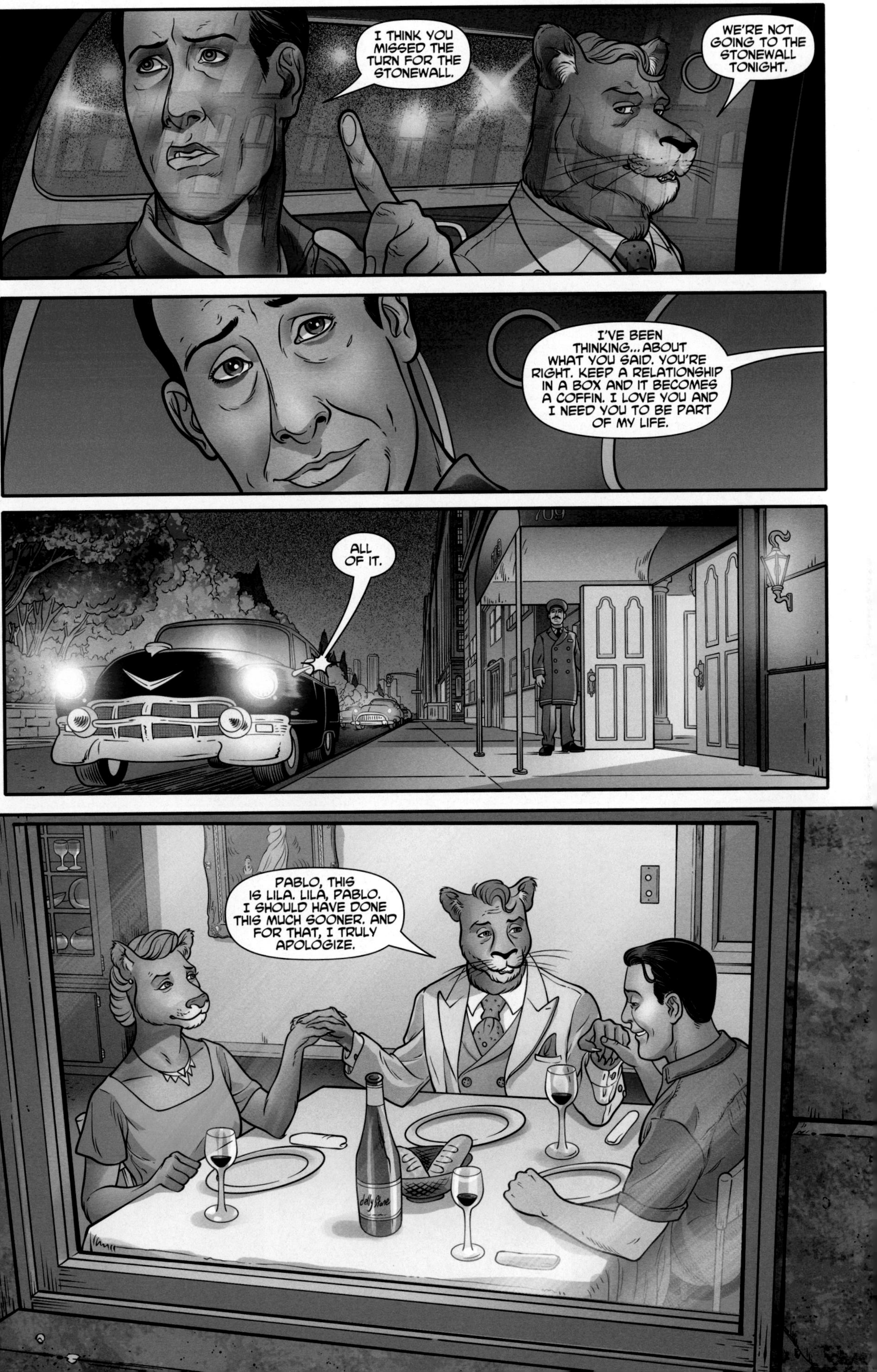
I THINK YOU MISSED THE TURN FOR THE STONEWALL.
WE'RE NOT GOING TO THE STONEWALL TONIGHT.
I'VE BEEN THINKING... ABOUT WHAT YOU SAID. YOU'RE RIGHT. KEEP A RELATIONSHIP IN A BOX AND IT BECOMES A COFFIN. I LOVE YOU AND I NEED YOU TO BE PART OF MY LIFE.
709
ALL OF IT.
PABLO, THIS IS LILA. LILA, PABLO. I SHOULD HAVE DONE THIS MUCH SOONER. AND FOR THAT, I TRULY APOLOGIZE.

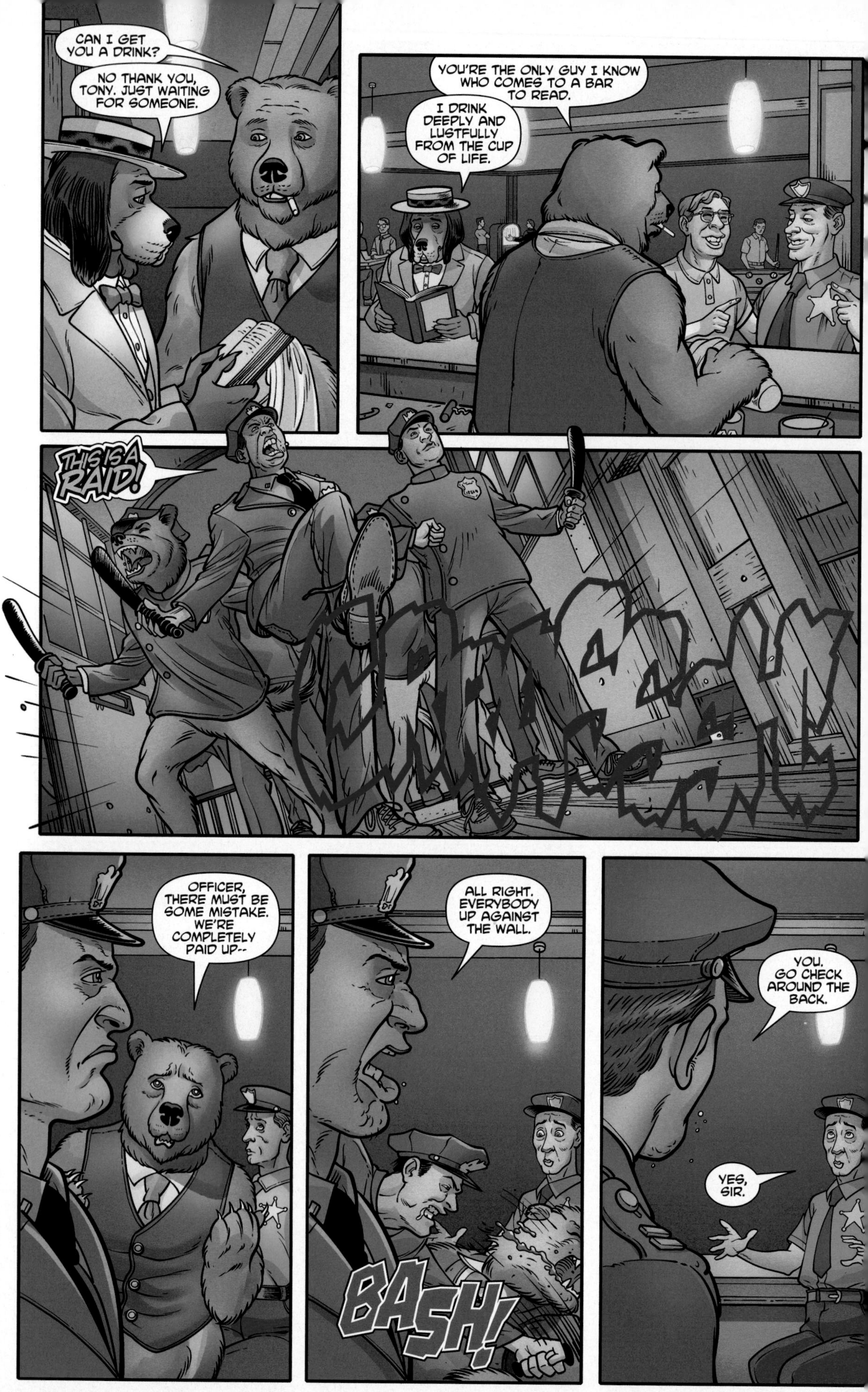
CAN I GET YOU A DRINK?
NO THANK YOU, TONY. JUST WAITING FOR SOMEONE.
YOU'RE THE ONLY GUY I KNOW WHO COMES TO A BAR TO READ.
I DRINK DEEPLY AND LUSTFULLY FROM THE CUP OF LIFE.
THIS IS A RAID!
OFFICER, THERE MUST BE SOME MISTAKE. WE'RE COMPLETELY PAID UP--
ALL RIGHT. EVERYBODY UP AGAINST THE WALL.
BASH!
YOU. GO CHECK AROUND THE BACK.
YES, SIR.

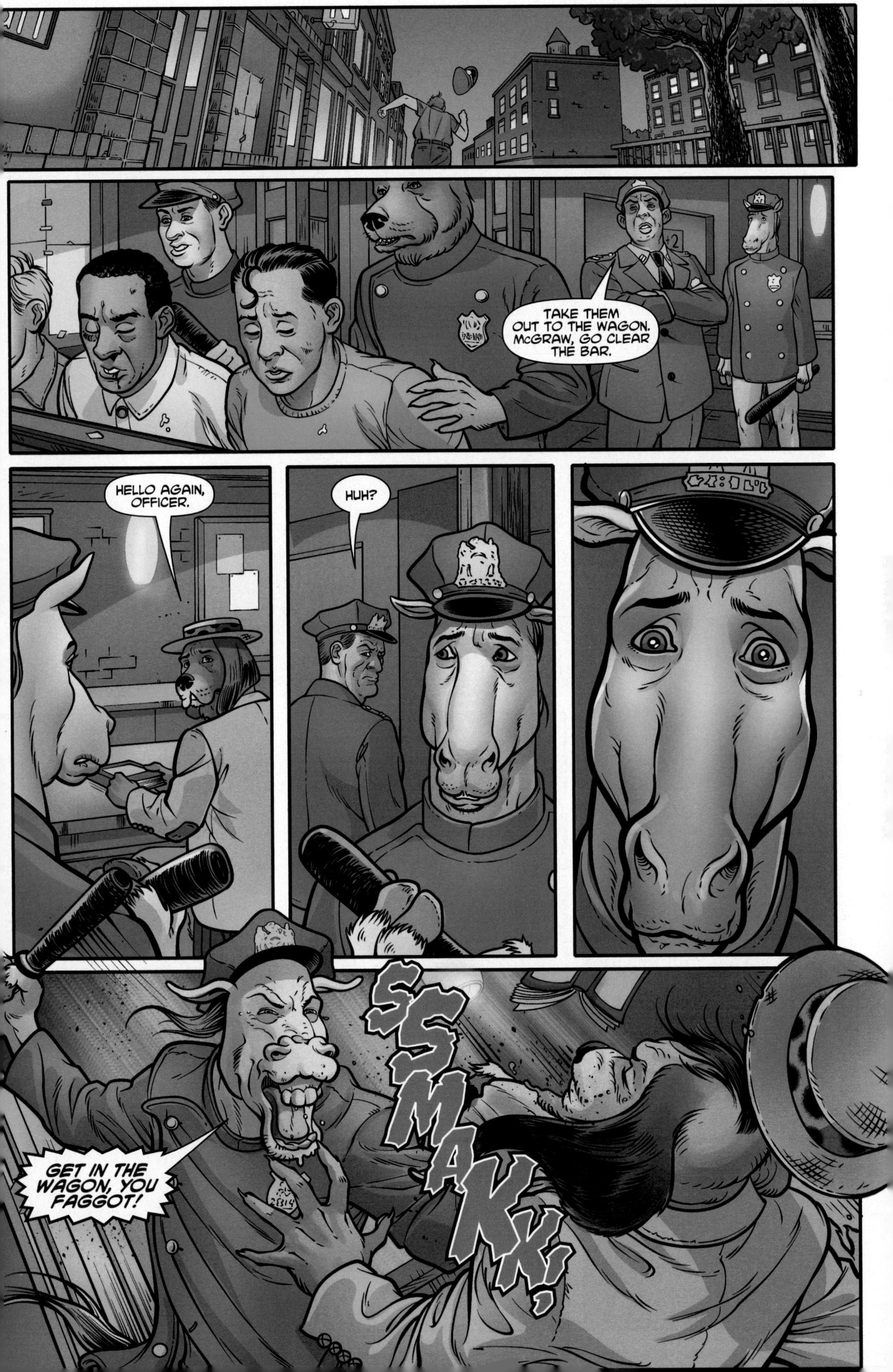
TAKE THEM OUT TO THE WAGON. McGRAW, GO CLEAR THE BAR.
HELLO AGAIN, OFFICER.
HUH?
SSMAKK!
GET IN THE WAGON, YOU FAGGOT!

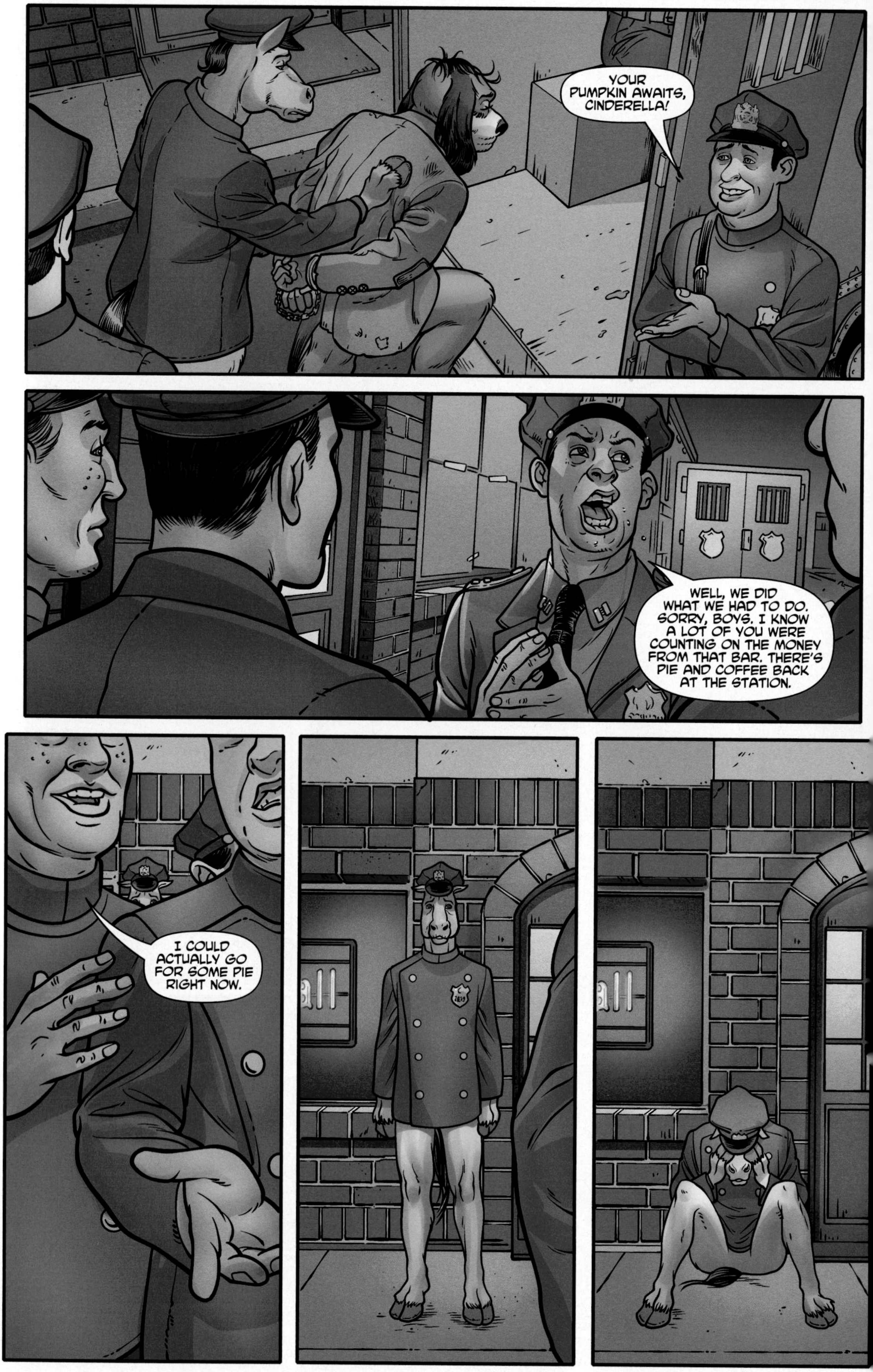
YOUR PUMPKIN AWAITS, CINDERELLA!
WELL, WE DID WHAT WE HAD TO DO. SORRY, BOYS. I KNOW A LOT OF YOU WERE COUNTING ON THE MONEY FROM THAT BAR. THERE'S PIE AND COFFEE BACK AT THE STATION.
I COULD ACTUALLY GO FOR SOME PIE RIGHT NOW.

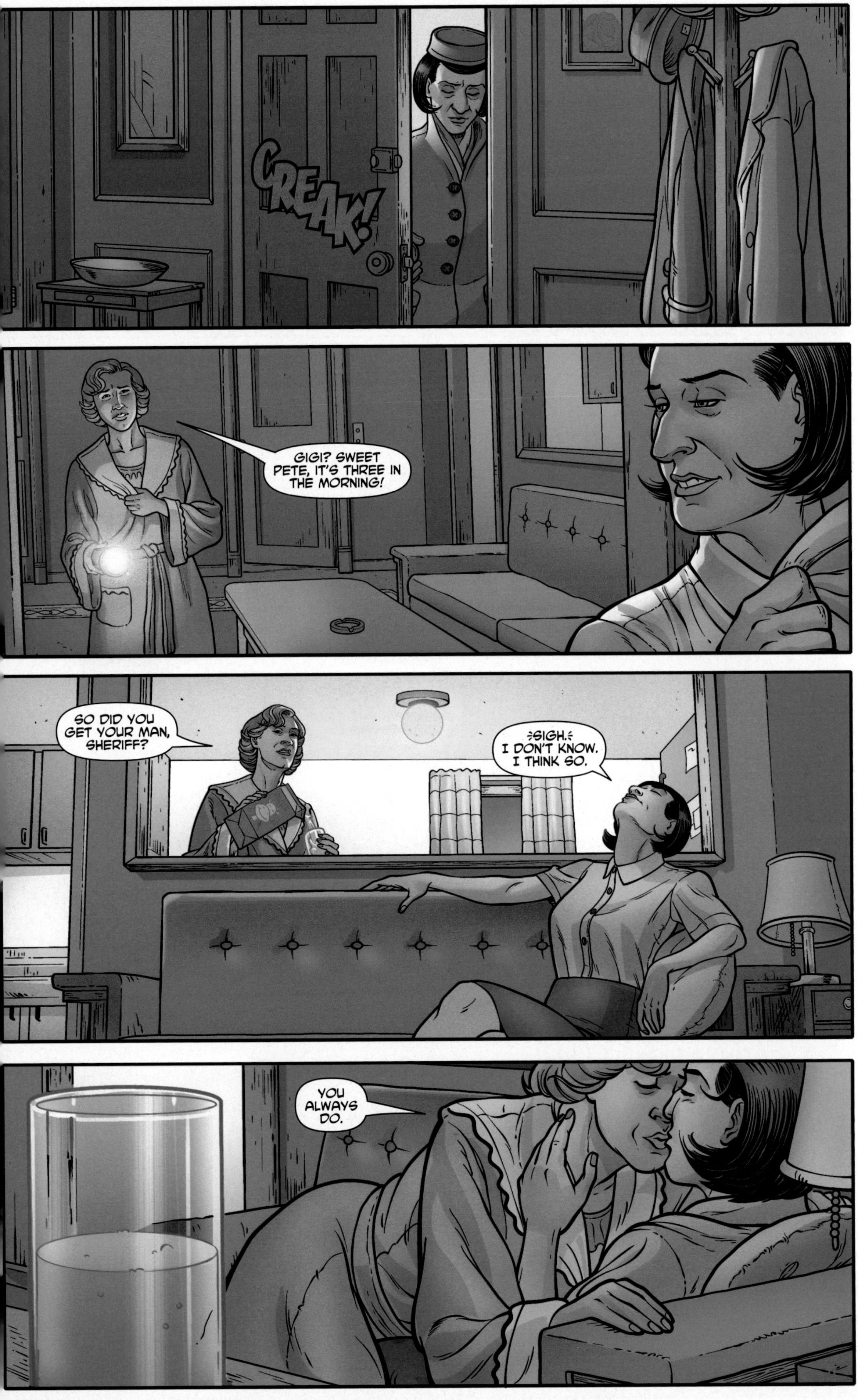
CREAK!
GIGI? SWEET PETE, IT'S THREE IN THE MORNING!
SO DID YOU GET YOUR MAN, SHERIFF?
SIGH. I DON'T KNOW. I THINK SO.
YOU ALWAYS DO.

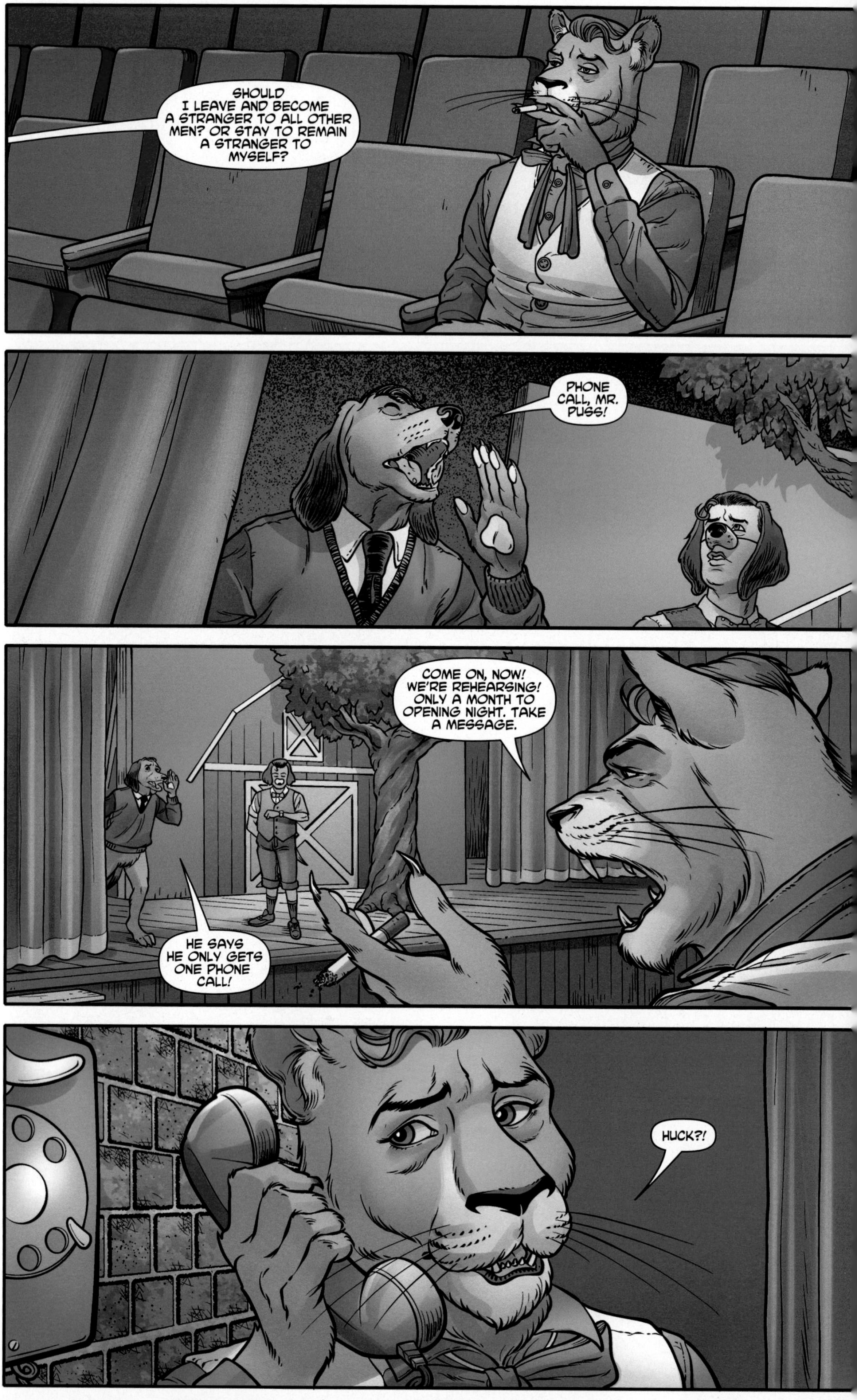
SHOULD I LEAVE AND BECOME A STRANGER TO ALL OTHER MEN? OR STAY TO REMAIN A STRANGER TO MYSELF?
PHONE CALL, MR. PUSS!
COME ON, NOW! WE'RE REHEARSING! ONLY A MONTH TO OPENING NIGHT. TAKE A MESSAGE.
HE SAYS HE ONLY GETS ONE PHONE CALL!
HUCK?!

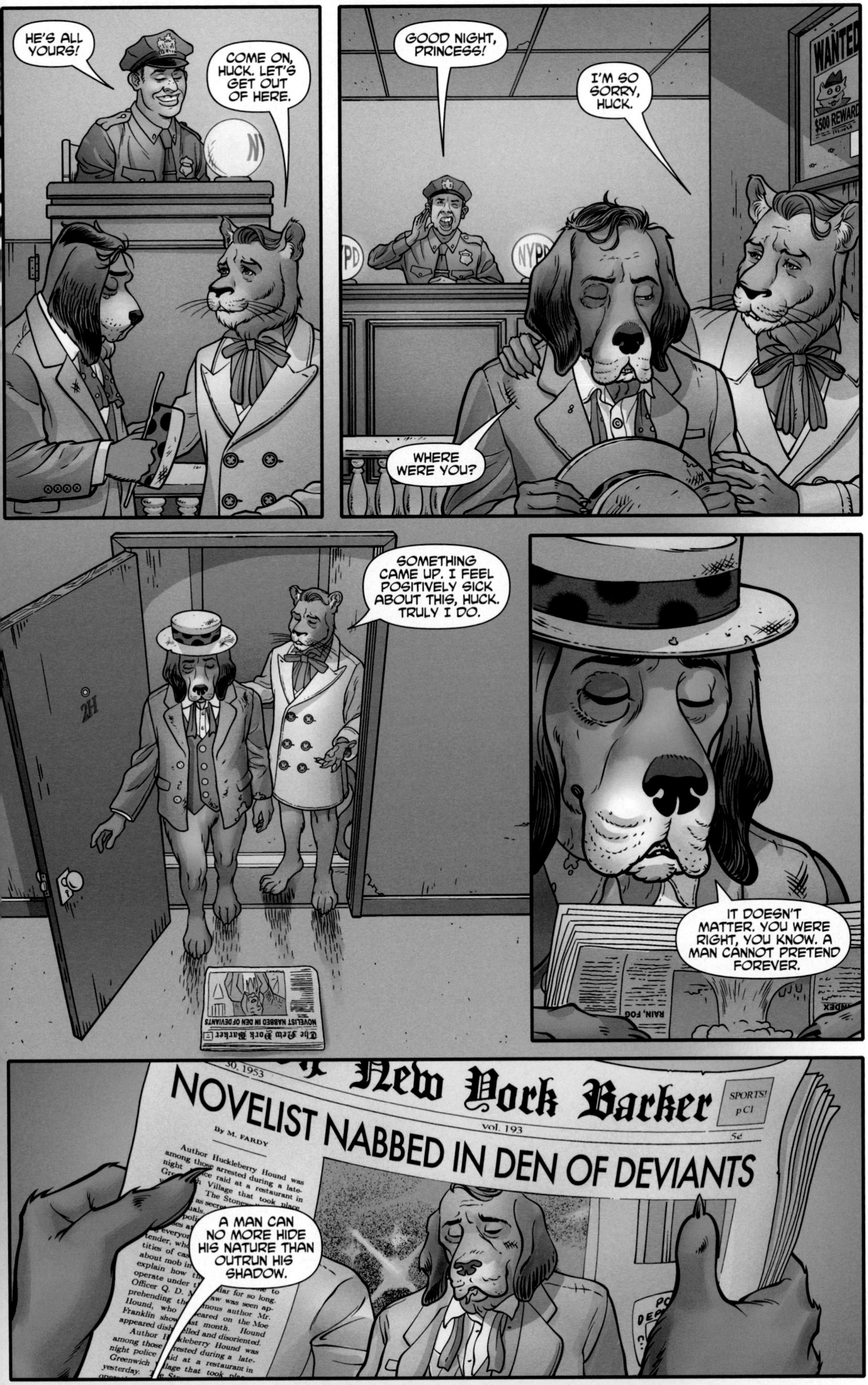
HE'S ALL YOURS!
COME ON, HUCK. LET'S GET OUT OF HERE.
WANTED
$500 REWARD
GOOD NIGHT, PRINCESS!
I'M SO SORRY, HUCK.
NYPD
WHERE WERE YOU?
SOMETHING CAME UP. I FEEL POSITIVELY SICK ABOUT THIS, HUCK. TRULY I DO.
2H
IT DOESN'T MATTER. YOU WERE RIGHT, YOU KNOW. A MAN CANNOT PRETEND FOREVER.
RAIN, FOG
New York Barker
SPORTS! pC1
vol. 193
5¢
NOVELIST NABBED IN DEN OF DEVIANTS
By M. FARDY
Author Huckleberry Hound was among those arrested during a late-night police raid at a restaurant in Greenwich Village that took place
A MAN CAN NO MORE HIDE HIS NATURE THAN OUTRUN HIS SHADOW.

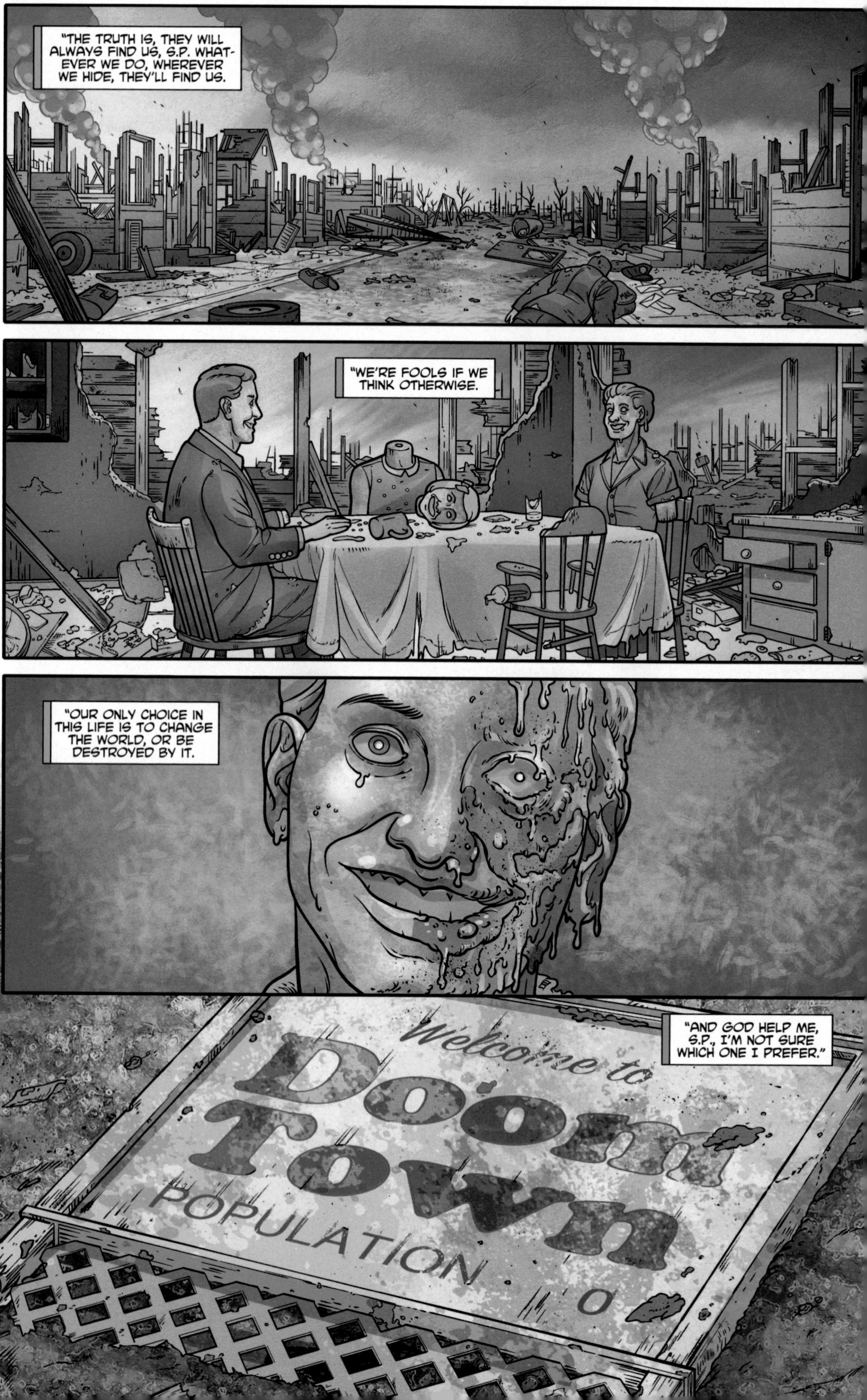
"THE TRUTH IS, THEY WILL ALWAYS FIND US, S.P. WHATEVER WE DO, WHEREVER WE HIDE, THEY'LL FIND US.
"WE'RE FOOLS IF WE THINK OTHERWISE.
"OUR ONLY CHOICE IN THIS LIFE IS TO CHANGE THE WORLD, OR BE DESTROYED BY IT.
"AND GOD HELP ME, S.P., I'M NOT SURE WHICH ONE I PREFER."
Welcome to
Doom Town
POPULATION
0

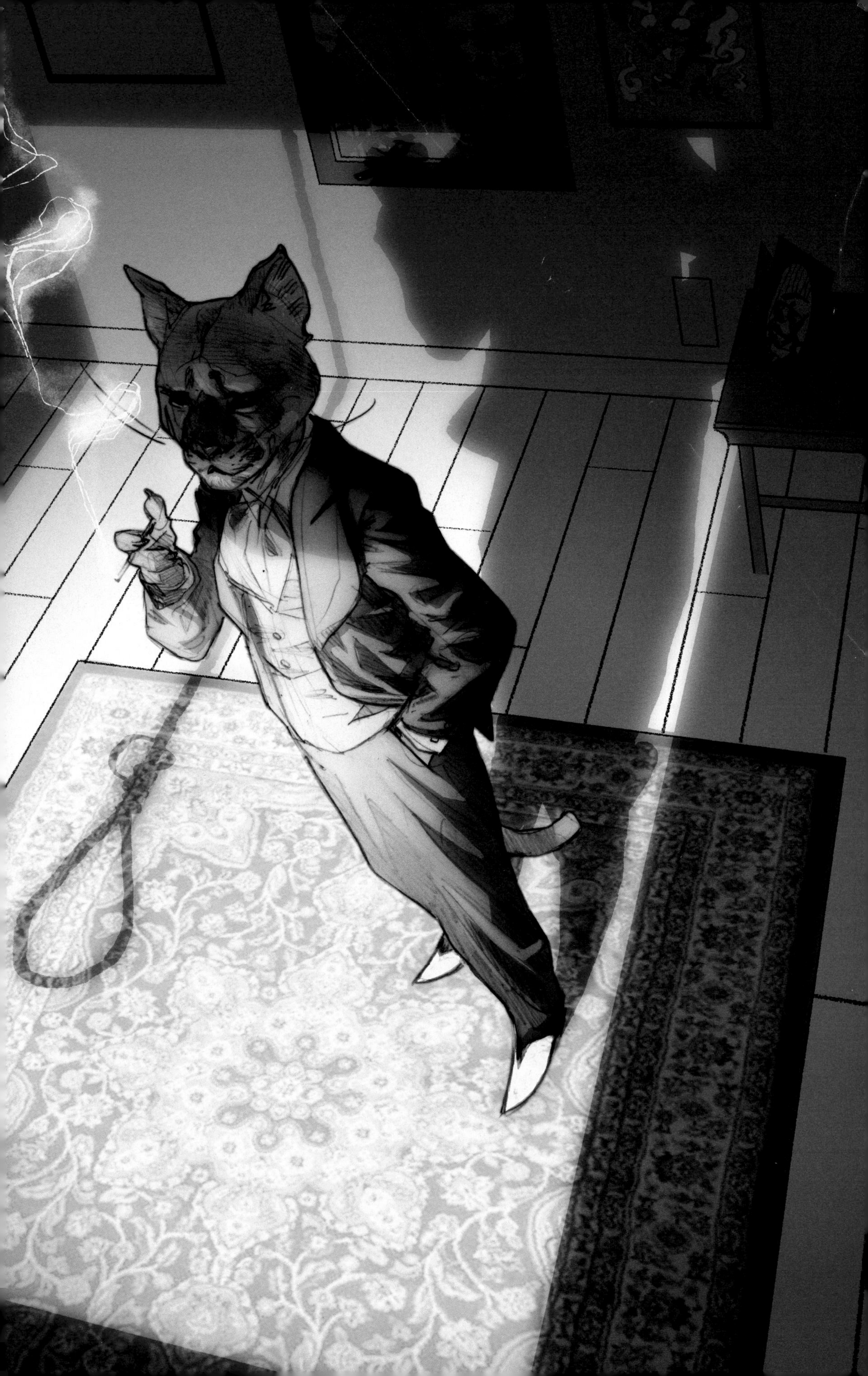

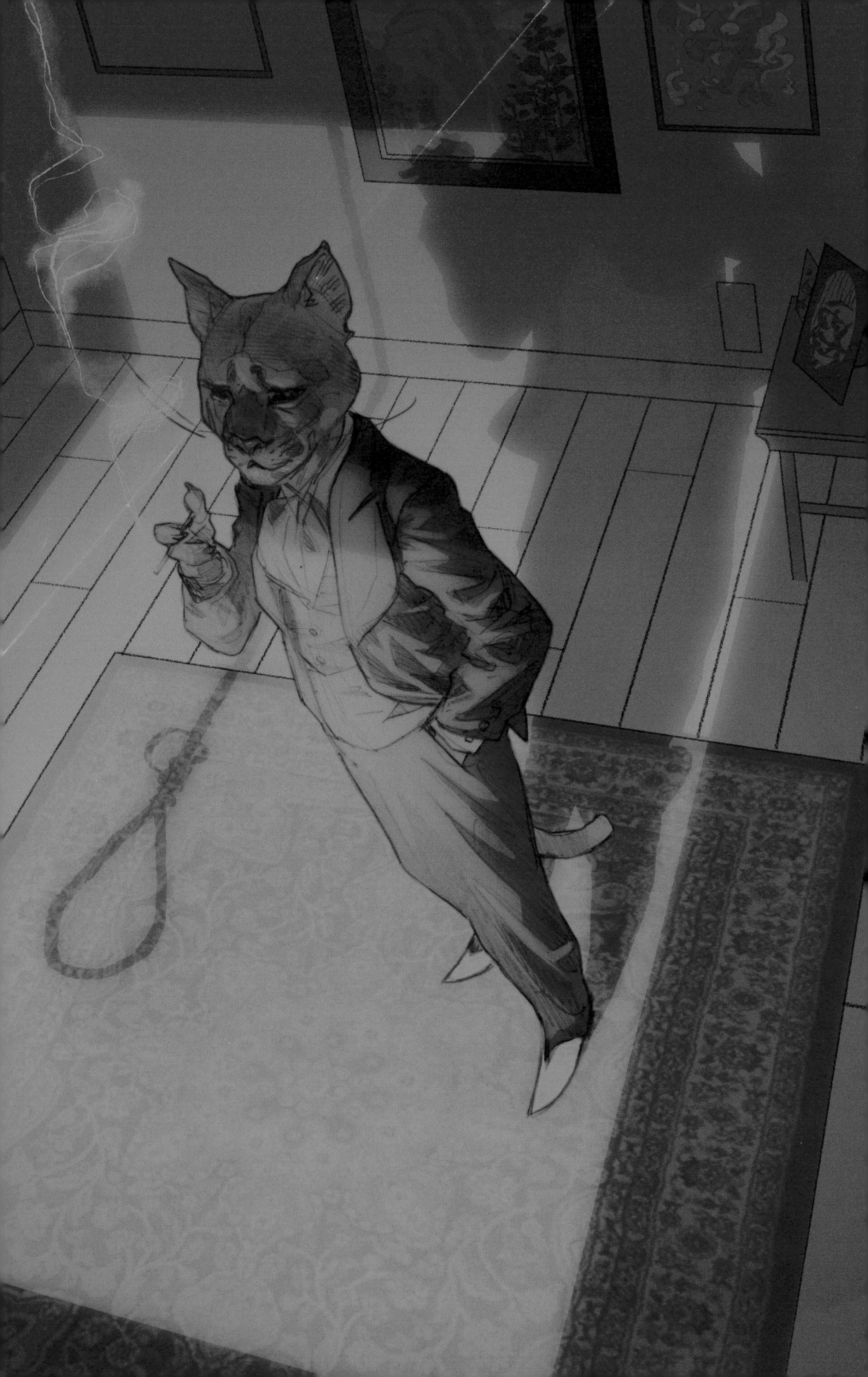

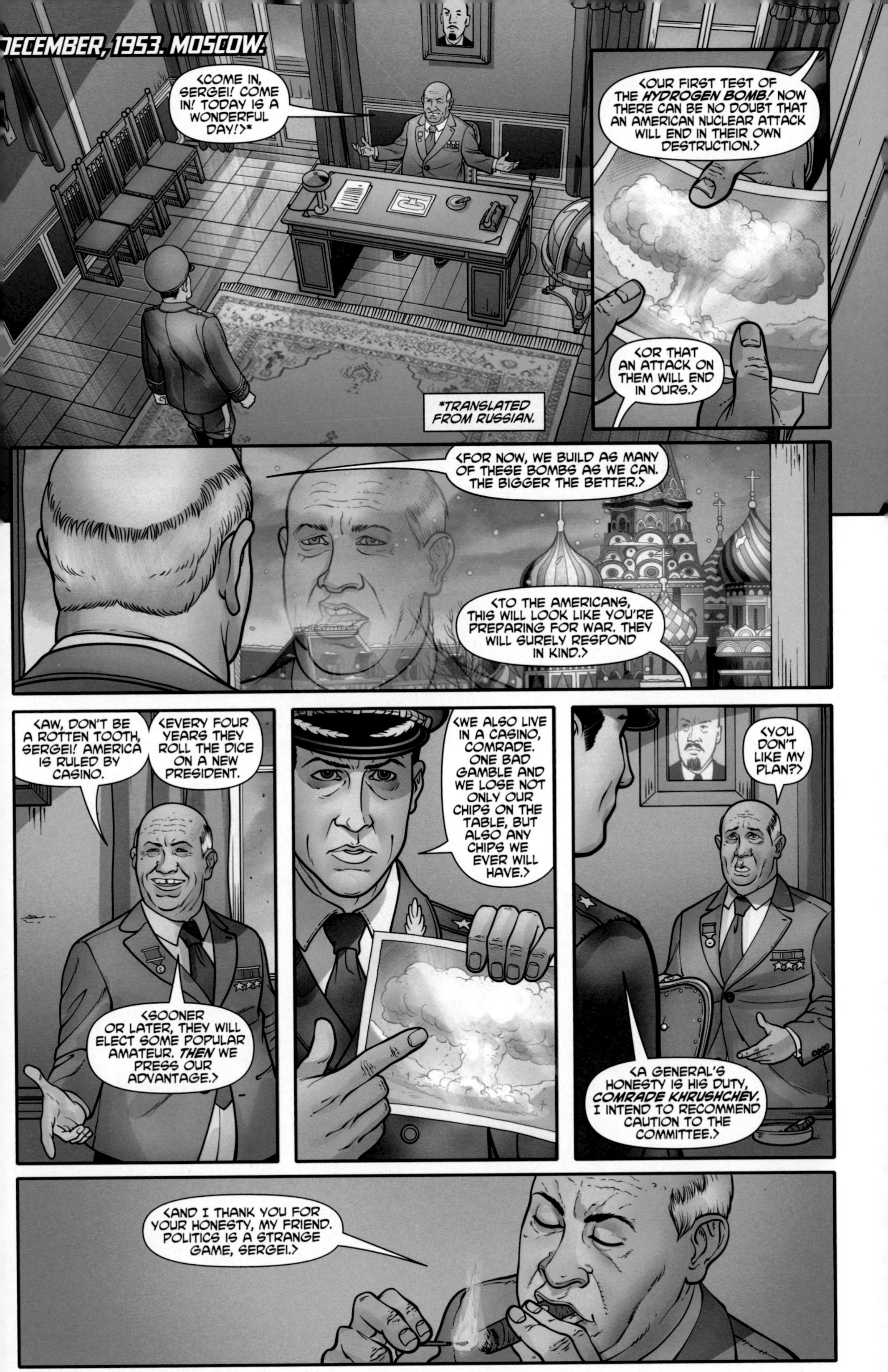
DECEMBER, 1953. MOSCOW.
<COME IN, SERGEI! COME IN! TODAY IS A WONDERFUL DAY!>*
*TRANSLATED FROM RUSSIAN.
<OUR FIRST TEST OF THE HYDROGEN BOMB! NOW THERE CAN BE NO DOUBT THAT AN AMERICAN NUCLEAR ATTACK WILL END IN THEIR OWN DESTRUCTION.>
<OR THAT AN ATTACK ON THEM WILL END IN OURS.>
<FOR NOW, WE BUILD AS MANY OF THESE BOMBS AS WE CAN. THE BIGGER THE BETTER.>
<TO THE AMERICANS, THIS WILL LOOK LIKE YOU'RE PREPARING FOR WAR. THEY WILL SURELY RESPOND IN KIND.>
<AW, DON'T BE A ROTTEN TOOTH, SERGEI! AMERICA IS RULED BY CASINO.
<EVERY FOUR YEARS THEY ROLL THE DICE ON A NEW PRESIDENT.
<SOONER OR LATER, THEY WILL ELECT SOME POPULAR AMATEUR. THEN WE PRESS OUR ADVANTAGE.>
<WE ALSO LIVE IN A CASINO, COMRADE. ONE BAD GAMBLE AND WE LOSE NOT ONLY OUR CHIPS ON THE TABLE, BUT ALSO ANY CHIPS WE EVER WILL HAVE.>
<YOU DON'T LIKE MY PLAN?>
<A GENERAL'S HONESTY IS HIS DUTY, COMRADE KHRUSHCHEV. I INTEND TO RECOMMEND CAUTION TO THE COMMITTEE.>
<AND I THANK YOU FOR YOUR HONESTY, MY FRIEND. POLITICS IS A STRANGE GAME, SERGEI.>

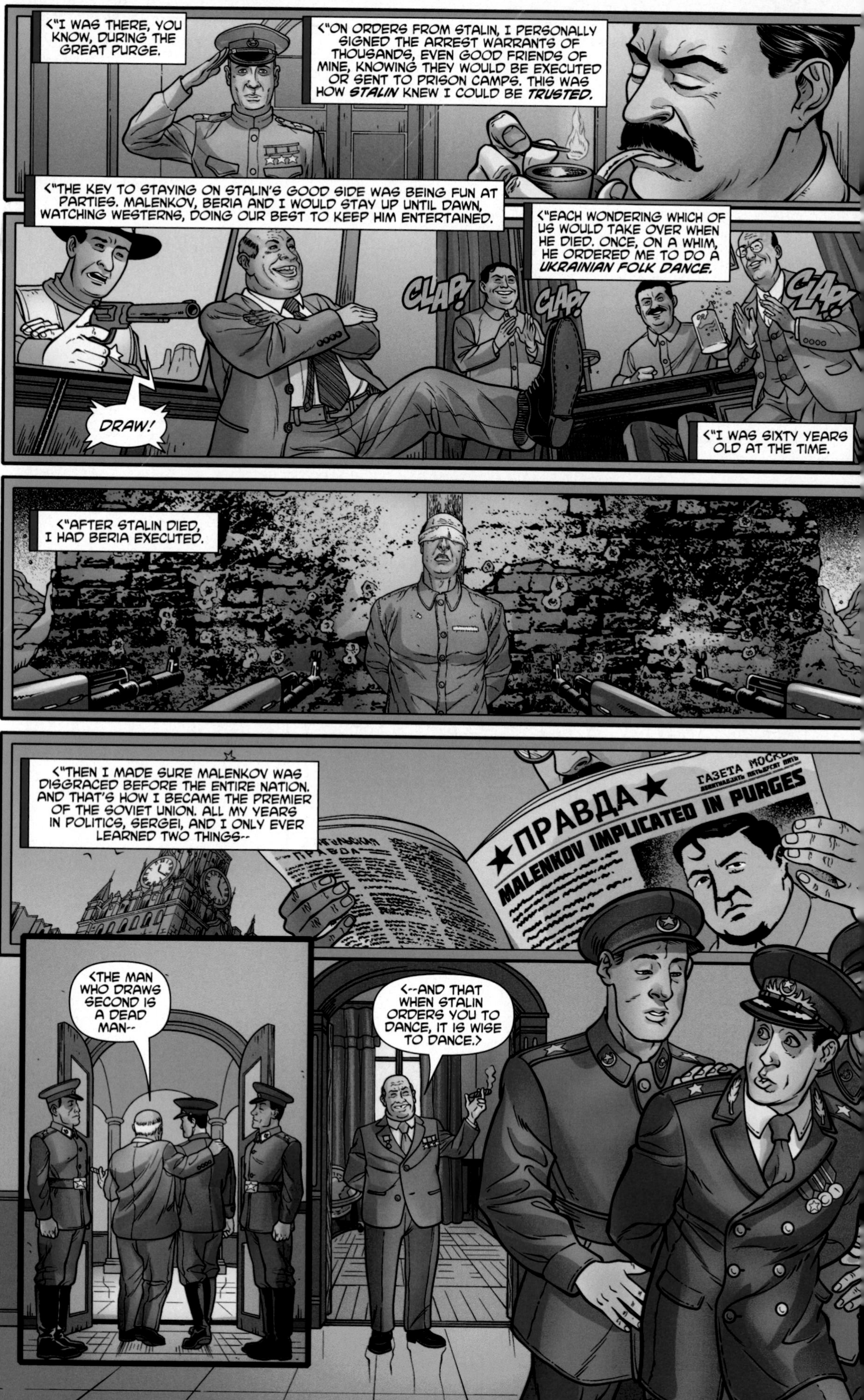

<"I WAS THERE, YOU KNOW, DURING THE GREAT PURGE.
<"ON ORDERS FROM STALIN, I PERSONALLY SIGNED THE ARREST WARRANTS OF THOUSANDS, EVEN GOOD FRIENDS OF MINE, KNOWING THEY WOULD BE EXECUTED OR SENT TO PRISON CAMPS. THIS WAS HOW *STALIN* KNEW I COULD BE *TRUSTED.*
<"THE KEY TO STAYING ON STALIN'S GOOD SIDE WAS BEING FUN AT PARTIES. MALENKOV, BERIA AND I WOULD STAY UP UNTIL DAWN, WATCHING WESTERNS, DOING OUR BEST TO KEEP HIM ENTERTAINED.
<"EACH WONDERING WHICH OF US WOULD TAKE OVER WHEN HE DIED. ONCE, ON A WHIM, HE ORDERED ME TO DO A *UKRAINIAN FOLK DANCE.*
DRAW!
CLAP!
CLAP!
CLAP!
<"I WAS SIXTY YEARS OLD AT THE TIME.
<"AFTER STALIN DIED, I HAD BERIA EXECUTED.
<"THEN I MADE SURE MALENKOV WAS DISGRACED BEFORE THE ENTIRE NATION. AND THAT'S HOW I BECAME THE PREMIER OF THE SOVIET UNION. ALL MY YEARS IN POLITICS, SERGEI, AND I ONLY EVER LEARNED TWO THINGS--
ГАЗЕТА МОСК
★ПРАВДА★
MALENKOV IMPLICATED IN PURGES
<THE MAN WHO DRAWS SECOND IS A DEAD MAN--
<--AND THAT WHEN STALIN ORDERS YOU TO DANCE, IT IS WISE TO DANCE.>

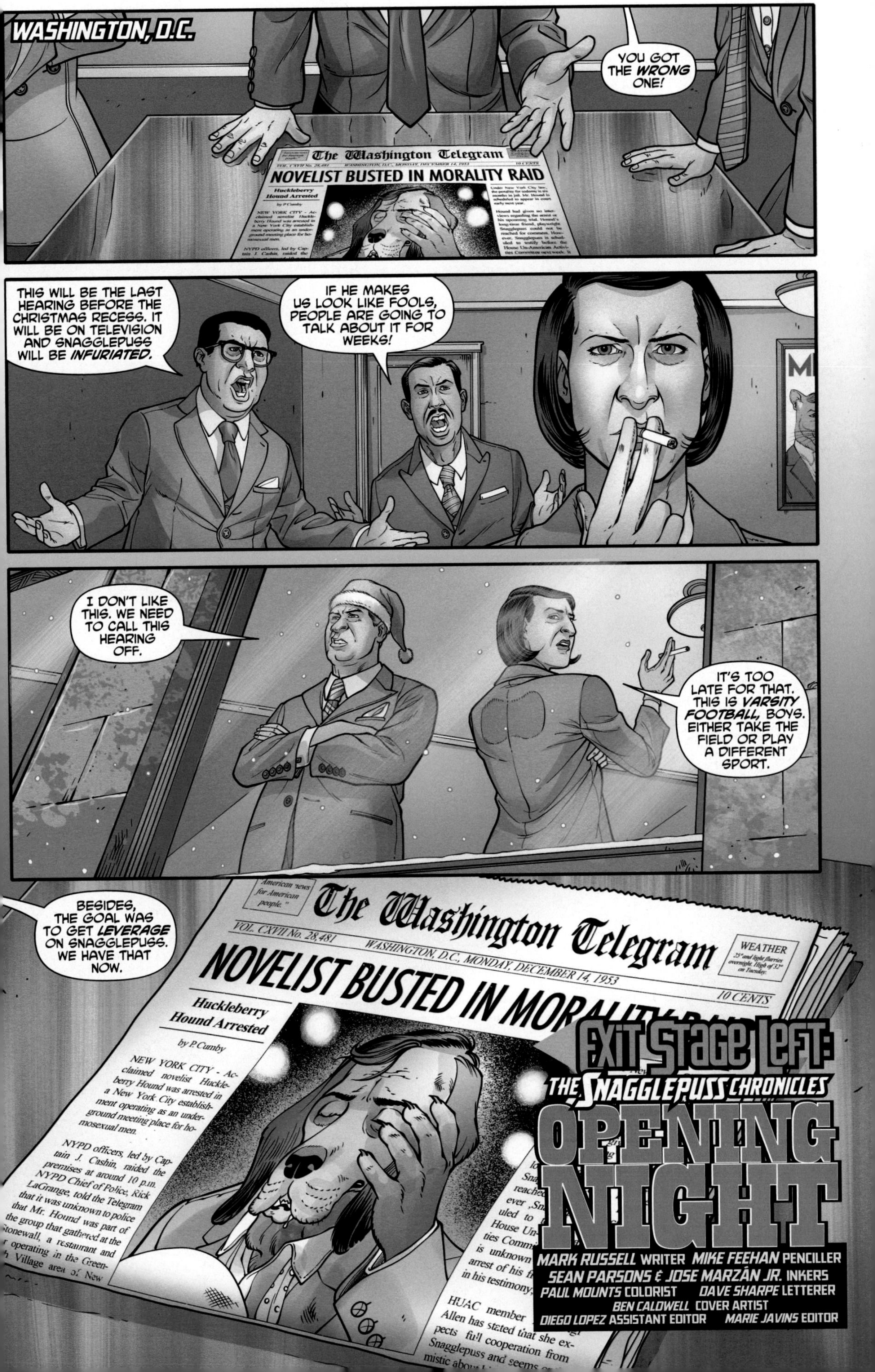
WASHINGTON, D.C.
YOU GOT THE WRONG ONE!
The Washington Telegram
NOVELIST BUSTED IN MORALITY RAID
THIS WILL BE THE LAST HEARING BEFORE THE CHRISTMAS RECESS. IT WILL BE ON TELEVISION AND SNAGGLEPUSS WILL BE INFURIATED.
IF HE MAKES US LOOK LIKE FOOLS, PEOPLE ARE GOING TO TALK ABOUT IT FOR WEEKS!
I DON'T LIKE THIS. WE NEED TO CALL THIS HEARING OFF.
IT'S TOO LATE FOR THAT. THIS IS VARSITY FOOTBALL, BOYS. EITHER TAKE THE FIELD OR PLAY A DIFFERENT SPORT.
BESIDES, THE GOAL WAS TO GET LEVERAGE ON SNAGGLEPUSS. WE HAVE THAT NOW.
"American news for American people."
The Washington Telegram
VOL. CXVII No. 28,481
WASHINGTON, D.C., MONDAY, DECEMBER 14, 1953
WEATHER
25° and light flurries overnight. High of 32° on Tuesday.
10 CENTS
NOVELIST BUSTED IN MORALITY RAID
Huckleberry Hound Arrested
by P. Cumby
NEW YORK CITY - Acclaimed novelist Huckleberry Hound was arrested in a New York City establishment operating as an underground meeting place for homosexual men.
NYPD officers, led by Captain J. Cashin, raided the premises at around 10 p.m. NYPD Chief of Police, Rick LaGrange, told the Telegram that it was unknown to police that Mr. Hound was part of the group that gathered at the Stonewall, a restaurant and bar operating in the Greenwich Village area of New
HUAC member Allen has stated that she expects full cooperation from Snagglepuss and seems op-timistic about
EXIT STAGE LEFT: THE SNAGGLEPUSS CHRONICLES
OPENING NIGHT
MARK RUSSELL WRITER MIKE FEEHAN PENCILLER
SEAN PARSONS & JOSE MARZÁN JR. INKERS
PAUL MOUNTS COLORIST DAVE SHARPE LETTERER
BEN CALDWELL COVER ARTIST
DIEGO LOPEZ ASSISTANT EDITOR MARIE JAVINS EDITOR

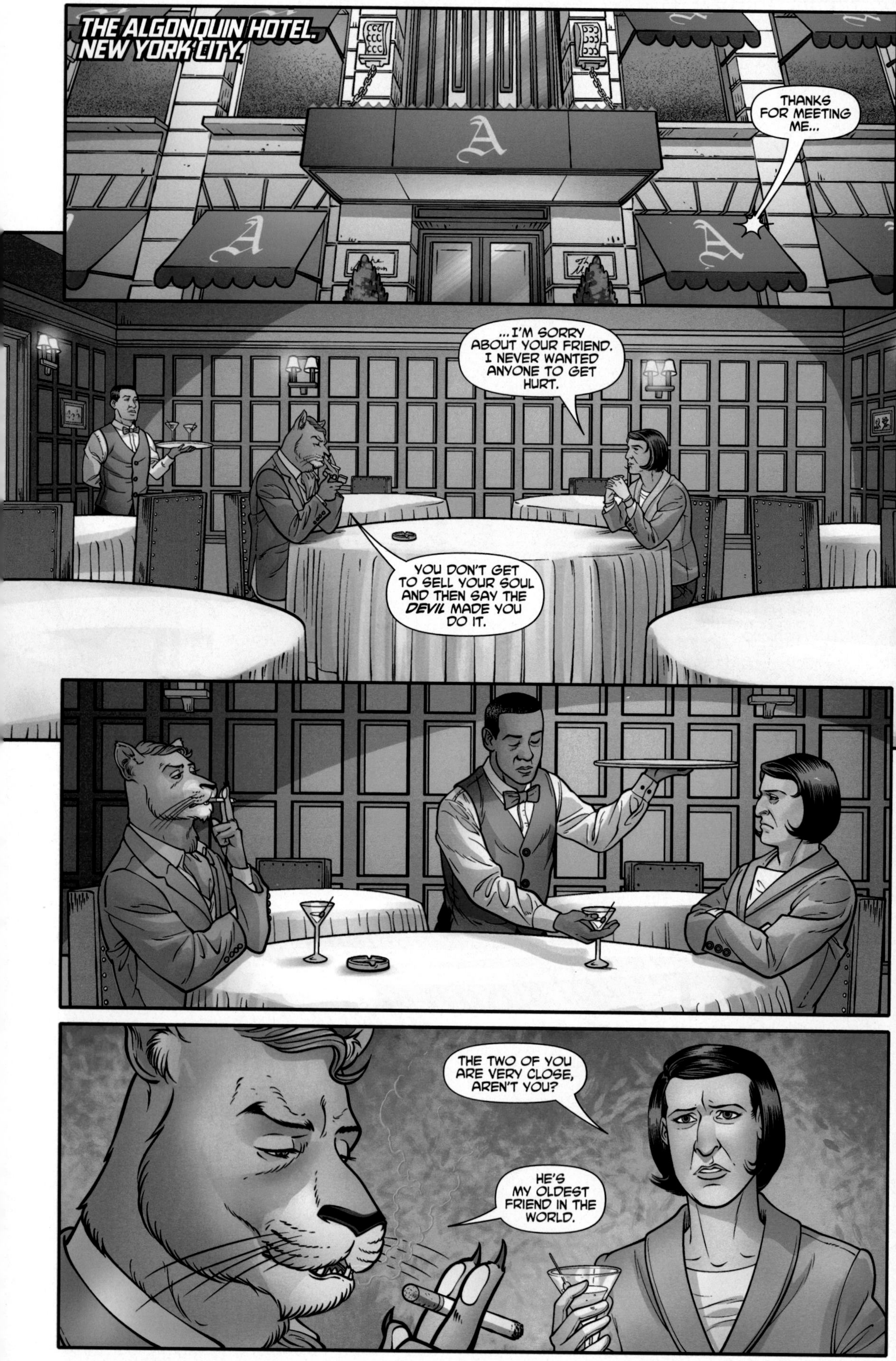
THE ALGONQUIN HOTEL. NEW YORK CITY.
THANKS FOR MEETING ME...
...I'M SORRY ABOUT YOUR FRIEND. I NEVER WANTED ANYONE TO GET HURT.
YOU DON'T GET TO SELL YOUR SOUL AND THEN SAY THE *DEVIL* MADE YOU DO IT.
THE TWO OF YOU ARE VERY CLOSE, AREN'T YOU?
HE'S MY OLDEST FRIEND IN THE WORLD.

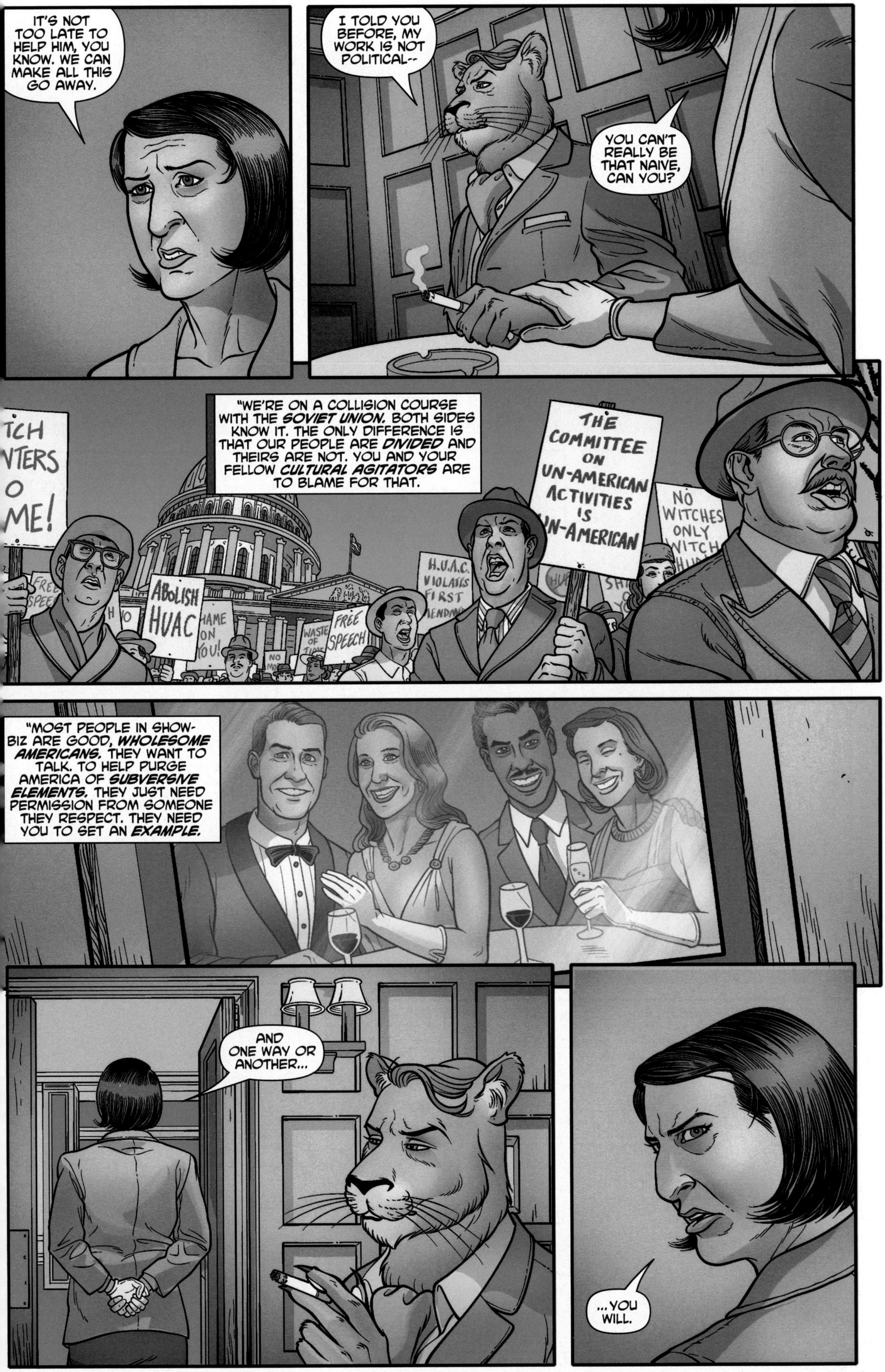
IT'S NOT TOO LATE TO HELP HIM, YOU KNOW. WE CAN MAKE ALL THIS GO AWAY.
I TOLD YOU BEFORE, MY WORK IS NOT POLITICAL--
YOU CAN'T REALLY BE THAT NAIVE, CAN YOU?
"WE'RE ON A COLLISION COURSE WITH THE SOVIET UNION. BOTH SIDES KNOW IT. THE ONLY DIFFERENCE IS THAT OUR PEOPLE ARE DIVIDED AND THEIRS ARE NOT. YOU AND YOUR FELLOW CULTURAL AGITATORS ARE TO BLAME FOR THAT.
THE COMMITTEE ON UN-AMERICAN ACTIVITIES IS UN-AMERICAN
ABOLISH HUAC
FREE SPEECH
"MOST PEOPLE IN SHOW-BIZ ARE GOOD, WHOLESOME AMERICANS. THEY WANT TO TALK. TO HELP PURGE AMERICA OF SUBVERSIVE ELEMENTS. THEY JUST NEED PERMISSION FROM SOMEONE THEY RESPECT. THEY NEED YOU TO SET AN EXAMPLE.
AND ONE WAY OR ANOTHER...
...YOU WILL.

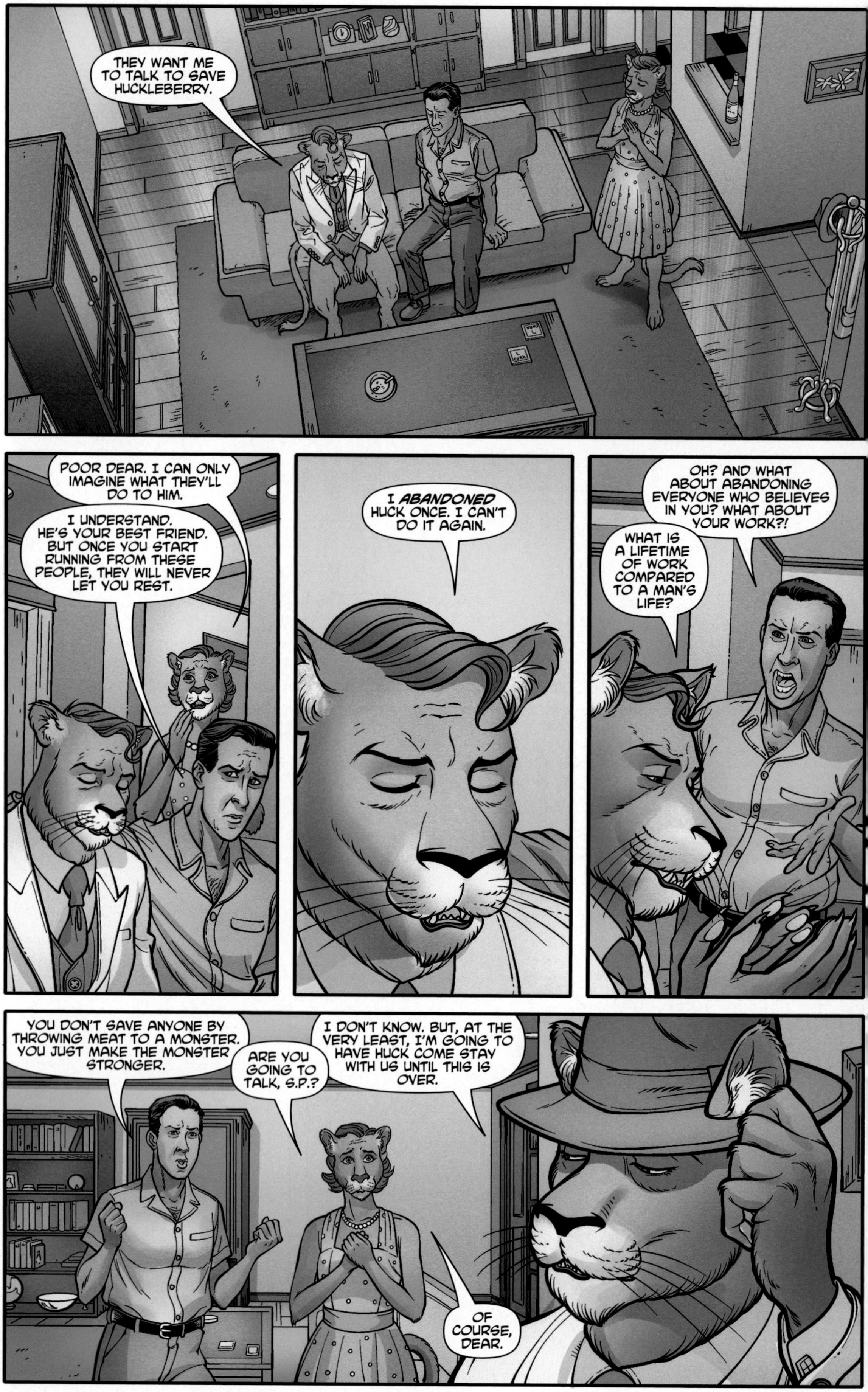
THEY WANT ME TO TALK TO SAVE HUCKLEBERRY.
POOR DEAR. I CAN ONLY IMAGINE WHAT THEY'LL DO TO HIM.
I UNDERSTAND. HE'S YOUR BEST FRIEND. BUT ONCE YOU START RUNNING FROM THESE PEOPLE, THEY WILL NEVER LET YOU REST.
I *ABANDONED* HUCK ONCE. I CAN'T DO IT AGAIN.
OH? AND WHAT ABOUT ABANDONING EVERYONE WHO BELIEVES IN YOU? WHAT ABOUT YOUR WORK?!
WHAT IS A LIFETIME OF WORK COMPARED TO A MAN'S LIFE?
YOU DON'T SAVE ANYONE BY THROWING MEAT TO A MONSTER. YOU JUST MAKE THE MONSTER STRONGER.
ARE YOU GOING TO TALK, S.P.?
I DON'T KNOW. BUT, AT THE VERY LEAST, I'M GOING TO HAVE HUCK COME STAY WITH US UNTIL THIS IS OVER.
OF COURSE, DEAR.

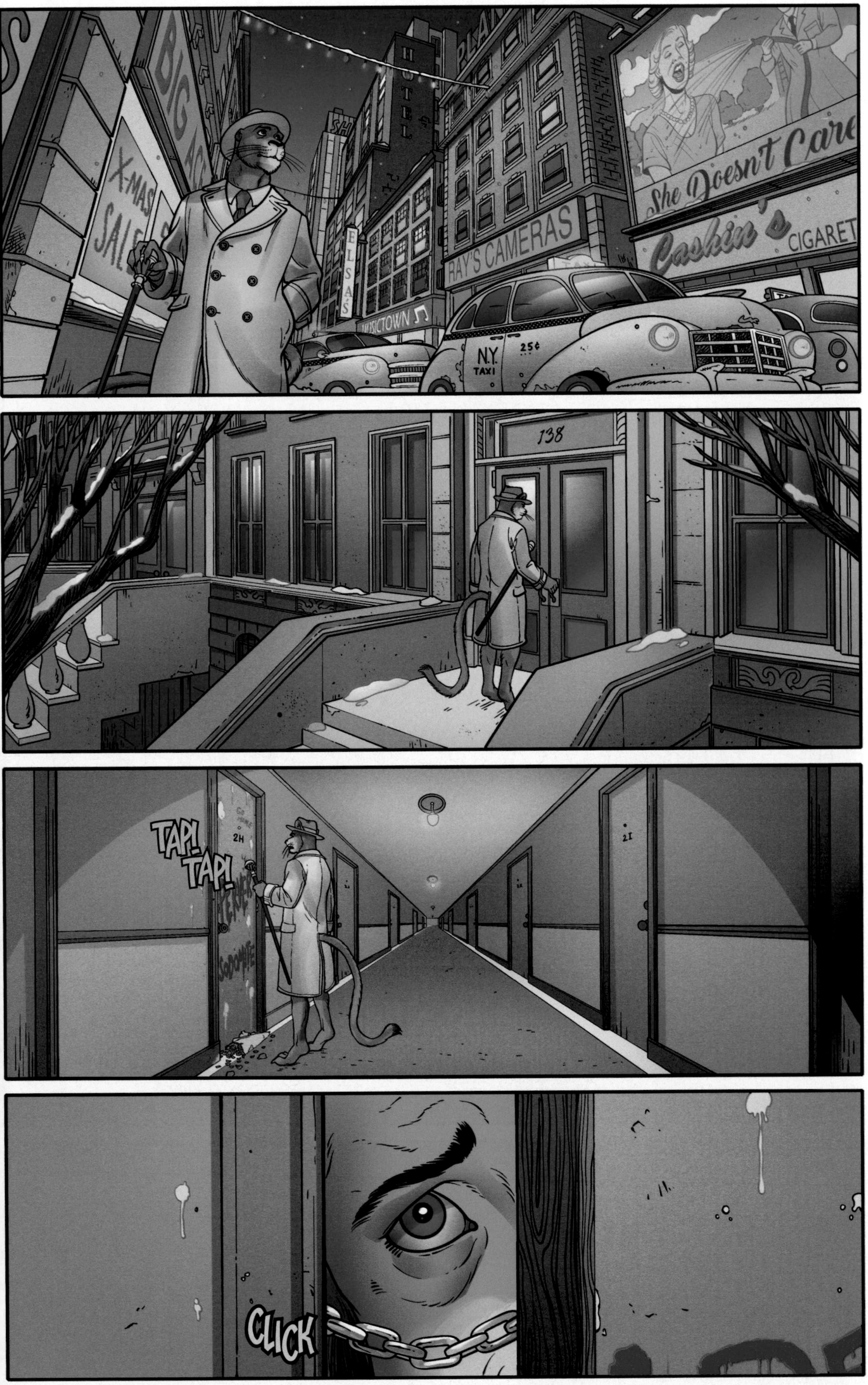

X-MAS
HOTEL
ELSA'S
MUSICTOWN
RAY'S CAMERAS
She Doesn't Care
N.Y.
TAXI
25¢
138
TAP!
TAP!
2H
2I
CLICK

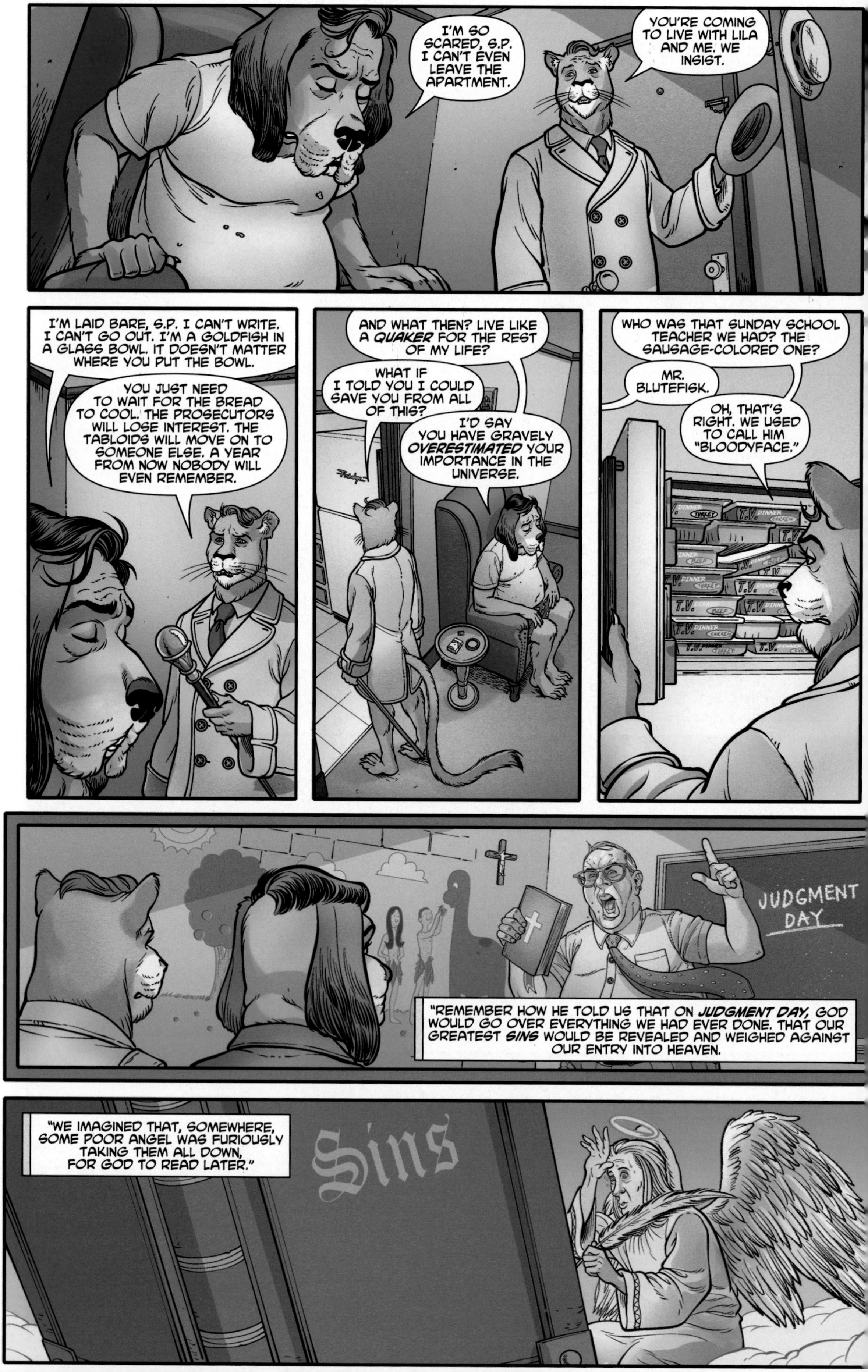
I'M SO SCARED, S.P. I CAN'T EVEN LEAVE THE APARTMENT.
YOU'RE COMING TO LIVE WITH LILA AND ME. WE INSIST.
I'M LAID BARE, S.P. I CAN'T WRITE. I CAN'T GO OUT. I'M A GOLDFISH IN A GLASS BOWL. IT DOESN'T MATTER WHERE YOU PUT THE BOWL.
YOU JUST NEED TO WAIT FOR THE BREAD TO COOL. THE PROSECUTORS WILL LOSE INTEREST. THE TABLOIDS WILL MOVE ON TO SOMEONE ELSE. A YEAR FROM NOW NOBODY WILL EVEN REMEMBER.
AND WHAT THEN? LIVE LIKE A *QUAKER* FOR THE REST OF MY LIFE?
WHAT IF I TOLD YOU I COULD SAVE YOU FROM ALL OF THIS?
I'D SAY YOU HAVE GRAVELY *OVERESTIMATED* YOUR IMPORTANCE IN THE UNIVERSE.
WHO WAS THAT SUNDAY SCHOOL TEACHER WE HAD? THE SAUSAGE-COLORED ONE?
MR. BLUTEFISK.
OH, THAT'S RIGHT. WE USED TO CALL HIM "BLOODYFACE."
JUDGMENT DAY
"REMEMBER HOW HE TOLD US THAT ON *JUDGMENT DAY,* GOD WOULD GO OVER EVERYTHING WE HAD EVER DONE. THAT OUR GREATEST *SINS* WOULD BE REVEALED AND WEIGHED AGAINST OUR ENTRY INTO HEAVEN.
"WE IMAGINED THAT, SOMEWHERE, SOME POOR ANGEL WAS FURIOUSLY TAKING THEM ALL DOWN, FOR GOD TO READ LATER."
Sins

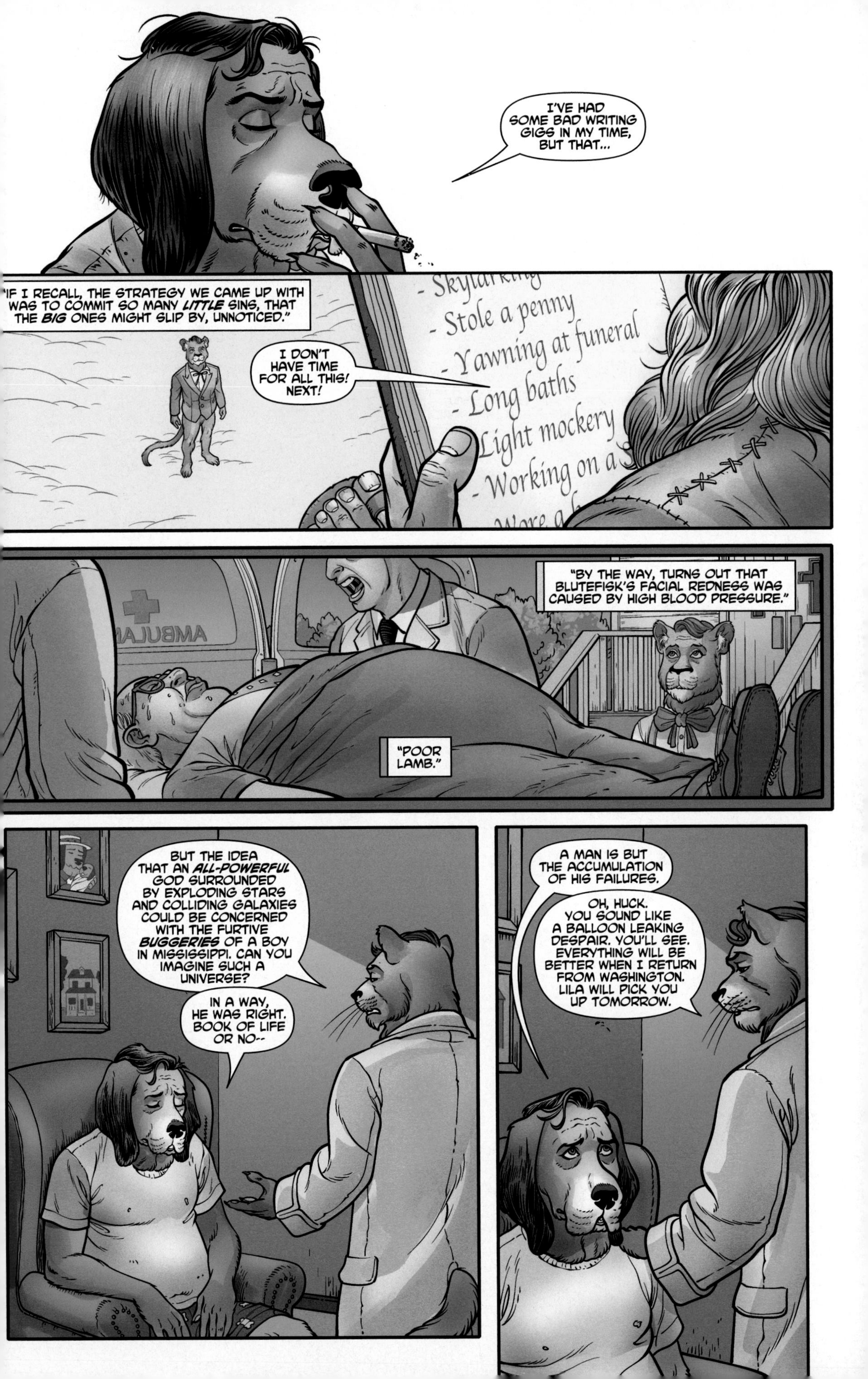
I'VE HAD SOME BAD WRITING GIGS IN MY TIME, BUT THAT...
"IF I RECALL, THE STRATEGY WE CAME UP WITH WAS TO COMMIT SO MANY *LITTLE* SINS, THAT THE *BIG* ONES MIGHT SLIP BY, UNNOTICED."
- Skylarking
- Stole a penny
- Yawning at funeral
- Long baths
- Light mockery
- Working on a
I DON'T HAVE TIME FOR ALL THIS! NEXT!
"BY THE WAY, TURNS OUT THAT BLUTEFISK'S FACIAL REDNESS WAS CAUSED BY HIGH BLOOD PRESSURE."
AMBULA
"POOR LAMB."
BUT THE IDEA THAT AN ***ALL-POWERFUL*** GOD SURROUNDED BY EXPLODING STARS AND COLLIDING GALAXIES COULD BE CONCERNED WITH THE FURTIVE ***BUGGERIES*** OF A BOY IN MISSISSIPPI. CAN YOU IMAGINE SUCH A UNIVERSE?
IN A WAY, HE WAS RIGHT. BOOK OF LIFE OR NO--
A MAN IS BUT THE ACCUMULATION OF HIS FAILURES.
OH, HUCK. YOU SOUND LIKE A BALLOON LEAKING DESPAIR. YOU'LL SEE. EVERYTHING WILL BE BETTER WHEN I RETURN FROM WASHINGTON. LILA WILL PICK YOU UP TOMORROW.

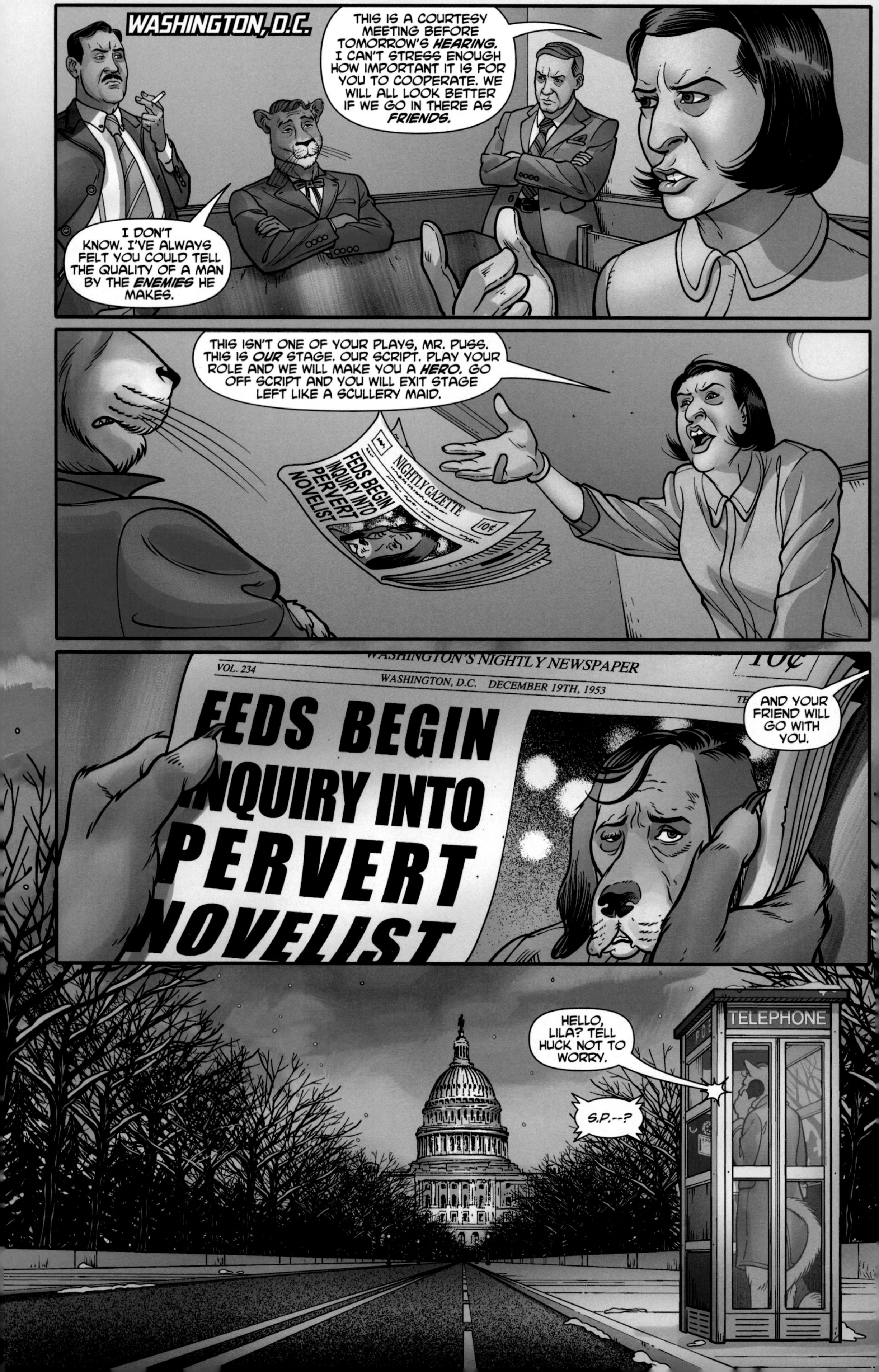
WASHINGTON, D.C.
THIS IS A COURTESY MEETING BEFORE TOMORROW'S HEARING. I CAN'T STRESS ENOUGH HOW IMPORTANT IT IS FOR YOU TO COOPERATE. WE WILL ALL LOOK BETTER IF WE GO IN THERE AS FRIENDS.
I DON'T KNOW. I'VE ALWAYS FELT YOU COULD TELL THE QUALITY OF A MAN BY THE ENEMIES HE MAKES.
THIS ISN'T ONE OF YOUR PLAYS, MR. PUSS. THIS IS OUR STAGE. OUR SCRIPT. PLAY YOUR ROLE AND WE WILL MAKE YOU A HERO. GO OFF SCRIPT AND YOU WILL EXIT STAGE LEFT LIKE A SCULLERY MAID.
NIGHTLY GAZETTE
FEDS BEGIN INQUIRY INTO PERVERT NOVELIST
10¢
WASHINGTON'S NIGHTLY NEWSPAPER
VOL. 234
WASHINGTON, D.C. DECEMBER 19TH, 1953
10¢
FEDS BEGIN INQUIRY INTO PERVERT NOVELIST
AND YOUR FRIEND WILL GO WITH YOU.
TELEPHONE
HELLO, LILA? TELL HUCK NOT TO WORRY.
S.P.--?

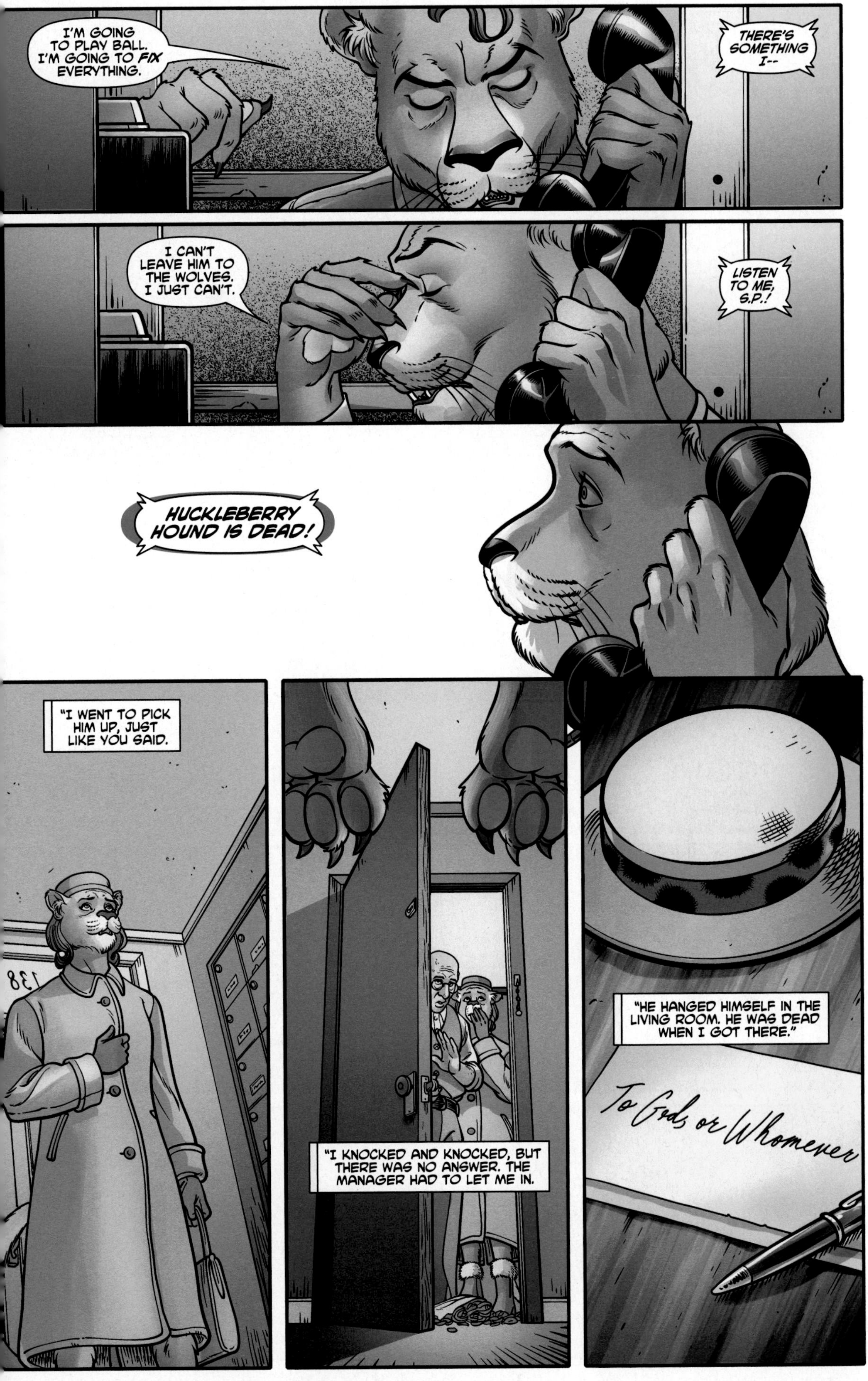

I'M GOING TO PLAY BALL. I'M GOING TO FIX EVERYTHING.
THERE'S SOMETHING I--
I CAN'T LEAVE HIM TO THE WOLVES. I JUST CAN'T.
LISTEN TO ME, S.P.!
HUCKLEBERRY HOUND IS DEAD!
"I WENT TO PICK HIM UP, JUST LIKE YOU SAID.
"I KNOCKED AND KNOCKED, BUT THERE WAS NO ANSWER. THE MANAGER HAD TO LET ME IN.
"HE HANGED HIMSELF IN THE LIVING ROOM. HE WAS DEAD WHEN I GOT THERE."
To Gods, or Whomever

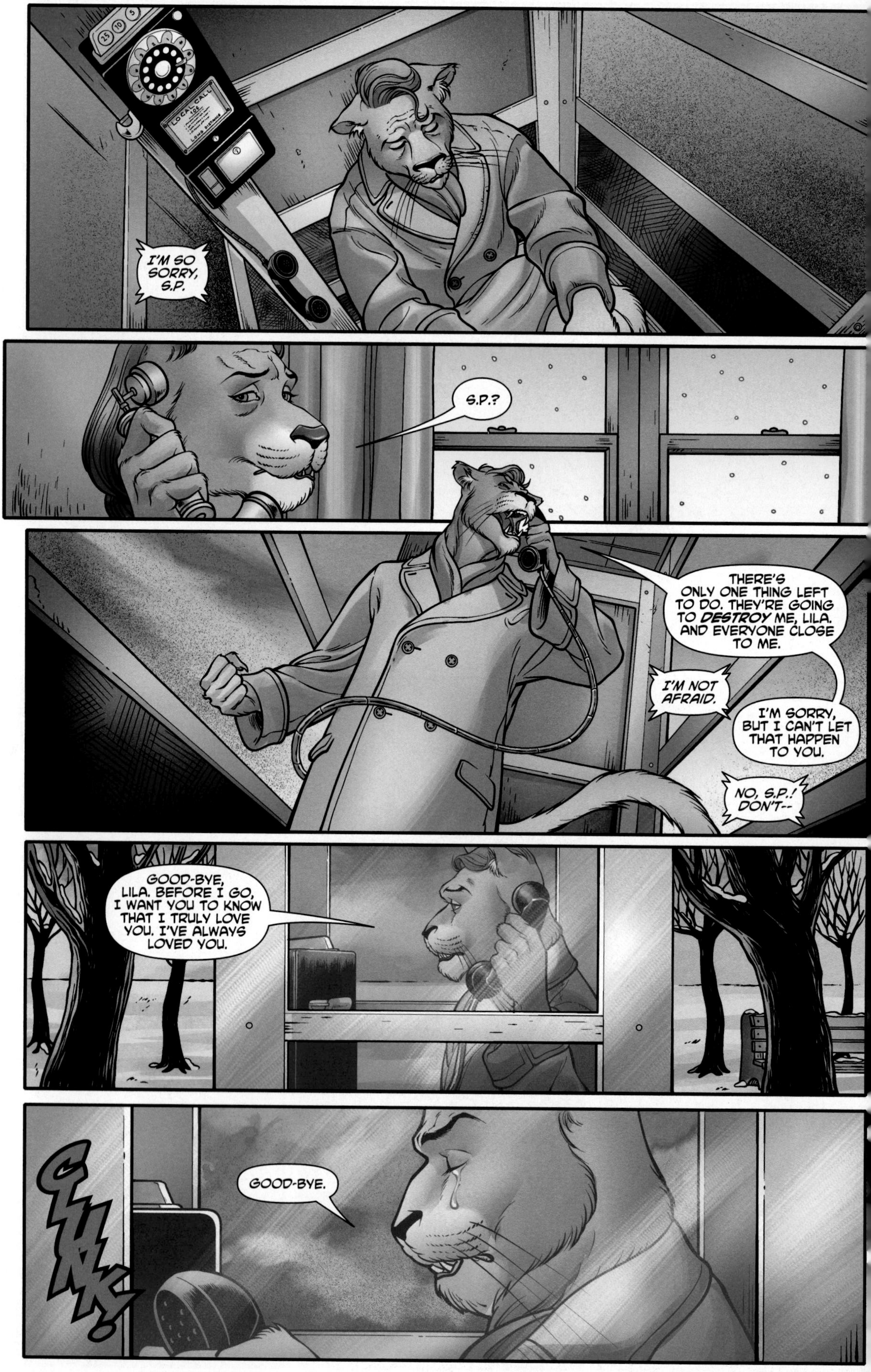
I'M SO SORRY, S.P.
S.P.?
THERE'S ONLY ONE THING LEFT TO DO. THEY'RE GOING TO *DESTROY* ME, LILA. AND EVERYONE CLOSE TO ME.
I'M NOT AFRAID.
I'M SORRY, BUT I CAN'T LET THAT HAPPEN TO YOU.
NO, S.P.! DON'T--
GOOD-BYE, LILA. BEFORE I GO, I WANT YOU TO KNOW THAT I TRULY LOVE YOU. I'VE ALWAYS LOVED YOU.
CLUNK!
GOOD-BYE.

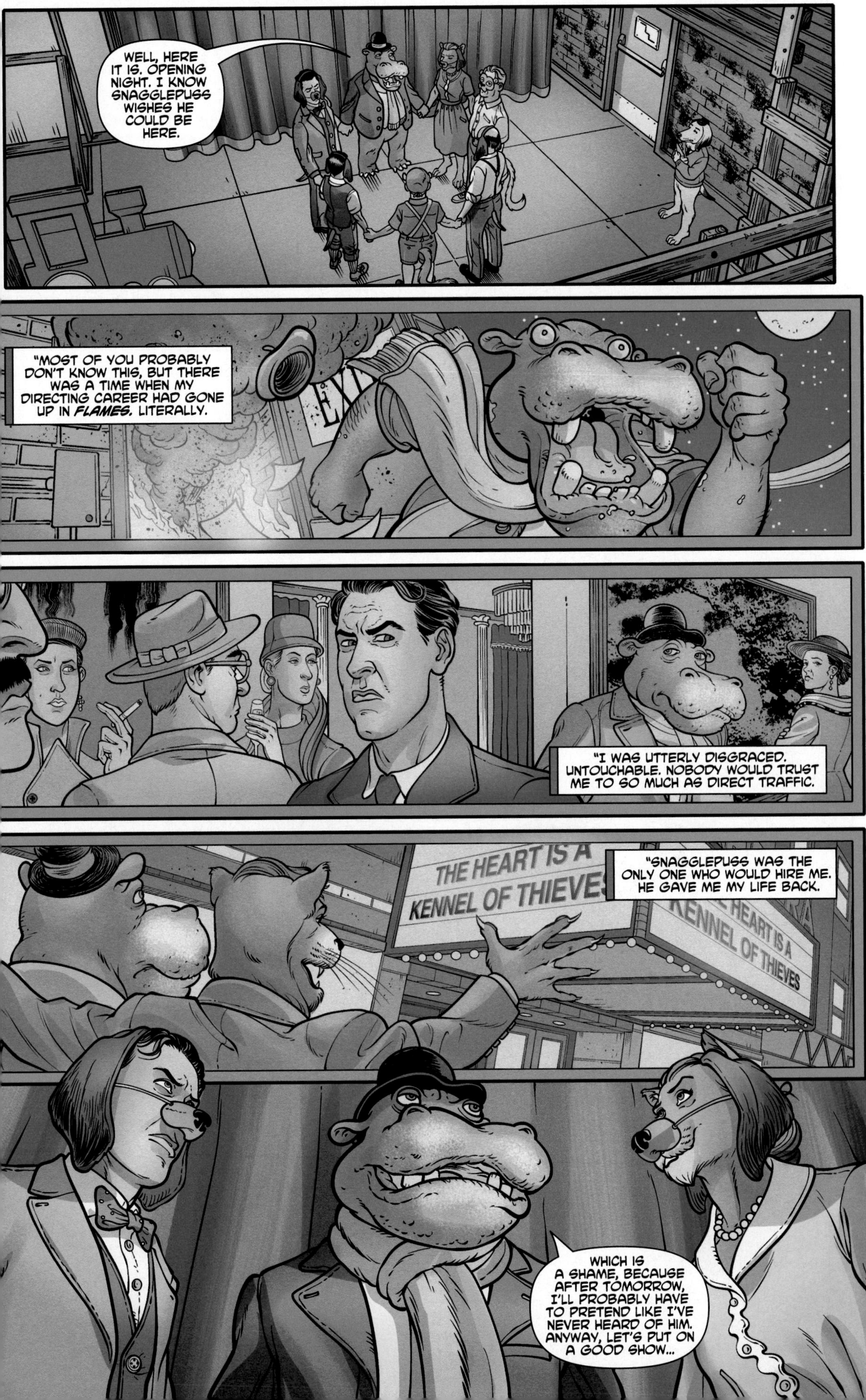
WELL, HERE IT IS. OPENING NIGHT. I KNOW SNAGGLEPUSS WISHES HE COULD BE HERE.
"MOST OF YOU PROBABLY DON'T KNOW THIS, BUT THERE WAS A TIME WHEN MY DIRECTING CAREER HAD GONE UP IN *FLAMES.* LITERALLY.
"I WAS UTTERLY DISGRACED. UNTOUCHABLE. NOBODY WOULD TRUST ME TO SO MUCH AS DIRECT TRAFFIC.
THE HEART IS A KENNEL OF THIEVES
"SNAGGLEPUSS WAS THE ONLY ONE WHO WOULD HIRE ME. HE GAVE ME MY LIFE BACK.
THE HEART IS A KENNEL OF THIEVES
WHICH IS A SHAME, BECAUSE AFTER TOMORROW, I'LL PROBABLY HAVE TO PRETEND LIKE I'VE NEVER HEARD OF HIM. ANYWAY, LET'S PUT ON A GOOD SHOW...

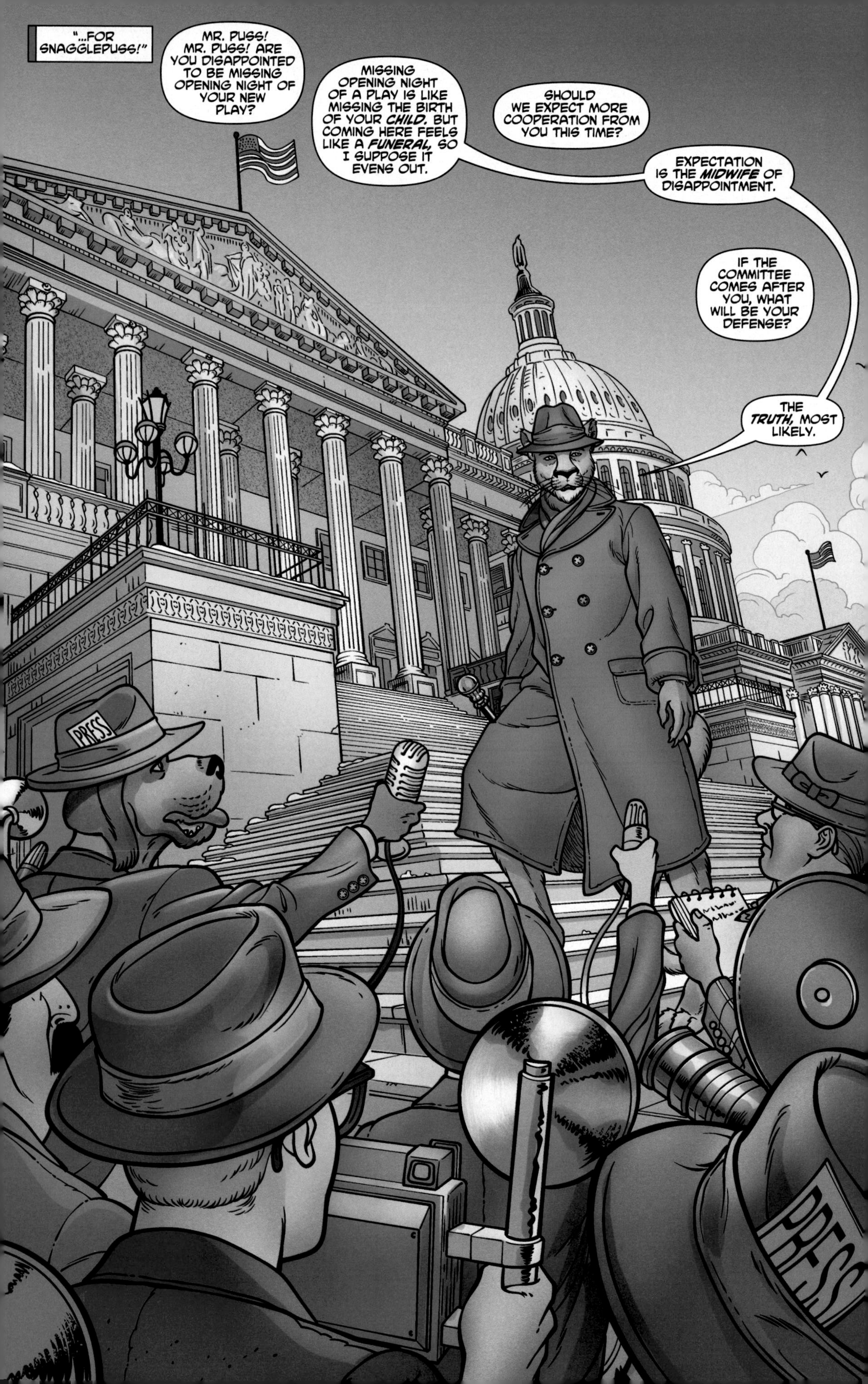
"...FOR SNAGGLEPUSS!"
MR. PUSS! MR. PUSS! ARE YOU DISAPPOINTED TO BE MISSING OPENING NIGHT OF YOUR NEW PLAY?
MISSING OPENING NIGHT OF A PLAY IS LIKE MISSING THE BIRTH OF YOUR *CHILD.* BUT COMING HERE FEELS LIKE A *FUNERAL,* SO I SUPPOSE IT EVENS OUT.
SHOULD WE EXPECT MORE COOPERATION FROM YOU THIS TIME?
EXPECTATION IS THE *MIDWIFE* OF DISAPPOINTMENT.
IF THE COMMITTEE COMES AFTER YOU, WHAT WILL BE YOUR DEFENSE?
THE *TRUTH,* MOST LIKELY.
PRESS
PRESS

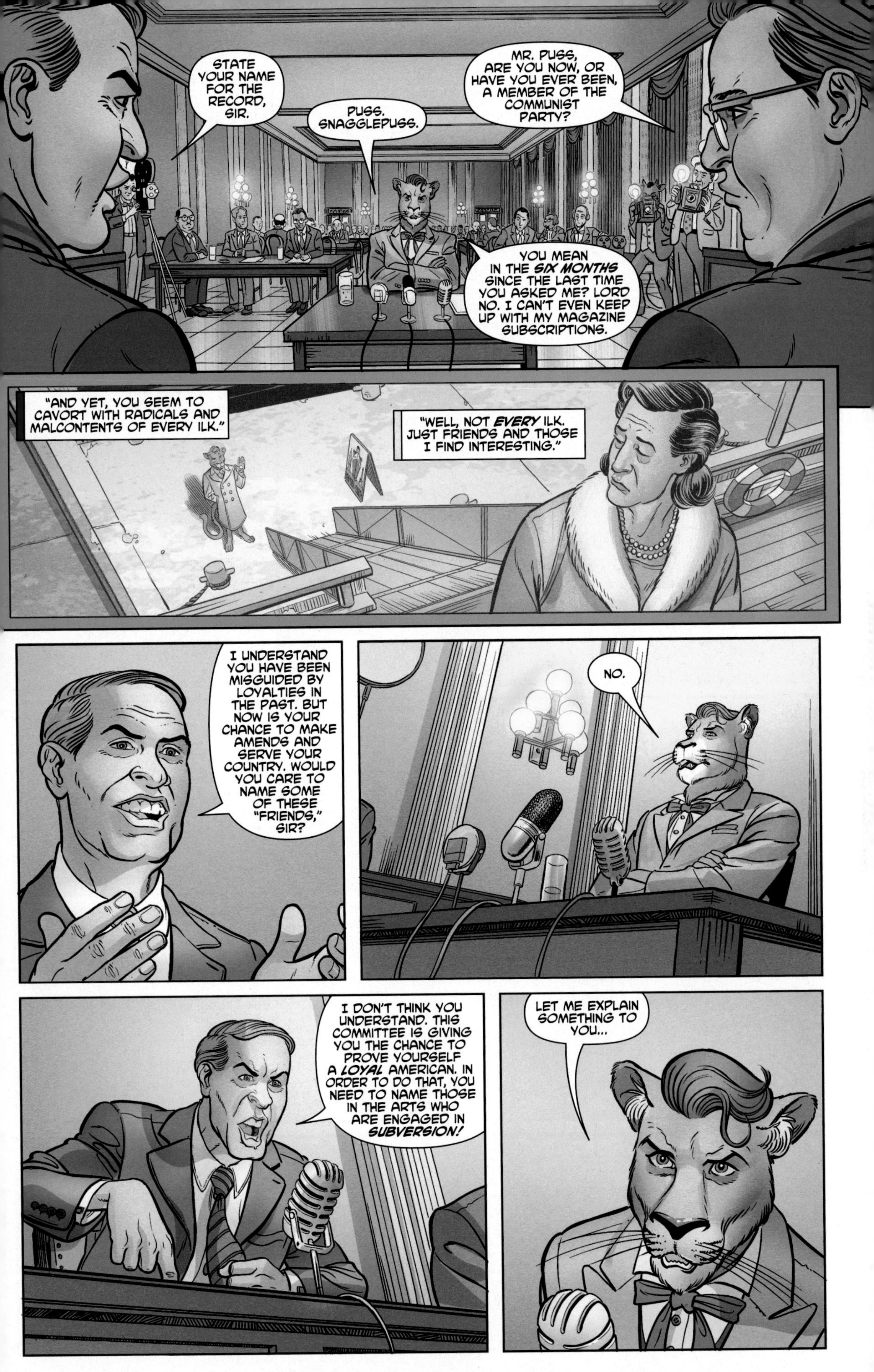
STATE YOUR NAME FOR THE RECORD, SIR.
PUSS. SNAGGLEPUSS.
MR. PUSS, ARE YOU NOW, OR HAVE YOU EVER BEEN, A MEMBER OF THE COMMUNIST PARTY?
YOU MEAN IN THE SIX MONTHS SINCE THE LAST TIME YOU ASKED ME? LORD NO. I CAN'T EVEN KEEP UP WITH MY MAGAZINE SUBSCRIPTIONS.
"AND YET, YOU SEEM TO CAVORT WITH RADICALS AND MALCONTENTS OF EVERY ILK."
"WELL, NOT EVERY ILK. JUST FRIENDS AND THOSE I FIND INTERESTING."
I UNDERSTAND YOU HAVE BEEN MISGUIDED BY LOYALTIES IN THE PAST. BUT NOW IS YOUR CHANCE TO MAKE AMENDS AND SERVE YOUR COUNTRY. WOULD YOU CARE TO NAME SOME OF THESE "FRIENDS," SIR?
NO.
I DON'T THINK YOU UNDERSTAND. THIS COMMITTEE IS GIVING YOU THE CHANCE TO PROVE YOURSELF A LOYAL AMERICAN. IN ORDER TO DO THAT, YOU NEED TO NAME THOSE IN THE ARTS WHO ARE ENGAGED IN SUBVERSION!
LET ME EXPLAIN SOMETHING TO YOU...

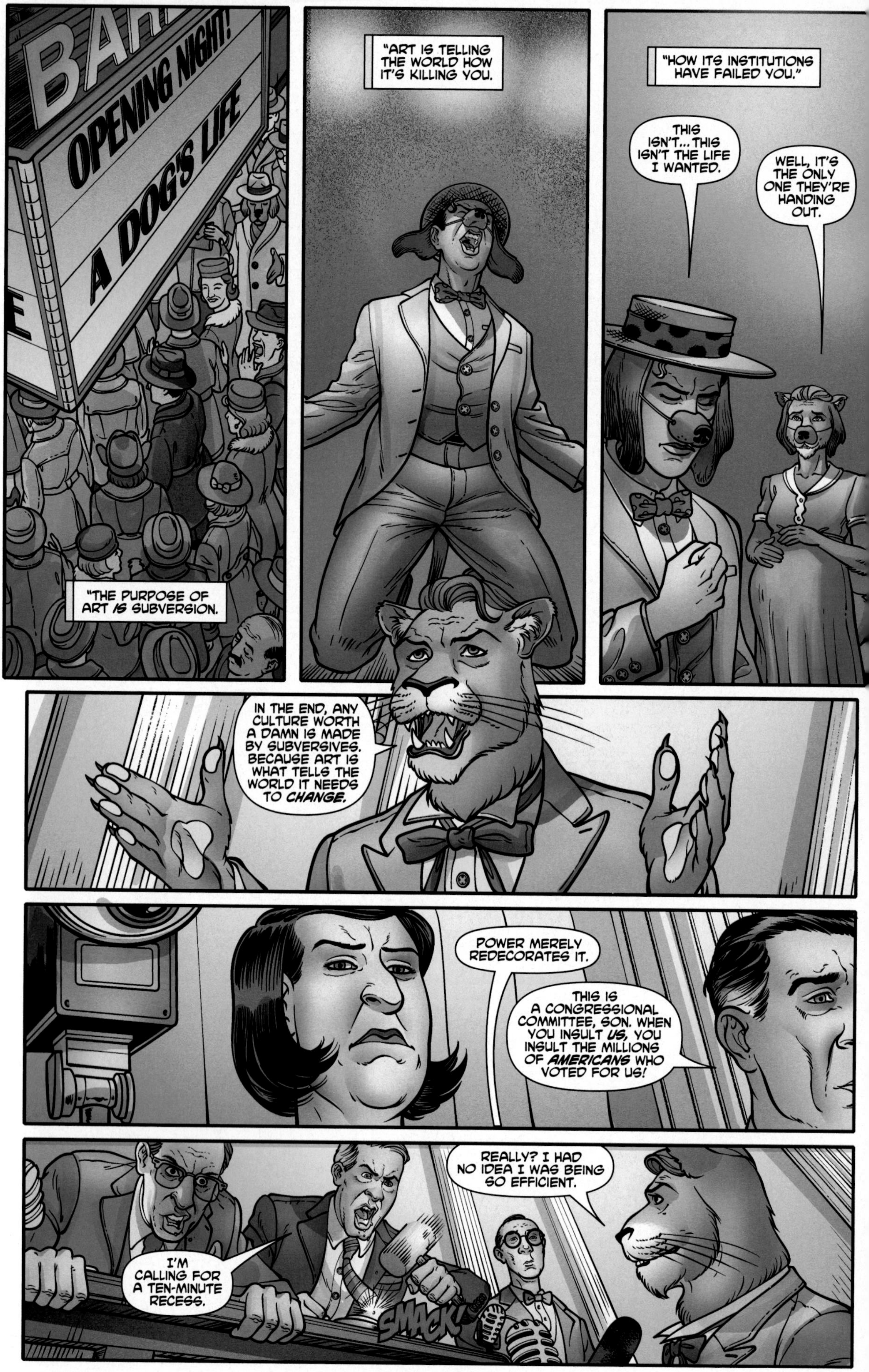
BAR
OPENING NIGHT!
A DOG'S LIFE
"THE PURPOSE OF ART *IS* SUBVERSION.
"ART IS TELLING THE WORLD HOW IT'S KILLING YOU.
"HOW ITS INSTITUTIONS HAVE FAILED YOU."
THIS ISN'T... THIS ISN'T THE LIFE I WANTED.
WELL, IT'S THE ONLY ONE THEY'RE HANDING OUT.
IN THE END, ANY CULTURE WORTH A DAMN IS MADE BY SUBVERSIVES. BECAUSE ART IS WHAT TELLS THE WORLD IT NEEDS TO *CHANGE.*
POWER MERELY REDECORATES IT.
THIS IS A CONGRESSIONAL COMMITTEE, SON. WHEN YOU INSULT *US,* YOU INSULT THE MILLIONS OF *AMERICANS* WHO VOTED FOR US!
REALLY? I HAD NO IDEA I WAS BEING SO EFFICIENT.
I'M CALLING FOR A TEN-MINUTE RECESS.
SMACK!

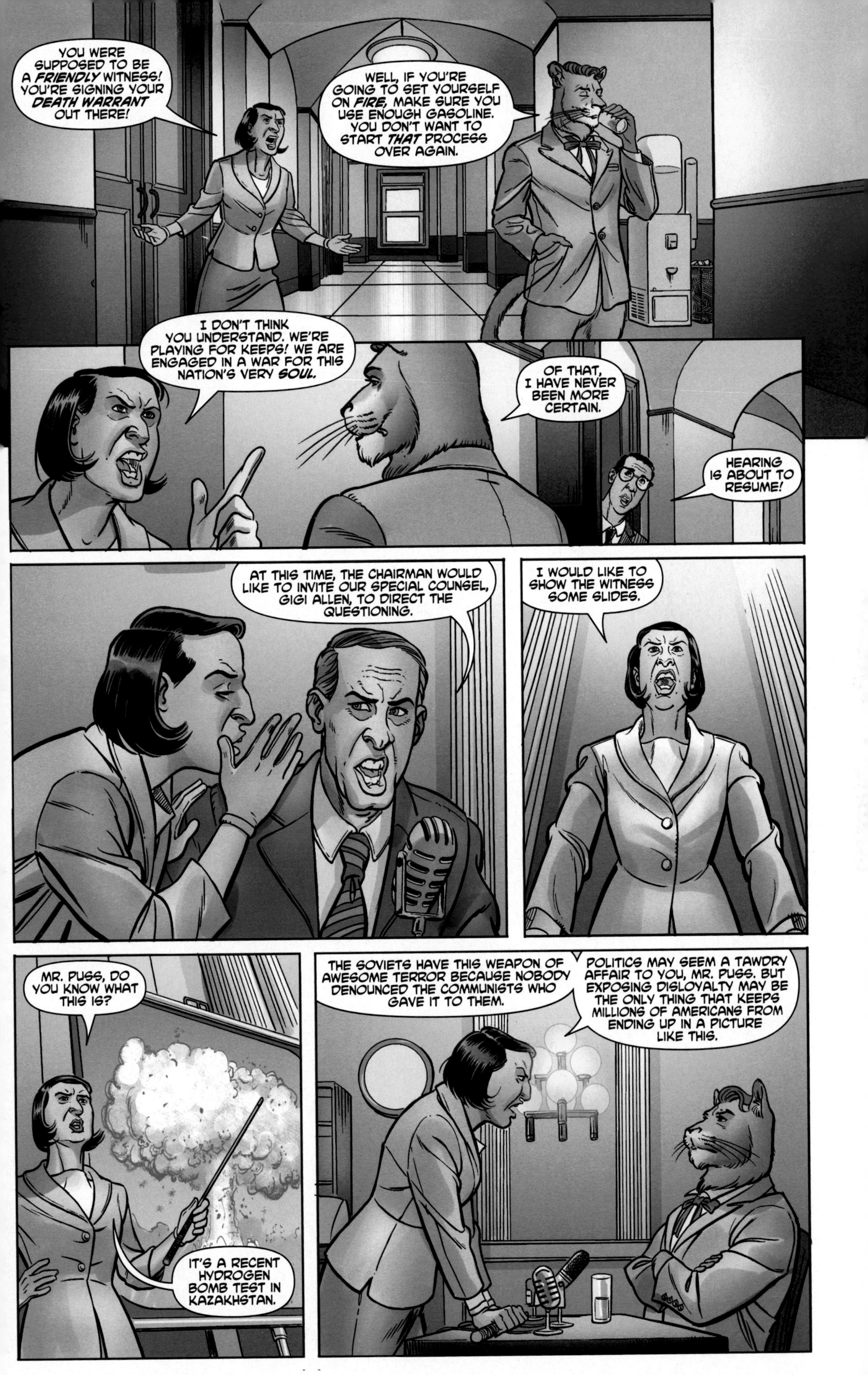
YOU WERE SUPPOSED TO BE A *FRIENDLY* WITNESS! YOU'RE SIGNING YOUR *DEATH WARRANT* OUT THERE!
WELL, IF YOU'RE GOING TO SET YOURSELF ON *FIRE*, MAKE SURE YOU USE ENOUGH GASOLINE. YOU DON'T WANT TO START *THAT* PROCESS OVER AGAIN.
I DON'T THINK YOU UNDERSTAND. WE'RE PLAYING FOR KEEPS! WE ARE ENGAGED IN A WAR FOR THIS NATION'S VERY *SOUL.*
OF THAT, I HAVE NEVER BEEN MORE CERTAIN.
HEARING IS ABOUT TO RESUME!
AT THIS TIME, THE CHAIRMAN WOULD LIKE TO INVITE OUR SPECIAL COUNSEL, GIGI ALLEN, TO DIRECT THE QUESTIONING.
I WOULD LIKE TO SHOW THE WITNESS SOME SLIDES.
MR. PUSS, DO YOU KNOW WHAT THIS IS?
IT'S A RECENT HYDROGEN BOMB TEST IN KAZAKHSTAN.
THE SOVIETS HAVE THIS WEAPON OF AWESOME TERROR BECAUSE NOBODY DENOUNCED THE COMMUNISTS WHO GAVE IT TO THEM.
POLITICS MAY SEEM A TAWDRY AFFAIR TO YOU, MR. PUSS. BUT EXPOSING DISLOYALTY MAY BE THE ONLY THING THAT KEEPS MILLIONS OF AMERICANS FROM ENDING UP IN A PICTURE LIKE THIS.

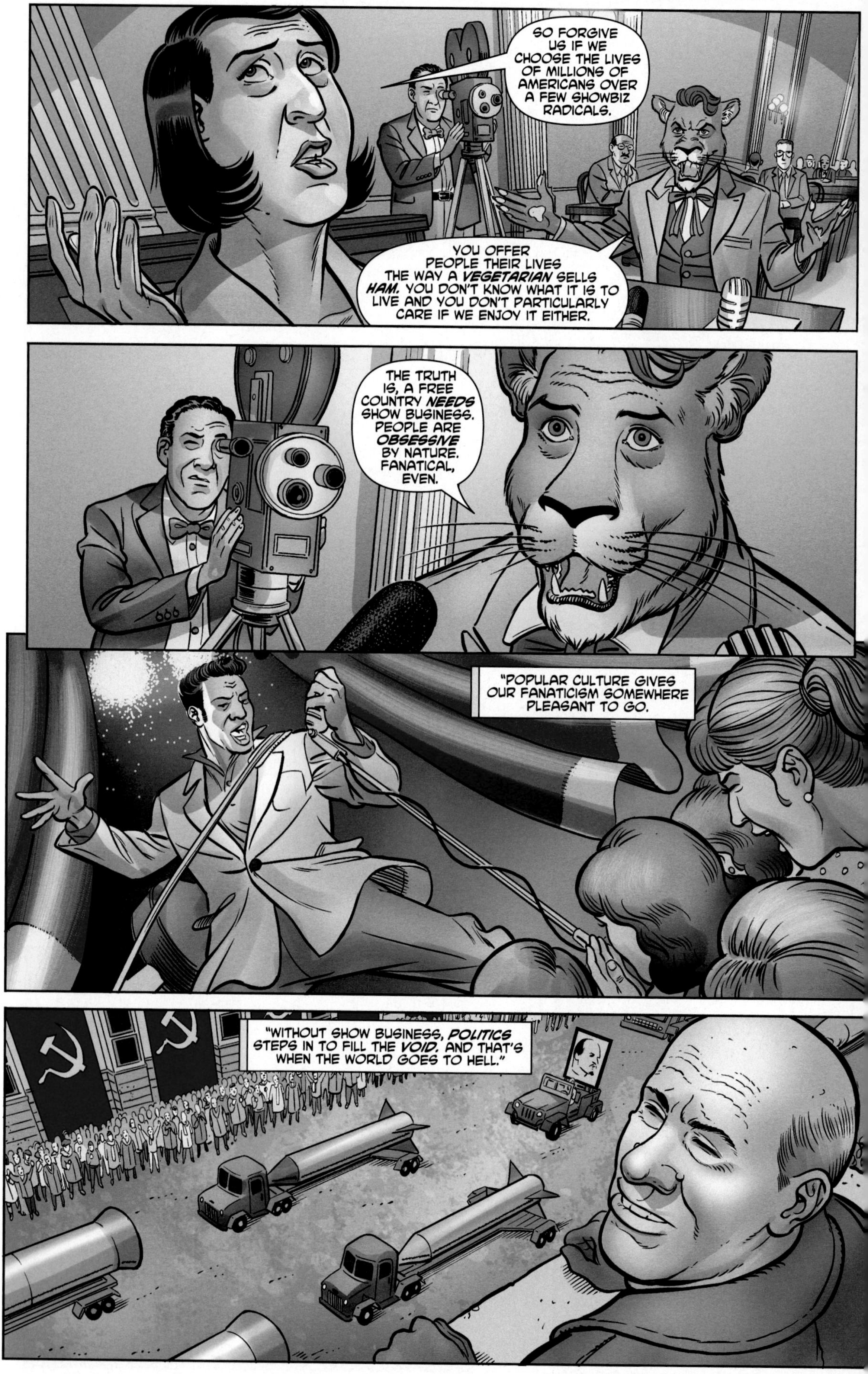
SO FORGIVE US IF WE CHOOSE THE LIVES OF MILLIONS OF AMERICANS OVER A FEW SHOWBIZ RADICALS.
YOU OFFER PEOPLE THEIR LIVES THE WAY A VEGETARIAN SELLS HAM. YOU DON'T KNOW WHAT IT IS TO LIVE AND YOU DON'T PARTICULARLY CARE IF WE ENJOY IT EITHER.
THE TRUTH IS, A FREE COUNTRY NEEDS SHOW BUSINESS. PEOPLE ARE OBSESSIVE BY NATURE. FANATICAL, EVEN.
"POPULAR CULTURE GIVES OUR FANATICISM SOMEWHERE PLEASANT TO GO.
"WITHOUT SHOW BUSINESS, POLITICS STEPS IN TO FILL THE VOID. AND THAT'S WHEN THE WORLD GOES TO HELL."

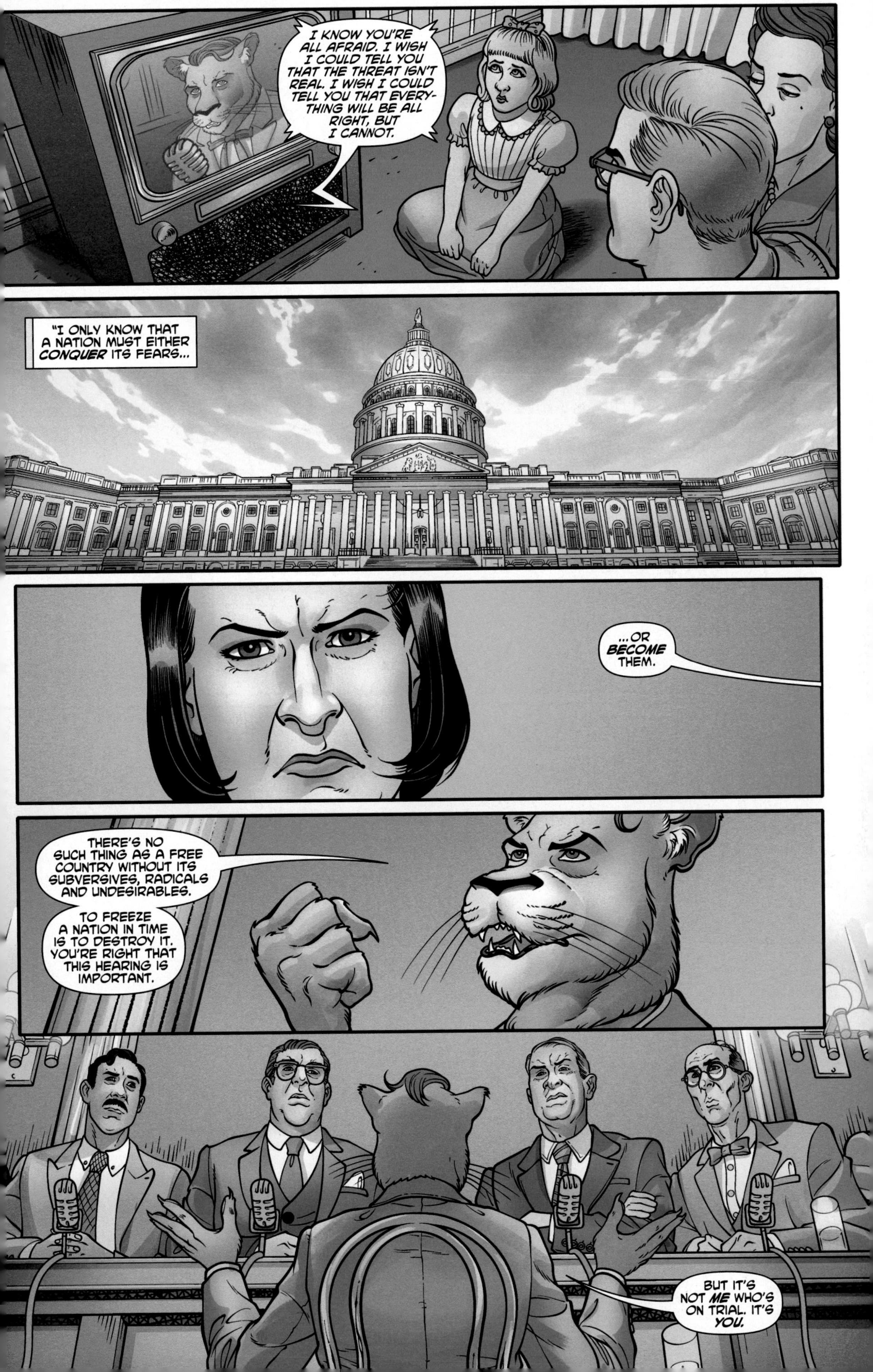
I KNOW YOU'RE ALL AFRAID. I WISH I COULD TELL YOU THAT THE THREAT ISN'T REAL. I WISH I COULD TELL YOU THAT EVERY-THING WILL BE ALL RIGHT, BUT I CANNOT.
"I ONLY KNOW THAT A NATION MUST EITHER CONQUER ITS FEARS...
...OR BECOME THEM.
THERE'S NO SUCH THING AS A FREE COUNTRY WITHOUT ITS SUBVERSIVES, RADICALS AND UNDESIRABLES.
TO FREEZE A NATION IN TIME IS TO DESTROY IT. YOU'RE RIGHT THAT THIS HEARING IS IMPORTANT.
BUT IT'S NOT ME WHO'S ON TRIAL. IT'S YOU.

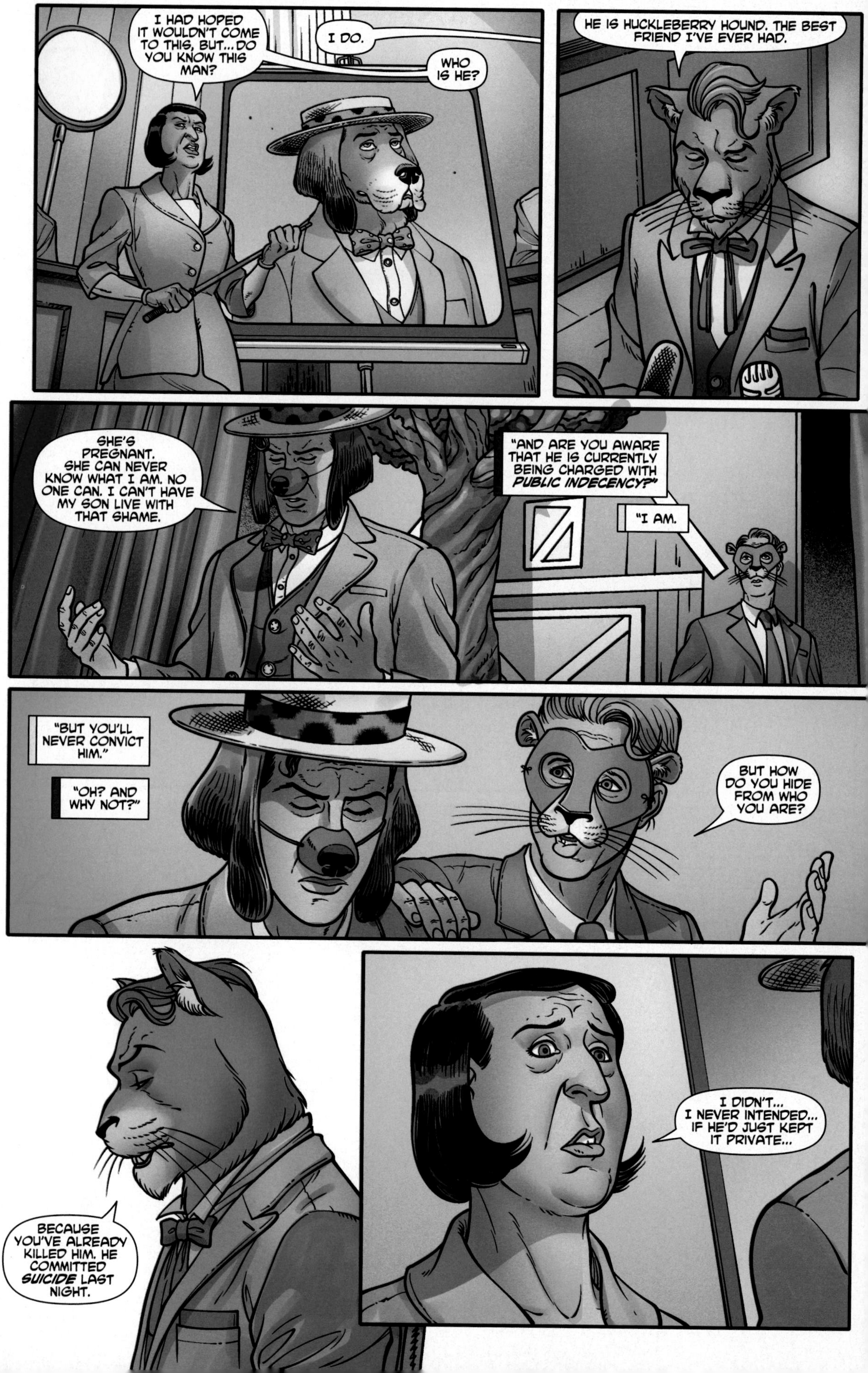
I HAD HOPED IT WOULDN'T COME TO THIS, BUT...DO YOU KNOW THIS MAN?
I DO.
WHO IS HE?
HE IS HUCKLEBERRY HOUND. THE BEST FRIEND I'VE EVER HAD.
SHE'S PREGNANT. SHE CAN NEVER KNOW WHAT I AM. NO ONE CAN. I CAN'T HAVE MY SON LIVE WITH THAT SHAME.
"AND ARE YOU AWARE THAT HE IS CURRENTLY BEING CHARGED WITH *PUBLIC INDECENCY?*"
"I AM.
"BUT YOU'LL NEVER CONVICT HIM."
"OH? AND WHY NOT?"
BUT HOW DO YOU HIDE FROM WHO YOU ARE?
BECAUSE YOU'VE ALREADY KILLED HIM. HE COMMITTED ***SUICIDE*** LAST NIGHT.
I DIDN'T... I NEVER INTENDED... IF HE'D JUST KEPT IT PRIVATE...

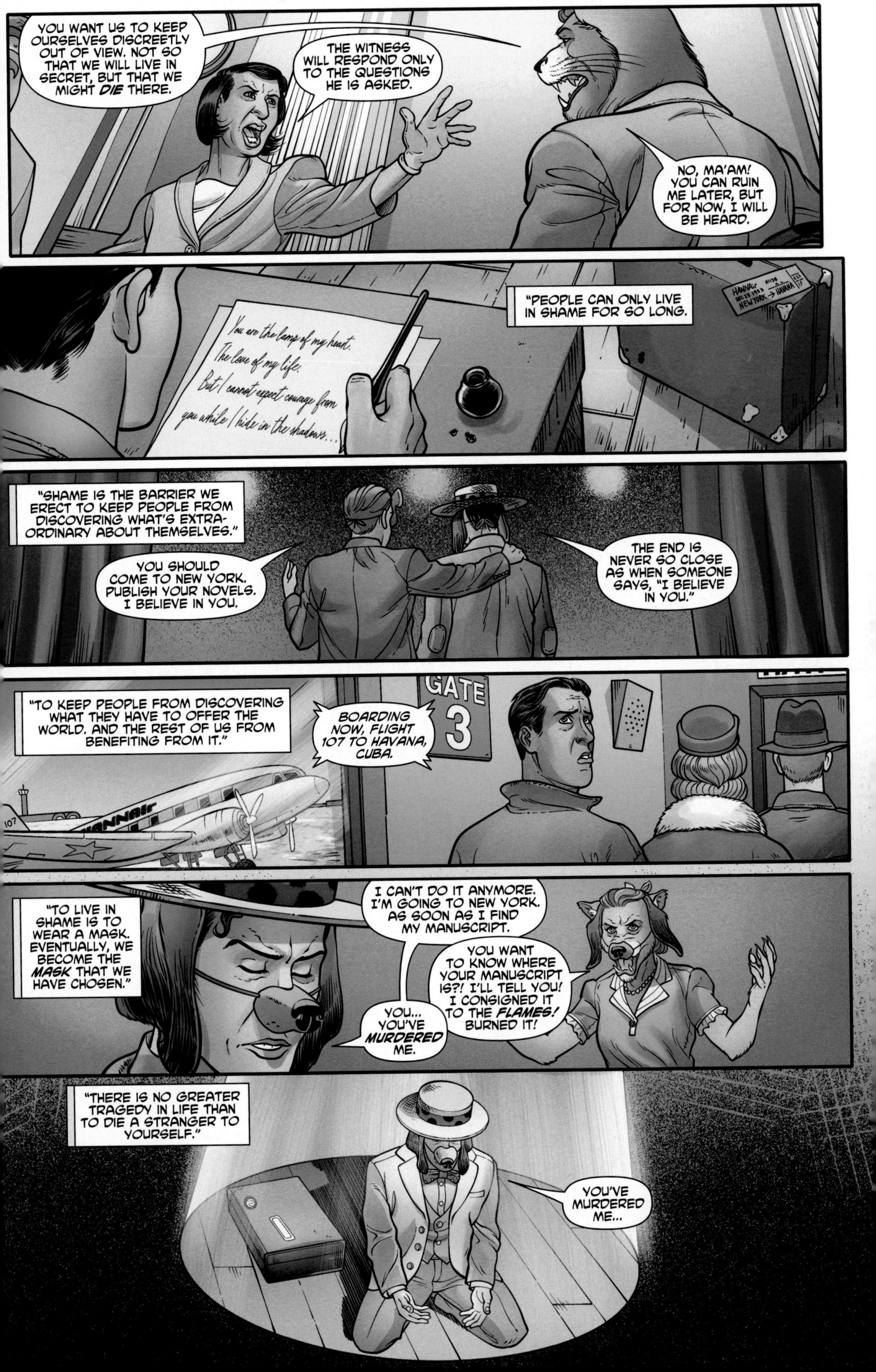
YOU WANT US TO KEEP OURSELVES DISCREETLY OUT OF VIEW. NOT SO THAT WE WILL LIVE IN SECRET, BUT THAT WE MIGHT *DIE* THERE.
THE WITNESS WILL RESPOND ONLY TO THE QUESTIONS HE IS ASKED.
NO, MA'AM! YOU CAN RUIN ME LATER, BUT FOR NOW, I WILL BE HEARD.
You are the lamp of my heart. The love of my life. But I cannot expect courage from you while I hide in the shadows...
"PEOPLE CAN ONLY LIVE IN SHAME FOR SO LONG.
"SHAME IS THE BARRIER WE ERECT TO KEEP PEOPLE FROM DISCOVERING WHAT'S EXTRA-ORDINARY ABOUT THEMSELVES."
YOU SHOULD COME TO NEW YORK. PUBLISH YOUR NOVELS. I BELIEVE IN YOU.
THE END IS NEVER SO CLOSE AS WHEN SOMEONE SAYS, "I BELIEVE IN YOU."
"TO KEEP PEOPLE FROM DISCOVERING WHAT THEY HAVE TO OFFER THE WORLD. AND THE REST OF US FROM BENEFITING FROM IT."
BOARDING NOW, FLIGHT 107 TO HAVANA, CUBA.
GATE 3
"TO LIVE IN SHAME IS TO WEAR A MASK. EVENTUALLY, WE BECOME THE *MASK* THAT WE HAVE CHOSEN."
I CAN'T DO IT ANYMORE. I'M GOING TO NEW YORK. AS SOON AS I FIND MY MANUSCRIPT.
YOU WANT TO KNOW WHERE YOUR MANUSCRIPT IS?! I'LL TELL YOU! I CONSIGNED IT TO THE *FLAMES!* BURNED IT!
YOU... YOU'VE *MURDERED* ME.
"THERE IS NO GREATER TRAGEDY IN LIFE THAN TO DIE A STRANGER TO YOURSELF."
YOU'VE MURDERED ME...

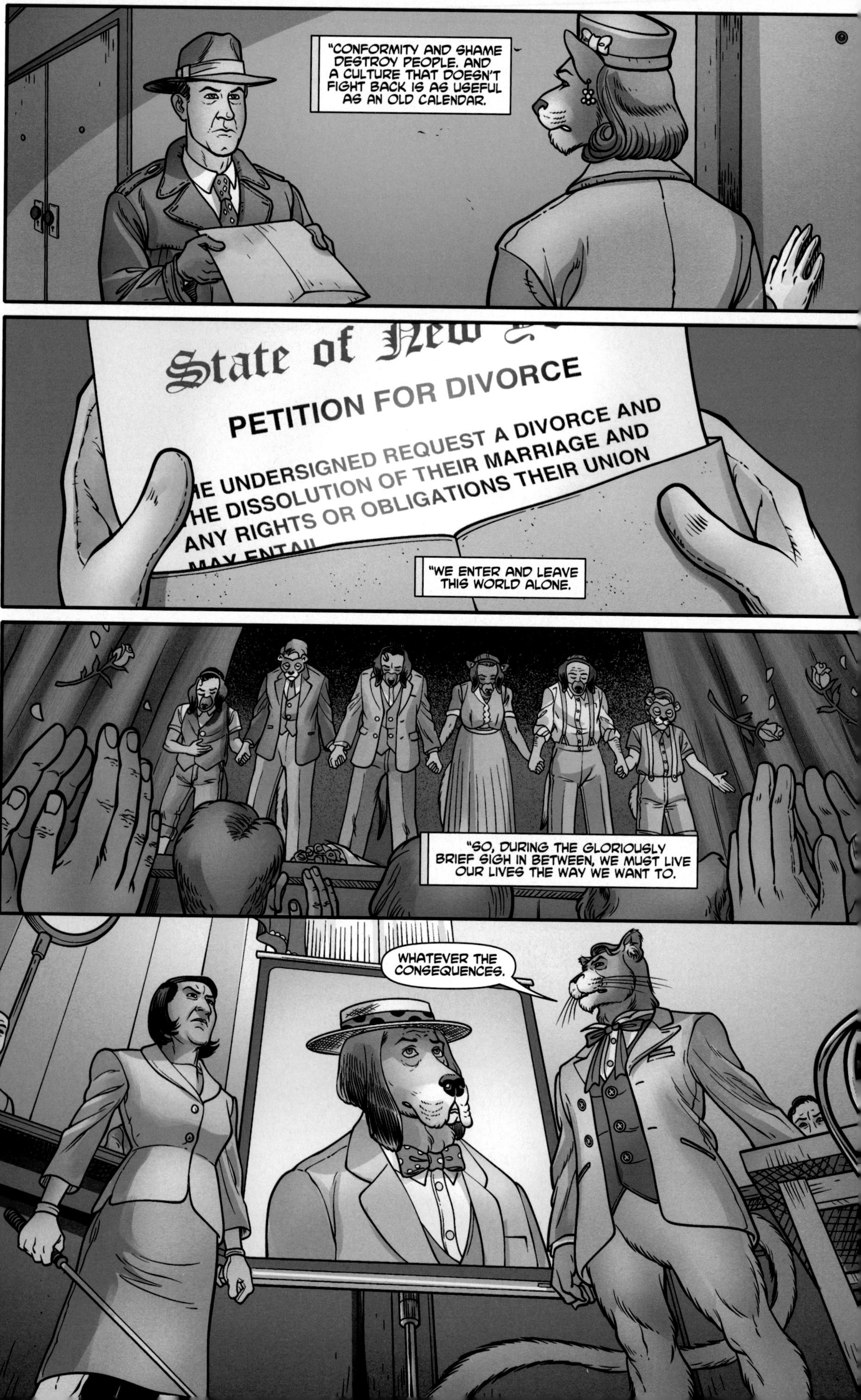
"CONFORMITY AND SHAME DESTROY PEOPLE. AND A CULTURE THAT DOESN'T FIGHT BACK IS AS USEFUL AS AN OLD CALENDAR.
State of New
PETITION FOR DIVORCE
THE UNDERSIGNED REQUEST A DIVORCE AND THE DISSOLUTION OF THEIR MARRIAGE AND ANY RIGHTS OR OBLIGATIONS THEIR UNION
"WE ENTER AND LEAVE THIS WORLD ALONE.
"SO, DURING THE GLORIOUSLY BRIEF SIGH IN BETWEEN, WE MUST LIVE OUR LIVES THE WAY WE WANT TO.
WHATEVER THE CONSEQUENCES.

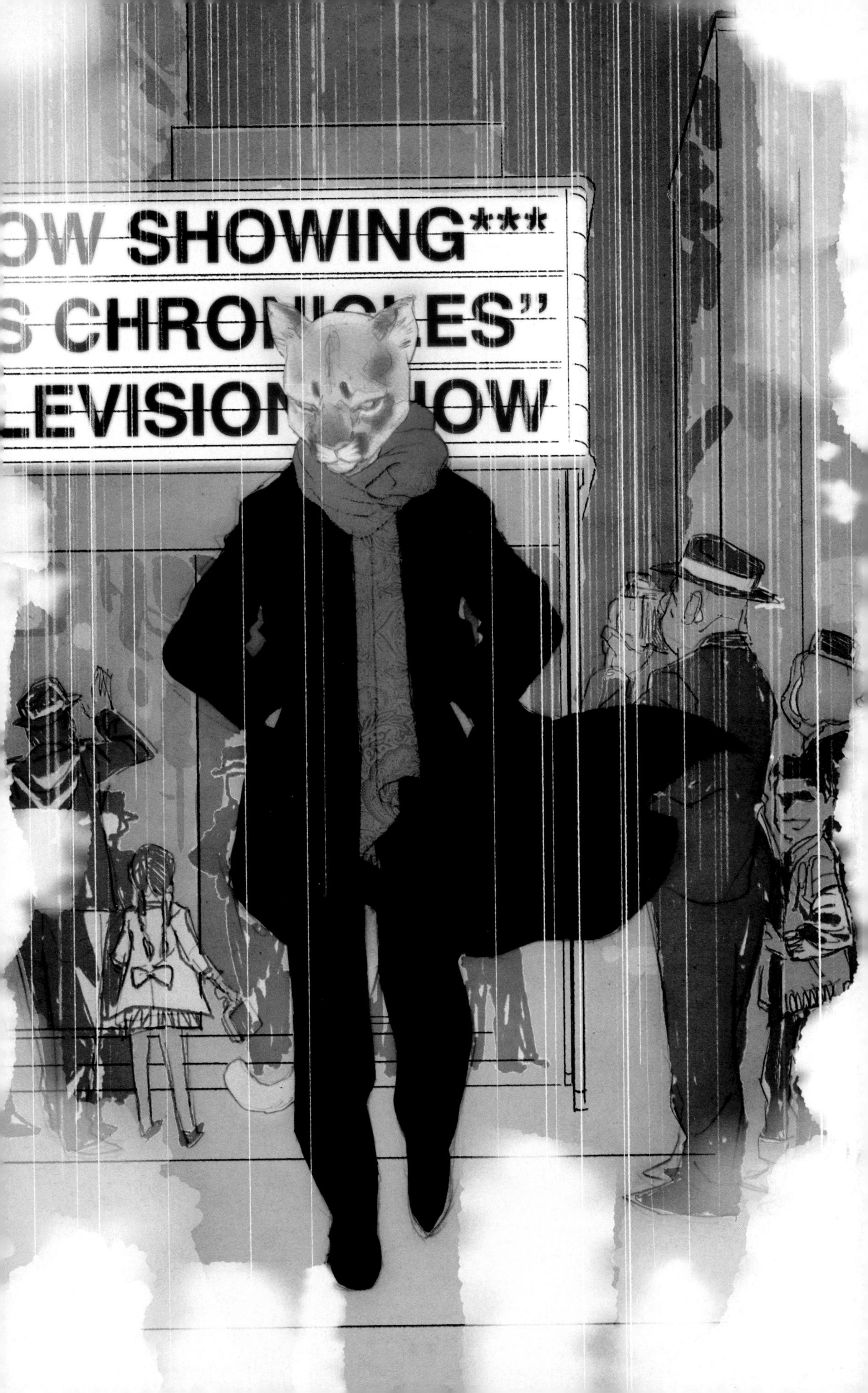
OW SHOWING***
S CHRON CLES”
LEVISION HOW

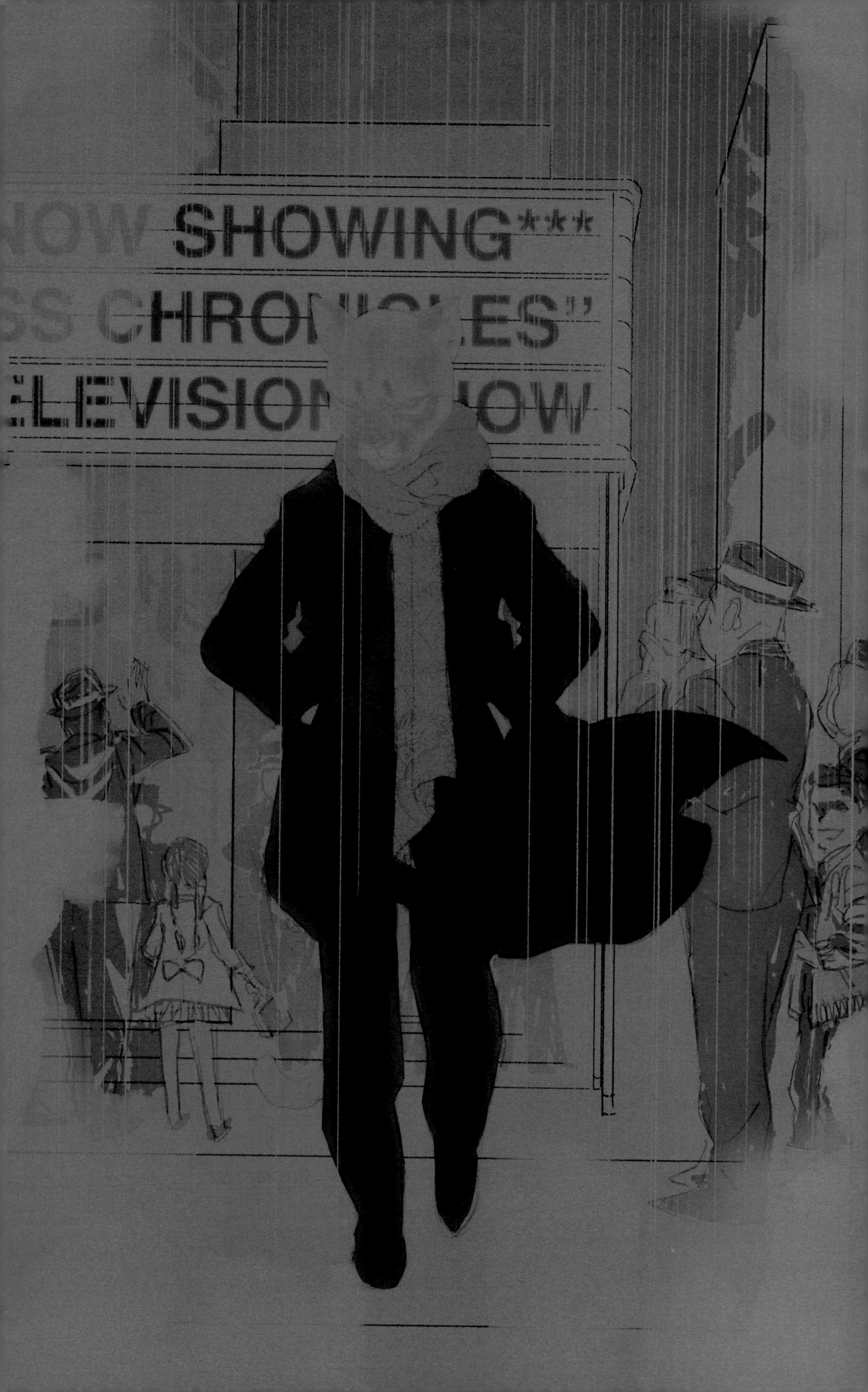
SHOWING

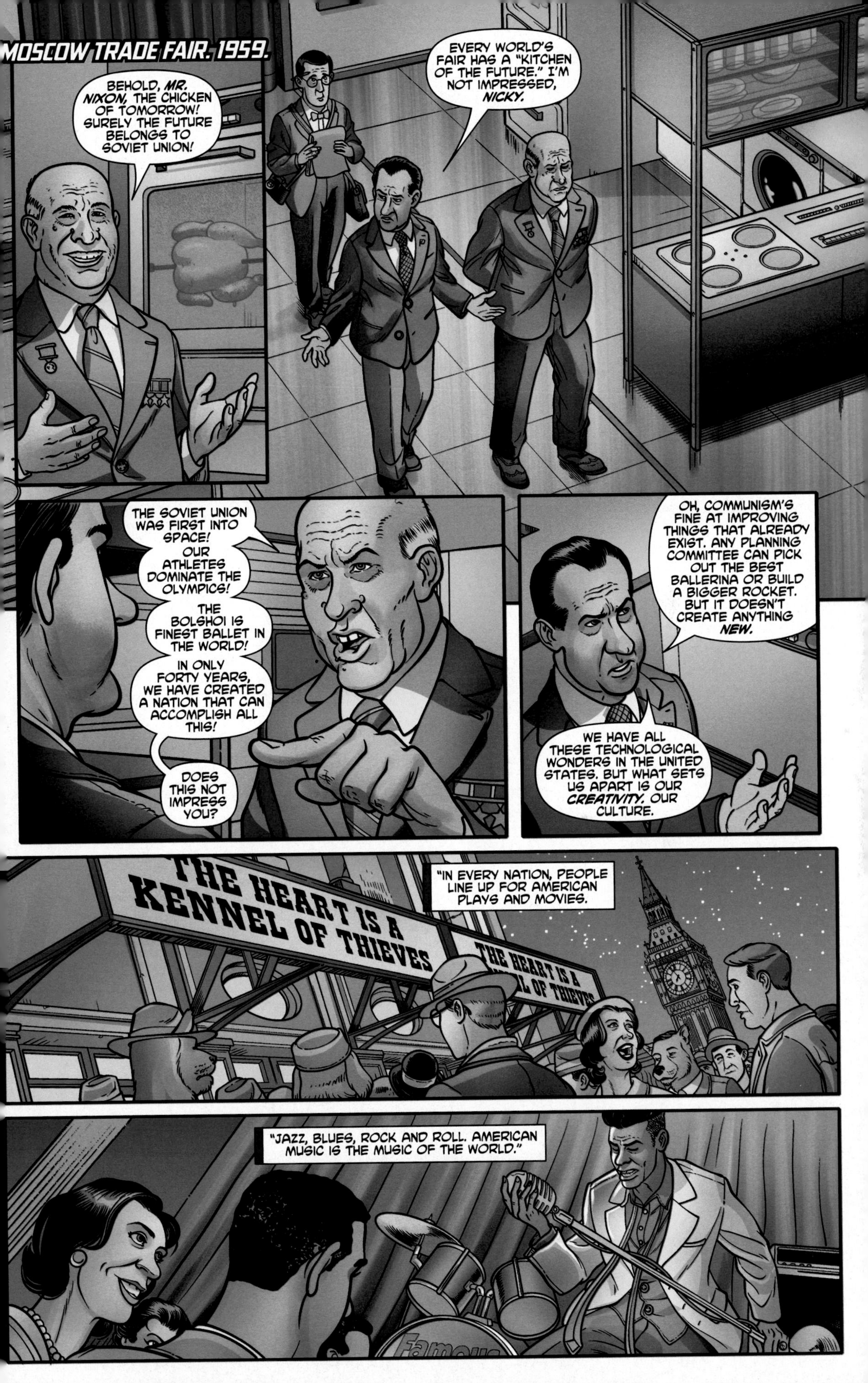
MOSCOW TRADE FAIR. 1959.
BEHOLD, MR. NIXON, THE CHICKEN OF TOMORROW! SURELY THE FUTURE BELONGS TO SOVIET UNION!
EVERY WORLD'S FAIR HAS A "KITCHEN OF THE FUTURE." I'M NOT IMPRESSED, NICKY.
THE SOVIET UNION WAS FIRST INTO SPACE!
OUR ATHLETES DOMINATE THE OLYMPICS!
THE BOLSHOI IS FINEST BALLET IN THE WORLD!
IN ONLY FORTY YEARS, WE HAVE CREATED A NATION THAT CAN ACCOMPLISH ALL THIS!
DOES THIS NOT IMPRESS YOU?
OH, COMMUNISM'S FINE AT IMPROVING THINGS THAT ALREADY EXIST. ANY PLANNING COMMITTEE CAN PICK OUT THE BEST BALLERINA OR BUILD A BIGGER ROCKET. BUT IT DOESN'T CREATE ANYTHING NEW.
WE HAVE ALL THESE TECHNOLOGICAL WONDERS IN THE UNITED STATES. BUT WHAT SETS US APART IS OUR CREATIVITY. OUR CULTURE.
THE HEART IS A KENNEL OF THIEVES
"IN EVERY NATION, PEOPLE LINE UP FOR AMERICAN PLAYS AND MOVIES.
"JAZZ, BLUES, ROCK AND ROLL. AMERICAN MUSIC IS THE MUSIC OF THE WORLD."

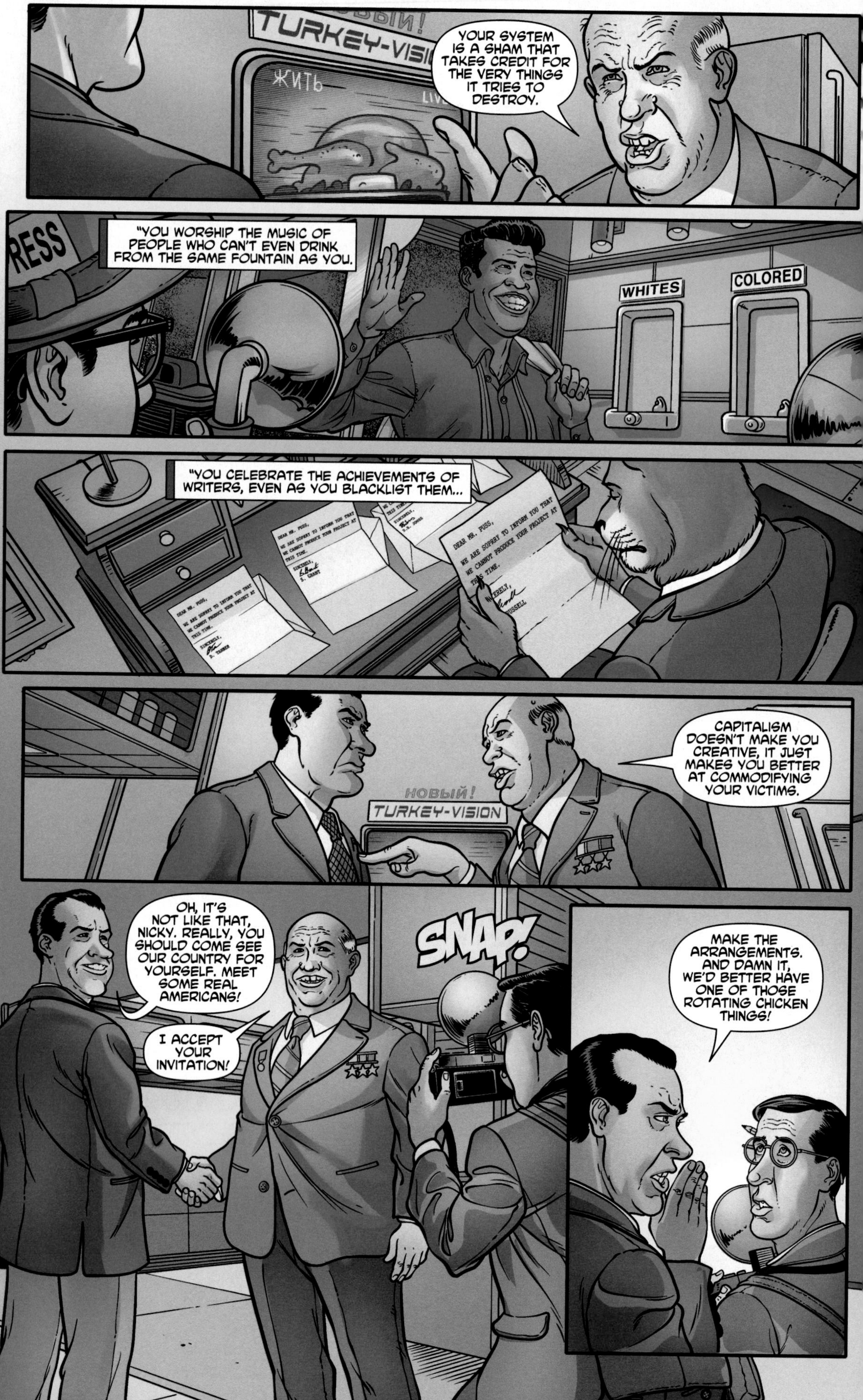

TURKEY-VISION
ЖИТЬ
YOUR SYSTEM IS A SHAM THAT TAKES CREDIT FOR THE VERY THINGS IT TRIES TO DESTROY.
RESS
"YOU WORSHIP THE MUSIC OF PEOPLE WHO CAN'T EVEN DRINK FROM THE SAME FOUNTAIN AS YOU.
WHITES
COLORED
"YOU CELEBRATE THE ACHIEVEMENTS OF WRITERS, EVEN AS YOU BLACKLIST THEM...
НОВЫЙ!
TURKEY-VISION
CAPITALISM DOESN'T MAKE YOU CREATIVE, IT JUST MAKES YOU BETTER AT COMMODIFYING YOUR VICTIMS.
OH, IT'S NOT LIKE THAT, NICKY. REALLY, YOU SHOULD COME SEE OUR COUNTRY FOR YOURSELF. MEET SOME REAL AMERICANS!
I ACCEPT YOUR INVITATION!
SNAP!
MAKE THE ARRANGEMENTS. AND DAMN IT, WE'D BETTER HAVE ONE OF THOSE ROTATING CHICKEN THINGS!

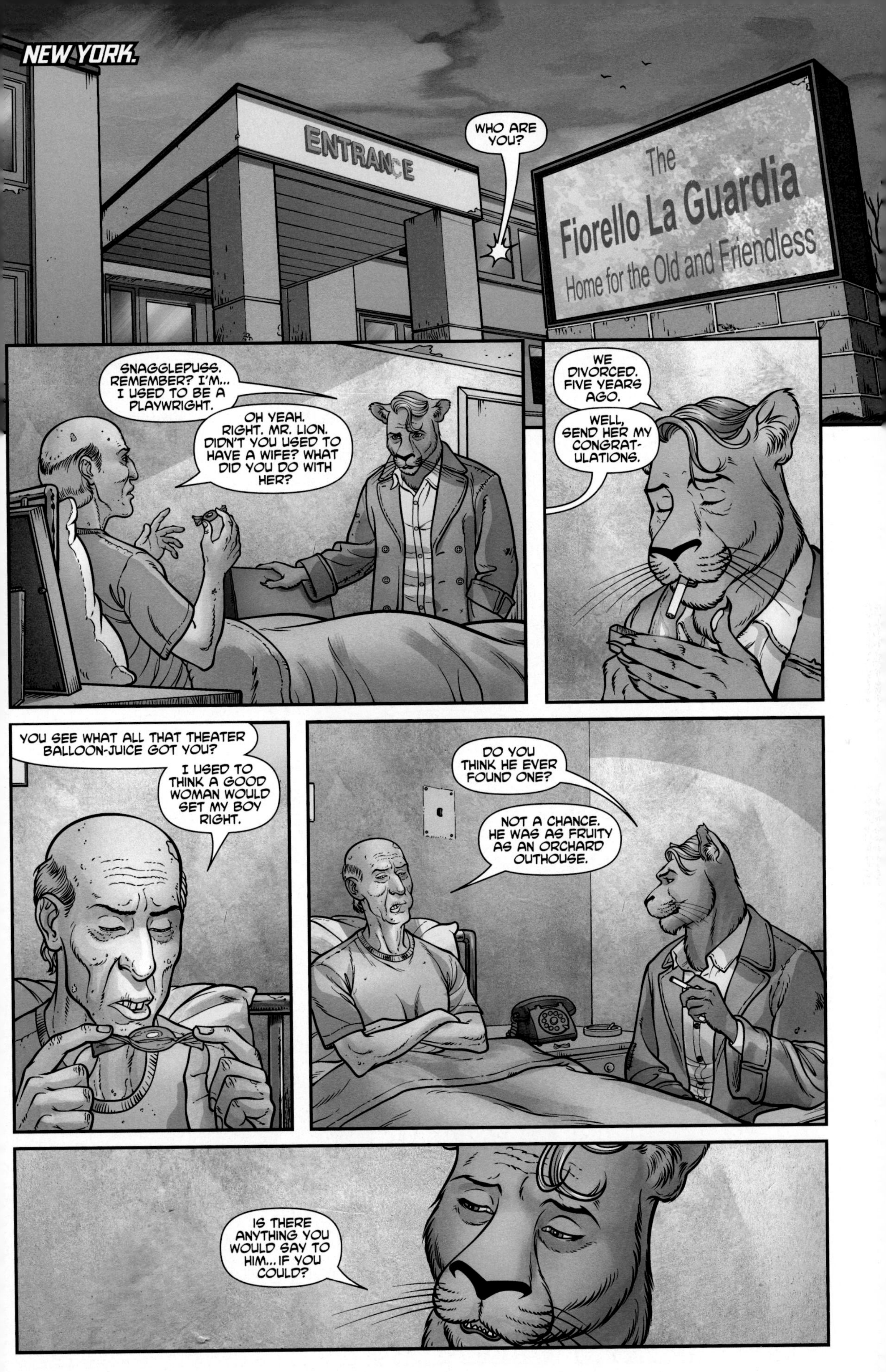
NEW YORK.
ENTRANCE
WHO ARE YOU?
The Fiorello La Guardia Home for the Old and Friendless
SNAGGLEPUSS. REMEMBER? I'M... I USED TO BE A PLAYWRIGHT.
OH YEAH. RIGHT. MR. LION. DIDN'T YOU USED TO HAVE A WIFE? WHAT DID YOU DO WITH HER?
WE DIVORCED. FIVE YEARS AGO.
WELL, SEND HER MY CONGRAT-ULATIONS.
YOU SEE WHAT ALL THAT THEATER BALLOON-JUICE GOT YOU?
I USED TO THINK A GOOD WOMAN WOULD SET MY BOY RIGHT.
DO YOU THINK HE EVER FOUND ONE?
NOT A CHANCE. HE WAS AS FRUITY AS AN ORCHARD OUTHOUSE.
IS THERE ANYTHING YOU WOULD SAY TO HIM...IF YOU COULD?

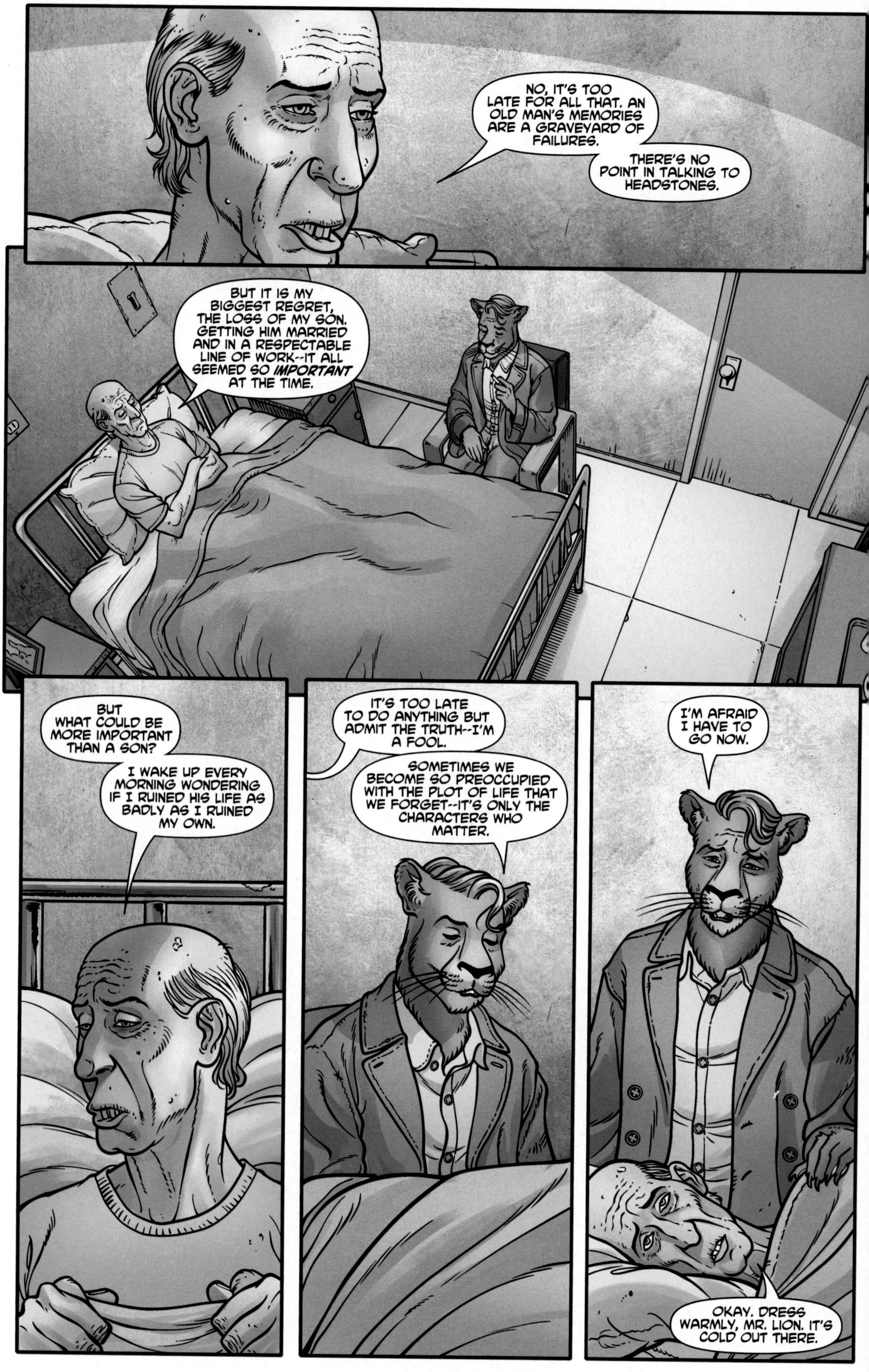
NO, IT'S TOO LATE FOR ALL THAT. AN OLD MAN'S MEMORIES ARE A GRAVEYARD OF FAILURES.
THERE'S NO POINT IN TALKING TO HEADSTONES.
BUT IT IS MY BIGGEST REGRET, THE LOSS OF MY SON. GETTING HIM MARRIED AND IN A RESPECTABLE LINE OF WORK--IT ALL SEEMED SO *IMPORTANT* AT THE TIME.
BUT WHAT COULD BE MORE IMPORTANT THAN A SON?
I WAKE UP EVERY MORNING WONDERING IF I RUINED HIS LIFE AS BADLY AS I RUINED MY OWN.
IT'S TOO LATE TO DO ANYTHING BUT ADMIT THE TRUTH--I'M A FOOL.
SOMETIMES WE BECOME SO PREOCCUPIED WITH THE PLOT OF LIFE THAT WE FORGET--IT'S ONLY THE CHARACTERS WHO MATTER.
I'M AFRAID I HAVE TO GO NOW.
OKAY. DRESS WARMLY, MR. LION. IT'S COLD OUT THERE.

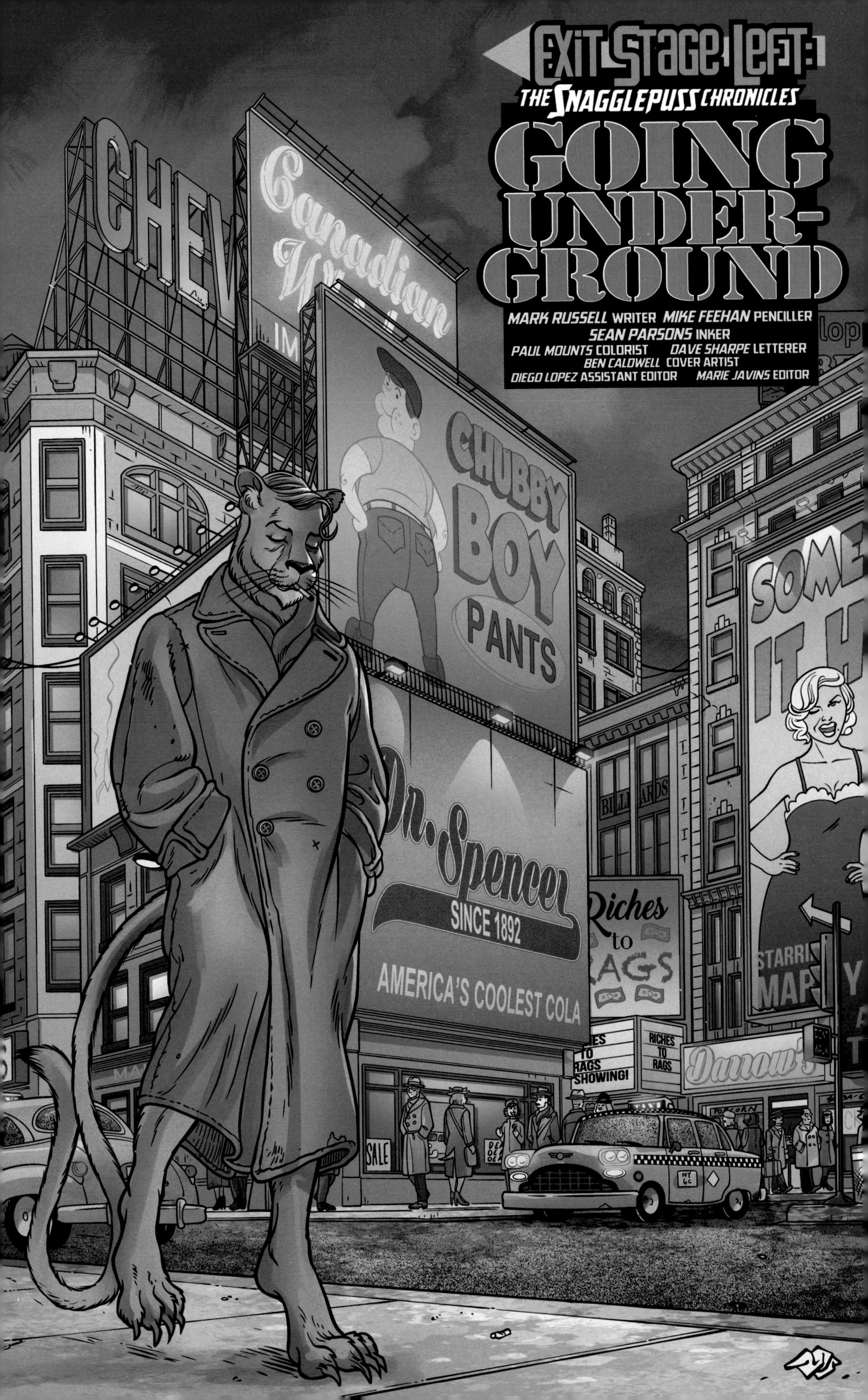
EXIT STAGE LEFT:
THE SNAGGLEPUSS CHRONICLES
GOING UNDER-GROUND
MARK RUSSELL WRITER MIKE FEEHAN PENCILLER
SEAN PARSONS INKER
PAUL MOUNTS COLORIST DAVE SHARPE LETTERER
BEN CALDWELL COVER ARTIST
DIEGO LOPEZ ASSISTANT EDITOR MARIE JAVINS EDITOR
CHEV
Canadian
CHUBBY BOY PANTS
Dr. Spencer
SINCE 1892
AMERICA'S COOLEST COLA
Riches to RAGS
RICHES TO RAGS
TO RAGS SHOWING!
BILLIARDS
SALE

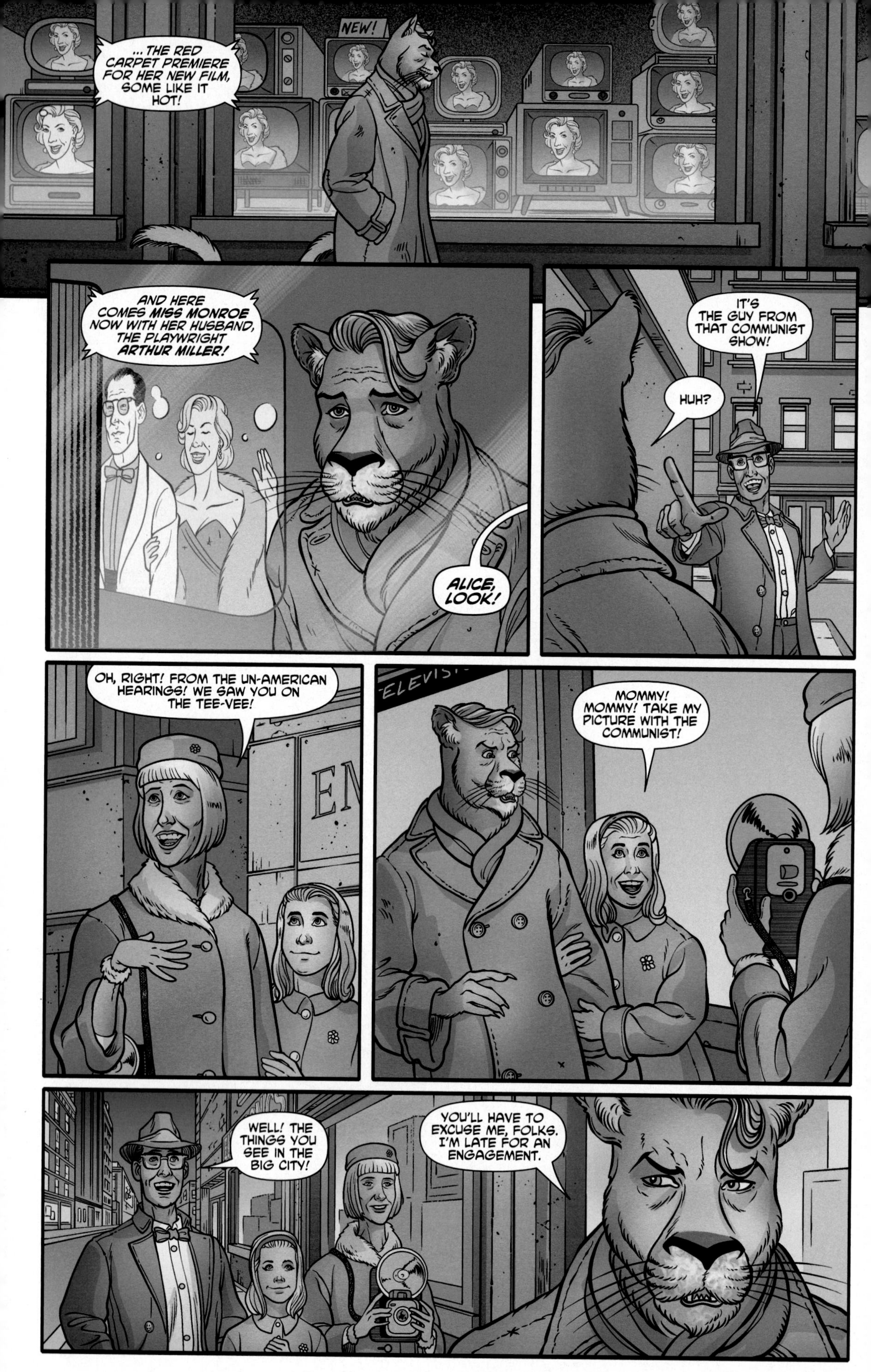

NEW!
...THE RED CARPET PREMIERE FOR HER NEW FILM, SOME LIKE IT HOT!
AND HERE COMES MISS MONROE NOW WITH HER HUSBAND, THE PLAYWRIGHT ARTHUR MILLER!
ALICE, LOOK!
IT'S THE GUY FROM THAT COMMUNIST SHOW!
HUH?
OH, RIGHT! FROM THE UN-AMERICAN HEARINGS! WE SAW YOU ON THE TEE-VEE!
MOMMY! MOMMY! TAKE MY PICTURE WITH THE COMMUNIST!
WELL! THE THINGS YOU SEE IN THE BIG CITY!
YOU'LL HAVE TO EXCUSE ME, FOLKS. I'M LATE FOR AN ENGAGEMENT.

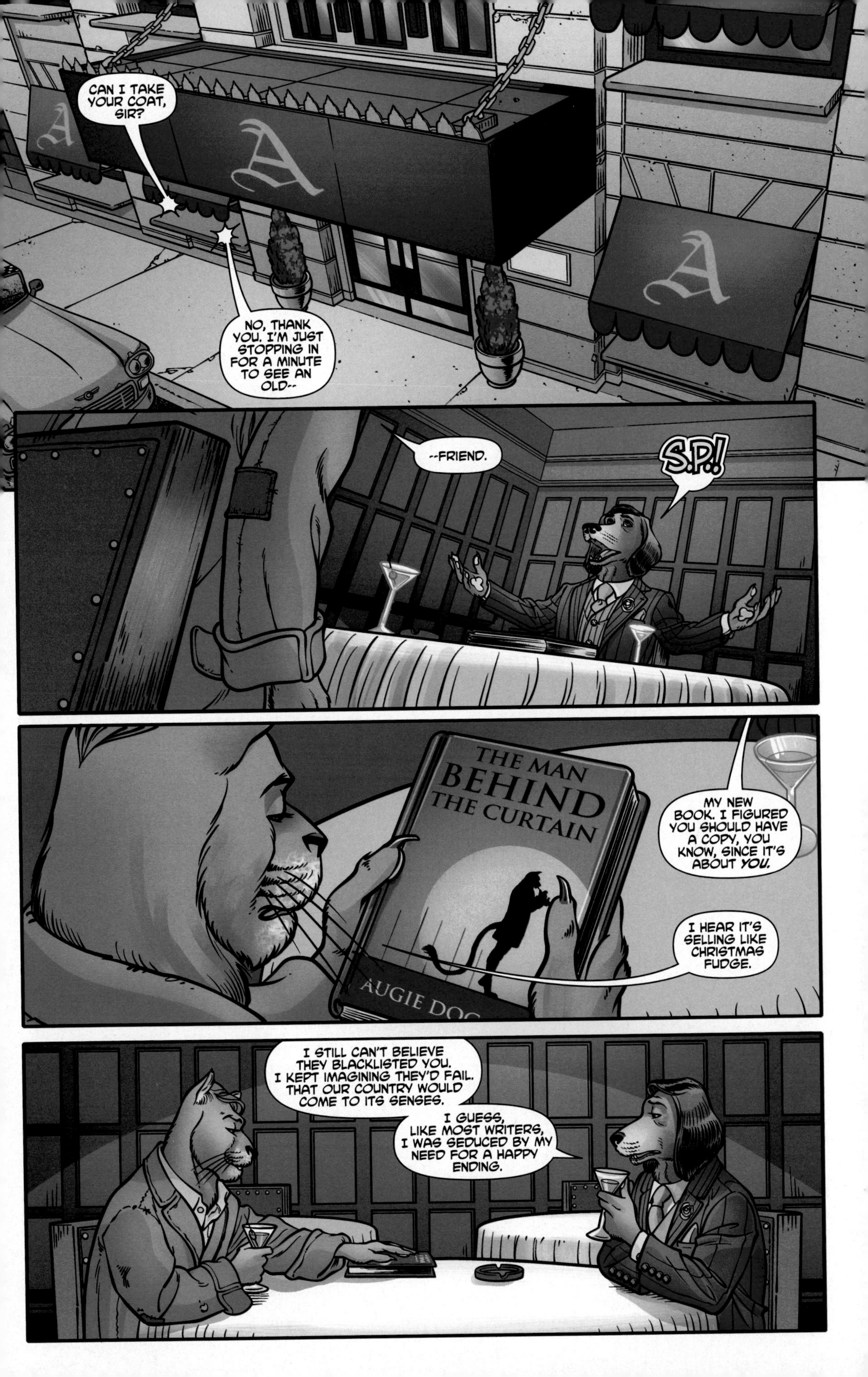
CAN I TAKE YOUR COAT, SIR?
NO, THANK YOU. I'M JUST STOPPING IN FOR A MINUTE TO SEE AN OLD--
--FRIEND.
S.P.!
THE MAN BEHIND THE CURTAIN
AUGIE DOG
MY NEW BOOK. I FIGURED YOU SHOULD HAVE A COPY, YOU KNOW, SINCE IT'S ABOUT *YOU.*
I HEAR IT'S SELLING LIKE CHRISTMAS FUDGE.
I STILL CAN'T BELIEVE THEY BLACKLISTED YOU. I KEPT IMAGINING THEY'D FAIL. THAT OUR COUNTRY WOULD COME TO ITS SENSES.
I GUESS, LIKE MOST WRITERS, I WAS SEDUCED BY MY NEED FOR A HAPPY ENDING.

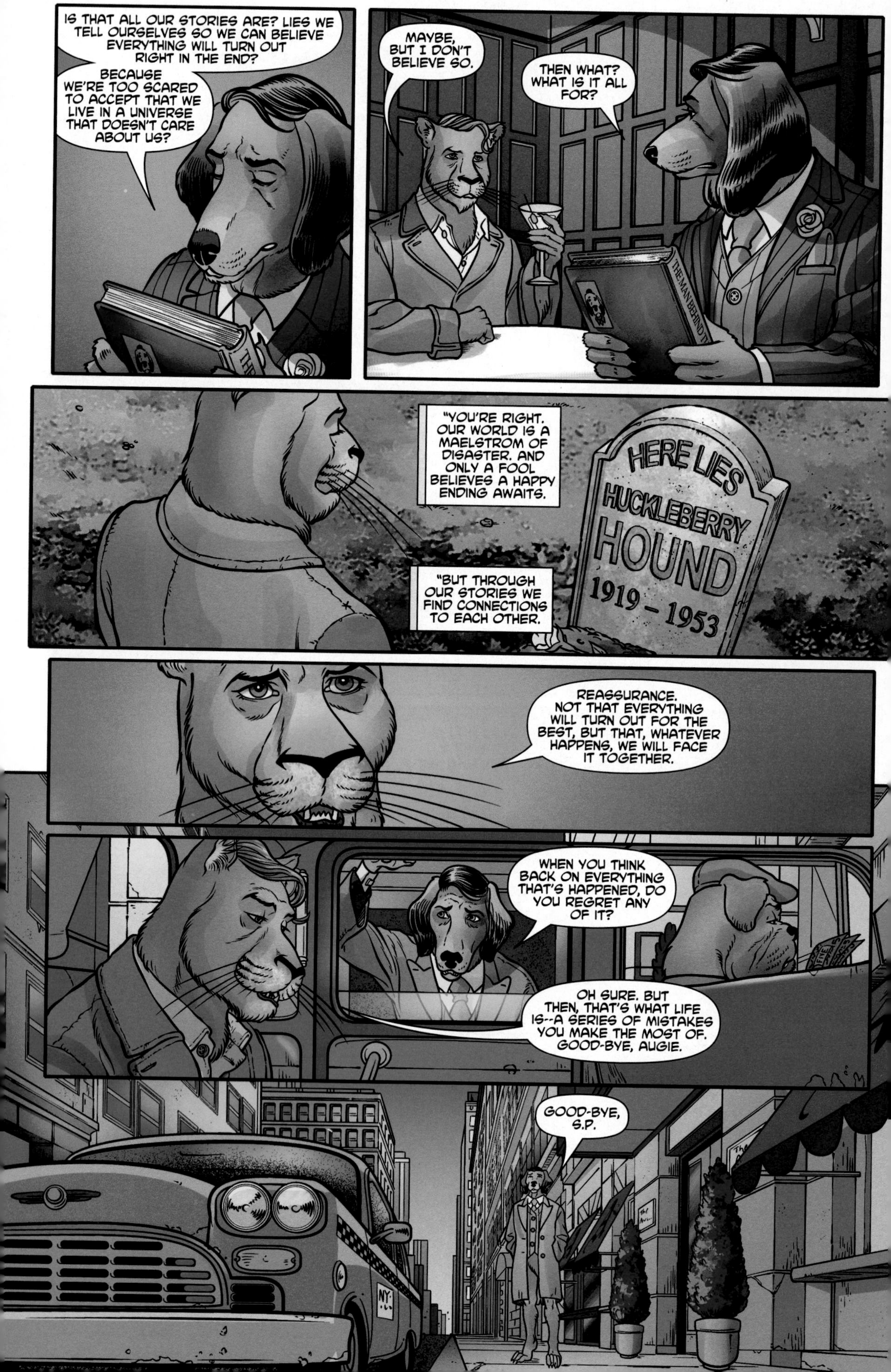
IS THAT ALL OUR STORIES ARE? LIES WE TELL OURSELVES SO WE CAN BELIEVE EVERYTHING WILL TURN OUT RIGHT IN THE END?
BECAUSE WE'RE TOO SCARED TO ACCEPT THAT WE LIVE IN A UNIVERSE THAT DOESN'T CARE ABOUT US?
MAYBE, BUT I DON'T BELIEVE SO.
THEN WHAT? WHAT IS IT ALL FOR?
THE MAN BEHIND
"YOU'RE RIGHT. OUR WORLD IS A MAELSTROM OF DISASTER. AND ONLY A FOOL BELIEVES A HAPPY ENDING AWAITS.
HERE LIES HUCKLEBERRY HOUND 1919 – 1953
"BUT THROUGH OUR STORIES WE FIND CONNECTIONS TO EACH OTHER.
REASSURANCE. NOT THAT EVERYTHING WILL TURN OUT FOR THE BEST, BUT THAT, WHATEVER HAPPENS, WE WILL FACE IT TOGETHER.
WHEN YOU THINK BACK ON EVERYTHING THAT'S HAPPENED, DO YOU REGRET ANY OF IT?
OH SURE. BUT THEN, THAT'S WHAT LIFE IS--A SERIES OF MISTAKES YOU MAKE THE MOST OF. GOOD-BYE, AUGIE.
GOOD-BYE, S.P.
NY

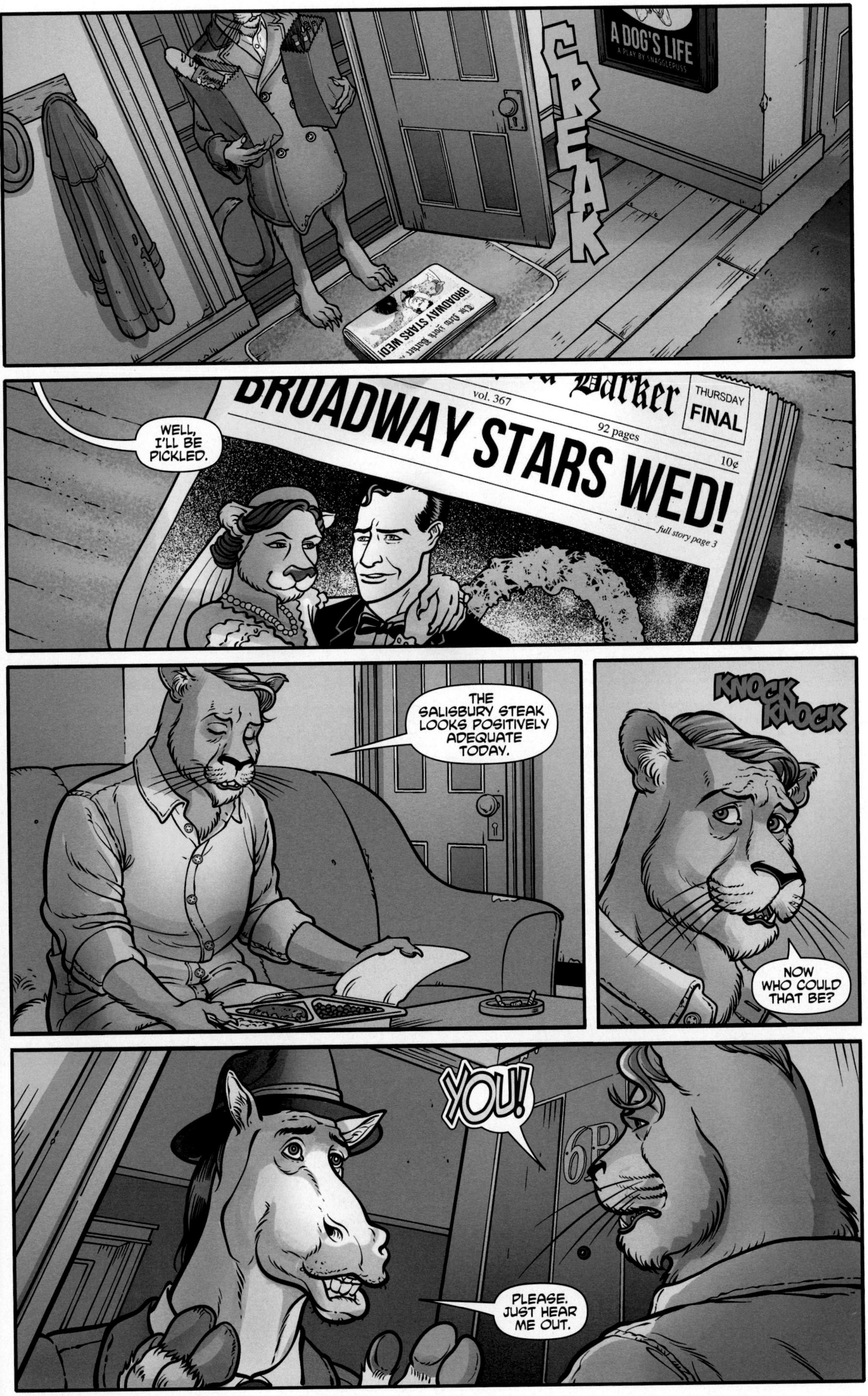
A DOG'S LIFE
A PLAY BY SNAGGLEPUSS
CREAK
BROADWAY STARS WED!
WELL, I'LL BE PICKLED.
Barker
vol. 367
THURSDAY
FINAL
92 pages
10¢
BROADWAY STARS WED!
full story page 3
THE SALISBURY STEAK LOOKS POSITIVELY ADEQUATE TODAY.
KNOCK KNOCK
NOW WHO COULD THAT BE?
YOU!
6B
PLEASE. JUST HEAR ME OUT.

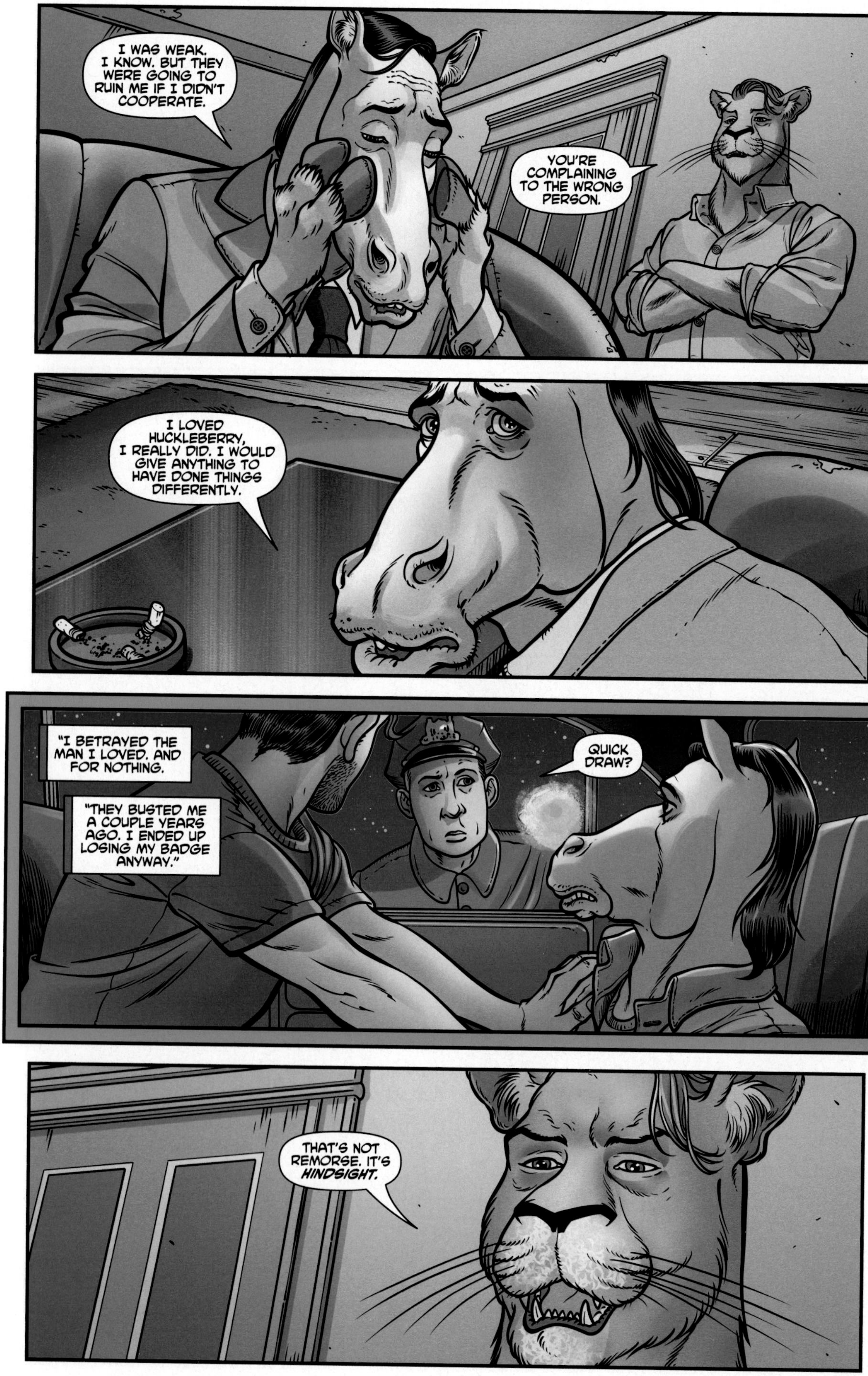
I WAS WEAK. I KNOW. BUT THEY WERE GOING TO RUIN ME IF I DIDN'T COOPERATE.
YOU'RE COMPLAINING TO THE WRONG PERSON.
I LOVED HUCKLEBERRY, I REALLY DID. I WOULD GIVE ANYTHING TO HAVE DONE THINGS DIFFERENTLY.
"I BETRAYED THE MAN I LOVED. AND FOR NOTHING.
"THEY BUSTED ME A COUPLE YEARS AGO. I ENDED UP LOSING MY BADGE ANYWAY."
QUICK DRAW?
THAT'S NOT REMORSE. IT'S *HINDSIGHT.*

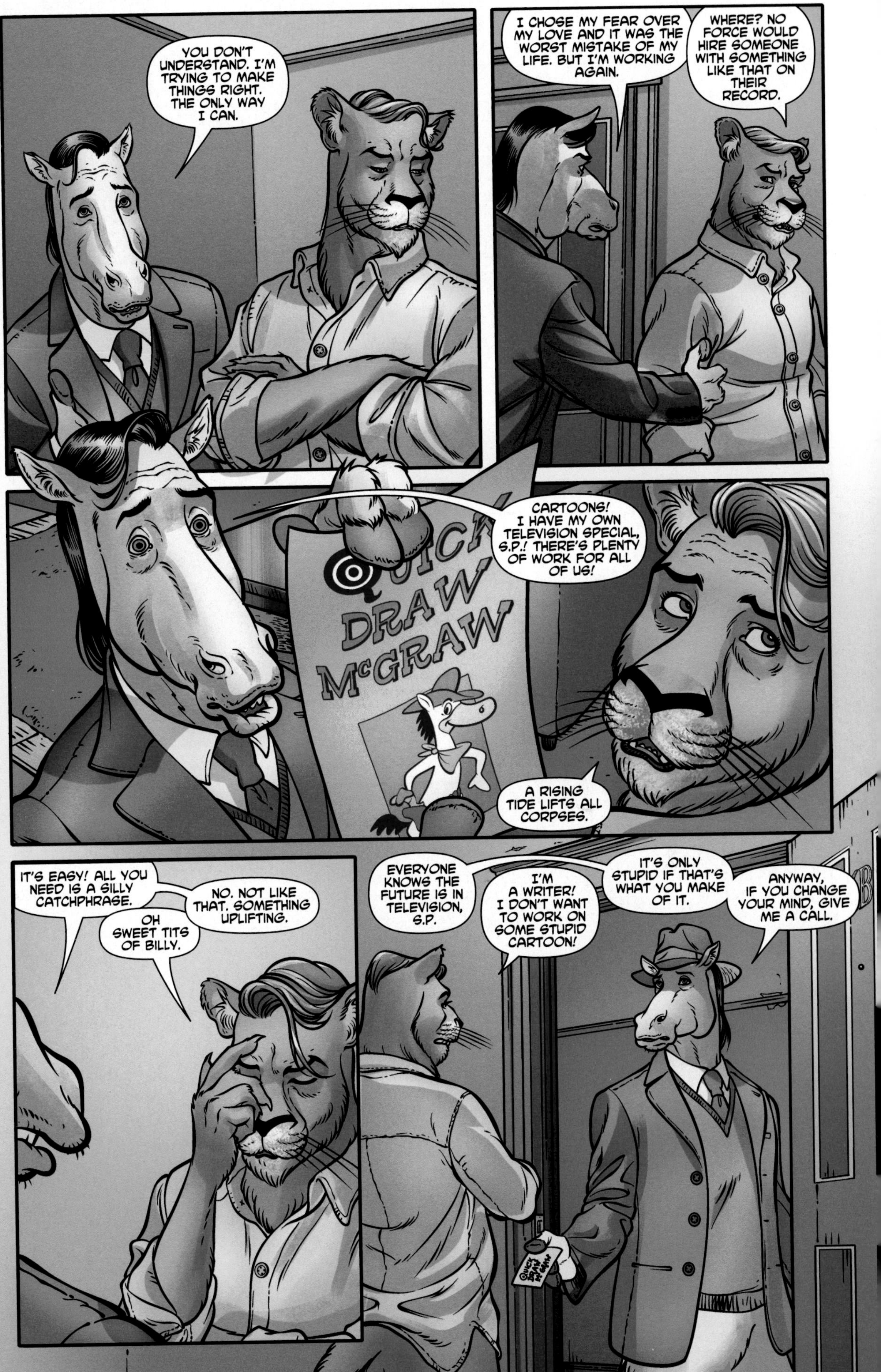
YOU DON'T UNDERSTAND. I'M TRYING TO MAKE THINGS RIGHT. THE ONLY WAY I CAN.
I CHOSE MY FEAR OVER MY LOVE AND IT WAS THE WORST MISTAKE OF MY LIFE. BUT I'M WORKING AGAIN.
WHERE? NO FORCE WOULD HIRE SOMEONE WITH SOMETHING LIKE THAT ON THEIR RECORD.
CARTOONS! I HAVE MY OWN TELEVISION SPECIAL, S.P.! THERE'S PLENTY OF WORK FOR ALL OF US!
QUICK DRAW McGRAW
A RISING TIDE LIFTS ALL CORPSES.
IT'S EASY! ALL YOU NEED IS A SILLY CATCHPHRASE.
NO. NOT LIKE THAT. SOMETHING UPLIFTING.
OH SWEET TITS OF BILLY.
EVERYONE KNOWS THE FUTURE IS IN TELEVISION, S.P.
I'M A WRITER! I DON'T WANT TO WORK ON SOME STUPID CARTOON!
IT'S ONLY STUPID IF THAT'S WHAT YOU MAKE OF IT.
ANYWAY, IF YOU CHANGE YOUR MIND, GIVE ME A CALL.

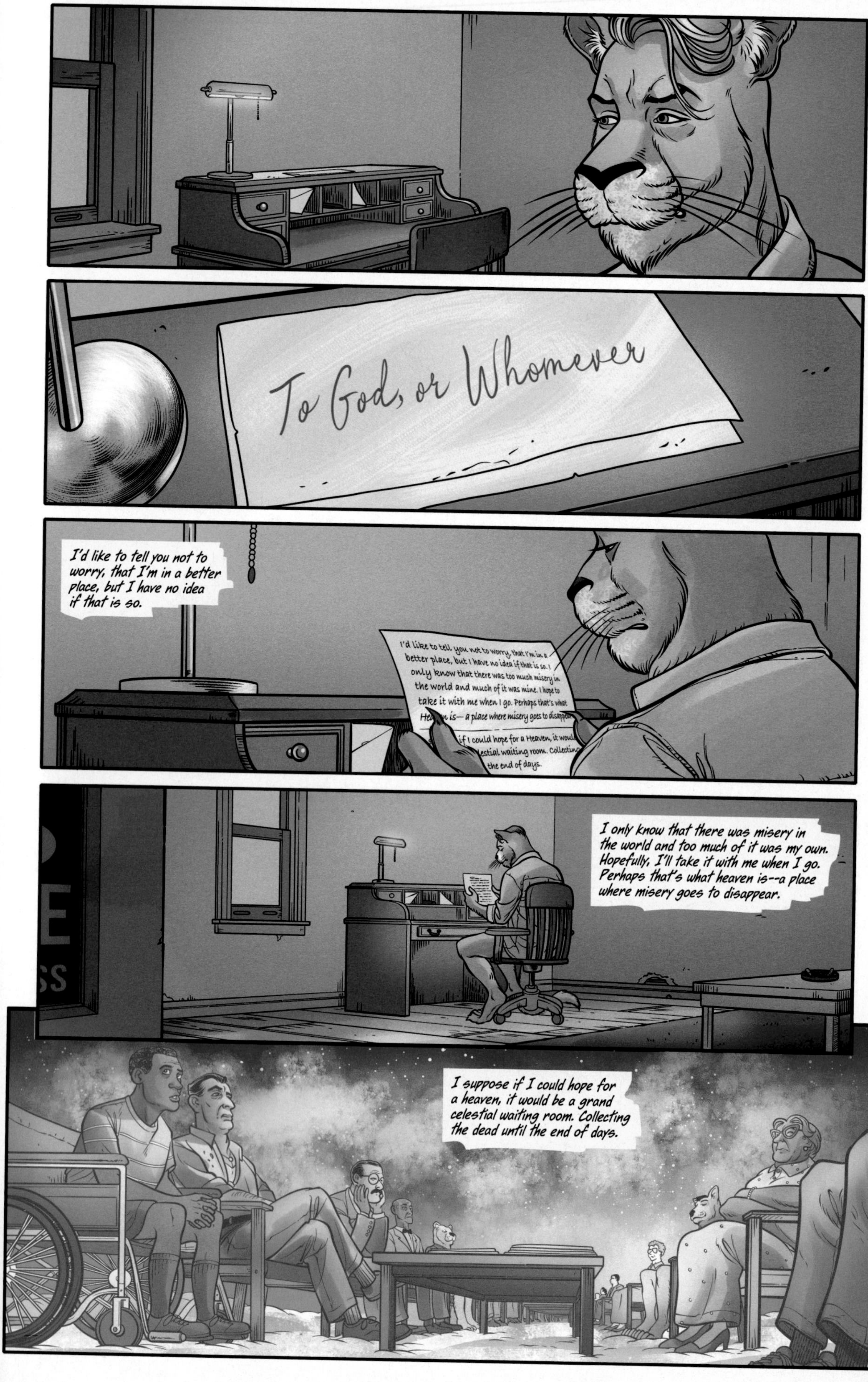
To God, or Whomever
I'd like to tell you not to worry, that I'm in a better place, but I have no idea if that is so.
I only know that there was misery in the world and too much of it was my own. Hopefully, I'll take it with me when I go. Perhaps that's what heaven is--a place where misery goes to disappear.
I suppose if I could hope for a heaven, it would be a grand celestial waiting room. Collecting the dead until the end of days.

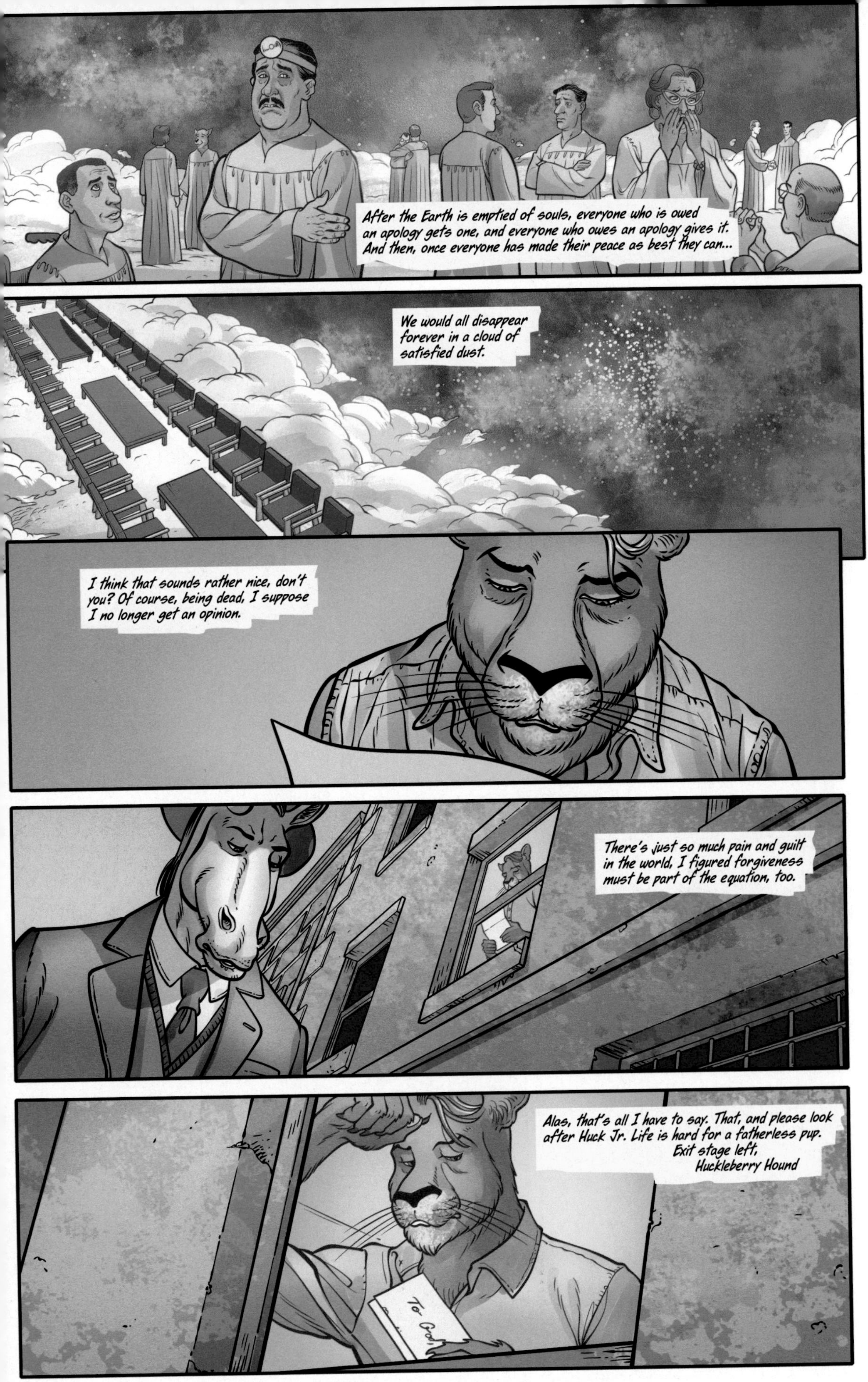
After the Earth is emptied of souls, everyone who is owed an apology gets one, and everyone who owes an apology gives it. And then, once everyone has made their peace as best they can...
We would all disappear forever in a cloud of satisfied dust.
I think that sounds rather nice, don't you? Of course, being dead, I suppose I no longer get an opinion.
There's just so much pain and guilt in the world, I figured forgiveness must be part of the equation, too.
Alas, that's all I have to say. That, and please look after Huck Jr. Life is hard for a fatherless pup.
Exit stage left,
Huckleberry Hound
To: God,

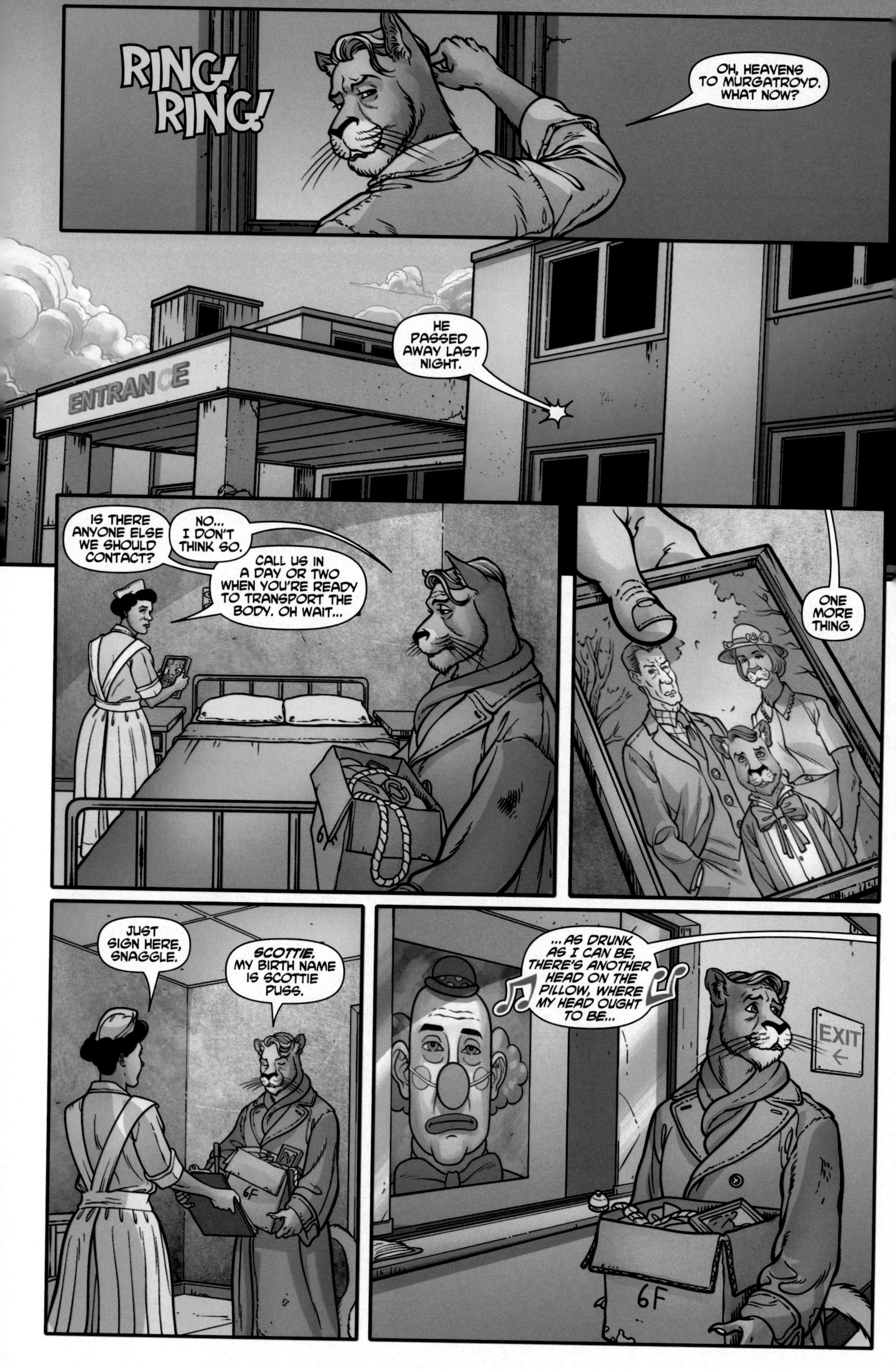
RING! RING!
OH, HEAVENS TO MURGATROYD. WHAT NOW?
ENTRANCE
HE PASSED AWAY LAST NIGHT.
IS THERE ANYONE ELSE WE SHOULD CONTACT?
NO... I DON'T THINK SO.
CALL US IN A DAY OR TWO WHEN YOU'RE READY TO TRANSPORT THE BODY. OH WAIT...
ONE MORE THING.
JUST SIGN HERE, SNAGGLE.
SCOTTIE. MY BIRTH NAME IS SCOTTIE PUSS.
6F
...AS DRUNK AS I CAN BE, THERE'S ANOTHER HEAD ON THE PILLOW, WHERE MY HEAD OUGHT TO BE...
EXIT
6F

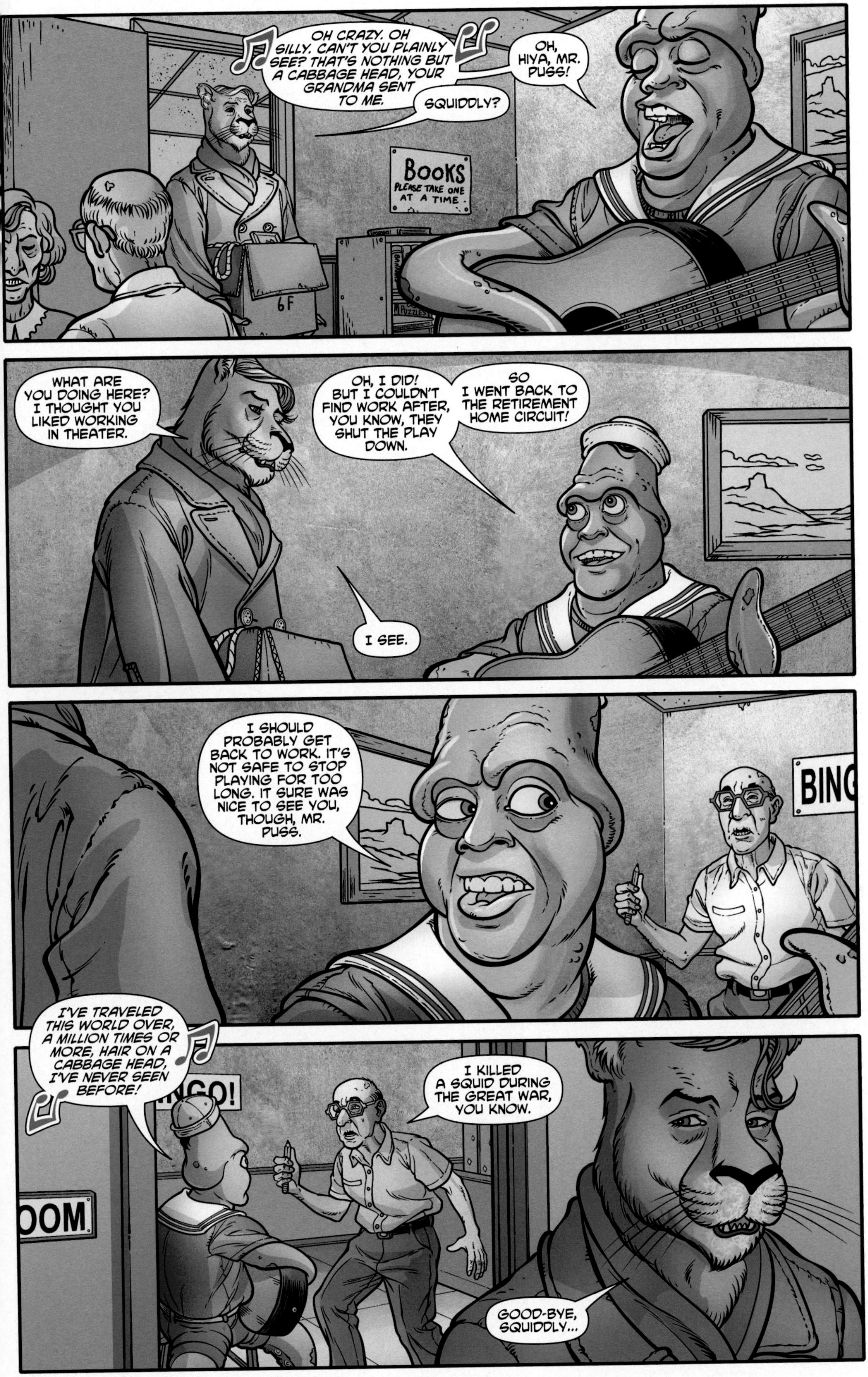
OH CRAZY. OH SILLY. CAN'T YOU PLAINLY SEE? THAT'S NOTHING BUT A CABBAGE HEAD, YOUR GRANDMA SENT TO ME.
OH, HIYA, MR. PUSS!
SQUIDDLY?
BOOKS PLEASE TAKE ONE AT A TIME.
6F
PUZZLES
WHAT ARE YOU DOING HERE? I THOUGHT YOU LIKED WORKING IN THEATER.
OH, I DID! BUT I COULDN'T FIND WORK AFTER, YOU KNOW, THEY SHUT THE PLAY DOWN.
SO I WENT BACK TO THE RETIREMENT HOME CIRCUIT!
I SEE.
I SHOULD PROBABLY GET BACK TO WORK. IT'S NOT SAFE TO STOP PLAYING FOR TOO LONG. IT SURE WAS NICE TO SEE YOU, THOUGH, MR. PUSS.
BING
I'VE TRAVELED THIS WORLD OVER, A MILLION TIMES OR MORE, HAIR ON A CABBAGE HEAD, I'VE NEVER SEEN BEFORE!
NGO!
OOM
I KILLED A SQUID DURING THE GREAT WAR, YOU KNOW.
GOOD-BYE, SQUIDDLY...

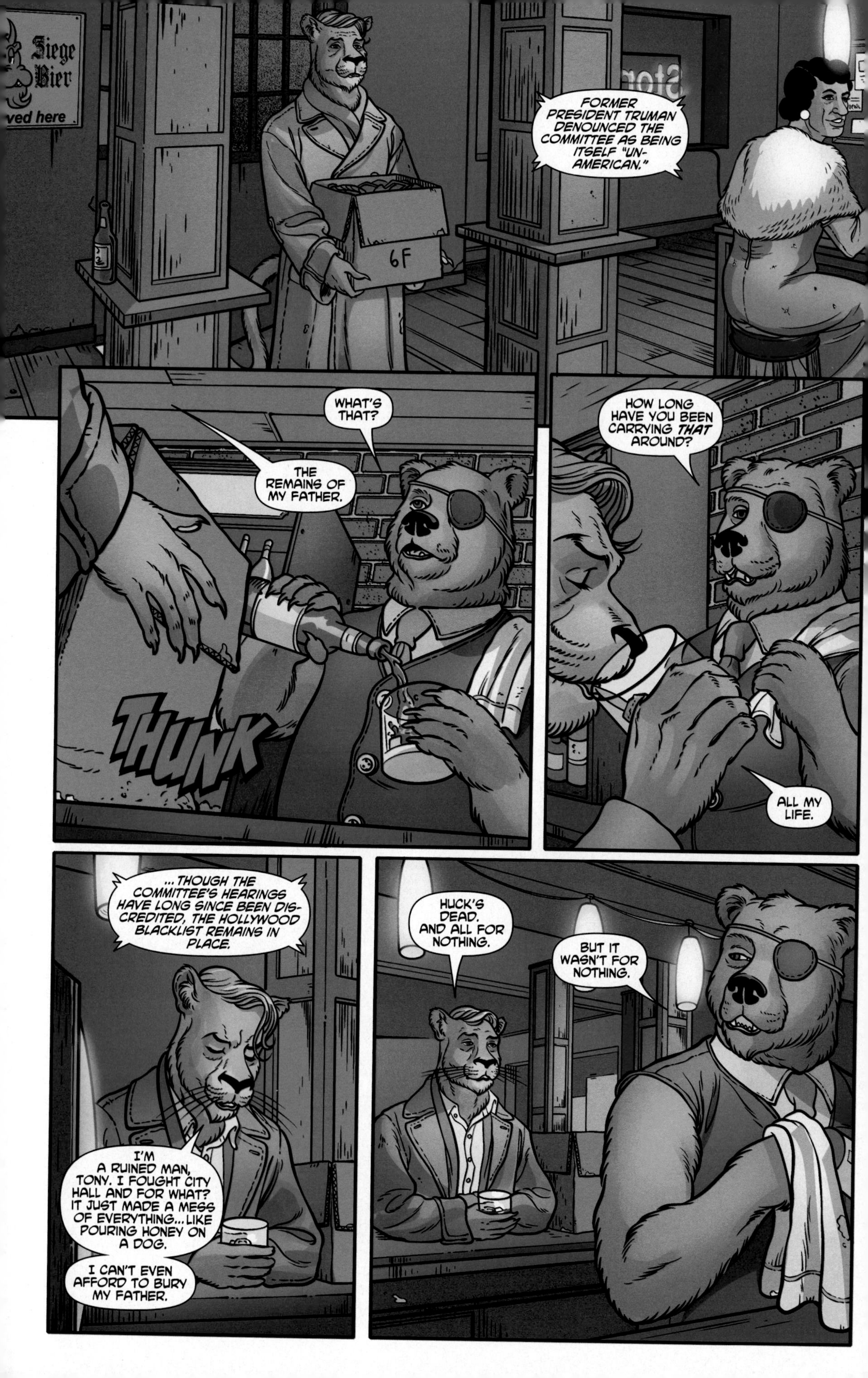
Siege Bier
ved here
FORMER PRESIDENT TRUMAN DENOUNCED THE COMMITTEE AS BEING ITSELF "UN-AMERICAN."
6F
WHAT'S THAT?
THE REMAINS OF MY FATHER.
THUNK
HOW LONG HAVE YOU BEEN CARRYING *THAT* AROUND?
ALL MY LIFE.
...THOUGH THE COMMITTEE'S HEARINGS HAVE LONG SINCE BEEN DISCREDITED, THE HOLLYWOOD BLACKLIST REMAINS IN PLACE.
I'M A RUINED MAN, TONY. I FOUGHT CITY HALL AND FOR WHAT? IT JUST MADE A MESS OF EVERYTHING...LIKE POURING HONEY ON A DOG.
I CAN'T EVEN AFFORD TO BURY MY FATHER.
HUCK'S DEAD. AND ALL FOR NOTHING.
BUT IT WASN'T FOR NOTHING.

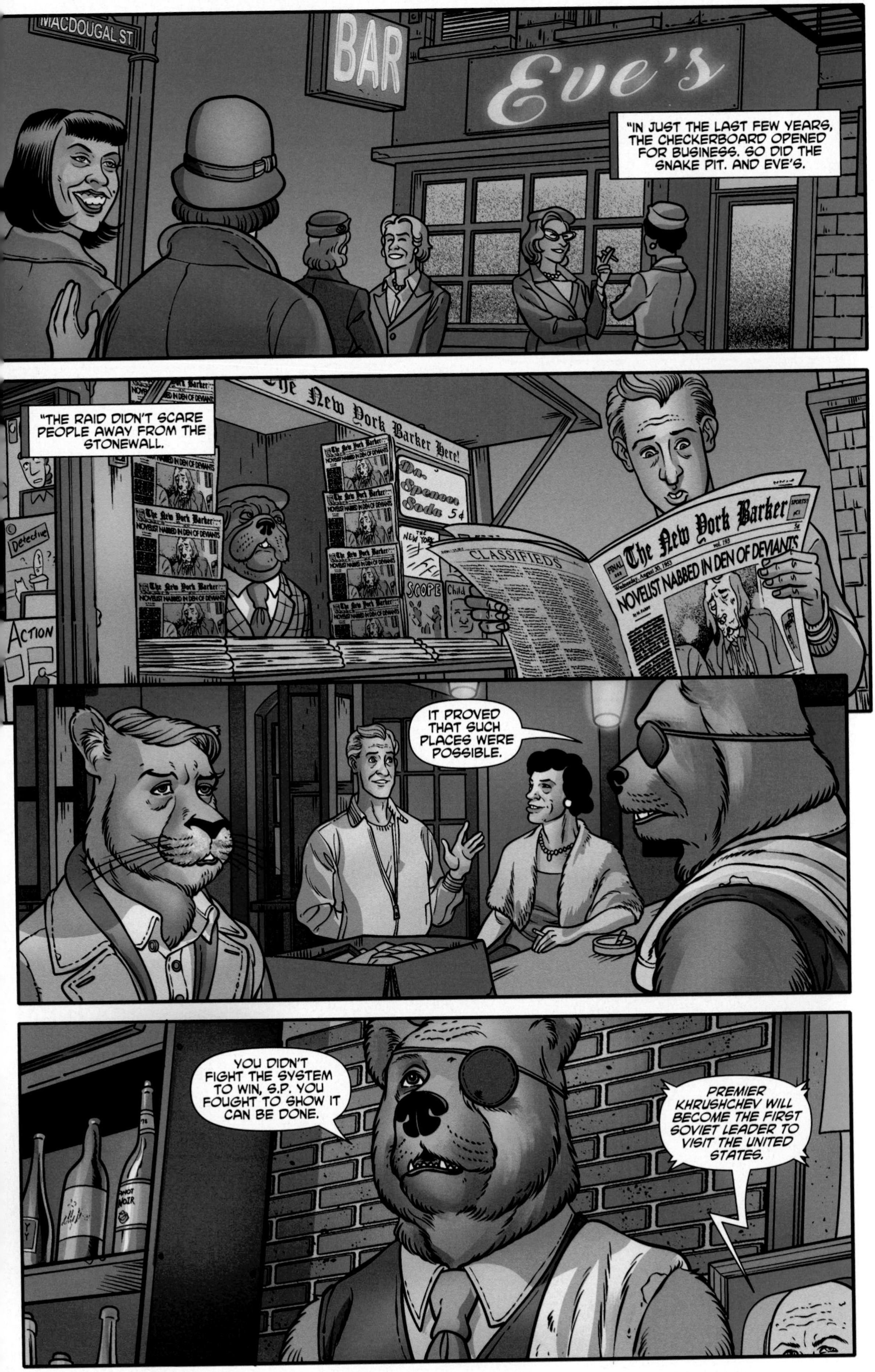
MACDOUGAL ST
BAR
Eve's
"IN JUST THE LAST FEW YEARS, THE CHECKERBOARD OPENED FOR BUSINESS. SO DID THE SNAKE PIT. AND EVE'S.
"THE RAID DIDN'T SCARE PEOPLE AWAY FROM THE STONEWALL.
The New York Barker Here!
Spencer Soda 5¢
The New York Barker
NOVELIST NABBED IN DEN OF DEVIANTS
CLASSIFIEDS
SCOPE
Detective
ACTION
IT PROVED THAT SUCH PLACES WERE POSSIBLE.
YOU DIDN'T FIGHT THE SYSTEM TO WIN, S.P. YOU FOUGHT TO SHOW IT CAN BE DONE.
PREMIER KHRUSHCHEV WILL BECOME THE FIRST SOVIET LEADER TO VISIT THE UNITED STATES.

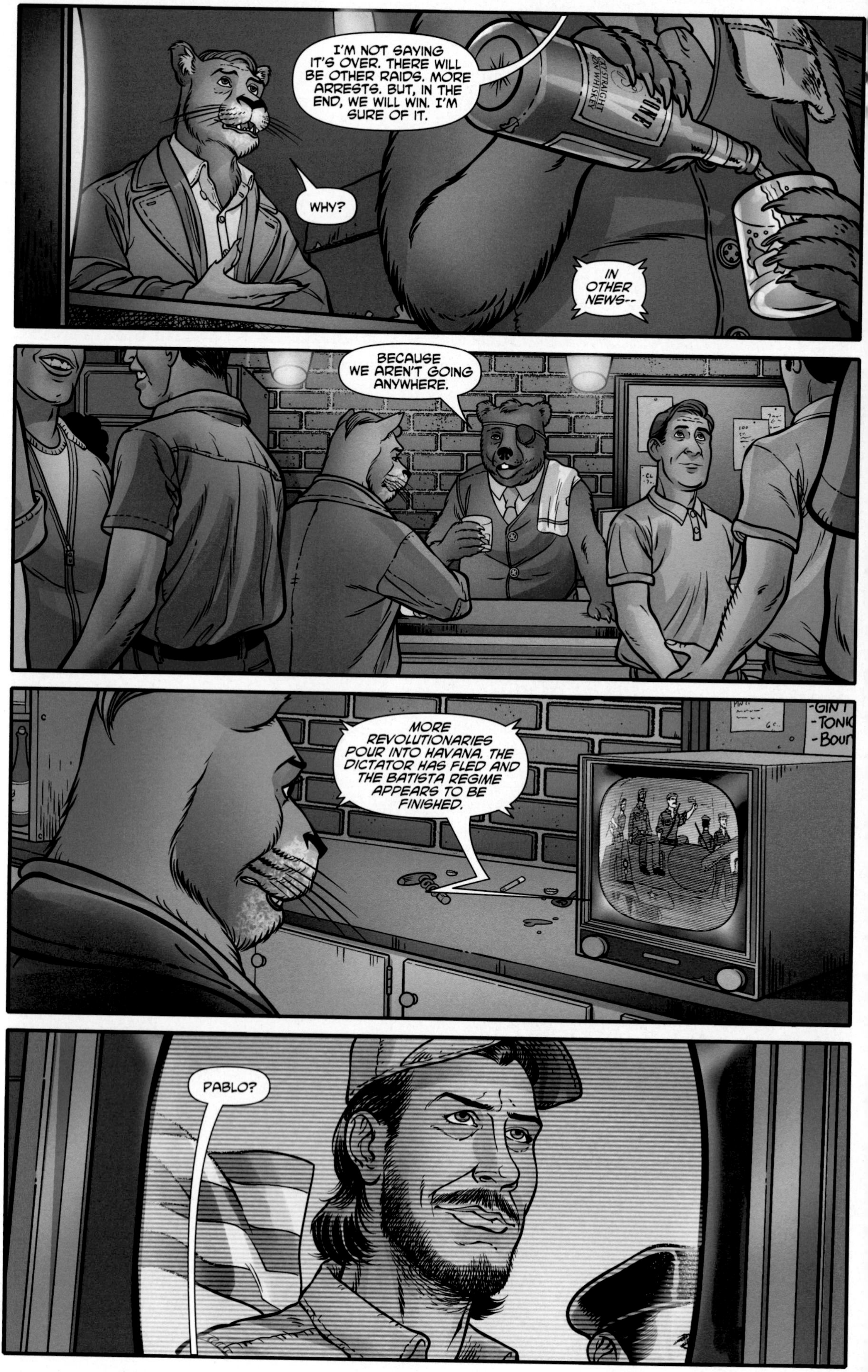
I'M NOT SAYING IT'S OVER. THERE WILL BE OTHER RAIDS. MORE ARRESTS. BUT, IN THE END, WE WILL WIN. I'M SURE OF IT.
WHY?
IN OTHER NEWS--
BECAUSE WE AREN'T GOING ANYWHERE.
MORE REVOLUTIONARIES POUR INTO HAVANA. THE DICTATOR HAS FLED AND THE BATISTA REGIME APPEARS TO BE FINISHED.
PABLO?

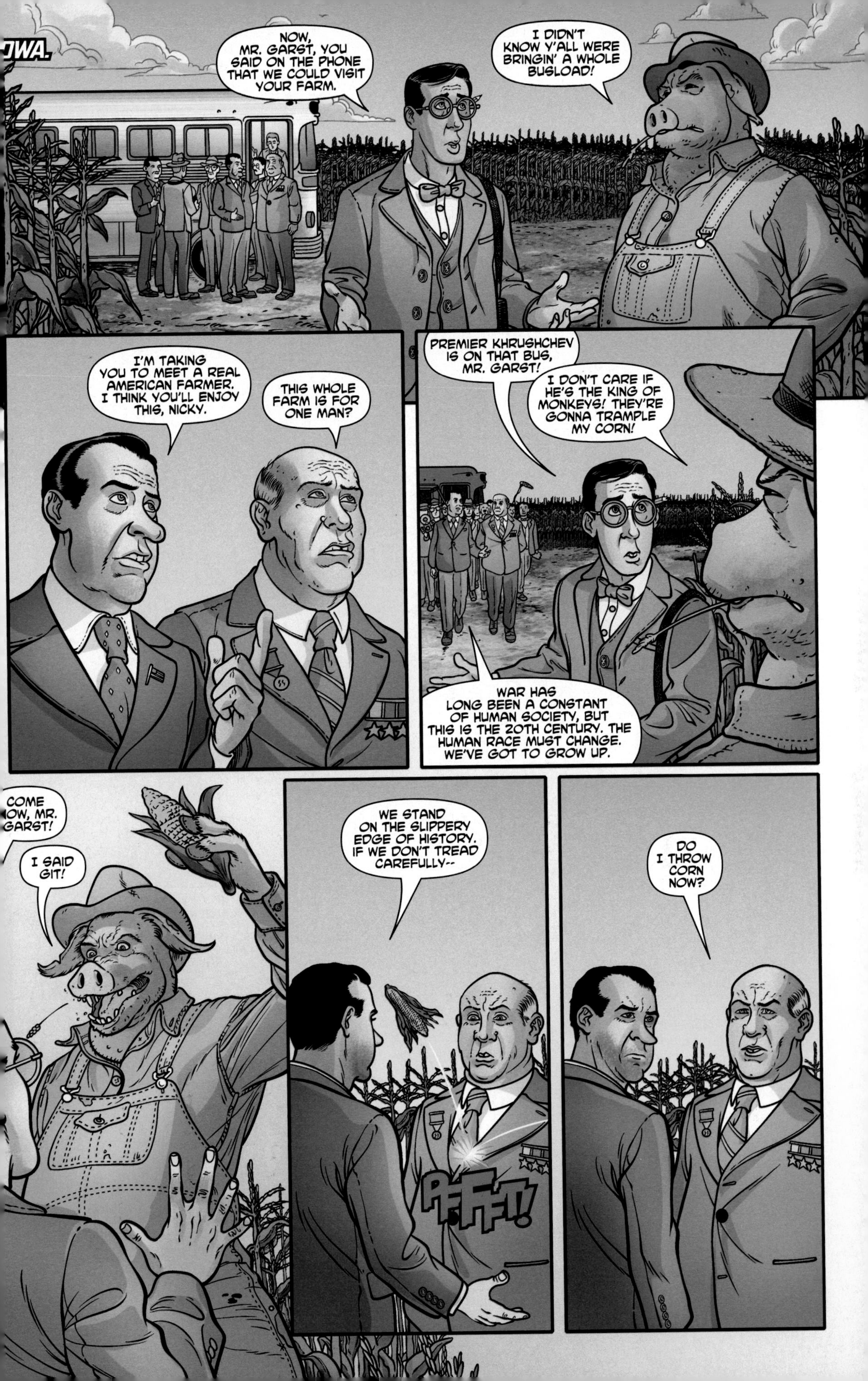
OWA.
NOW, MR. GARST, YOU SAID ON THE PHONE THAT WE COULD VISIT YOUR FARM.
I DIDN'T KNOW Y'ALL WERE BRINGIN' A WHOLE BUSLOAD!
I'M TAKING YOU TO MEET A REAL AMERICAN FARMER. I THINK YOU'LL ENJOY THIS, NICKY.
THIS WHOLE FARM IS FOR ONE MAN?
PREMIER KHRUSHCHEV IS ON THAT BUS, MR. GARST!
I DON'T CARE IF HE'S THE KING OF MONKEYS! THEY'RE GONNA TRAMPLE MY CORN!
WAR HAS LONG BEEN A CONSTANT OF HUMAN SOCIETY, BUT THIS IS THE 20TH CENTURY. THE HUMAN RACE MUST CHANGE. WE'VE GOT TO GROW UP.
COME ON, MR. GARST!
I SAID GIT!
WE STAND ON THE SLIPPERY EDGE OF HISTORY. IF WE DON'T TREAD CAREFULLY--
PFFFT!
DO I THROW CORN NOW?

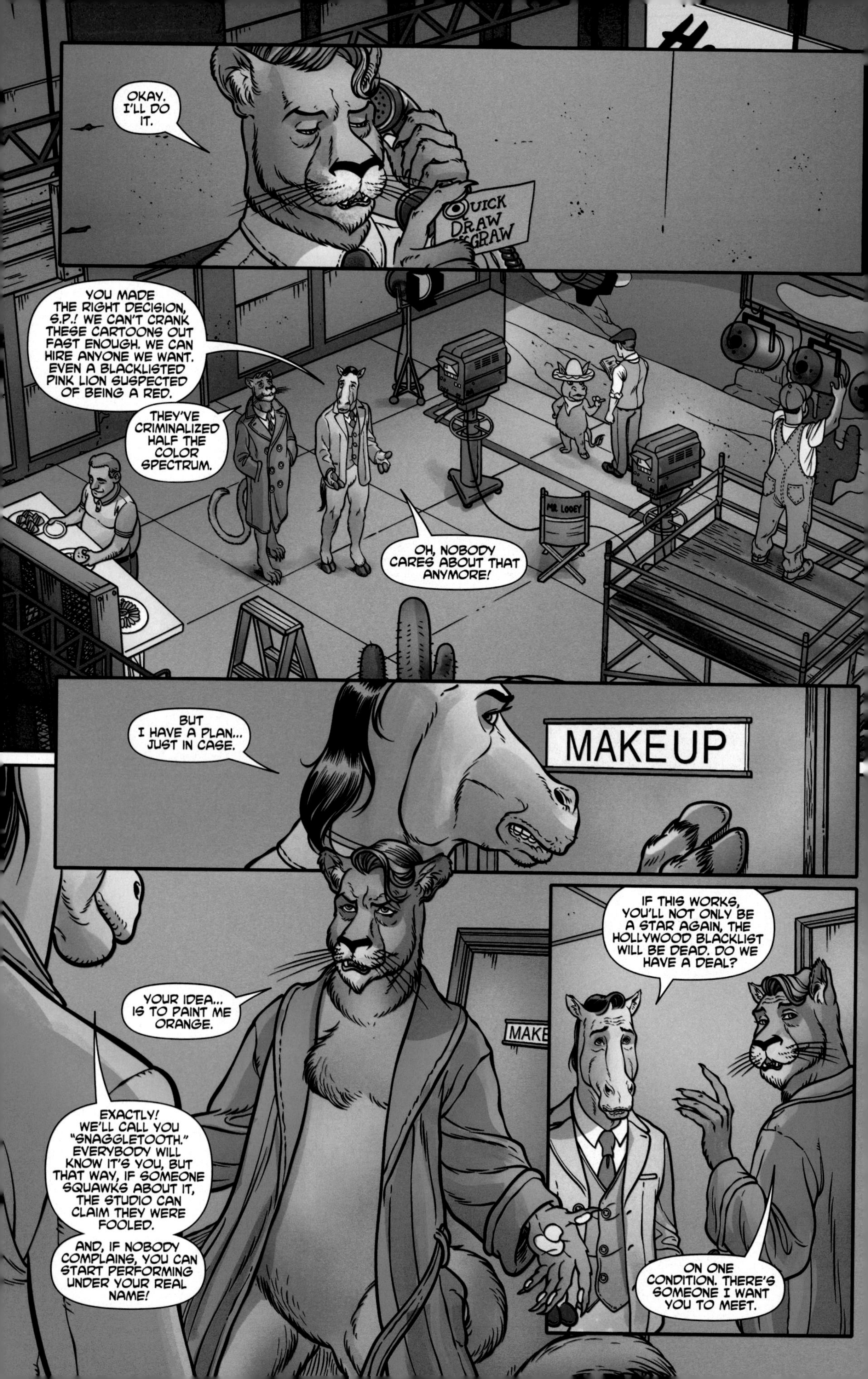
OKAY. I'LL DO IT.
QUICK DRAW McGRAW
YOU MADE THE RIGHT DECISION, S.P.! WE CAN'T CRANK THESE CARTOONS OUT FAST ENOUGH. WE CAN HIRE ANYONE WE WANT. EVEN A BLACKLISTED PINK LION SUSPECTED OF BEING A RED.
THEY'VE CRIMINALIZED HALF THE COLOR SPECTRUM.
MR. LOGEY
OH, NOBODY CARES ABOUT THAT ANYMORE!
BUT I HAVE A PLAN... JUST IN CASE.
MAKEUP
YOUR IDEA... IS TO PAINT ME ORANGE.
EXACTLY! WE'LL CALL YOU "SNAGGLETOOTH." EVERYBODY WILL KNOW IT'S YOU, BUT THAT WAY, IF SOMEONE SQUAWKS ABOUT IT, THE STUDIO CAN CLAIM THEY WERE FOOLED.
AND, IF NOBODY COMPLAINS, YOU CAN START PERFORMING UNDER YOUR REAL NAME!
IF THIS WORKS, YOU'LL NOT ONLY BE A STAR AGAIN, THE HOLLYWOOD BLACKLIST WILL BE DEAD. DO WE HAVE A DEAL?
ON ONE CONDITION. THERE'S SOMEONE I WANT YOU TO MEET.

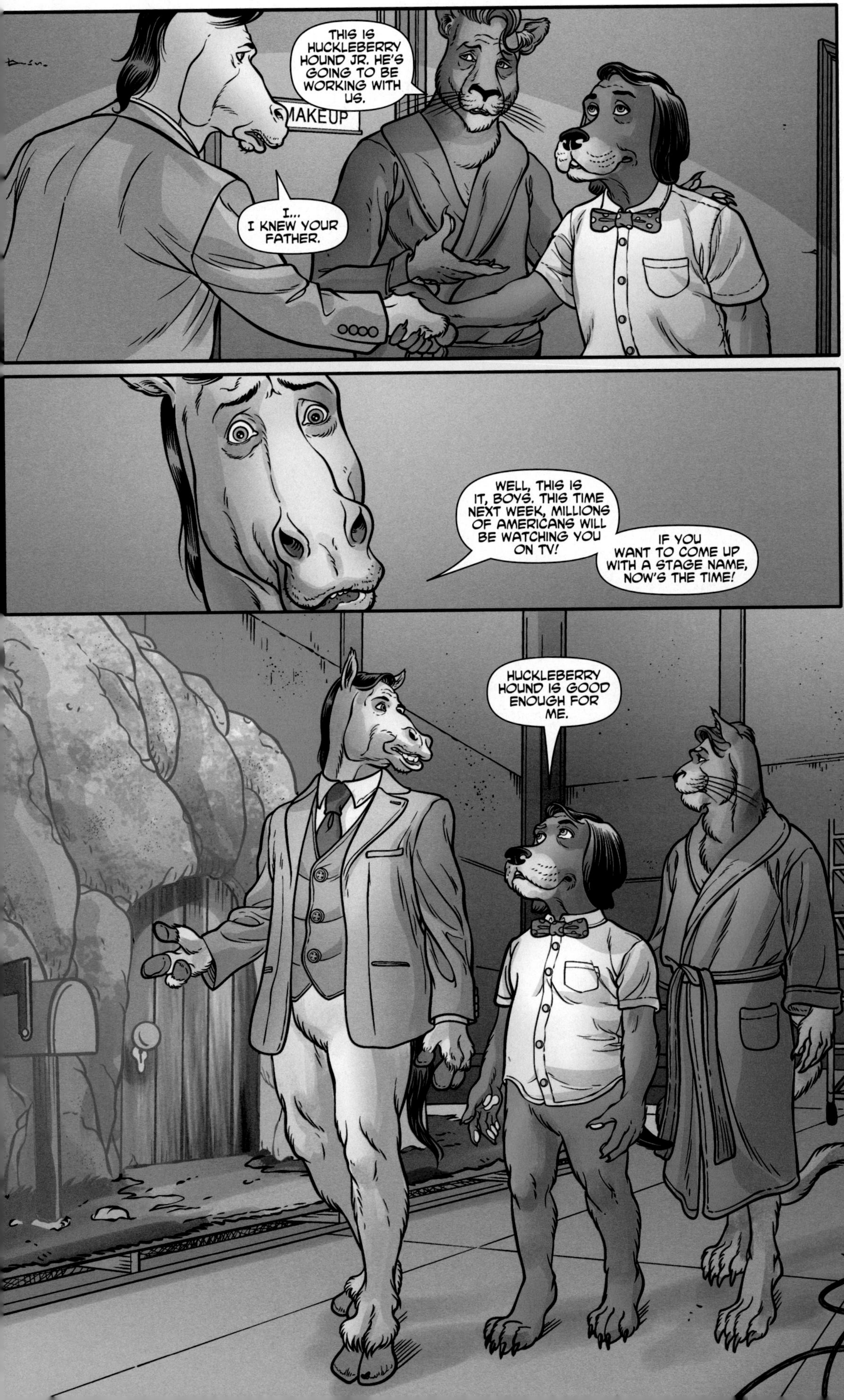
MAKEUP
THIS IS HUCKLEBERRY HOUND JR. HE'S GOING TO BE WORKING WITH US.
I... I KNEW YOUR FATHER.
WELL, THIS IS IT, BOYS. THIS TIME NEXT WEEK, MILLIONS OF AMERICANS WILL BE WATCHING YOU ON TV!
IF YOU WANT TO COME UP WITH A STAGE NAME, NOW'S THE TIME!
HUCKLEBERRY HOUND IS GOOD ENOUGH FOR ME.

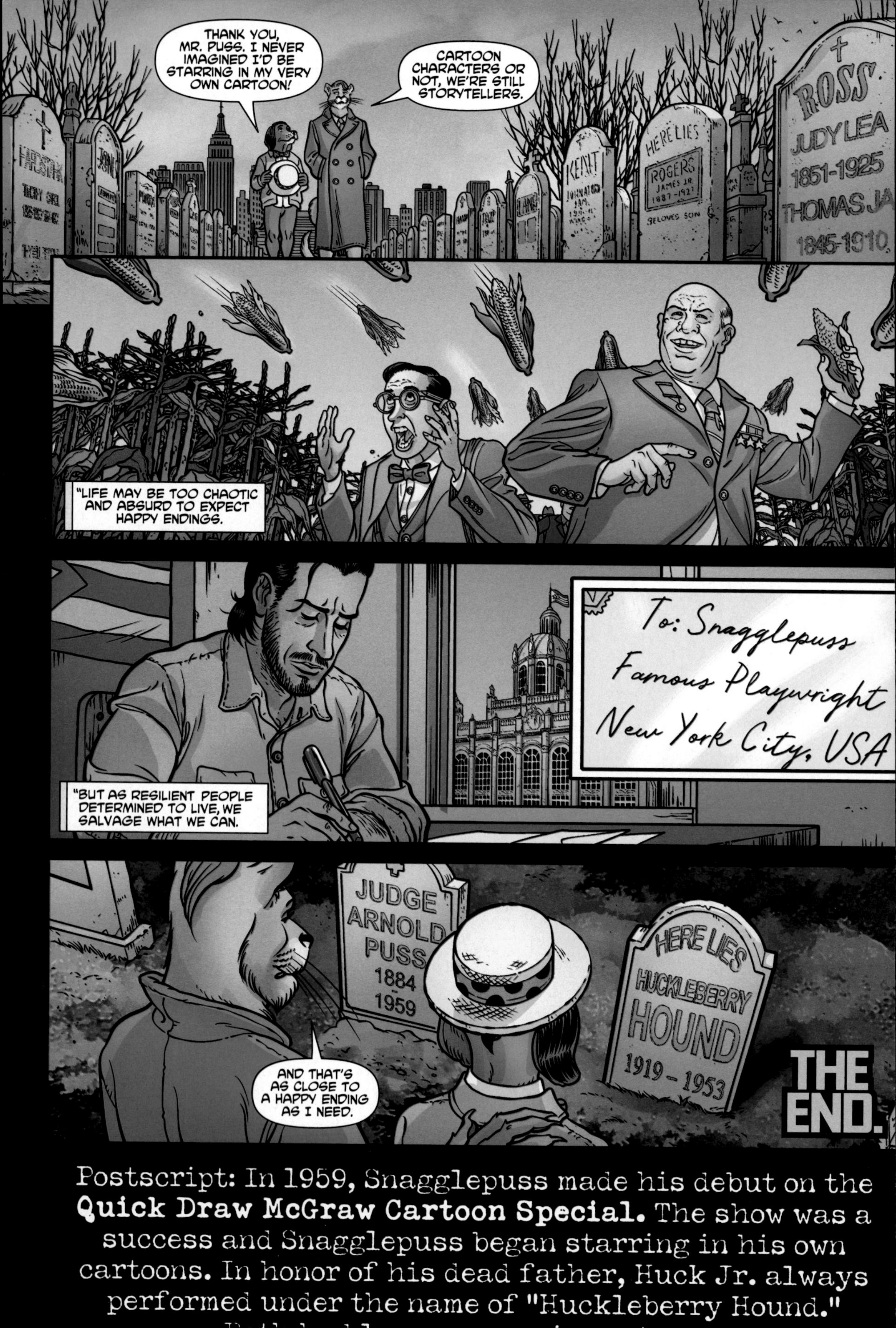
THANK YOU, MR. PUSS. I NEVER IMAGINED I'D BE STARRING IN MY VERY OWN CARTOON!
CARTOON CHARACTERS OR NOT, WE'RE STILL STORYTELLERS.
ROSS
JUDY LEA
1851-1925
THOMAS JA
1845-1910
HERE LIES
ROGERS
BELOVED SON
"LIFE MAY BE TOO CHAOTIC AND ABSURD TO EXPECT HAPPY ENDINGS.
To: Snagglepuss
Famous Playwright
New York City, USA
"BUT AS RESILIENT PEOPLE DETERMINED TO LIVE, WE SALVAGE WHAT WE CAN.
JUDGE ARNOLD PUSS
1884
1959
HERE LIES
HUCKLEBERRY HOUND
1919 – 1953
AND THAT'S AS CLOSE TO A HAPPY ENDING AS I NEED.
THE END.

Postscript: In 1959, Snagglepuss made his debut on the **Quick Draw McGraw Cartoon Special.** The show was a success and Snagglepuss began starring in his own cartoons. In honor of his dead father, Huck Jr. always performed under the name of "Huckleberry Hound." Both had long careers in cartoons, as did many of their friends.

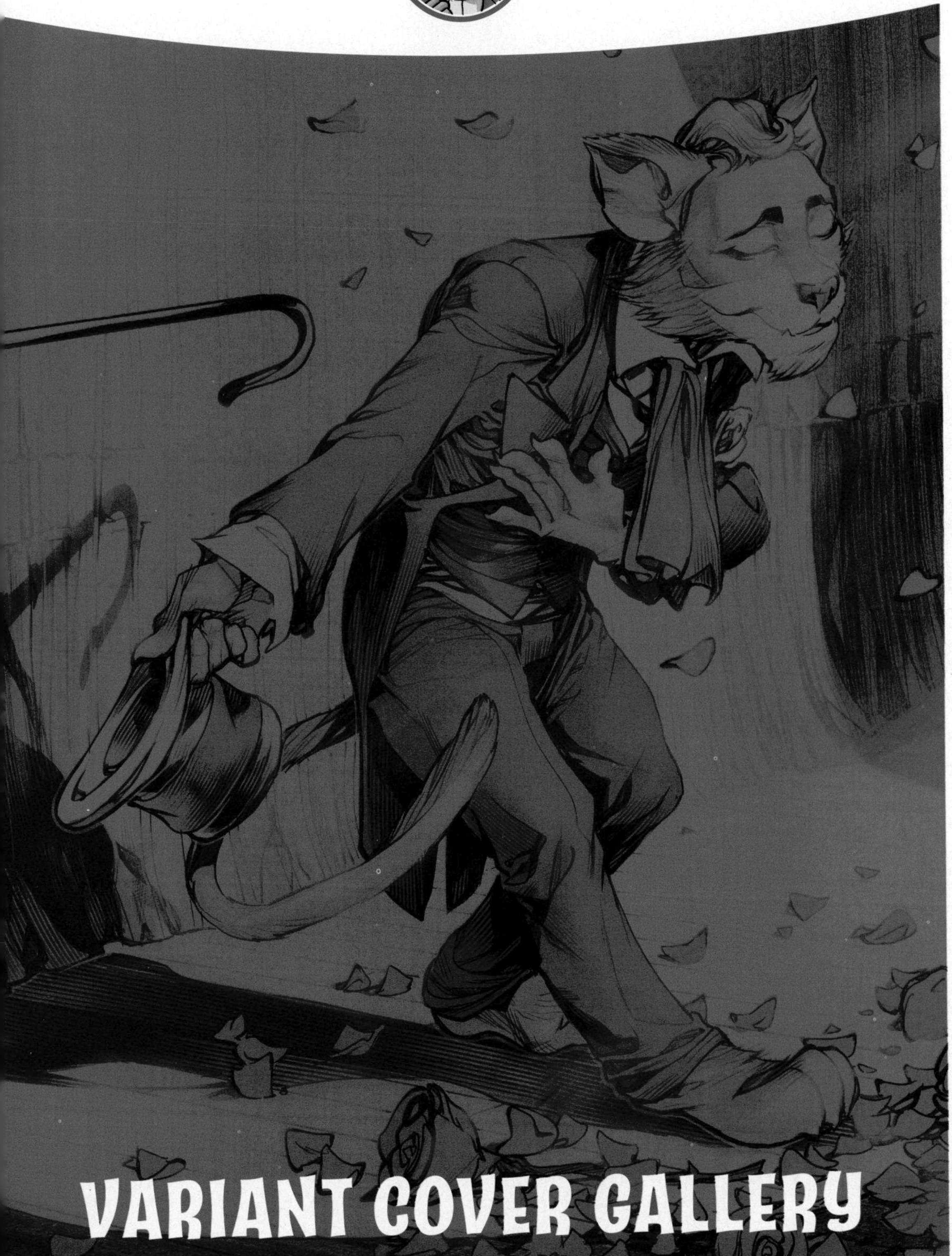

VARIANT COVER GALLERY

EXIT STAGE LEFT: THE SNAGGLEPUSS CHRONICLES #1
variant cover by EVAN "DOC" SHANER

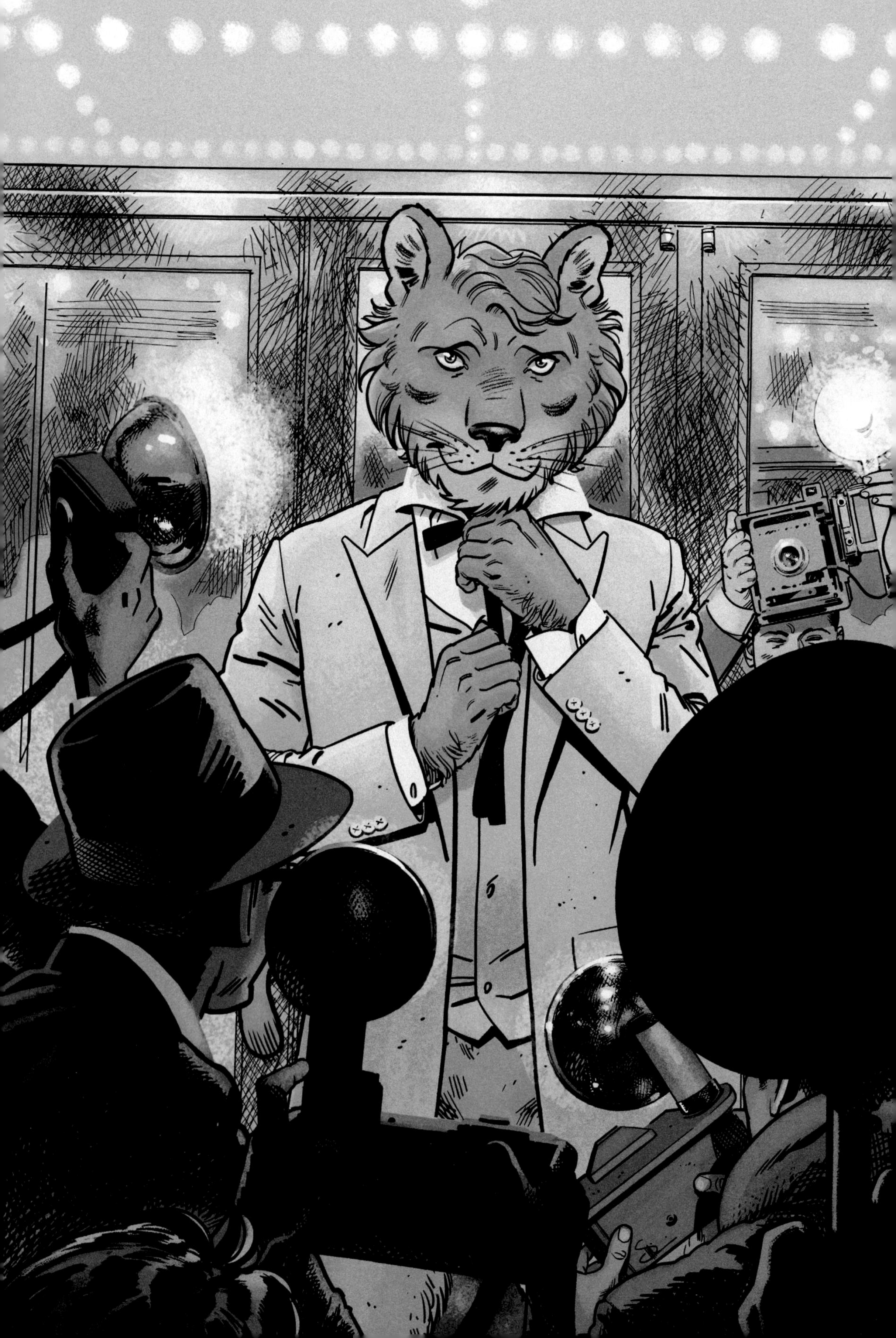

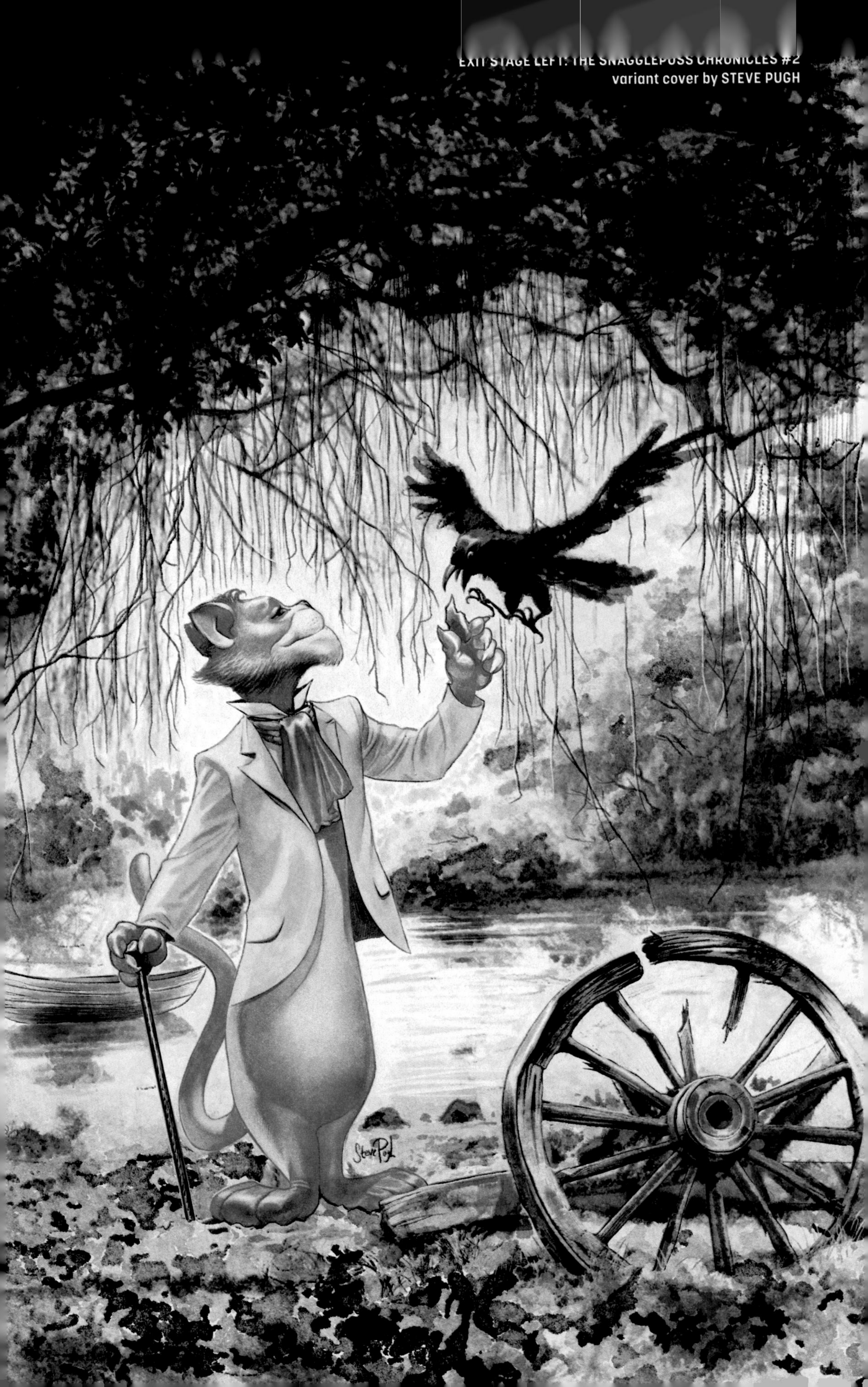

EXIT STAGE LEFT: THE SNAGGLEPUSS CHRONICLES #2
variant cover by STEVE PUGH

EXIT STAGE LEFT: THE SNAGGLEPUSS CHRONICLES #3
variant cover by DAN PANOSIAN

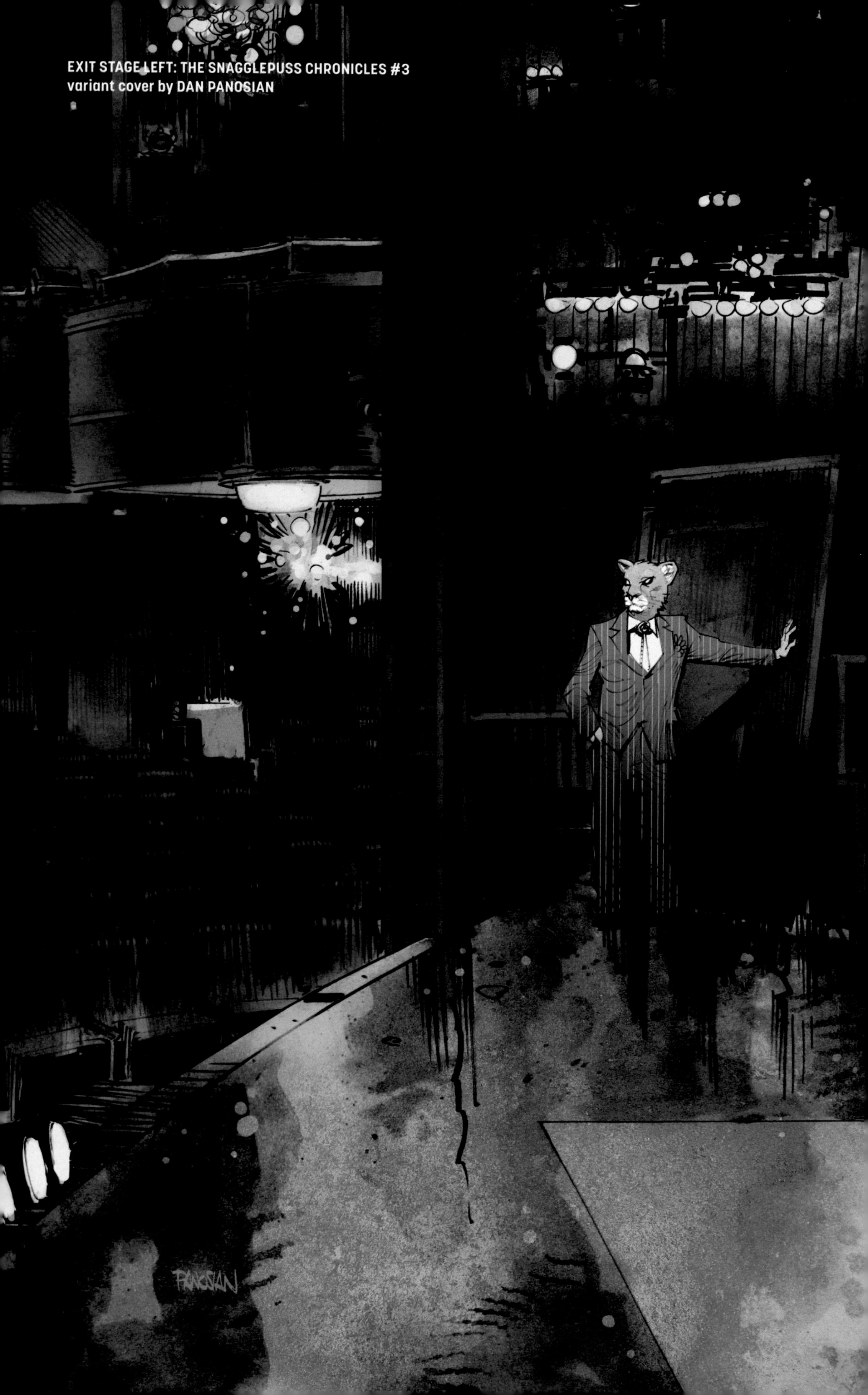
PANOSIAN

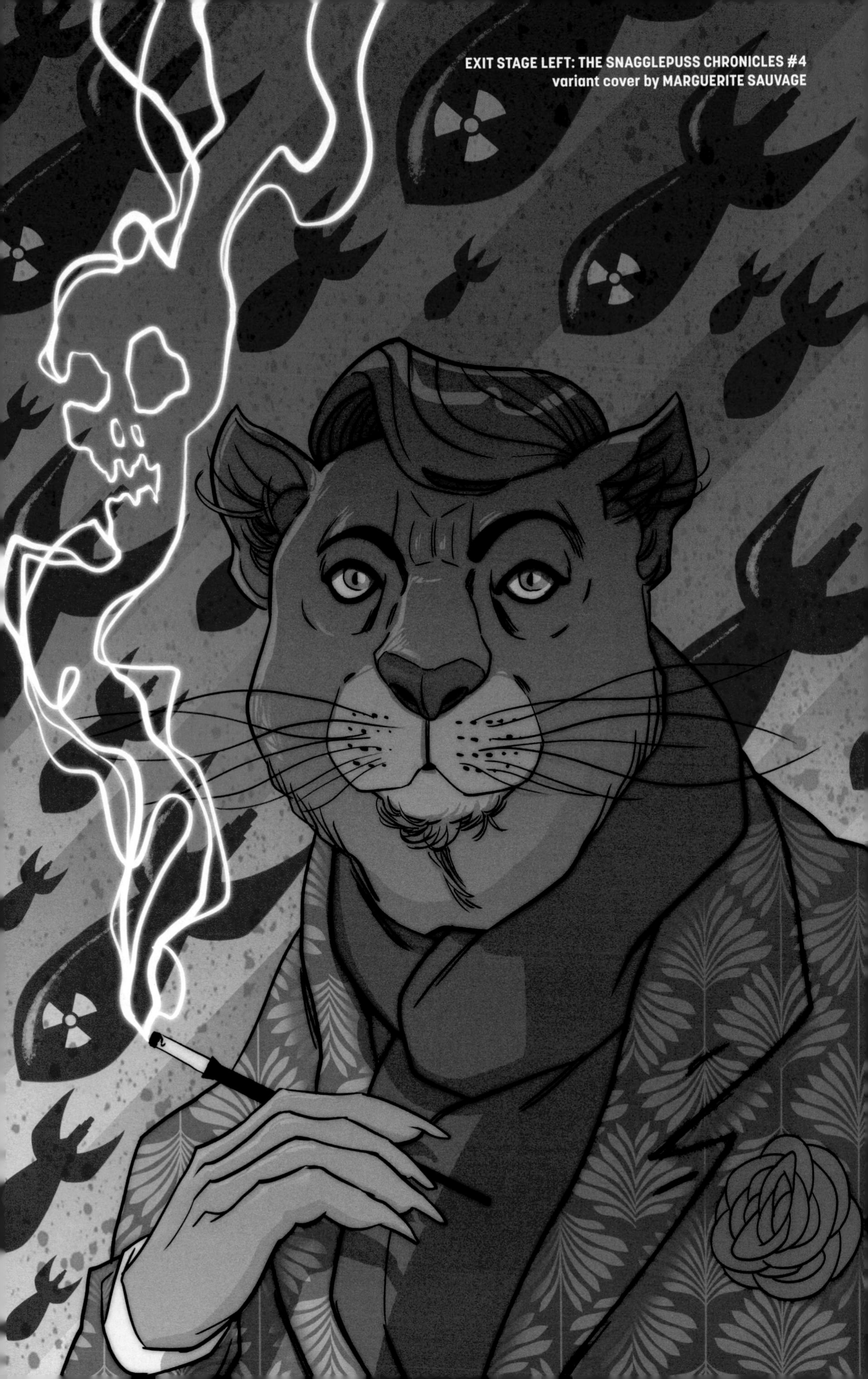

EXIT STAGE LEFT: THE SNAGGLEPUSS CHRONICLES #4
variant cover by MARGUERITE SAUVAGE

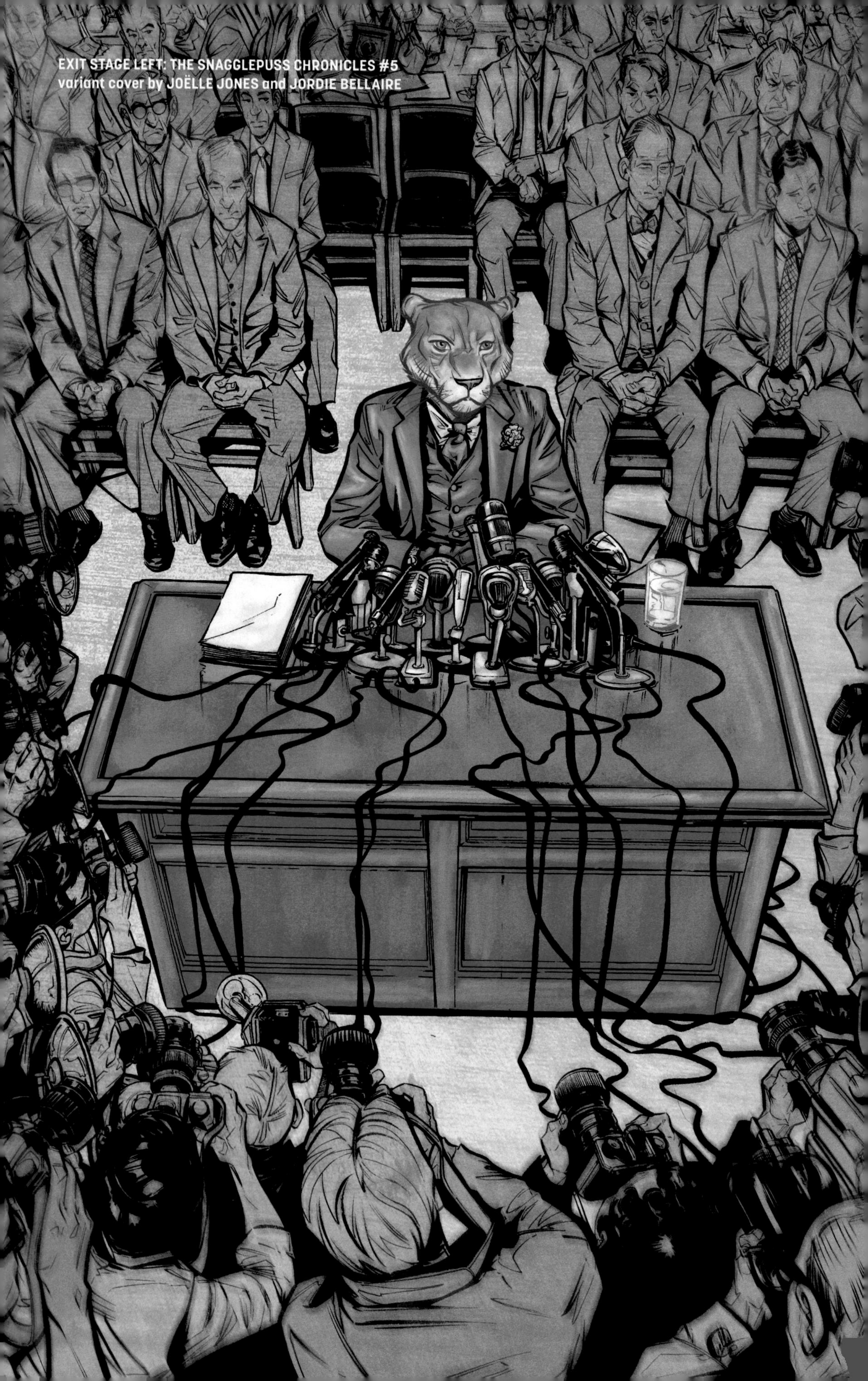

EXIT STAGE LEFT: THE SNAGGLEPUSS CHRONICLES #5
variant cover by JOËLLE JONES and JORDIE BELLAIRE

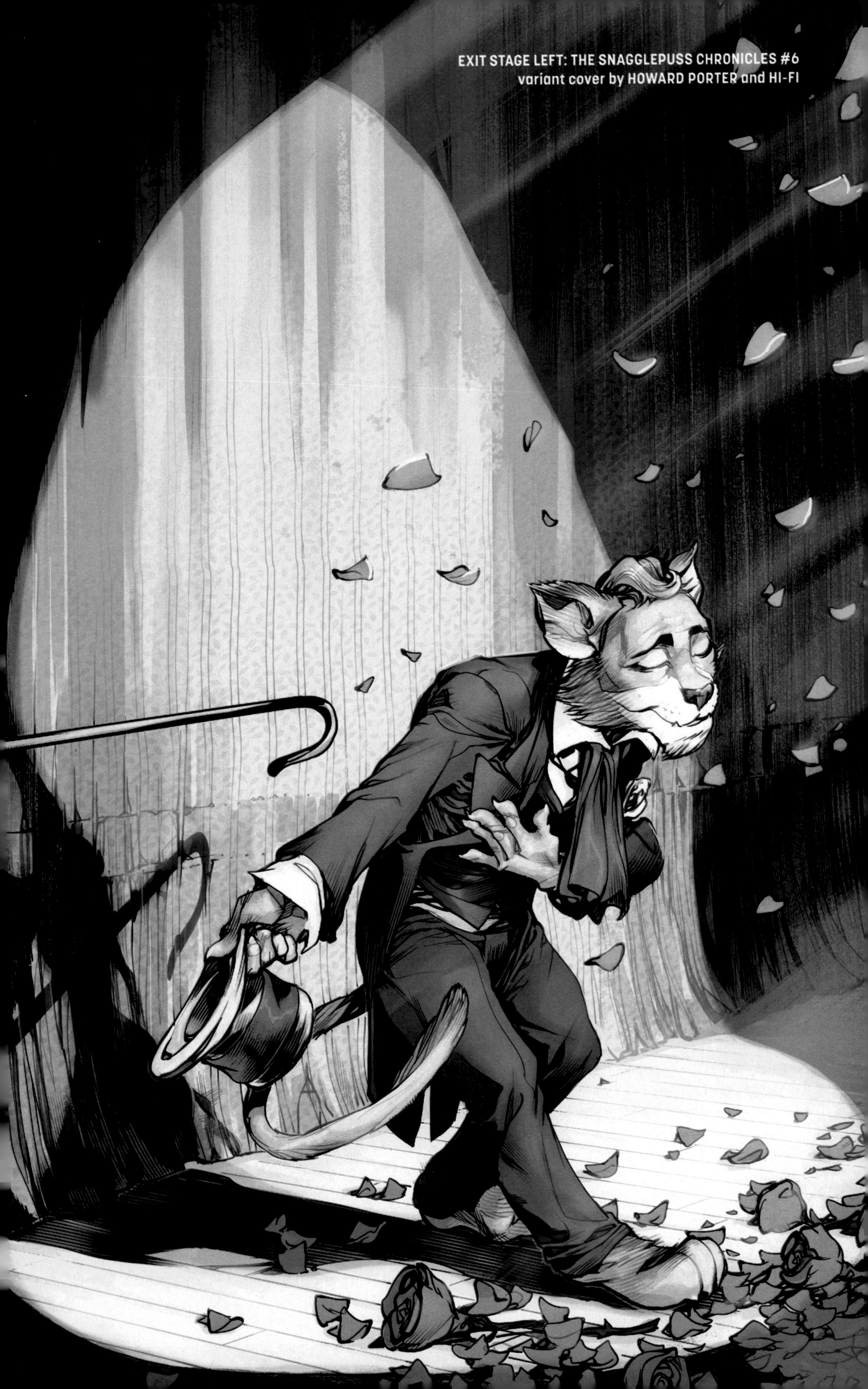

EXIT STAGE LEFT: THE SNAGGLEPUSS CHRONICLES #6
variant cover by HOWARD PORTER and HI-FI

SNAGGLEPUSS Historical Glossary:

What follows is a brief glossary of various historical figures and events referenced in
EXIT STAGE LEFT: THE SNAGGLEPUSS CHRONICLES.

Issue 1

SNAGGLEPUSS:

Several attributes of Snagglepuss are loosely inspired by the Southern Gothic playwright Tennessee Williams, best known for plays such as *Cat on a Hot Tin Roof* and *A Streetcar Named Desire*. Like Snagglepuss, Williams was born in Mississippi and later moved to New York City, where he traveled within a social circle of fellow gay men and artists. Williams is one of the most revered playwrights in American history.

HUCKLEBERRY HOUND:

Huckleberry Hound possesses a few traits loosely inspired by the novelist William Faulkner. The author of *The Sound and the Fury* and *As I Lay Dying*, Faulkner won both the Nobel Prize and multiple Pulitzer Prizes for literature, though he spent most of his career in relative obscurity. He was a contemporary of Tennessee Williams, and like Huckleberry Hound, he was born and spent most of his life in Mississippi. Though unlike the relationship between Snagglepuss and Huckleberry Hound, Faulkner and Williams were not childhood friends, and in fact were born 14 years apart.

THE STONEWALL INN:

The Stonewall Inn was operating as a restaurant in 1953, during the events of this series, but it would not become a Mafia-run gay bar until the mid-1960s, after the original restaurant was destroyed in a fire. Though there were numerous police raids on the Stonewall Inn throughout its history, it was one particular raid in 1969, when patrons refused to surrender the bar to the police, that touched off the Stonewall Uprising, becoming an important catalyst for the Gay Rights Movement.

HOUSE UN-AMERICAN ACTIVITIES COMMITTEE (HUAC):

Both the House of Representatives and the U.S. Senate conducted hearings designed to investigate, expose and intimidate Communists and other subversive elements living in the United States. Though created in 1938, the House Un-American Activities Committee gained a lot of power after World War II as the public began to worry about possible Soviet influence on American government and culture. Being investigated and placed on the committee's "blacklist" made it next to impossible to find work in the United States. While Lillian Hellman was questioned by the committee as shown in this series, she was never blacklisted or forced to move abroad, though more than 300 other artists were. HUAC remained active throughout the Vietnam War, though it lost most of its credibility once Hollywood started ignoring the blacklist in 1959.

THE BATISTA REGIME:

Fulgencio Batista had been the democratically elected president of Cuba from 1940-44 and would probably be remembered very differently by history if he had been content to become the *former* president of Cuba. However, facing near-certain electoral defeat in 1952, he staged a military coup and canceled the elections. He then ruled Cuba as a dictator for the next seven years under a brutal and corrupt regime. The incident with the soldiers kicking the gay men out of the park actually happened as described in issue #1, though not in Cuba. That happened in Panama around the same time, as related to me by a woman whose father witnessed it as a member of the Panamanian military.

PEGGY GUGGENHEIM:

An heir to the Guggenheim fortune, Peggy Guggenheim was an ardent supporter of the arts, going so far as to even marry the painter Max Ernst. She dedicated much of her personal fortune to collecting and producing art and often threw lavish mixers–inviting writers, artists and musicians from New York's bohemian and avant-garde scenes.

ROSENBERG EXECUTIONS:

As depicted in this series, Julius and Ethel Rosenberg were executed for treason on June 13, 1953, for giving American nuclear secrets to the Soviet Union. Though later historical evidence would confirm their espionage, Ethel Rosenberg was executed with her husband despite not actively transmitting any information to the Soviet Union herself. They were prosecuted by Roy Cohn, the inspiration for the character of Gigi Allen.

Issue 2

THE HYDROGEN BOMB:

In 1953, when most of this series takes place, the hydrogen bomb was less than a year old. Unlike its predecessor, the atomic bomb, the hydrogen bomb's thermonuclear power had almost unlimited capacity for destruction. The first hydrogen bomb had a yield of 10.4 megatons, almost 500 times more powerful than the atomic bombs dropped on Japan at the end of the Second World War. The destructive power of the hydrogen bomb rendered any attempts to survive a bomb blast comically inadequate, though officials continued to promote civil defense efforts to give both the Soviet Union and the American public the illusion that the U.S. government believed a thermonuclear war would be survivable.

Issue 3

THE JOE FRANKLIN SHOW:

Joe Franklin (or Moe Franklin, as he is referred to in the series), hosted a seminal and popular television talk show in New York City. *The Joe Franklin Show* made its television debut in January of 1951, and remained on the air for nearly 50 years. Franklin counted Marilyn Monroe, Salvador Dalí, Elvis Presley and five U.S. presidents among his guests, along with thousands of others.

MARILYN MONROE/ JOE DIMAGGIO/ARTHUR MILLER:

While the relationship between Marilyn Monroe and Arthur Miller as depicted in this series is fictional, in 1955 Monroe would embark on a love affair with Miller while still married to Joe DiMaggio. She divorced DiMaggio in October of that year and married Miller seven months later. And according to DiMaggio, Heinz did offer to pay him $10,000 to endorse their ketchup if his record-setting hitting streak made it to 57 games. As depicted in the series, his hitting streak ended at 56.

THE RAID ON THE MONCADA BARRACKS, SANTIAGO CUBA:

On July 26, 1953, Fidel Castro led a group of rebels in a raid on the Moncada Barracks, the second-largest military installation in Cuba. Though the raid itself was a failure, it would become the start of a revolution that would eventually topple the Batista regime in Cuba.

Issue 4

DOOM TOWN:

"Doom Town" was the colloquial name given to small artificial towns in the Yucca desert of Nevada. Populated by mannequins and built to resemble average American suburbs, doom towns were used to test the effects of nuclear detonations on nearby towns and the outskirts of major cities. *Doom Town* is also the title of a Jack Chick religious tract condemning homosexuality.

HERMAN KAHN:

Herman Kahn, who gives Gigi Allen a tour of the Nevada nuclear test site in issue #4, was a strategist and game theorist who worked for the RAND Corporation and was influential in creating the American nuclear strategy during the 1950s and '60s. Even as scientists created increasingly more powerful hydrogen bombs, Kahn clung to his belief that the United States could survive, and even win, a nuclear war by adopting such tactics as developing a second-strike capability and feeding radioactive food supplies to the elderly. He was one of the inspirations for the titular character in the film *Dr. Strangelove or: How I Learned to Stop Worrying and Love the Bomb*.

GIGI ALLEN:

The character Gigi Allen is loosely based on the lawyer Roy Cohn, who served as special counsel to Senator Joseph McCarthy during the McCarthy Era. During the Lavender Scare, Cohn extorted and blacklisted dozens of people for their homosexuality, despite the fact that he was himself a gay man. In 1973 Cohn represented a young Donald Trump after the federal government accused him of violating the Fair Housing Act by discriminating against black tenants. In 1986 Cohn was disbarred for unethical conduct. He died of AIDS later that year.

Issue 5

NIKITA KHRUSHCHEV:

In the aftermath of Stalin's sudden death from a stroke in 1953, Nikita Khrushchev ambitiously maneuvered his way into power as described at the beginning of issue #5.

Though unlike the events in the series, he would not successfully undermine Georgy Malenkov until 1955, after which he emerged as the sole and indisputable leader of the Soviet Union. Khrushchev developed a reputation as a bit of a loose cannon, however. After his standoff with John F. Kennedy in the Cuban Missile Crisis nearly embroiled the Soviet Union in nuclear war, the Central Committee decided to forcibly retire him, after which he remained in obscurity until his death in 1971. *Pravda*, the official newspaper of the Soviet Union, announced his passing with a single sentence.

Issue 6

THE KITCHEN DEBATE:

During a trade fair in Moscow in 1959, an impromptu debate broke out between Premier Khrushchev and Vice President Nixon about the relative merits of the Soviet versus the American way of life during a visit to a futuristic model kitchen. The debate was recorded on color video cassette, itself a futuristic recent invention, and was broadcast in both nations. The debate resulted in an invitation for Khrushchev to visit the United States, which he accepted, the first Soviet premier to do so. Khrushchev sought to test the young American, but was impressed both by Nixon's performance in the debate and his confidence in inviting him to visit the United States. In 1959 Khrushchev fully expected that he would be dealing with Nixon as the next president of the United States. When the even younger and less experienced John F. Kennedy was elected instead, Khrushchev decided to press his advantage and test the resolve of the young president with an ultimatum to remove American armed forces from West Berlin and by deploying Soviet nuclear missiles in Cuba.

THE GARST CORNFIELD WAR:

During Khrushchev's visit to the United States, Nixon wanted to show him a successful American farm to demonstrate the superiority of American agriculture and to give him a chance to mingle with some ordinary Americans. Arrangements were made to visit the Iowa farm of Roswell Garst. When busloads of reporters and photographers arrived behind Nixon and Khrushchev, though, Garst began to have reservations about the tour. Insisting that all those people walking through his fields would destroy his corn, he refused to let the press on his property. When the reporters refused to leave, Garst began throwing ears of corn at them. Khrushchev, however, thought this was part of the tour and began throwing corn himself. A corn fight ensued, after which Khrushchev and Garst became friends. Khrushchev later began using some of Garst's techniques in Soviet agriculture.

THE QUICK DRAW McGRAW SHOW:

The Quick Draw McGraw Show first aired in the fall of 1959. Quick Draw was usually accompanied by his donkey sidekick, Baba Looey, who also makes a brief cameo in the series. Augie Doggie also featured prominently in *The Quick Draw McGraw Show*, along with his father, Doggie Daddy. As mentioned in the series, *The Quick Draw McGraw Show* marked the debut of Snagglepuss, though in this initial iteration he was called "Snaggletooth" and was orange rather than his now-familiar pink. Snagglepuss would begin starring in his own cartoons in 1961.

SNAGGLEPUSS character sketches by MIKE FEEHAN

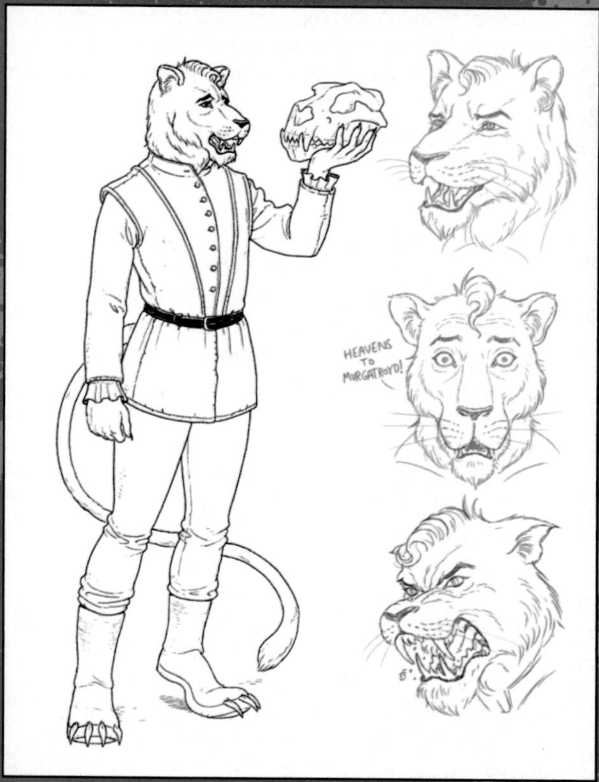
HEAVENS TO MURGATROYD!

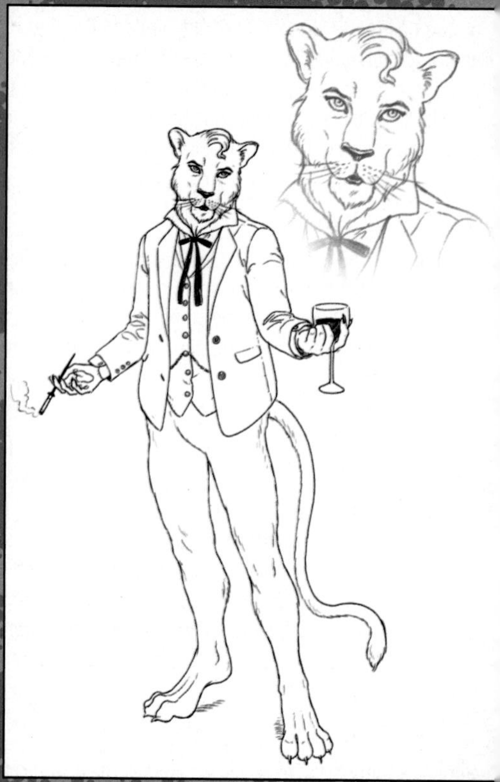

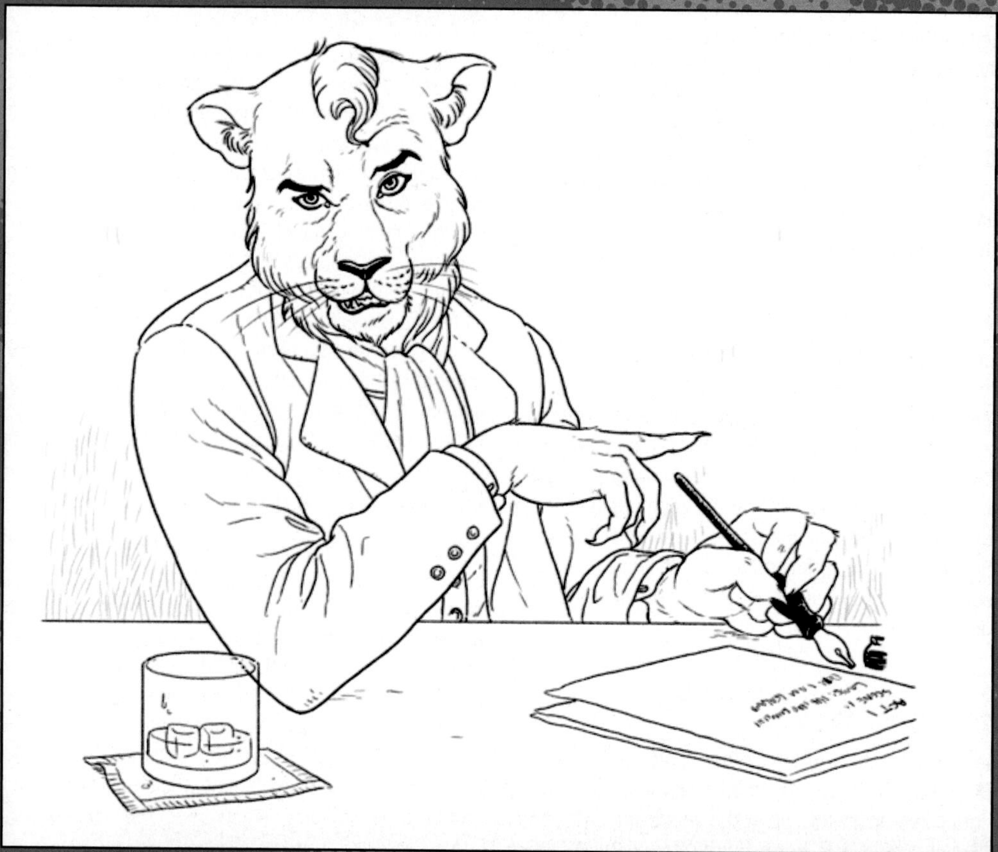

Cover roughs by BEN CALDWELL

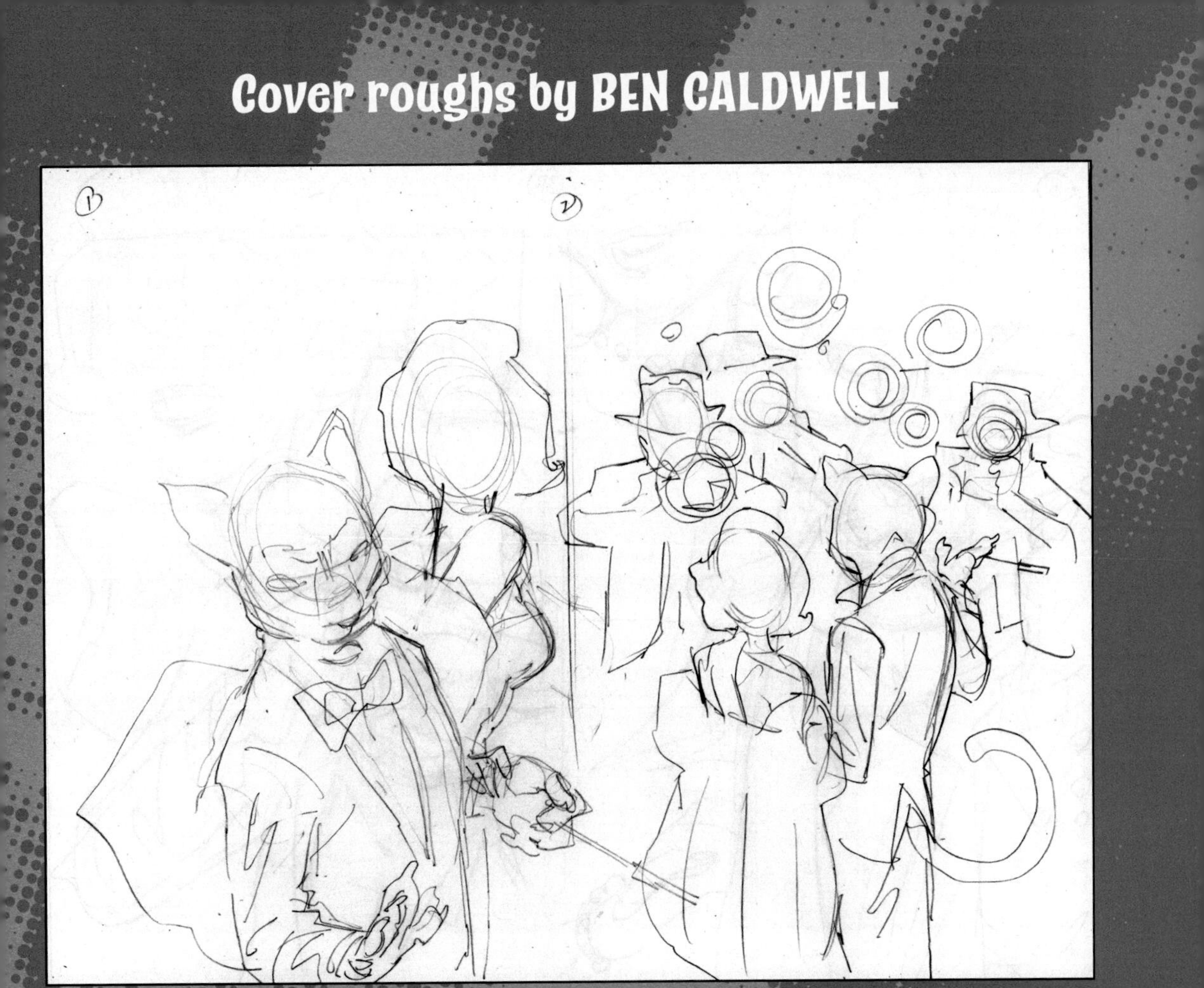
1
2

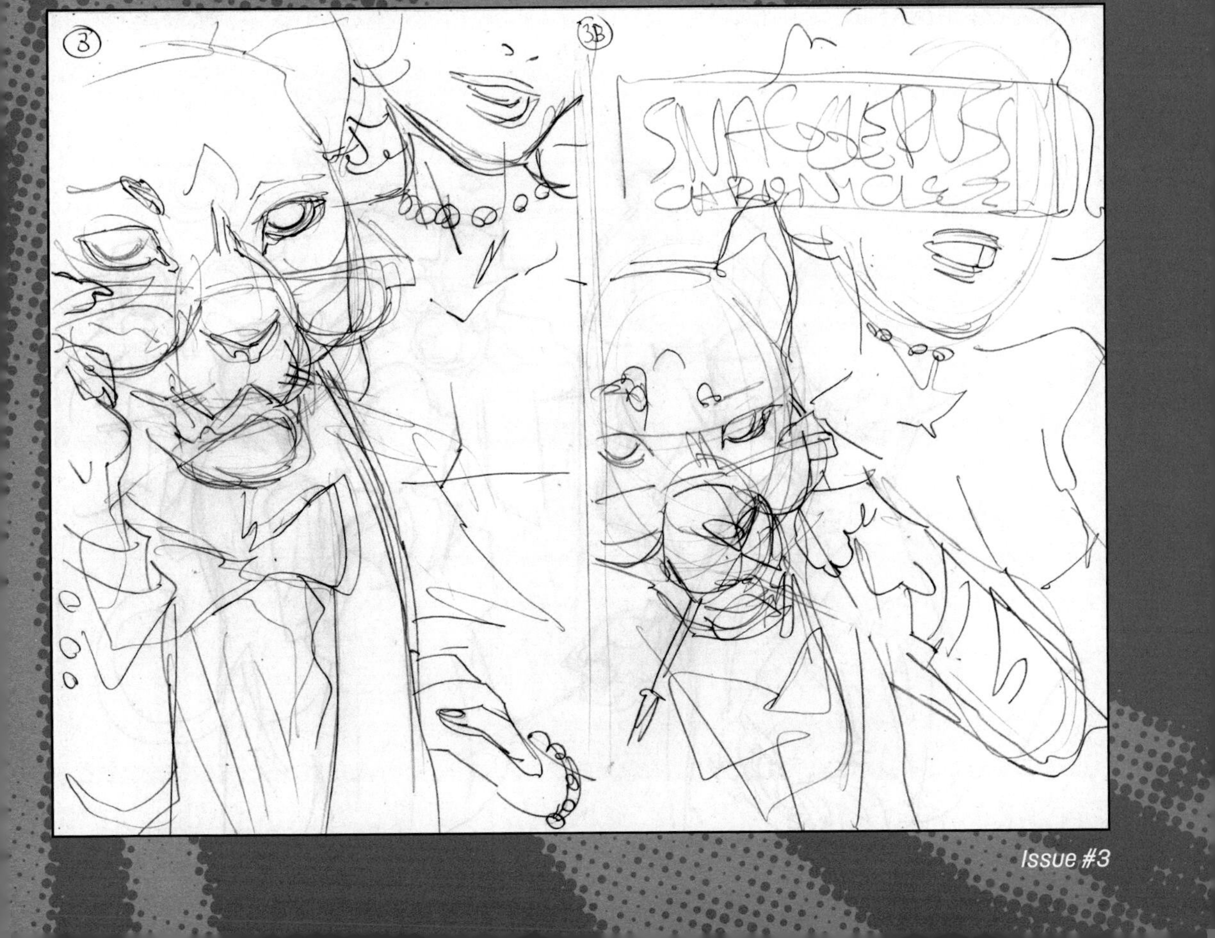
3
3B

Issue #3

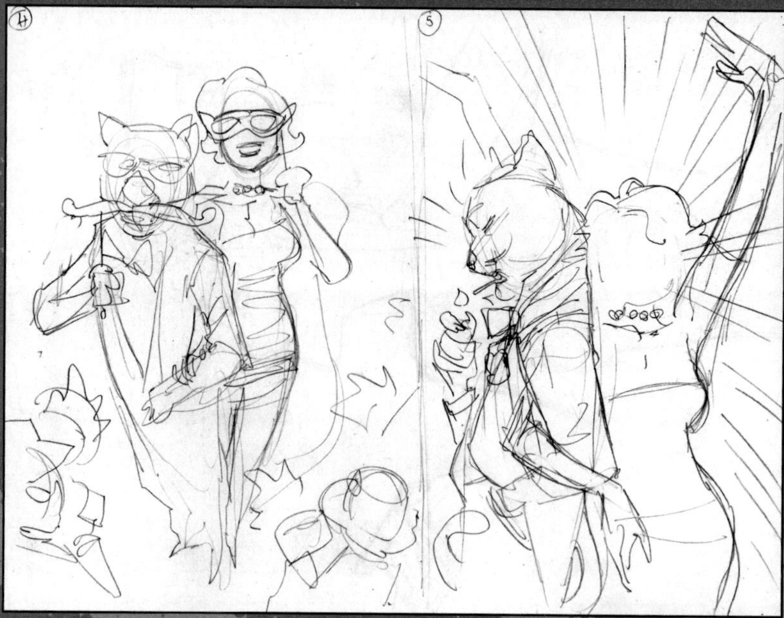

Issue #3

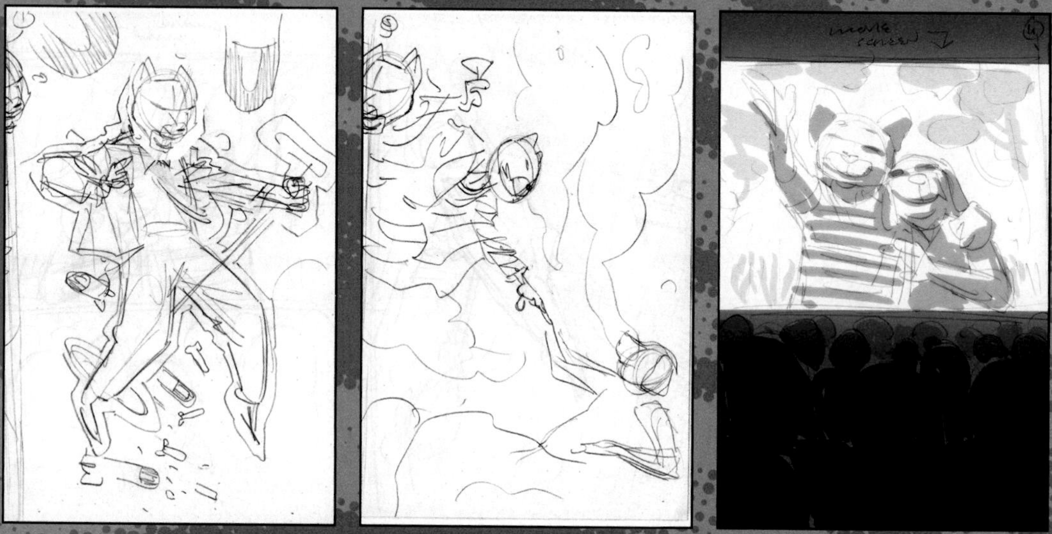

Issue #5

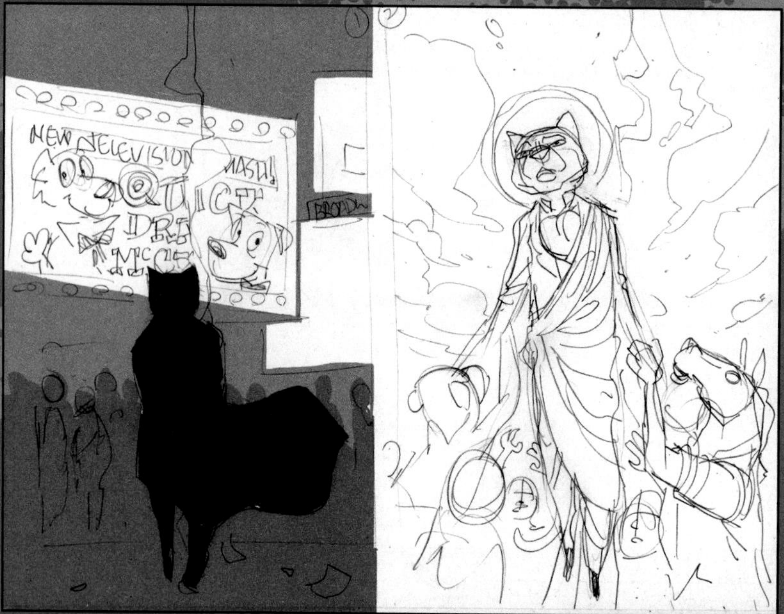
NEW TELEVISION
MASH!
BROADW

Issue #6

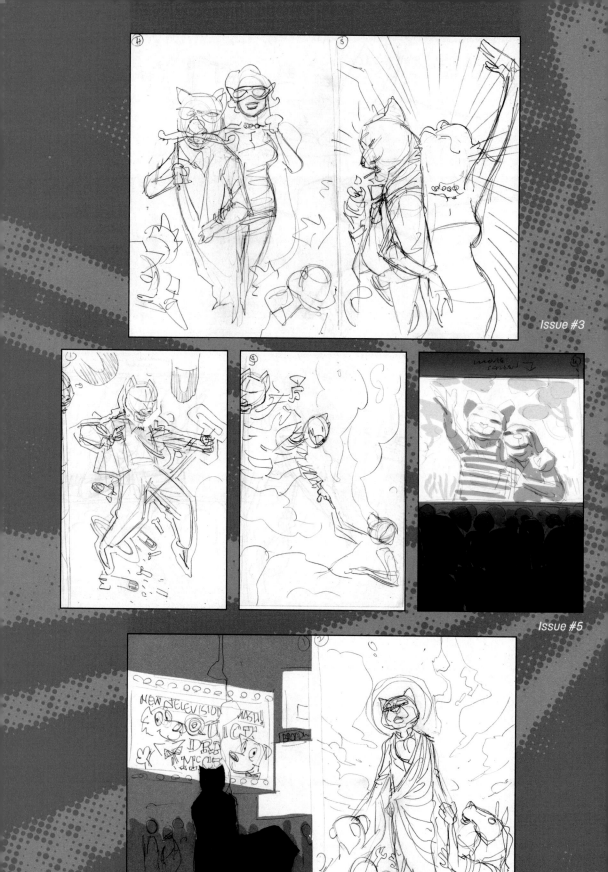